Dougie McHale

The Homecoming

Copyright © Dougie McHale 2015

The right of Dougie McHale to be identified as the author of this work has been asserted by him in accordance with the Copyright, Design and Patents Act 1988.

This is a work of fiction. Names and characters are the products of the author's imagination and any resemblance to actual persons, living or dead is entirely coincidental.

All rights reserved. No part of this publication may be reproduced, stored in a retrieval system, or transmitted, in any form or by any means, electronic, mechanical, photocopying, recording or otherwise, without the prior permission of the author.

'I am at last determined to go to Greece it is the only place I was ever contented in.' Lord Byron, 1823.

Prologue

1941

The sky is lacquered in milky clouds and a watery sun. They amble along a farm track bordered by hedgerows; birdsong accompanies their progress. He frantically flaps his hand around his head, irritated by the continuous drone.

'The bees are attracted to your brylcream.' She grins. She pulls her hand along a grass stem and rubs the dislodged seeds between her fingers.

'We're going to France soon.'

'When are you going?' A slight panic rises in her voice.

'In a few days; the lads are saying that it'll be over in six months.'

'Six months is still a long time,' she says with a tremor of anxiety.

'It will go by quickly enough. Before you know it, I'll be back home. We were told yesterday. Our basic training is over now and, once our leave is finished, we're off to France.'

Her heart begins to pound. He burns with excitement.

'I've never been to France. Ayr is the furthest I've been from home. I went there on holiday one summer when I was still at school. It rained every day.' He laughs.

She looks at him seriously. 'This won't be a holiday. You're going to war. This isn't a game you're playing.'

'I've been well trained. It's not as if we don't know what we're doing,' he says, offended by her accusation.

'I'm sorry,' she placates. 'It's just that my mind's been occupied lately. I was going to wait awhile longer before I told you, but it seems I don't have the luxury of time now.'

'Tell me what?' He frowns, still recoiling from her rebuke.

She takes a deep breath, reaches out and takes his hand. 'I'm pregnant. I've already been to see the doctor.'

His eyes widen. 'You're having a baby. You're having a baby,' he repeats.

'That's what it means.' She smiles.

He pulls her towards him. 'Have you told your mum and dad?' There is a slight panic in his voice.

She shakes her head. 'No, not yet. I'm dreading it.' She feels her heart sink.

'They'll have to be told. But you can't do it on your own. I'll be there with you. We'll need to do it soon.'

'It's all happening too quickly. I haven't even got used to the idea myself. A baby... me.'

He holds her face in his hands. 'You'll make a wonderful mum and when I get back from this war, we'll get married and be a family.'

'You'd better come back to me Robert Williams.'

He kisses her forehead. 'All the wars in the world won't keep me from you.'

***

A determined concentration crosses the doctor's face as he stares with intent at the protruding mound of matted hair that glistens between the girl's trembling legs. He has rolled the sleeves of his white shirt above the elbow, yet speckles of blood stain the fabric, like paint flicked from a brush.

'One more push lass, that should do it,' he encourages through tobacco-stained teeth. It is the deliverance of a prayer, not a fact.

Flickering candles illuminate the blackness of another power cut in a soft light that splays a dance of elongated shadows across the wall. Ice cold air seeps through the window frame and floats over the small room. The doctor feels it on the back of his neck, like breath whispered against his skin. Her skin, coated in sweat, is flushed, apple red, in contrast to the white night dress crumpled and creased across her thighs.

Huddled in murmured prayer, two tenebrous figures lurk in the corner. Irritated, the doctor looks over his shoulder.

'Get me a towel,' he barks and adds impatiently, 'Quickly.'

The contractions seem endless, the involuntary waves that move inside her are a constant and painful reminder that the life within is eager to escape its confines.

When it is over, she is delicately placed on her mother's chest.

From the shadows they move and, like thieves, snatch the baby from her.

'The necklace,' she pleads.

'Don't worry, my dear, I'll see to it.' The doctor's words are soft, apologetic and heavy with shame.

Edinburgh 2002

Two Seconds to Steal a Lifetime.

Louis ran through sheets of rain, regretting his decision not to have hailed one of the ubiquitous black taxis that patrolled Edinburgh's George Street, now conspicuous by their absence.

His fingers, wet and numb, clenched the collar of his coat. He cursed his attempt to stem the flow of irritant droplets staining his shirt in damp dark patches and moulding the cold material uncomfortably to his chest.

Escaping the constant deluge, he finally entered the warm hallway with an involuntary shiver. Rainwater dripped from him, forming globular beads on the floor. A sudden stillness settled around him, he felt tired and quickly removed his drenched jacket with a welcome relief.

Louis had enjoyed a few drinks with work colleagues in a city bar, and now his taste buds stirred for more. In the kitchen, he plucked a beer from the refrigerator. He savoured the cold sensation as it caressed his throat and wondered why the first drink from a bottle was always the best.

It took a few moments for the contours and shapes of accustomed objects to gradually unfold, emerging from the darkness, as the refrigerator's thrum washed over him, reminding him, as it always did, of the purring of a contented cat.

He placed the half-drained bottle on a work surface and slid his feet from the confines of his shoes, a release that enabled him to curl and stretch his chilled toes. He considered making something to eat. Emma would be asleep, and the satisfying appeal of sliding beneath the sheets, and feeling the warmth of her body against his skin, pulled him towards the bedroom. The door stood ajar. Revelling in anticipation, he peered through the dull light. Gently, he pushed the door, which protested with a tired creak.

The crisp white sheet provocatively rose, like a solitary

hill, shrouding the bed, and sparing his eyes. The sheet slid from entwined bodies, exposing their nakedness. Louis felt himself drowning as if rushing water had engulfed his lungs, stealing his words of reprisal with involuntary gulps for air. He stared at them incomprehensively, paralysed.

Emma lifted her head. 'Oh shit, Louis… I'm sorry.'

The words hang in the air, taunting him. Instinctively, she covered herself and her shame. His world suddenly stopped upon its axis. This kind of thing did not happen to him, to Emma, and then a profound rage grasped him, multiplying in his mind, electrifying every nerve and sense, urging him to tear the sheet from her.

He moved into the room, a demented animal, and his life of intricacy and detail, the life he identified as his own was ripped from him, it ceased to exist. Two seconds to steal a lifetime.

Ambers

A week had passed. Closed blinds illuminated the room in a soft rim of light, concealing the outside world. As much as possible, Louis avoided entering the bedroom, preferring instead the uncomfortable hardness of the sofa. He had slept in his clothes, and now they stuck to his skin becoming unwelcome and oppressive. He rose from his slumber and caught his reflection in the mirror. For a second he was undecided which of the two left him the most uncomfortable, the clinging fabric or the stranger that stared back at him. They were both equally alien; a hot shower would purify his skin, the stranger, would need more than the cleansing qualities of water to slide down the plug and disappear.

    He showered and dressed. The process was mechanical and routine and, with it, Louis rediscovered a reassuring familiarity that had previously deserted him. He felt an urge to escape his self-imposed house arrest. He found the confines of each room suffocating, as if their walls were slowly closing in on him. That morning, he went out for breakfast.

    He emerged from the stairwell of the basement flat where Lansdowne Crescent curved, hugging elegant townhouses and verdant lush trees. A mantle of freshly cut grass searched out his nostrils with its mint fragrance. As he walked, he gazed at St. Mary's Cathedral, whose tapering spires seemed to scrape the slate grey Edinburgh sky. Years of endless traffic fumes stained and darkened the cathedral's façade, engraining its stone with pollution's modern trademark. Perversely, he now considered, it had been this disfigurement that had first lured him towards the cathedral's imposing grandeur.

    He crossed a busy street, alert to the traffic. He followed a path next to the cathedral, where a mass of scaffolding and tarpaulin was erected around its sidewalls, scaling every contour and fixture as if a huge bandage had been applied to attend to its wounds.

    Louis imagined the miniature side chapels inside the

cathedral, where worshipers contemplated their worries or celebrated life's pleasures. Like small islands, they were unattached and distinct from the main altar, their profound stillness and mystic qualities lay waiting to be discovered, and, on occasions, Louis found himself seduced by the refuge that such places offered.

He navigated one more street before encountering the slate-coloured cobbles of William Street. He had always thought of this area as a self-contained village hidden within the heart of the city. Its small and elegant juxtaposed shops, diverse and eloquent in their appeal, were the main attraction towards this thinking. It was here, in its several pubs, he spent long ardent evenings with Emma, illuminated by conversation and the laughter of friends. Life was balanced, insulated, and predictable, properties that cocooned him in a warm security that seemed impregnable. That life had now been swallowed, digested and spat out.

Over the years, Louis and Emma had become regular visitors to '*Amber's Café and Deli*' preferring its blend of unpretentious and intimate surroundings. A friendly and familiar voice greeted him.

'It's nice to see you Louis, your usual?'

'That would be nice thanks, Carla.'

He sat at a table by the window. A disregarded issue of that day's Scotsman lay on its surface. Normally he would scan the sports pages, looking for any mention of Hibernian Football Club in a header. The paper lay unopened.

'You know I never seem to get anything done these days, I'm not complaining, it means the place is busy, you just missed the breakfast rush. Anyway, how are you, Louis?' Carla placed a coffee on the table.

He leant back in his chair. 'I've felt better. I'm all over the place really.' He paused. 'She's moved out, packed most of her things and left. He was waiting for her in his car.'

She nodded without looking up. 'I know.' Her voice held a trace of guilt.

Louis said nothing, but nodded an acknowledgement. Of

course, Emma would confide in Carla. He felt a moment of betrayal.

'It's starting to feel real now,' he said finally. 'There's still a few of her things left in the flat. I've been holding on to the thought that sooner or later she'll realise she made a mistake. I would have taken her back you know. That's not going to happen, not now.'

'No, I suppose not.'

He stared out of the window. 'Every morning I wake into a nightmare, Carla.'

'It'll get easier. I'm sure it will.'

She reached out and touched his arm. Their relationship had initially comprised of coffees, small talk and scanning the surface of each other's histories. It was part of Carla's job description to be pleasant, sociable, and interested in her customers. At first, Louis and Emma fitted into this neat package but, with time, it developed from following the manual of customer care into a mutual friendship that the three of them had grown to value.

That morning, Louis noticed a sparse somnolence about Amber's. Two businessmen seated in a corner wore the regulation uniform of the city, non-descriptive suit, and briefcases. The older of the two displayed a proficient air of dominance about his demeanour. He spoke, while barely drawing breath between self-indulgent sentences. Louis noted his companion nodding robotically at intervals, well-rehearsed from experience, a self-imposed silence only punctuated by the occasional agreement.

The older man's face was rounded and portly; a beetroot complexion spread across his exaggerated cheeks while protruding folds of skin escaped the neck of his starched shirt. His prodigious shoulders stretched the material of his jacket, which gave the impression that his suit was ill-fitting and too small for his accentuated frame. A lighter and a packet of cigarettes appeared from his pocket and were placed on the table by short stumpy fingers complementing Louis' impression of a lifestyle that did not agree with an already overworked heart; a pulsating time bomb on the countdown to zero, Louis thought.

Carla sat opposite him.

'Louis if there's anything I can do, or if you feel the need to talk, don't hesitate. I'm a good listener as you know.'

He smiled warmly, welcoming her words.

'I feel like the clown in Emma's circus. Everyone seemed to know, most of her friends knew. It's funny; you think you know people until something like this happens. I would've called a lot of those people friends. It looks like I was the last to know. How could I not have known?'

'It's not unusual Louis. It usually works out that way. If it's any consolation, I'd no idea either. Although it can't compare to what you're going through, in a way, I feel cheated as well. She kept her secret from me too - until you found out that is. God, she's a good actor. She called me and said she'd been seeing someone else and that you'd found them together. Seemingly, you broke his nose; it was the least he deserved. She didn't go into the details at first. We agreed to meet, and she told me the whole thing. I was stunned. I couldn't believe it. I was so angry with her, but she wouldn't listen. She thought I would be a sympathetic ear; she got that wrong.'

'I keep going over it, trying to work out just what went wrong and why. What did I do that made her want to go with someone else? When did she start to feel like that?'

'You're not to blame Louis. Everyone knew you worshipped her.' Carla touched his hand. 'Think of it in this way, and I say this as a friend, if this was going to happen then maybe it was better it happened now. You wouldn't want this to be any more complicated than it already is. Would you?'

Louis knew this was a reference to children. There had been a time when both he and Emma discussed and contemplated having children. Louis had always instigated these one-sided conversations, knowing he was pulled in that direction more than Emma ever was. She was not comfortable in the presence of children; she preferred to live in the adult world. 'I was not born with motherly instincts,' she often retorted. She rarely applied her affections towards her friend's children, and on the occasions she did, it was with the minimum of interest. She was not cold towards them, but it was made obvious that the barriers she put in place were there to be observed. Without an invitation, her space was not to be invaded.

The equation was not could she fit into the world that a child brings, but rather, could a child be neatly packaged into her world with minimal disruption?

Before Emma, the potent call to the priesthood was alluring and consistent. Louis' journey predicted a childless path married to Catholicism and his prospective parishioners. The church and its consumption of study, prayer and reflection consumed his life as he attended seminary at Blair's College, Aberdeenshire and then the Pontifical Scots College in Rome.

It was while in Rome, that Louis met Emma Myers. She was on holiday in the city with friends. Her brother Jez, a friend of Louis and fellow student at the Pontifical Scots College, invited Louis along to meet Emma in one of the many cafes that populated the square where they often spent their free time away from their studies. An immediate attraction was born and a cordial relationship ensued. Emma spent most of her time with Louis whenever the demands of his studies allowed. They would meet at her hotel and amble around the sites and venues the city offered, Louis acting as her guide. On her last night, the physical attraction between them was confirmed, by a fumbled and embarrassing kiss within the Piazza Navona.

When Emma returned to Edinburgh, their correspondence became more frequent and detailed. The secular world, and in particular, Emma's world became magnetic; they occupied Louis' thoughts, their consistency held his emotions in a state of conflict. He fought the battle, yet his allies of church and vocation subsided, removing themselves from the fabric of his life, as the potent allure of a woman reverberated around every aspect of his being.

His prayers for guidance became intense. He confided in close friends. There was no manifestation of comfort, just emotive storms of volcanic proportions. His faith was not in question, it was the expression of that faith that troubled him. Emma had become the central aspect of his life, to the Church of Rome's detriment.

Within six months of them first meeting, they were living in Edinburgh, Louis earning his living as an architect, his profession for five years before he joined the priesthood.

Chocolate speckled froth camped itself on the tip of the younger businessman's nose as he placed his cup on the table. He boyishly wiped the cause of his embarrassment; his eyes sweeping the surrounding area to gauge if his dignity was still intact.

'The only times we ever argued were around Emma's refusal to even consider having children. And now it doesn't matter anymore, how ironic is that. It's a joke. I'm so fucking angry. Sorry, Carla.' Louis sighed.

'That's all right Louis, at least that's the healthy way to express your anger. It doesn't get you into trouble,' Carla said with some sincerity. 'I heard Paul was pressing charges against you for breaking his nose.' She shook her head disbelievingly. 'What a self-indulgent creep. I don't know what Emma sees in him.'

'She persuaded him to drop the charges.'

'Well, that's something at least. Trying to appease her guilt I suppose,' Carla said, satisfied.

A sudden thought crossed his mind. This was one of only a few times he had been in Amber's without Emma and from now on it would be a reoccurring theme he realised.

'I thought I knew everything there was to know about her. Sometimes I even knew what she was thinking just by looking at her expression or gesture, but really I didn't know her at all. The person I thought she was wouldn't have done this.'

'Look, why don't we go out for a drink one night or come over to my place. I'll cook a meal or we could get a carryout, you look like you haven't been eating much.'

Louis rose from his chair, abandoning his coffee. It was time to go. He was not ready to socialise.

'That would be nice, but just now I wouldn't be good company. I'll see you soon, Carla.'

Carla's lips curved into a smile. 'You haven't ordered

your breakfast yet. Sit down and I'll make some toast and eggs. I'll even poach them for you,' she added.

'I'm fine. Honest.'

'Well remember to call. I meant what I said.' She rose from her chair.

'I will.' He paused, holding the door open.

The warmth of the cafe immersed him in the smells of palatable food and the exuberant aroma of strong coffee momentarily rooted him to the spot. It was in cold contrast to the chill that nipped at his feet, unwelcoming and intruding. A suitable metaphor that depicted his life, he thought.

Carla moved to the counter and attended to the businessmen's food; both were salads. He must be on a diet, Louis thought; was his friend offering a gesture of moral support? Louis wondered for how much longer the overburdened suit would take the strain.

Carla glanced at him and smiled. For the first time, he saw her differently. He registered an assurance in their friendship that she would always be there for him. He felt compelled to linger a moment longer.

He valued her counsel. He had his mother to thank for that. The memory of it brought a slight smile to his lips. His mother's taste in coffee did not accustom her to the rich fine beans of the coffee world. This caused some amusement between Louis and Emma, and upon their weekly visits to his mother, they would first frequent Amber's, topping up their caffeine levels, before the unpalatable onslaught of a cup of Tesco's own make.

The cold air seeped through his clothing. He must go, he thought.

Gizmo's Charms

In the palm of a hand, the rodent sniffed the air with an intensity and purposefulness that left its senses inebriated. The object that triggered this fermentation, a half consumed burger, sat in a yellow polystyrene carton. A small cluster of children willed and urged the creature to pacify their anticipation by devouring their offering. An intense shriek reverberated around them, as the rodent appeased their excitability by attacking the food. It exposed two sharp implements that tore at the meat. Two small-clawed legs expertly held the food in position while the rodent expeditiously chewed its humble meal.

An elated resonance of approval emanated from the children like a shock wave from an exploding bomb. The rodent gave out an alarmed shriek and sought refuge inside its owner's sleeve, a worm-like tail the only discernible part of its body viewable to its now deflated audience.

Louis witnessed this scene from a few yards away. The number of children was now depleted due to the absence of the creature and, as he approached, the last of them were being shuffled away by exorable parents. The rodent's owner sat on steps that led to a prodigious doorway. He exhibited an expansive smile as he tried to coax the creature from his sleeve.

Louis' first impression was that the man resembled a street beggar, but he noted that his clothing was clean and well-kept and not stained from the appearance that suggested a street life.

A bulky and hooded army jacket draped the man's body which would have covered his knees when he stood. Green combat trousers were tucked neatly into a large pair of Doctor Martin boots and a large rucksack, more akin to mountaineering, rested at an angle against a door as if it was stopping it from toppling. A few days of facial growth exaggerated a pristine shaven head that shone in the fading light as if it had been meticulously polished. Louis calculated that the man was slightly younger than himself, possibly in his mid-twenties.

His curiosity urged him to ask, 'Is that a mouse?'

'No. This is a rat, my friend,' the man replied, retrieving the rat from his sleeve.

'You can come out now the scary children have gone,' he said softly.

The rat sniffed the air apprehensively.

'I've had her for a few years now,' he said with a slight cockney accent.

'Has it got a name?'

'Gizmo, after the rat in that film, what's it called again? I can never remember.' The rat disappeared under the fabric of the sleeve. 'She keeps me company and never answers back.'

'Not your typical female then,' Louis remarked ingratiatingly.

They both laughed. It served Louis as a release valve, recent circumstances not affording him a sense of humour.

'Unfortunately, my current position doesn't allow me to meet many members of the opposite sex. The only chance I get these days is when they offer me money for my services.' The man smiled faintly.

'Oh, services?' Louis tried to keep his look passive.

'We entertain.' His smile broadened. 'Well, I like to think of it as entertainment. It's Gizmo that does the entertaining really. I'm just the assistant.'

Louis asked if the man was sleeping rough or staying at a hostel.

'That depends on your interpretation of rough. I think of the sky as my roof. At night, the stars and moon are my light and my tent and sleeping bag are my shelter and warmth. This way of life feeds my heart and mind, while Gizmo feeds both our stomachs with her charm.'

'It sounds a good way of living when you describe it like that.'

'I wouldn't live any other way mate, anyway, I've lived like this for years. I like to think of myself as a professional traveler, it's what I do. It keeps me happy and contented. I could never return to the fucking rat race.' He nuzzled his nose in Gizmo's fur. 'Sorry, Gizmo, no pun intended.'

'So what made you come to Edinburgh?'

'Now there's a story. I got my timings all wrong.' He laughed. 'I thought I'd come for your famous festival but I'm too early, silly bugger. I thought they'd cancelled it when I got here. Anyway, it's been a profitable mistake. Imagine the competition I'd have had to put up with if the city was bursting at the seams with street acts. Easy pickings mate. Gizmo just needs to make an appearance and they throw money at us.' He looked at the hamburger. 'And burgers too.' He offered Gizmo the hamburger. Louis watched the rat nibble its meal.

'So, where were you before you came here?'

'In the last couple of weeks, I've been up the west coast, breathtaking scenery but a bit bloody wet at times. The midges! I got bitten to death. Then I made my way to the capital of the Highlands - Inverness. I thumbed a lift down to Perth. Walked across the Forth Road Bridge and now my home for the foreseeable future is your wonderful city.'

'Where will you go next?' Louis asked intrigued.

'York's nice at this time of year, always lots of tourists,' he replied matter of fact.

Louis found himself attracted to this choice of existence. He favoured its sense of freedom, its hints of romanticism, but most of all he wanted to feel its escapism. It kindled in him the genesis of an awakening, the fruition of which he was just beginning to realise.

He plunged his hand into his pocket and pulled out a five-pound note, bent over and placed it into a polystyrene cup. The man raised his eyebrows while contemplating the unexpected gesture.

'Fucking hell. Gizmo's charm must've wrapped itself around you in a big way.'

'Not exactly,' Louis replied, 'but you could say something else did.'

For several days after their meeting, Louis took a detour from his normal route to work, to see if the man still sheltered in the doorway. Each visit brought a sense of disappointment and unfulfilled expectation. On his last visit, Louis became aware that he had not asked the traveller his name and he wondered if he had indeed ventured to York.

An Arranged Meeting

They met in Amber's. Conversing in a public place was the option that suited them both as opposed to the confined environs of the flat, their reasoning being to defuse any unhealthy confrontation between them.

He ordered a coffee and took his usual seat by the window. Carla smiled encouragingly, medicine to calm them both and tame the air of anticipation.

Days had turned into weeks, merging with a month and then another, stolen time.

It transpired Emma had planned to leave him, but Louis' untimely discovery had brought those plans forward, excusing Emma the anguish inherent in choosing an appropriate moment.

His thoughts could not let her go as the imagery of that night replayed a thousand times in his head. Memories of their past became like ghosts, daily visitations that haunted him, lurking in every corner of every room. Louis remained in the flat. He had bought it before joining the priesthood and then, when he studied in Rome, he let it out to friends, ensuring himself a monthly income which was deposited into an account and left to accumulate. On his return to Edinburgh, it became the home he shared with Emma.

As the years passed, they weaved their identity into its very fabric, leaving him now with the only tangible thing in his life that corresponded to a solid foundation.

On the occasions when they spoke, usually in order for Emma to retrieve her mail from those still unaware of her new address, he learnt she now lived with Paul. The knowledge that Paul was once an occasional acquaintance who frequented the company of his friends applied another layer to Emma's deception, as it was when Louis was with Emma that her attraction to Paul had breathed its first taste of life.

They had picked this time of day as Amber's would be quiet, the lull before lunchtime. He noticed a young couple, students he thought, and a lone woman absorbed in The

Times crossword. He saw Emma crossing the street. She looked tired and pensive.

She entered Amber's. A fire started in the pit of her stomach, the embers of panic washing over her as her eyes travelled the room and fell upon Louis. She smiled hesitantly while crossing the floor.

He suddenly felt exposed; it left him uncomfortable, tinged with an apprehension about what was to follow. He clasped the warmth of the cup, an action he hoped would defuse or at the least mask his discomfort.

Louis was drawn to her eyes, he always had been. This instinctive response echoed shades of their first encounter. Emma had been amused at his efforts in describing their colour, *'Luxuriating a sandy blue texture.'* She responded that he sounded like an art critic reviewing a painting. Louis had taken this as a compliment, undaunted by her satirical tone.

She now sat opposite him. Louis had prepared for this. He observed she had put on a little weight in the face; he thought the effect complemented her.

The familiar scent of her perfume, luscious in its aroma, stirred him, the abundance of hair, neatly tied back from her face, evoked within him images of her curls, coiled like snakes around his seeking fingers. Several strands rested on her cheek, which she nervously flicked behind her ear.

'Hello Emma, you're looking good,' he finally said, this being the first thought that entered his head.

'Thank you,' she replied with a nervous smile.

'Would you like a coffee?'

'I'd love one, yes. That would be nice.'

Not a bad start, he thought, civility being the best policy... The only one, throughout the worst of times, he had always held on to achieving a sense of dignity, a trait welded onto him by his father.

Under the pretence of studying a till roll, Carla assiduously monitored her two friends. They both looked in her direction. To save herself any embarrassment, she acknowledged the attention they afforded her.

'Would you like your usual Emma?' she asked

'Yes, as long as you give the making of the coffee some attention.' The satire in Emma's voice crossed the space between them like a poisoned arrow.

'Shit,' Carla murmured through clenched teeth. 'Was it that obvious?'

'Don't take it out on her, she means well,' Louis said, in her defence. 'She's concerned... for the both of us. Carla's a good friend. This has implications for others too.'

'I know, I'm sorry. God... it feels like I'm living in a fish bowl.'

'One of your own making. It's Carla you should say sorry to, not me.'

'I will. That was unfair, so... how have you been?'

Louis noted a sincere and genuine tone in the conveying of the words.

How have I been? The words danced around his head. To hell and back, as if I had just suffered a bereavement. Devastated comes to mind, like the old cliché, 'your world comes crashing down,' the implications of it are you have no world. The one you lived in, breathed in, does not exist anymore, you take on the demeanour of a zombie, untouchable, your emotions are caught up in a whirlpool, it feels like a nuclear warhead metaphorically exploded in your life, fragmenting... no ... annihilating every aspect and you sit in the ashes that are left, shell-shocked, muted, unable to comprehend, unwilling to comprehend the reality of the situation. Your heart burns, like a fire in your chest. It consumes you, suffocates you, until you struggle to breathe and the will to breathe sometimes deserts you, frightens you...

'I'm ok I suppose, you know, I'm trying to get back to normal, whatever that is now. They say time's a great healer and all that.'

His last words surprised even him, for if it were true, he had not tasted its medicine, not yet anyway. He still felt the pangs of her betrayal, a betrayal he hated but he could not hate her.

'I never intended for this to happen.' Emma paused, reflecting on the meaning of her words. 'I didn't want to hurt you. There would never have been a right time to tell you. How could there be? God, it is such a mess. I'm not a bad person. I made a mistake by not telling you sooner.'

Louis stared out of the window.

'We were becoming a habit Louis, a caricature of the things we said we'd never be.'

She reached for his hand but he withdrew it. 'I'm so sorry Louis, I never intended it to end in the way it did. Paul and I are happy.'

He flinched at the mention of his name. She continued. 'It was becoming impossible living each day as a lie, I felt suffocated, I needed...'

Carla placed a cup on the table beside Emma, who touched her wrist.

'I'm sorry Carla... will you forgive me?'

'Of course, it's fine, honest,' she replied.

'I'm not myself.'

'Look it's fine, I understand. I'll speak to you later,' Carla said, her voice cracking.

They embraced.

Emma composed herself and rearranged her jacket, her eyes' glazed composition conducive in conveying her exposed emotion. This was not how she envisaged the proceedings; it was not going well. She reminded herself that she had to keep a perspicacious mind to tell her reason for agreeing to this meeting. She now regretted coming to Amber's; they should have gone somewhere neutral. Too many memories claimed this space. This was not the place to impart such words, the ones she had rehearsed and fashioned in an attempt to dilute and desensitise their impact.

'I'd forgotten how good Carla's coffee tastes.'

'It's better than my mum's coffee?'

She laughed softly. 'How could I forget?'

An awkward silence fell between them.

Just then, a tall woman swept into Amber's, exchanging a loud animated greeting with the lady who had been engrossed in her crossword. From her bag, she produced a crossword cut from a newspaper and with a solitary finger slipped her spectacles up the bridge of her prodigious nose and hunched over the paper cutting. They both proceeded to discuss its contents in a euphoric flurry.

The tall lady suddenly began a fit of coughing, her throat rattling like an old car refusing to start on a cold morning.

'Water dear, I need water,' she spluttered in a cracked voice.

'Of course, I won't be a minute.'

This unexpected, yet welcome intrusion defused the inquietude between them. Emma shifted in her chair.

'There's not an easy way to say this,' she said, suddenly feeling uncomfortably hot.

The countenance on Louis' face depicted the accused awaiting a jury's verdict, and she sensed his desperation as his stone expression forced her to breathe more deeply as if the oxygenated air would release her from this burden.

Her rehearsed speech and the massaging of the words now seemed extraneously inappropriate. She made the decision, in that moment, to abandon her insipid approach.

'I'm pregnant Louis!'

The imparting of the words sounded foreign, an unintelligible language devoid of meaning and substance.

There followed an elongated pause. The silence encased them. Louis rubbed his temple with his right hand, hoping to erase the words she had just spoken, but their weight seeped into him like a sponge consuming water.

She could not bear the silence. A voice inside her implored him to speak and, when he eventually did, there was not the sense of release that her conscience craved.

'You're pregnant,' Louis spat. 'You are having his child. My God, how ironic.'

He sat back in his chair staring at her. 'What about all of those conversations, the soul searching, the explanations and your bloody excuses... I always wanted children, our child. You refused me, you left me for him and now this... I can't believe it, Emma.'

'Louis please...' she pleaded, craving his forgiveness.

He leant forward, a sardonic smile crept across his face.

'Do you want to know the first thought that came to me...

well, I'll tell you.' His voice was pierced with sarcasm. 'Will she keep the baby? Or will she get rid of it? Just like all of those other irritating intrusions that don't comply with the neat and organised boxes that fill your life. And how long have you known?' He threw the words at her. They struck like a stone.

'I'm sixteen weeks.' Emma looked away.

Louis stared at her, calculating the time. She was pregnant before he found out about the affair. Louis pushed the chair away as he attempted to rise. His head swirled. Emma grabbed his wrist.

'I know how this must look, but believe me, Louis it wasn't intentional... God, I know how much you wanted children and I know I always sidestepped the issue... This might sound crass, but maybe it was supposed to be. I feel ready now.'

Although he was numb, he was not going to prevaricate any longer. His voice was angry now.

'Listen to yourself, for God's sake! You hardly know him. You've lived together for five minutes and now you're having his child... Well done Emma, you've excelled yourself this time.'

His reproachful tone faded into a precarious silence as an unbearable heaviness fell upon him. She seemed a stranger to him.

Emma searched his face for the slightest sign of forgiveness, but there was none forthcoming, his eyes were like stone. The chair scraped the floor as he stood.

'Please Louis. Please don't leave like this,' she pleaded.

He moved towards the door, he glanced at Emma who sat with her head in her hands muffling her sobs.

By now the students had left, leaving only Carla and the two ladies immersed in their crossword. A state of nausea came over him. Carla moved towards Emma.

Outside, torrents of rain fell, causing people to scurry for shelter, their words of protest effaced by the sudden downpour and in that moment Louis contemplated if and when he would find his shelter.

A Spirit of Adventure

The morning light consumed night's blanket and transformed foreign shapes and peculiar outlines into familiar objects and furnishings, the ornamentation of a life shared.

He lay with his arms outstretched, supine like a cross, reflecting the moment Emma's revelation left his sensibilities crucified. He studied his horizontal arms. They exaggerated a sense of spaciousness, a reminder of his loss stirring within him the reminiscences of a time when she would have lain beside him.

He recollected her warmth, that absorbing invitation to envelop her with an arm, his stomach resting against her back, his legs touching the back of her legs, moulded together, like a piece of a jigsaw. His face nestled into the nape of her neck, her scented hair tickling his skin before drifting off to sleep again.

The soft tapping of rain against glass penetrated this world of memories he often revisits. The world that is now lost to him.

Louis slid from the warmth of the duvet to take a shower. He stood naked, droplets of water evaporating on his body, drying in the moist air. He listened in expectation for the song that greeted him each morning. However, on this morning, its inaudibility compelled him to stretch and open the window causing a rush of steam to be expelled as if inhaled by the outside air. On his skin, shafts of hair stood erect in objection to the glacial air. The bird song remained silent. For several weeks, it had accompanied his morning ritual with an intermittent repetition of notes that were now familiar to him. Louis wondered if birds migrated during this time of year; it was a concept he found appealing. A melancholy wave licked at him; he would miss his good morning call.

Breakfast consisted of toast, coffee and his daily consumption of The Scotsman. He read the back pages first, usually to digest the football coverage. It was then his habit to scan the front page for a headline that caught his interest.

Emma called these his '*ritual.*' Today saw him dispense with convention, as the paper lay unread.

He was an early riser, a habitual behaviour that went back to his seminary days, now a lifetime away. Today was an appropriate day to rise early. He was going to meet Jez, Emma's brother, now Father Myers, the parish priest at St John's in the village of Glen Craig in Fife. Jez knew of his sister's forthcoming appointment with motherhood and he had been a welcome support that Louis had capitalised on.

During one of their regular phone calls, Louis expressed a desire to meet, offering to come to Fife, hinting at a revelation that would be inappropriate to impart unless told in person.

He drove along Queensferry Road, which took him through the suburbs and out into the green belt. Overhead, a plane majestically descended, wheels already in the landing position, the thunder of its engines masked by the pervasive tones of Lenny Kravitz emanating from the car's speakers.

He was soon crossing the Forth Road Bridge. To his right, the much older rail bridge loomed ominously, shedding its rustic paint over the River Forth. It triggered the memory of a bitter cold millennium New Year's Eve with Emma, in South Queensferry, anticipating the customary countdown to the new millennium from a large digital clock perched on the top of the rail bridge, its structure lit up by scores of powerful lamps like a sprawling metal Christmas tree.

Louis often thought of these bridges as giant metal arteries transporting thousands of people and goods on a daily basis across the River Forth, both icons of engineering to their own respective eras. Even as a child, he envisaged the two elephantine towers of the Road Bridge as imposing and majestic gateways to the Kingdom of Fife.

Further images stirred within him as they always did when he visited this part of the country, family holidays at St. Andrews, with his sister, two brothers, Italian father and Irish mother. The former contributing to his olive complexion and surname, Satriani, the latter being instrumental in his lifelong love affair with a particular football team from Leith.

Pastel tones decorated the morning sky in virgin light tingeing wispy clouds in silver shafts, like a celestial fan.

It was such spectacular scenes that infused Louis with the omnipotence of God and, as he drove, an imperceptible smile crept across his face. A warm sensation radiated from his abdomen, a glow of well-being that was constant and intense, elation more powerful than any drug. And, from the car's speakers, Lenny Kravitz sang, '*God is love.*'

He passed through villages and towns, preferring to avoid the main dual carriageway that by-passed them. These communities owed their existence to the digging of coal, an industry they had once prospered under, where father and son worked and toiled side by side and, in sombre times, may have died together. Less than a generation ago, score upon score of mines had populated the landscape, becoming part of its fabric, feeding and clothing whole communities, representing all aspects of life, work, social and play. Now, as he passed through the villages, Louis was aware that the giant slept, its lifeblood drained, its body decimated, its people scattered.

He arrived in Glen Craig and negotiated a tree-lined track that led to St John's Church, the clarity of light influenced by low descending cloud and the onset of a precipitous downpour.

Several cars stood parked in an area of fine gravel. Louis eased into space and stopped. He extinguished the ignition and the obstreperous music was immediately superseded by rhythmic droplets of rain drumming on the bodywork of the car.

A magazine lay on the passenger seat, opened at the depiction of a serene aqua blue sea where a whitewashed village ascended a steep hill and basked in sunlight. Louis had scanned every detail and digested every word he could now recite the content as if it were a poem.

He began to read.

A potent fire burnt within, lighting a corner of the soul and, with each visit to these islands, a marriage of in perpetuity was consummated. A way of life, whose qualities and characteristics are the product of indigenous culture, clothes the visitor with its ubiquitous exorbitance, pacifying the senses into submission.

Prolific landscapes impinge upon the traveller a spiritual ambience like manna from heaven's garden, profoundly addictive to the eye. By day, whole villages dream under a somnolent shroud, while at night they awake to the flush of music, conversation and soft light.

The salubrious climate cleanses the spirit and massages the body under the cover of an ever-expanding azure sky. The smells and natural perfumes are carried on warm currents, becoming healing potions, medicine for a troubled mind. The rhythmic beat of the cricket takes on a whole new perspective, becoming a chant, a prayer, a mantra, even a celebration.

Churches, with their white bell towers and blue domed roofs, are an ever-present feature in the Greek village, town, and landscape, representing stability and a way of life that feeds the soul and mind. Likewise, the deep azure sky, the golden sun and the beckoning call of the fine sand and clear seas, are temples of worship that attract many pilgrims.

Zakynthos is an island that not only casts a spell upon the visitor through its scenery and ambience, one is also exposed to the awakening of a self-realisation. I have confronted situations and experiences that, by their nature, forced me to re-evaluate my makeup and chemistry and therefore my relationship with my environment. This was not a fleeting reaction, it held substance and was tangibly exuberant of the wealth of insight it resonated as if forcing one to wear their clothes inside out, exposing the parts that are hidden from view and seldom seen. Zakynthos can be many things to many people, depending on how the individual uses their time to explore its offerings.

Vivacious Laganos, the haven of the night owl, pulsates to the hypnotic, invariable and ubiquitous beat of dance music, where the tribes of the young party until dawn.

The capital, Zakynthos town, with its cosmopolitan

ambience, offers a slower pace where culture, shopping, and pavement cafes entice the visitor against the backdrop of a picturesque harbour and a flotilla of boats. Viewed from the capital, Mount Skopos dominates the landscape, rising audaciously, puncturing the sky. It is here, that one can escape civilisation and breathe one's fill of the silence and absorb the panoramic views where meditation is an inevitable part of the experience. Tranquil and voluptuous, spiritual and scenic, Mount Skopos resonates with the verities of Greece.

The island's countryside is an undulating sea of life, a kaleidoscope of colour, whose mantle of lavish vegetation carpets the land in an abundant display of opulence. The myriad characteristics that Zakynthos harbours, is an Aladdin's treasure waiting to be discovered.

It is in the aspect of discovery, of the new and unfamiliar that the essence of life is attainable and appreciated to the full. In Zakynthos one just has to look, it is there; I found it, wrapped it around my soul and drank my fill of its infinite warmth.

Zakynthos is a member of the Ionian group of islands and is the most southerly...

He stopped reading and looked outside. Small streams of rain weaved their passage down the glass of the windscreen and, outside, an array of puddles populated the liquidised ground. From inside the church, he could hear an organ playing and singing.

He negotiated the ponds of water, sidestepping the large puddles and jumping the small ones. Briskly, he made progress towards the church entrance.

Once inside, he shook rivulets of rain from his jacket. He was in a foyer where a small shop sold religious books, children's bibles, mass books, an assortment of crosses, rosary beads, pictures and postcards depicting Christ, Mary and a variety of biblical scenes. Aware that his presence might disturb those inside, he tentatively opened another door and, upon stepping forward, he habitually blessed himself before taking a seat at the nearest pew. Around thirty people celebrated mass. Louis noted that the majority were elderly and female. They shuffled exorbitantly, filing towards the altar where a sombre Jez distributed communion. Louis watched this snail-like procession, envisaging himself in the place of his friend. How different his life would be then, a simple life attending to the needs of his parishioners.

A hand touched his shoulder. He turned around to see an old man smiling.

'You must be Louis, I've been waiting for you,' the old man said in a hushed voice. He lowered his head towards Louis. 'Father Myers will see you in the manse after mass... the housekeeper will look after you. Follow me.'

'Thanks,' Louis said, as he rose and followed the man's outstretched palm, inviting him to exit the church.

The manse sat on its own a few yards from the church. There was no garden at the front of the house. However, a large mantle of grass, dotted with trees, flourished to the side of the building and beyond; the sprawling Fife countryside emanated a greyish complexion in the wet drizzle.

As he approached the front door, it opened to reveal a tall woman, a feature that deceived her advancing age. She smiled at Louis and he smiled back. Her hair, silver-streaked and well groomed, was tied back from her face. She smiled with her eyes, he noticed, her glance more eloquent than any word and Louis immediately warmed to the elegant aura she projected.

'Come on in out of the rain, I've just boiled the kettle, Louis isn't it? Such an exotic name... French? Would you like some tea or coffee Louis? I'll show you into the study. What a dreadful day and it started out so promising as well.'

Louis smile widened as he wiped his wet shoes on the doormat. He was going to like this woman.

She shepherded him to a large front room. 'Make yourself comfortable. Father Myers shouldn't be too long... you're old friends? I suppose you'll just call him Jez?'

'Yes, we studied together in Rome.' Louis elected to sit

on one of two brown leather sofas.

'Oh, you're a priest as well, Father Myers never said. It must've slipped his mind. He's been awfully forgetful lately, probably worrying too much about all that business concerning his sister.'

'Well no, I wasn't ordained.' The reference to Emma caught him unexpectedly.

'Oh, I see. That's me putting two and two together and getting five. You would think I should've learnt by now. I've had plenty of time to practice.'

'No harm done. I would've thought the same.'

'That's kind of you. I didn't mean to intrude, I'll see to the coffee now... it was a coffee?'

'Yes. Just a little milk, that would be great.'

As she left, Louis sat back into the seat. Its leather creaked as he considered his surroundings. A neat flower arrangement speckled an unattractive tiled fireplace in a flurry of brilliant colour. The housekeeper's touch, he thought. A slight chill hung in the air. Louis shivered. To further compound this disconcerting sensation, dark mahogany furniture tempered the room's natural light. A desk sat at the window, cluttered with paper, a diary, a laptop, a pile of books sitting at such an angle that Louis was sure they were about to topple at any minute and, in the middle of this unkempt confusion, sat a framed photograph. Louis crossed the room and picked it up. Jez, Louis and a group of friends sat at a street cafe in Rome. It brought a smile to his face and he remembered it being taken. He retreated into his thoughts. Approaching footsteps jolted him back to the present.

'Let me help. I'll take that,' Louis offered, taking the weight of the tray from the housekeeper and placing it on the small table in front of him.

'Thank you, Louis. Oh, I've turned the heating on. You wouldn't think we were in the middle of June would you? The air's got quite a nip to it, and this rain doesn't help either.'

'It's turning out to be another typical summer,' Louis said, reaching for a flower-patterned china cup.

They could see people hurrying to their cars under umbrellas.

'It looks like mass has finished. Help yourself to a wee chocolate biscuit. I'd get one quick while there's still some left,' she said jokingly.

'Ah, Jez and his sweet tooth?'

'I'm afraid so.'

'I'm sorry, but I didn't ask your name?'

'Oh you don't have to be sorry Louis, where are my manners? Imagine not introducing myself. My name is Carris.'

'What a lovely name. You're the first Carris I've ever met.'

'It's my privilege. Actually, I have the distinction of being the only person in the village with the name. I don't know of a single person in the village who's shared my name in all the time I've lived here and I've lived here all my life.'

The sparkle in her eye subsided as if extinguished by some unheard thought.

'The coffee's nice. Thank you.' Louis held her gaze and the compulsion to do so overwhelmed his civility. Although Carris was studious and courteous, Louis glimpsed a sadness in her eyes, the unfolding of regret perhaps and, in that moment, it occurred to him he could have been looking at a reflection of himself. Why had the mention of a name, her name, stirred such a reaction?

'Oh forgive me,' she said, bending forward to pick up the tray. 'Hold on to your memories Louis. There may come a time when the pictures from the past will be all you have. Ah, there I go again, melancholic old fool.'

Louis passed the tray to Carris, a small smile creased her lips and, as she straightened, she composed herself and, once again reflected in her demeanour, was a woman of propriety. 'Thank you, Louis, enjoy your coffee.' She turned and left the room.

Jez swept into the room like a herd of elephants.

'I'm gasping for a smoke, hope you don't mind Louis? It's my only addiction...'

'But one of your many pleasures,' Louis interrupted. 'Are you still using that line to justify killing yourself?'

Jez stretched out his arms smiling expansively. 'It's the only good one I've got.'

Louis stood and they embraced. 'And you've only had ten years to come up with a new one.'

Jez was now dressed casually. He wore a light blue shirt which hung untidily over his prominent waistline. Red blood vessels fought for space on his puffed cheeks and his receding hairline emphasised his forehead to the detriment of his small rounded eyes.

He crossed to the window. 'I'll open this a bit. It'll keep the dragon at bay while I have a puff. She smells the smoke a mile off, doesn't approve you see - says it's bad for my health. Look at me.'

He gestured with his hands. 'It can't get any worse.'

Jez relaxed in the chair opposite Louis, lit a cigarette, and drew heavily on it. He tilted his head back, filling the air with blue smoke which coiled above him like an industrial chimney. He looked at Louis with interest.

'Under the circumstances, you're looking good. Sorry, I've not had the chance to visit; they're keeping me busy here.'

This was Jez's second year at the parish.

'I feel bad I haven't visited more,' Louis said.

'What do you mean visited more? This is your first time.' Jez laughed.

'Consider it an apology then.'

'I prefer visiting you.' Jez smiled. 'It gives the older ladies of the parish some spice to add to their daily gossip. It's rife you know. *Why would he be going to Edinburgh without his dog collar on*? You wouldn't believe it, Louis. Anyway, I'd go stir crazy if I didn't get over to Edinburgh once in a while. I can't exactly let my hair down in the local pub.'

'The purple-dye brigade are keeping their eye on you then? Surely you don't have to gallivant off to the capital to generate gossip, not Jez Miles? Are your bad ways finally behind you and you've retired gracefully?' Louis grinned.

'It'll take a lot more than a few old woman and their poisoned tongues, I can assure you of that.' Jez drew on his cigarette. 'So what's so important that you can't tell me about it over the phone?'

The photograph of the village in the magazine, nestling around a hill and brilliant white in the sun's glare, sharpened Louis' mind. He sensed a slight fluttering that swelled in his stomach, born from the knowledge he was wiping clean a stained window to view a landscape that beckoned him, invited him, to feel it, taste it and be a part of it. Louis found it irresistible. He shifted in his chair.

'I read somewhere about a mother's relationship with her child. She described that relationship by saying happiness is like a butterfly, yet it's a different butterfly for each of us. The butterfly that the mother was trying to capture wasn't the same as the one her daughter was chasing. It struck a chord with me, it perfectly described both Emma and I. We were both searching for different butterflies if you like. I realise that now. I thought we were looking for the same one.' Louis' throat tightened.

'If you gave Emma the moon Louis, she'd want the sun as well, she was like that as a child. She was never happy with what she had, always looking for the next best thing.'

'I knew that when we moved in together God, it was her flirtation I was attracted to in the first place. Even in the early days, I knew she didn't want children. She had always argued she was not that kind of woman. She could never give up her life for such a commitment, but I always thought that one day I would change her mind. I was wrong, you see, we were chasing different butterflies right up until the end, or that's what I thought until she told me about the baby.'

'Ah yes. Emma's little bombshell. I'm going to be an uncle, can you imagine? Do you fancy a real drink?' Jez asked, rising from his seat. He opened a drawer at his desk.

'Carris doesn't know about my hiding place.' He grinned and pulled out a bottle of whisky. 'My little treasure trove.'

'I'd better not, just to be on the safe side... on you go, though.'

'Don't worry my man, I intend to.'

Jez filled his glass and studied Louis.

'You've not come all this way just to tell me that you and Emma were running around Edinburgh scaring the butterfly population half to death.' He tilted his head back and drew heavily on his cigarette. 'Come on man, out with it.'

By now, sunlight had bathed the room in a permeable tone, flooding every corner. Louis felt marginally uplifted. The sun's unsuspected presence encouraged him.

'It's difficult to put into words. I thought we shared the same hopes and dreams. There was a time when we did and we strived for them. We had our ups and downs, our good times and bad, but that's what relationships are all about, aren't they? You've got to nurture a relationship before it can grow and I really thought we had something special. The promise of a life together has gone and now that she's pregnant, with his baby, well it's not going to happen. I can't believe I'm saying these words. You can't even begin to imagine what that feels like, Jez. It's as if someone one has just ripped my insides from me. I've thought a lot about my future. Where am I going now with my life? What does it hold for me? I've decided I need to put myself first. I don't have anything to keep me here, not now. That was anchored in Emma, but not anymore.' He leant forward as if to give meaning to his words. 'For the first time in months, I've decided that I'm going to be in control of the decisions and choices I make. They're not going to be influenced by other people and their actions.'

Jez was seated once more; he extinguished his cigarette and drained the contents of his glass. It produced a dull thud as he placed it on the table.

'Come on then. Tell me, what has caused this transformation? Christ Louis.' He crossed himself, a habit that had stuck ever since his days in Rome, where the other trainee priests had daily bets on how many times a day Jez would take Christ's name in vain.

'Another habit I see you haven't lost.' Louis grinned.

'I thought you were considering some dreadful deed and in need of my pastoral guidance... you had me worried there, Louis.'

'No, I've passed that stage. I know people care about me and that's what's got me through this. Knowing that I could speak to others has helped to get me to where I am now. It took time to feel ready to speak about it but I've found it to be invaluable. It's given me the strength to take control of my life to the point where I can now embrace it and see where it takes me.'

He thought of the traveller and their meeting. He knew even then that his life would not return to how it once was, how could it? He had been given a key to a door whose possibilities were too tempting to refuse, and he had willingly pushed it open.

'Ah, I sense a spirit of adventure. I wonder what that might entail?'

Jez scrutinised his friend.

'Recently I've been thinking a lot about places I've become drawn to. There is a magnetism about Greece. I need to go there and breathe the air, surround myself in the landscape, the colours, the climate and the people. I don't know if this makes any sense to you Jez, but I need to do this. I want to leave my old life behind and all that it has become. I don't want to feel I just exist from day to day. I've now got this wonderful opportunity to do exactly what I want when I want and go where I want. Just the thought of it makes my insides tingle; it's become infectious.'

Jez smiled. 'It's certainly got a hold of you, I can see that.'

'When Emma told me about the baby, I knew I'd lost her and, from then on, the reality of transforming my life became real; from that moment it just kicked in. I've never known a feeling like this. Even when I decided to join the priesthood it didn't feel like this; this is a release.'

'And have you thought about it... I mean really thought it through? What about your job, your flat?'

'The company has been really supportive throughout all of this. They said they'd keep my job open, they will officially treat it as extended leave, unpaid of course, and, as for the flat, I'm going to rent it out to a friend at work who has been looking for somewhere to live, so if things get tight while I'm away I'll have that income to tide me over.'

'In a way, I envy you Louis. From this tragedy, comes a great opportunity. There are many people who'd give their right arm to do what you're about to do, although I think it takes great courage. I know it's a cliché Louis, but in your case, God indeed works in mysterious ways.'

Louis shrugged. 'The decision was an easy one to make. If Emma and I were still together I'd not have even thought about it.'

'So where in Greece do you plan to go?'

'I'm going to Athens first, then I might travel through the mainland, before trying out some of the islands. There's that many, I'm spoilt for choice.'

'Do you think it would be to your advantage to have a familiar face around just in case you start to feel homesick?' Jez grovelled jocularly.

'You might have a point there. It would make sense to have a familiar face around... maybe I should ask Carla.' Louis smirked.

They both laughed and Louis was reminded why he loved to hear Jez laugh. It started as a high pitch cackle, a short pause, followed by another inexorable episode.

'When are you going?'

'Tomorrow.'

'You're not hanging about then. How long do you plan to go for?' Jez asked.

'I don't know. I'll take each day at a time and see where it leads me.'

The sharpened click of shoes on tiles announced the imminent arrival of Carris.

'Will you be staying for lunch Louis?' Carris asked, instinctively running a finger along the polished surface of the sideboard before inspecting it for particles of dust. She smiled.

'If it's no trouble, I'd be delighted,' Louis replied.

'That's settled then. It would be a pleasure. There's plenty of food and it would seem a shame for it to go to waste.' Carris gave Jez a stone look. 'That would be unusual in this house.'

Jez laughed. 'It could be your last supper, well lunch, before leaving your old life behind.'

Carris cleared the empty cups, paying particular attention to the glass that had contained the whisky. She swayed a disapproving glance towards Jez, who looked like a child caught stealing sweets from a shop.

Louis found the episode amusing, disguising his amusement with a halfhearted cough.

'She keeps you on your toes,' Louis said, once Carris had vacated the room.

'She does,' Jez agreed. 'Always catches me out, though.'

'Never mind my last supper I have a feeling that might have been your last drink of the day.'

Carris' appearance had reminded Louis of the sadness he had discerned in her eyes.

'Tell me about Carris,' Louis enquired.

'What do you want to know?'

'She reacted oddly when I asked her name?'

Jez lit another cigarette, sat back, and cleared his throat.

'Carris once had a degree of notoriety in the village. When she was younger, much younger, sixteen I think, during the Second World War, her childhood sweetheart was called up into the army and sent to France. Carris was pregnant... well you can imagine the scandal, in those days, the shame of it became public knowledge, an altogether different world. Her parents were originally from Ireland who came here to find work; her father worked in the pits. He had a brother who was a priest back in Ireland and it was this brother who arranged the whole thing. They sent her to Ireland to a place run by nuns. The baby was born there and then adopted. The church has failed many people, Louis, and regrettably it's slow to confess its own sins.'

'And what became of the father... did they continue to see each other?'

'Sadly no, he never returned from France... 'missing in action' was the official line. The body was never found, or if it was, he was never identified.'

'That's so sad. I can't imagine what she must have gone through. How could a young girl cope with such tragedy?'

'She never married nor had any more children. She's told me that when she thinks of the baby she calls it Carris, this was her grandmother's name as well. I don't think she ever forgave her parents, but she's become one of the most respected members of the community.'

'So her community didn't judge her, they accepted her for the person she was.'

'As I understand it, some were more forgiving than others. Most condemned the sin but not the sinner, unlike her parents, unfortunately.'

The Discernment of Loss

She sat at the kitchen table, her shoulders rising and falling with every sob, her breathing erratic, her eyes stained with charcoal tinged mascara smudged by tears that stung, sticking her eyelashes together, wet and salty, weaving their path down her shiny skin like small streams. Her eyes were puffy; she began to sniff in involuntary waves. Her throat ached and felt as if it was being wrenched out of her skin. The mobile phone sat a few inches from her hand. She contemplated the number and tentatively reached out.

Paul entered the kitchen and she retracted her hand, an instinct of survival. She had never seen this manifestation of his personality. She realised the once familiar face was a stranger that now stared at her heinously. The stale and stagnant odour of tobacco haunted his breath, while alcohol awakened his demons.

'You were fucking seen with him.' He spat the words with venom, his eyelashes blinked profusely.

She turned in frustration, looking out of the window.

'I don't think that conversing with someone constitutes a relationship.'

She now regretted her unwillingness to inform Paul of her intention to meet with Louis but then, if she had, his reaction, she now understood, would have been similar.

'I just felt it was the right thing to do, to tell Louis that I was pregnant. I owed him that at least.'

'Oh I see, so it wasn't to tell him that he was the father... well, was it? And fucking look at me when I'm talking to you.' His eyes bulged.

'Of course not... it's your baby,' Emma replied in her defense. 'Why are you being like this?'

He glanced at the phone, hissing through his teeth. 'Have you phoned him?' It was not spoken as a question but rather, an accusation. Incredulity masked her face.

'No, No.' Emma said, her head fell into her hands, surrendering to the futility of speech. He was beyond rationalisation and inebriated by resentment and rage. She suddenly felt a wave of encapsulating fear, like the rush of cold air and, in that moment, she longed for Louis. She craved his voice, his tender touch but, above all, the discernment of loss, her loss, crushed her with its weight.

Emma looked up, just as his fist broke her jaw. She could no longer see his hate as her vision blurred and glazed over. The force of the blow projected her sideways, like a loose floppy doll. Her hand collided with the mobile phone, sending it spinning off the table. She did not hear it clatter to the floor, as her temple collided with the edge of a worktop unit.

Emma lay motionless; a dark red tide of blood stained the floor tiles, like an oil slick, draining the life from her. Paul towered over her, now sobbing uncontrollably, the return of his senses substantiated by the pulsating pain in his knuckles. Falling to his knees, he cradled her in his arms.

'Oh God... Oh God. Emma speak to me, I'm sorry. I believe you, honestly I do. Say something, anything.'

The irrevocable nature of his action seeped into him as his sobriety was forced upon him. Where her head rested, his shirt was damp and he became aware of an exorbitant amount of dark blood filtering through the fabric. Helplessly he watched as the life faded from her eyes, like slipping into quicksand and, from the back of her throat, she whispered, 'Louis.' Devoid of life, she stared at him with eyes like marble.

Two Bridges

The invitation to accept lunch had extended to dinner. The two friends spent the day reminiscing, conjuring images and stories of Rome, of sultry weekends and beaches on the Italian coast. In his conversation with Jez, Louis confided his anxiety regarding the desertion of his faith but gradually, like the return of a lost friend, he had seen God in the actions and faces of others and due to these experiences he felt a renewed affiliation with his faith. He confessed being devoured by betrayal at the news of Emma's pregnancy, while feeling solicitous about her wellbeing.

They wrapped themselves in the memories their words painted,
sporadic laughter puncturing the air as they recalled nights that none of them wanted to end, meals shared under the velvet blanket of the night sky, wine that dulled their senses and the untouchable temptations of vivacious young women who conversed with Louis in Italian, perceiving him to be one of their own with his proficiency in the language. (His father made it a house rule that only Italian could be spoken in the home, to remind his children they might be Scottish by birth, but it was Italian blood that populated their veins. That it was diluted by their Irish mother did not constitute a conflict of interest in his reasoning and, as long as Hibernian was the football team supported by her siblings, a small part of Ireland would always prevail. Therefore, to his mother's way of thinking, the emphasized tones and colourful vocabulary that resonated through the household was a small price to pay).

For the first time in months, Louis felt happy.

The need to urinate was becoming an overwhelming urgency. His initial calculation of making it to the other side of the Forth Road Bridge was not the promising prospect he envisaged; he now conceded it redundant, as a piercing sensation in his bladder forced him into a re-evaluation and sharp exit from the M90.

Trees straddled the road, their branches merging into a

tunnel constructed by nature. The entrance to the hotel was how he remembered it, the kind that if you did not know it was there, it was easy to miss and drive past. He took the first left along an inclining and twisting road.

The car park was busy. He found a vacant space and parked. The hotel basked in an inviting and warm yellow light. Louis noticed the fading clarity of light that had descended unsuspectingly.

In his haste, he fumbled with the car keys, locked the car and ran towards the entrance. Once inside Louis ascended a flight of stairs that led into a spacious reception area. To his left, two doors opened into a large room where a bride and groom danced to a live band. The bride's dress swayed as if the wind had moved and brushed its fabric like an invisible partner in the dance. He noticed her eyes sparkle, emanating a contentment, like a smile that catches a sunrise on the birth of a new morning.

Guests with radiant smiles and inebriated laughter hugged the periphery of the floor, enthusiastically clapping in accompaniment to the music.

Louis turned and spotted the sign for the toilet, hovering above a sea of extravagant ornamental hats. He weaved a cautious passage through the large proliferation of feminine profligacy, excusing himself several times.

The queue snaked out of the toilet, forcing the urgency of his predicament upon him. Conversations about the secrecy of the honeymoon suite unfolded. Some devised plans, like detectives, on whom to interrogate to reveal the information that would tell them the room in which they could hatch their boyish plans.

His stomach felt extended, and he was alarmed at the stabbing pain in his bladder. The encroaching demeanour of an impostor unfolded upon him as Louis imagined his embarrassment if asked his connection to the newlyweds. He indulged in a small prayer pleading for his identity to be concealed. He realised the hypocrisy in turning to God to spare his humiliation. It had become easy to abandon him and easier still to crave his protection.

To his relief, the queue gradually subsided as he drew

closer to the toilets. Most of the urinals were used by men wearing kilts, the ubiquitous dress code for a Scottish wedding. To his relief, he didn't have to wait long before releasing his discomfort with a long sigh.

It was then that the unsuspecting whoosh of air, blown into a bagpipe startled him, as a piper, dressed in full highland regalia rehearsed his tune.

The sound resonated and bounced off every wall and floor tile, amplifying the volume, tone, and pitch of the notes. Louis was left struck by its intense power, surrounding him, entering and saturating his every pore with its haunting and ancient sound. The experience was surreal as he became enveloped in ancient music that, for centuries, had stirred and fortified the hearts and senses of men and women whilst he stood relieving himself.

He became acutely aware of its hypnotic qualities and in that moment realised why generations of men had gone to their deaths accompanied by its trance. Yet, there was another face to this metaphoric coin. It pronounced times of celebration fused within a performing cocktail of national identity and cabaret.

As Louis washed his hands, the piper left, the music fading with distance as the piper drew closer to his theatre, his audience, and the electric anticipation.

On leaving, Louis once again passed through the reception area. It was now almost deserted, apart from solemn looking waiters cleaning tables of disregarded glasses and overflowing ashtrays. The air was oppressive and stagnant in stale smoke. He passed a young couple draped over a settee, engulfed in a passionate and absorbing kiss. The young woman's skirt had risen ungraciously, exposing the white skin of her thigh.

Once again Emma visited him, entering his thoughts, provoking images of friends' weddings and shared gestures of love and passion. Louis glanced to his right and, through the opened doors, he noted that the piper's spell had worked its magic, inviting willing participants to its celebratory dance.

Once outside Louis welcomed the freshness of the night

and filled his lungs with chilled exhilarating air.

Louis decided not to go to his car; instead he walked along a rising path that led to a viewing area with undisturbed views of the bridge he had crossed earlier that day.

The sounds of celebration from the hotel were now distant as he stood in the still quiet night. The headlights from traffic crossing the Forth Road Bridge reminded Louis of the illuminated eyes of insects at night. During the day, in comparison, he imagined swarming parties of Japanese tourists, enthusiastically composing photographs of the bridges with cameras that seemed permanent extensions of their arms.

Louis watched clouds race across the sky, smudging the moon as if it had just been painted and was still wet upon a black canvas.

He wondered about Carris and the path she took, no, was forced to endure, knowing her child would never know her or be insulated by her love. Louis tortured himself with an image of Emma, cradling her baby. He longed to be a part of such a world but, in that longing, was the realisation that such a world would not be his. He tried to recollect the picture in the article that lay in his car, the detail and colour depicted a sense of serenity, a peacefulness that he could not touch in his own life.

Louis thought of his parents and their outward spilling of disbelief and incomprehension that their son could abandon his marriage to the church for the physical love of a woman. Their son, the priest, was now just their son, the man. He thought of Jez and how parallel their lives could have been if fate had not decreed that he was to meet Emma. Louis thought of how one simple decision could engineer and map lives and destiny. It was such an action that found him standing alone, dwarfed by the sheer presence of two bridges, that now held significance in his life, for he could never lose the memory of this moment, this defining instance.

He turned and walked back down the path, its steep gradient forcing him into a light jog, revealing an insular and therapeutic comfort, as he accepted that this was the start of the rest of his life and he knew such a decision would touch and have a profound influence on the lives of others, even those who were unfamiliar to him.

Zakynthos

The Flower of the East

'Kalimera Maria, we've been waiting for you. Luckily your paying customers have been patient. We should have left ten minutes ago.'

'Kalimera Marios, you worry too much, it's not good for your heart. Remember what the doctor told you about stressing your heart… anyway they're like puppies, give them what they want and they behave themselves.'

'That's all very well Maria. Remember, puppies can nip.'

She mounted the steps of the coach. 'I appreciate your concern, Marios, but their bark is louder than their bite. Anyway, give them ten minutes viewing our beautiful island and my lateness will pale into insignificance.'

Marios threw his head back and expelled a hearty laugh, admiring her retort and display of confidence.

'She always gets the last word,' he muttered while putting the coach into gear.

The coach moved slowly, increasing its speed, as Marios negotiated a cautious path through a cluster of parked vehicles. Maria picked up a microphone, switched it on and surveyed the passengers.

A gallery of nationalities met her vision: British, German, French and Italian. She spoke in English, her delivery proficient and fluent.

'Good morning ladies and gentlemen. My name is Maria and I am your guide for today's trip. Our driver today is Marios. As we proceed through the island, I'll draw your attention to places of historic value and do my best to portray the character and culture of Zakynthos and its people. If you have questions, please don't hesitate to ask. We will reach our first stop, the village of Macherado, to view its main attractions, the church of the Saint Agio Mavara and the icon of the saint in about thirty minutes. So, in the meantime, relax and enjoy our beautiful island from the comfort of the coach. Thank you.'

Maria replaced the microphone and sat in the seat next to

Marios. He looked at her through black sunglasses and although she could not see his eyes, a mischievous smile gave away his thoughts.

'Maria, speak to me in English, your voice sounds so sexy...'

'Marios,' she remonstrated. 'Pay attention to the road, I won't be very sexy if I'm dead and that's exactly what you'll be if your wife finds out about your filthy tongue.'

He put his hand to his heart as if wounded. 'I suffer a fate worse than death when each morning I wake and find her laying next me. Driving this coach is my only escape. Have some pity, Maria, don't mention my wife.'

'Marios how long have you been married? Thirty years... did you not marry for love? You have beautiful grandchildren...'

'And they take after their grandfather with their looks, thank God... Love is like beauty, it fades with the years, except me of course. Don't you think so Maria?'

She shook her head. 'Trust me Marios, you don't want to know what I think,' and, with a wry smile, she said, 'If your head was any bigger, we'd all suffocate with the lack of oxygen.'

'Tell me, Maria, how is your mother? Now there's an image of beauty, beauty personified, your father, may he be at peace with all the saints in heaven was the luckiest man in Zakynthos on the day he married your mother and he knew it. He was the envy of every man.'

'She's well, but still desperate for more grandchildren.' Maria smiled at the thought.

'Now, there will stand a lucky man ... ah if only I was just a few years younger.'

'Try decades Marios. Your poor wife must know the meaning of suffering, married to the likes of you.'

Marios scratched his nose, creasing the skin. He had known Maria since she was a child and they had worked together for four years, so he knew the current lull in their conversation meant she intended to be alone with her thoughts.

Maria weaved a slender hand through honey coloured

hair. A small scar, the result of a childhood accident, sat at an angle, barely discernible to the right of her upper lip. It was an imperfection that had been conducive to staining teenage vanity and viewed at the time to be a detestable and detrimental curse, coating and subduing her personality, leaving it reticent. Then, by her late teenage years, these implications were replaced by a sense of blossoming and womanhood, erasing her perception of ugliness, eclipsed by a fondness towards her minor impairment she now (in her twenties) thought of as contributing to, by its presence, an imperfection that defined her looks.

   The coach travelled through countryside that Maria never tired of gazing upon, primrose houses and terracotta roofs flashed into view and just as suddenly disappeared again. In places where the sea hugged the shore, saturated blue and turquoise gave way to a deep sapphire that stretched towards the horizon, its colours once again evolved, owing to the azure sky and the occasional solitary white cloud that invaded the vast space of dominant blue.

   Maria thought, there could be no other place on earth, that provoked such beauty, definite and crystallising, as her island.

The Letter

The smell of cooking permeated the upper floors of the house, like rising smoke from a fire. Maria watched an insect crawl across an ocean of whitewashed wall as an image of her mother, cooking breakfast and singing while she worked, entered Maria's thoughts. The closeness in the room confirmed it was already another warm day as shafts of light penetrated the shutters, like long silver spears, invading the room and exposing particles of floating dust normally hidden and unseen.

   She slid from the sheet and, already missing the insular comfort of her bed, wrapped a towel around her, secured it and opened wooden shutters and glass panelled doors. At once, the bedroom was washed in virgin light as she stepped onto the somnolent balcony. Her space.

   Ceramic pots, flush in a colourful bazaar of flowers, are set at sporadic intervals, populating the balcony that wrapped around the top floor of the house. Maria smiled. Two black cats precariously weaved their slight, shiny bodies in and out of decorative wooden spokes upon the ledge of the balcony as if playing a game of 'follow the leader.'

   She called their names. They came to her with arched backs and erect tails, rubbing against her legs with amplified purrs, projecting their contentment. She sat on a wicker chair, drew her legs to her chest, and watched, as an unfortunate insect snagged the cat's curiosity. They crouched on all fours, masked in a pensive study. Their impatience deserted them and they pounced, theatrically and cumbersomely; a flash of tumbling fur and entangled limbs, they knocked each other off balance, surfaced in a disorientated stupor, and disappeared around the corner to resume the chase.

   In the garden, the sun drew long distinct shadows over the dry earth. The light, having a certain subtle and infectious quality inherent to the ambience of the time of day, painted and basked objects and landscapes in an explosion of colour. The music of nature sang its song.

Birds, like the chorus line in a stage show, penetrated the air, their melodies surfing on the warm currents, filling the garden with a soft therapeutic song. A warm breeze gently rustled leaves, as if an invisible hand had tentatively shaken them.

The same breeze exhilarated and refreshed Maria, like a fan blowing air across her skin. She breathed contentedly as the murmuring soundtrack of waves drew her attention to the sea. She brushed a stray wisp of hair behind her ear and massaged her neck in a continuous motion before yawning and then the gentle and serene introduction to the start of her day was broken.

'Maria, are you awake? Your breakfast is cold, are you remembering you promised your brother you'd take him fishing today.'

'I'm coming... and yes, I haven't forgotten,' she sighed, her solitude broken. One last look, she thought, as she caught sight of a ferry, negotiating the waves and the entrance to the harbour. From her balcony, it looked like a motionless toy and she imagined reaching out and plucking it from the sea.

The kitchen was the nucleus of the house, a large room that functioned as the hub of the Nasiakos' family activity. It was the kind of place that always hugged you, Maria thought.

Maria's first memories are of this room: her mother cooking, cleaning, washing and the family eating. It seemed to always claim her mother's time. Maria remembered sitting at the table and reading out loud from a book, often homework, she thought, as her mother cooked the evening meal and listened attentively. It had become the place of reprimand for her older brother, Stelios, when childhood pranks and misspent adventures backfired, where the teaching and value of manners and good behaviour were enforced by her father, and good fortune celebrated and bad news endured and suffered. It became a place of haven for the family pet dog that, as a stray, wandered into the kitchen and was immediately adopted by Maria and Stelios.

The kitchen was dominated by a large wooden table that

sat in the middle of the floor space. It had been in the family for generations, on her father's side, bearing the marks her grandfather had made when he was just a boy and then the weight of his coffin and then latterly, her father's coffin. It was now only used to its full potential on Sundays when Stelios, his wife, and children visited for lunch and the heavy table was lifted into the garden. Maria's mother refused requests from Stelios to buy a new table for the garden, 'it's a family tradition,' she said sternly, and that was the end of that.

The summer months witnessed these family gatherings, under the shade of the fig tree that was said to be just as old as the kitchen table itself. When Maria was a child, her father teased his children by suggesting that the tree would one day make a grandiose table. They, however, viewed this suggestion with horror; the tree had become a friend where they spent their days playing in its contorted branches and the perpetual shade it offered, like an umbrella, from the broiling sun.

Maria had lived in the house all of her life, except for two years, which she spent with a boyfriend, living in the centre of Zakynthos Town, in a small cramped flat, to the disapproval of her mother who reminded her, if her father was still alive, he would insist on a long engagement and then marriage. Whereupon Maria took great satisfaction in reminding her mother she had only known her husband to be for three weeks before they married. Her mother retorted that times were different then, and theirs was a unique case.

Maria's relationship with her boyfriend was like a ship on the ocean, calm and serene, yet exposed to the occasional storm. However, the storms gathered more frequently, more verbal than violent, and the ship eventually sank. She returned home, like the prodigal son or, in her case, daughter and, just like the parable, her mother welcomed her unconditionally without resorting to the pious remark of 'I told you so.'

Maria entered the kitchen and caught sight of the scene that met her each morning, her mother preparing breakfast. Her mother wore a lilac dress that brushed her ankles.

'Good morning,' Maria said, sitting at the table.

Clare turned and smiled at her daughter. 'It wouldn't do to keep Michalis waiting. If you said you were leaving at nine o'clock, then nine o'clock it will be.'

'I know, I know,' Maria mused.

Clare poured dark coffee into two white cups. Clare was in her early sixties. She had tied back her strawberry chestnut hair, highlighting the texture and polish of her skin. Faint lines fanned from the corner of her eyes and it was only when she laughed or frowned that they announced their presence. Light freckles speckled her complexion, dusting her forearms.

She offered Maria a cup, reminding her to be careful as it was hot.

Lifting the cup to her lips Maria blew into it, causing delicate ripples to seek the edge of the rim. She studied her mother. A doleful and absent look masked Clare's face, a preoccupation at odds with her normal demeanour that often saw her enquire about Maria's day, offer a commentary on the latest social news of neighbours and friends, and deliberate on the list of household chores that demanded her attention. She sat in silence within a stony glare.

'Are you feeling alright?' Maria asked.

The words seeped into Clare; the discernment of their meaning invaded her thoughts, her concealed world, and drew her back to the kitchen and the aroma of coffee and her daughter's searching eyes.

'Oh, I'm sorry Maria, I was miles away.'

'You seem preoccupied,' Maria said, with a raised eyebrow.

'Yes, I suppose I am.' She cupped both hands around her cup. 'In fact, I was years away. Today's the anniversary of when I first met your father. It seems like yesterday but, at the same time, it feels he has been gone from us for so long. I miss him so much.'

A current of loss resonated in her mother's voice.

'I know you do, we all do.' Maria stood, sliding the chair backwards; she moved around the table and embraced her mother. Both women held on to each other as if doing so would squeeze the grief from each of them, knowing they had lost a father and husband but not the love they felt for him.

'Come now, let's sit, and enjoy our coffee while it's still hot,' Clare said.

Maria sat at the table and sipped her coffee.

'Oh, I almost forgot there's a letter for you on the table. It has an Athens postmark. It might be important.'

Maria felt hesitant and excited at the same time.

'Well, are you going to open it?' Clare said, after a time.

Maria hesitated. 'I will, after my coffee.'

She touched the white envelope. 'I remember dad saying we should follow our dreams but always be there for family.'

'He did, both were important to him, but what's that to do with the letter?'

If I go to Athens I can't do both, Maria thought.

Adjustment

Maria is fifteen minutes older than her brother, Michalis yet, the course of that time sets them apart and was instrumental in influencing the life that Michalis was to inherit. The medical diagnosis disclosed by the doctor to shade light on Michalis' inability to reach his expected developmental milestones was offered in cold and mechanical rhetoric as if read, word for word from a medical encyclopedia.

'Mental retardation, Mrs. Nasiakos,' the doctor inquired. *'Are you familiar with the implications of such a condition?'*

Maria's mother later remarked that the doctor, with his clinical white coat, greased hair and youthful complexion, did not look old enough to have graduated from school, never mind medical college.

The lugubrious air that impregnated the small and cluttered office crushed her chest and caused her to gasp for air as the doctor commented that her son's brain had been starved of oxygen due to the complicated and unforeseen nature of the birth. This, he remarked, was a major contributing factor to his present condition and then, as if as an afterthought, he continued, there was no cure for their son, as part of his brain did not work as it should and never would. He concluded that he was sorry; the words imparted were devoid of feeling and had an air of finality about them that announced the end of their meeting.

It was an experience that remained vivid and potent; her mother would recall it with clarity, even years after the event. Her descriptions depicted a traumatic wave that swept over her life that became the catalyst for a whirlpool of emotional crisis and the re-evaluation of hopes and expectations. She initially rejected the diagnosis, a symptom of her psychological adjustment which, she read about later, depended on how the news was given to the parents.

Maria would always be a reminder to her parents of the child they lost in that stuffy and oppressive room. This emotional impact would manifest in their changed expectations for their son, their altered perspectives for the future, the realisation of being a different family from their neighbours, from friends. To their knowledge, there was not another single family on the island that shared their life-shattering circumstance, there was no one they could turn to for advice or for guidance and they were adamant that Michalis would not end up in an institution on the mainland.

They grieved the loss of the normal child. Clare later learned, from her avid research and encyclopedic reading, that their sense of bereavement and mourning was part of the process that highlighted the stages they would go through as they advanced from shock to a coming to terms with and adapting to their new situation. She knew these stages well, where a plethora of negative emotions and reactions consumed her life. Like a natural disaster, there was no escaping the unwritten rules she would experience.

An avalanche of unrelenting stages ravaged her emotions. She felt herself being assaulted by confusion and living from day to day within a sensation she could only describe as numbness. Each morning when she awoke, she lay in bed and prayed through stinging tears she had awakened from a nightmare and then the guilt would creep upon her and envelop her, like quicksand.

She felt part of her being devoured until nothing was left but emptiness, a shell of what she had once been. Her questions appeared to have no answers. The months fell upon each other like dominoes. Then calmness descended upon the family like the contentment felt when one is absorbed in a task. The family developed a preoccupation of inner searching and forced self-development. They set about redefining their goals and priorities, asking questions, and finding they were becoming realistic about Michalis' abilities and taking enormous pride and joy in the things he could achieve. This forged a sense of realism and hope, there was an air of reconciliation, an ambience of acceptance that moulded itself into the heart of the family where they felt blessed to experience the gifts he shared with them, that enabled his personality to develop and flower and the scent he offered, such as his smile, laughter and sereneness were, inhaled with vigour and cherished, as if they were life themselves.

A Beautiful Fish

They walked together, down the slight gradient of the hill where a ribbon of somnolent houses snaked towards the centre of town. Above them, the incandescent sun, already claiming the vast oasis of blue as its own, followed their progress.

In his hand, Michalis held a fishing rod; on his back, a rucksack which contained the rudimentary equipment for his excursion - fishing lines, hooks, a reel, a knife and several small fish he would cut up later and use to entice the bigger fish that were the objects of his desire. Michalis had a tall stature and, although there was a stoop to his neck, he stood six foot in his bare feet. His left eye sat further from the bridge of his nose when compared to the right eye and this made it difficult to decide whether he was looking at you or around you. Michalis' hair was short and thinning and, although it was a deep black, hinting at blue, speckles of silver grey had appeared. His lips were always curled in a hesitant smile and, as he walked, his steps were small, yet determined. His command of language was limited therefore he relied on signing with his hands to make his needs known. In accomplishing this, he had devised his own unique system with which to communicate with others. People who knew Michalis (which seemed to be the whole of the island, as his personality preceded any communication difficulty) had become familiar with his self-styled sign language and were, in most cases, proficient in forming a two-way source of communication, stimulating their sense of achievement, which boosted Michalis' self-esteem, who, in typical animated style, took great pleasure in reminding people he was responsible for their new found skill.

Due to Michalis' popularity, their walk was not lonely. A woman, absorbed in her task of sweeping dried leaves, lifted her head and seeing them approach offered an enthusiastic and convivial wave as a freak gust of wind blew her source of labour into an unkempt mass, to the delight of an amused Michalis.

Above them, neighbours spoke on decorative balconies amongst an explosion of colour and earthy terracotta vases and pots. Seeing the approaching Michalis, they bellowed warm greetings with expansive gestures.

As they progressed, an item of clothing in a fashion boutique caught Maria's eye; she leisurely ambled brushing the fabric and scanning the price tags as the coolness of the air conditioning impelled her to linger longer. Such unplanned excursions frustrated Michalis who viewed them as a distraction to the eventual purpose of his walk, to reach the harbour and fish.

He wrestled with his restlessness by swinging his fishing rod, like a sword, cutting the air with a whipping sound that held his attention until the ache of the harbour forced him to retrieve his sister who relented to his persistence by letting him pull her by the arm and onto the street.

They reached Solomos Square and found themselves straddled by elegant buildings, palm trees and, a little further, pavement cafes that vibrated with the foreign tongues, the enticing aroma of cooked food and the purposeful posturing of waiters.

Tasting salt upon his lips Michalis sensed the nearing of the harbour. He brought his hands to his lips, palm to palm as if praying and shook them from side to side blowing on them, tapping both feet on the ground in a dance of anticipation and excitement.

Several people tore themselves from their food and stared, their inhibition evaporating like the curiosity of children.

'Nearly there now,' Maria said, placing a reassuring hand on Michalis' shoulder.

Maria's work brought her to the square twice a week and, on her days off, if she frequented the square, it became her habit to recite in English the commentary she imparted to her tour party.

'When the reconstruction of the capital began, after the earthquake of 1953, the builders and architects stayed true to the old Venetian designs of grandeur and elegance. The museum is an impressive example of the splendour and

affluence the Capital enjoyed before the earthquake struck. It houses memorabilia from the lives of the island's poets, Solomos and Phoskols, and island life before 1953. As well as the museum, we will be looking at other buildings which were also faithfully restored, such as the Library and Art Gallery...'

The waterfront vibrated with pavement cafes and enticing shops; they looked intimate and cosmopolitan amongst the volatile nature of the traffic. Crossing the road was precarious. However, once on the other side, the ambience was pleasant and calm, as if an invisible wall was constructed, absorbing the noise.

Fishing boats hugged the harbour wall. Their mustard nets spilled onto the quayside in mountainous mounds, emptied of their catch as their owners skillfully sewed and repaired them.

Maria noticed two young boys fishing at the harbour wall. Theirs was a primitive style compromising of a line of gut with a hook tied to the end and small pieces of fish as bait. She observed their simple device had not borne them the fruits of success, yet this did not diminish their enthusiasm and contentment as their legs dangled over the water, happy to be fishing.

A little further, a ferry emptied its hulk of articulated vehicles, trucks, cars, and motorbikes. A disturbance of engines, horns, and screeching brakes swirled in a crescendo, as the arms of a policeman swept the air in graceful waves, like a music conductor, bringing harmony and order to the tumultuous exodus of vehicles.

'Michalis, Maria... at last! Where have you been?' The deep and resonating timbre of the voice always reminded Maria of Louis Armstrong singing, 'What a Wonderful World.' It belonged to an old friend of her father, Alexandros, a portly man in his late sixties who made his living ferrying tourists to and from the various sightseeing attractions of the island.

The question hung in the air. As they approached the boat, Michalis quickened his pace.

'I'm sorry Alexandros, blame me. It was my fault, I was

window shopping,' Maria confessed.

Alexandros laughed, revelling in Maria's discomfort.

'Never mind, you're here now. Anyway, it's not as if the fish have anywhere else to go.' A smile tugged at the edges of Michalis' mouth. He walked the length of the small brow that connected the impressive boat with the shore. Alexandros greeted him warmly, guiding him onto the deck with a playful slap on the back.

Michalis waved at Maria, before ascending the steps to the upper deck of the boat. Alexandros pulled in the brow, as Maria untied the moorings and threw them onto the boat. Alexandros laboriously climbed the steps to the bridge before bringing the engines to life with a splutter and a burst of smoke and then he eased the boat towards the open sea.

He turned towards Maria and confidently shouted above the drone. 'I'll have him back by five, don't worry about lunch. Our bellies will be full once I cook the fish we're about to catch.'

Maria studied the boat, absorbing every detail as if viewing its shape for the last time. She focused on her brother, savouring the moment, digesting it, absorbing her instinct to protect him. Maria trained her eye on the two figures who were by now steadily merging into the watery landscape. She knew the tallest figure was Michalis, and she retained the image, storing it and processing it to be replayed later in her mind, to be held on to and cherished. The lines and colours, the shades and tones were precious; she strained as long as she could until her vision became blurred. Maria stood and watched; eventually the boat grew smaller, shrouding its occupants, as it finally rounded the harbour wall and disappeared from view. A knot tugged at her and she hoped the sea would remain calm.

'Protect him and keep him safe,' she whispered.

Her feet were swollen, a mixture of walking and the rising heat. She slipped off her shoes, stretched her legs, and curled her toes backwards and forwards until they felt like they belonged to her again. The relief was immediate and gratifying, as was the shade the parasol offered as she sipped her coffee at a pavement café looking out over the shimmering and placid water of the harbour.

Beyond this, rolling pined-fringed hills rose towards a limitless blue sky. The church of St. Dionysios, the dominant figure of a tower and the sprawling buildings of the capital, lay like building blocks against the silhouetted hills of the island's interior.

Maria crossed her legs and rested the cup on her lap. Its radiating warmth was immediately pleasant, almost sensual. This awareness was not lost on her. Life had been devoid of any serious relationship since her *'two years in the wilderness,'* as she referred to that time, that failure.

Maria waved away an irritant fly. She bore a rooted aversion to them for as long as she could remember.

When she was younger, her phobia became the subject of amusement for Stelios, her older brother, who chased her around the house with a squashed fly stuck to tissue paper. Maria recalled these episodes (as the fly seemed intent on entering her ear, again she flicked it away with her hand) and the stricken panic that consumed her with a clarity that defined the years in-between: running blindly, screaming at such a volume it filled the house with her fear, until she reached the sanctuary and open space of the garden.

Maria could now smile at these childhood pranks with fondness. However, such civility did not stretch to the present fly that once again bombed towards her before landing on the table.

A sudden whoosh and a bang, startled Maria, she involuntary jumped in her chair and looked just in time to see the lifeless fly swooped from the table by a magazine.

'Oops... sorry Maria. I didn't mean to frighten you.'

Maria squinted in the glare of the invariable sun.

'Zoe! I almost jumped out of my skin... God, you scared me half to death.' Maria protested, embodying the merest suggestion of hurt.

Zoe sat opposite Maria, placing the magazine on the table. She smiled with moon white teeth, an expression that remained intact when she spoke, animating her face. Her hair, tied back from her face, hung down the middle of her shoulders where the sun elaborated its natural shine.

'I saw your attempt at getting rid of the fly,' Zoe said, flicking her hand in the air with an exaggerated arc. 'Pathetic. I thought you needed a more decisive tactic.' She gestured towards the magazine.

'I'm sorry, I didn't mean to give you such a fright, but it was funny. You should've seen the look on your face. Oh, Maria, it was a picture.' Zoe squeezed the words out as they both surrendered to the comedy with bouts of laughter.

'Two emotional extremes in the one day. I don't know if I cope with that,' Maria stated jovially.

'Oh dear, I haven't laughed so much in ages,' Zoe said, wiping small droplets of tears from the corners of her eyes. 'I saw Michalis on Alexandros' boat.'

'Yes, they're going fishing; they should be back by five.'

'And what do you have planned?'

'Oh, I don't know. After all that excitement, a little chilling out sounds appealing.'

'Well, how about some shopping therapy to chill out to?' Zoe asked, her ever-present smile curled in expectancy. 'Well?'

'Mmm... I think I could cope with that.' Maria rose from her chair. 'Let's go,' she urged.

'Are you not forgetting something?' Zoe pointed to the abandoned shoes and Maria's shoeless feet. 'You'd better put them on first.'

'I thought you said shopping therapy, I'll buy a new pair.' Maria grinned and fell back into her chair, the playful satire of her voice echoing in her head.

'I'm starving,' Maria said, slipping on her shoes. 'What about a bite to eat? Oh and take this with you.' Maria grinned, handing the magazine to Zoe. 'Your aim is better than mine.'

***

'I need your advice.'
'What about?'
'A job I've been offered.'

'Wonderful. I didn't know you were looking for another job.'

'That's the point. I wasn't.'

'So,' Zoe said, intrigued. 'What is this job?'

'I went to a conference in Athens last week. Our company sends us there every year, new developments in the travel industry, job fairs, that sort of thing. Anyway, I bumped into an old friend whom I shared a room with when I was at university in Athens. She's started her own tour guide business and she offered me a job.'

'A job? Just like that?'

'Well, there would be an interview but she said it would just be a formality. The job was mine if I wanted it.'

Maria drank her wine. She felt invigorated, a mixture of wine and the prospects that such an offer may unfold. She was also thinking of her mother and of Michalis; it brought a conflict into her world of contentment, a knotted ache that lurked in her chest.

They were sitting outside under a parasol, the café bar being one of Maria's favourites. A waiter took their order and moved on to another table.

Zoe raised an eyebrow. 'You're not sure are you?'

'Oh, I don't know what to think. Part of me is excited about it.' Maria sighed. 'I can't imagine living in a city... Athens, the noise and the crowds. It would be such a major change.'

'Think of the nightlife, the restaurants, the people, you would meet new friends and there's the shopping.'

'I know. When you put it like that what would there not be to like about it?'

'What's keeping you here Maria? You need to be honest with yourself. Is it worth staying for or do you want to grab this opportunity by the balls and see where it leads you?'

Maria avoided Zoe's eyes. Her hand clutched the stem of her glass.

'You haven't told your mother yet, have you?'

'No.'

'You need to start thinking about yourself, Maria. For once put yourself first.'

'I know, I know. I've lived away from home before as you know, but Athens.'

'It's not that far. You can both take turns at visiting each other.'

'She's a bit fragile at the moment, emotionally that is.' Maria's voice strained.

Zoe noticed how hard this was for Maria and relented. She smiled. 'If you do decide to go, pick your moment with caution; after all, if you hadn't met your friend you wouldn't be contemplating this job offer and moving to Athens.'

'I know, but a letter arrived this morning. There is a date set for the interview.'

***

Maria stood looking out towards the Ionian, her hands laden with bags, the spoils of her shopping. Her attention was drawn towards a swirl of white cloud and an airplane, its white vapour trailing across the sky like a child's chalk mark.

Maria checked the time. Ten past five. She scanned the line of moored boats, looking for one in particular; her disappointment encapsulated by an uneasy frown that dissolved when she caught sight of a familiar approaching boat. Maria squinted, concentrating hard, now regretting drinking too much wine at lunchtime. Drawing closer, the boat revealed itself. A heavy feeling crushed her chest and her stomach began to churn. She felt light headed.

'Oh Michalis. Where are you?' she sighed.

A pain stabbed her behind the eyes. She paced the quayside, anxious thoughts racing. Should she phone her mother? No, she would only worry. Does Alexandros have a mobile? What if he did, she did not know the number. Has one of them fallen overboard? What if there has been an accident, a collision involving another boat and they cannot radio for help? What if Alexandros has had a heart attack and Michalis is on the boat afraid and alone? Maria's heart pounded. Rivulets of sweat populated her forehead, like small streams. She wiped them with the back of her hand and murmured, 'This is crazy. Get a grip, Maria.'

She glanced again at her watch. Five twenty. 'I'll give them until half past,' she placated herself. 'He did say five o'clock? Yes of course he did, they'll be here soon.'

The light softened, a reminder of Michalis' late return. She watched as a ferry docked on the other side of the harbour. Again she consulted her watch. She cried to herself, 'This is not good, something must have happened.' Her throat felt like a rock inside her, her eyelashes sticky, wet with tears that floated on her eyelids, visible and glistening. She tried to calm her thoughts.

Maria glanced around. On one of the other boats, Maria saw a man. She ran towards him. Reaching the boat she gasped for air, feeding her aching lungs.

'Hey... excuse me. Are you able to contact other boats?'

He looked up, the sight of the women unexpected, her distress startling yet it interested him, drawing him away from his work. He stood up, rubbing his hands on an old cloth, stained with blotches of white paint.

'Yeh, I can do that... why?'

Maria removed strands of hair that stuck to her face. She tried to steady her voice. 'I need you to try... it's my brother, he should be back by now... he's gone fishing, something must have happened... Oh God, make them be safe.'

'Slow down, slow down. What's your brother's name and whose boat is he on?'

'Michalis... it's Alexandros' boat.'

'Ah Alexandros... no problem. On you get, watch your step, let's see what we can do.'

'You know Alexandros?' Maria asked, the knowledge of this was comforting; her anguish began to subside.

Once she had reached him, he was already talking on the radio. The smell of paint overpowered Maria, she swallowed hard; Maria felt light headed in the small confines of the cabin. Maria's eyes fixed on a dark sweat line that ran down the middle of the boat owner's back.

'I have a worried young lady here, Alexandros.'

There was a fluttering in Maria's abdomen, like trapped butterflies. She covered her mouth, her lower jaw loosened, she bit a finger and a sound escaped her, predicting an expected reply. She craned forward.

'Tell her I'm sorry.' The voice was tinny over the crackle that emanated from the small speaker, yet it was unmistakably that of Alexandros, gravelly and resonant.

'We overslept after lunch, our stomachs full of fish.'

'Look,' said the man, pointing with a finger. 'There they are.' With no reply forthcoming, he turned to see Maria sprint along the quayside.

As the boat drew closer, and the expansive smile on Michalis' face came into view, Maria felt her anxiety drain from her. She felt exhausted. Michalis stood at the front of the boat, holding a huge fish that swung from his hand, like a pendulum, sparkling as the sun caught its scales. With his free hand, he waved then stumbled, regained his balance and continued to wave, his expansive smile undiminished. Alexandros glided the boat to a stop, the engine died and the sea gently lapped its side.

'Kalispera Maria. Look, we've emptied the sea of fish.' Alexandros gestured to a bucket, its contents filled to the brim with their shiny lifeless catch.

Michalis indicated intently with his head for Maria to look at his handheld trophy.

Maria looked up from the bucket, unable to laugh or cry.

'Yes,' she panted. 'It's a beautiful fish.'

Athens

A Sense of Clarity

It is morning. She is lying next to him, in their bed, the blinds are still drawn and a subtle ambience permeates the room. The warmth from her body feels a natural part of wakening up. It is something he has become used to, like shaving each morning; it is part of the day's routine. However, today it is different as if this is their first time together. There is a sense of the unknown, fuelled by anticipation and the desire to be united in a physical union. It seduces each pore, and it is enthralling and irresistible.

A warm sensation radiates from his abdomen and flows through him, like an electrical current. She is smiling, baring white teeth. Her arms are stretched above her head, as if to initiate an invitation, an offering, and the giving of herself, unconditionally.

He has moved onto his side, one arm under him, steadying him, taking the weight of his body. With his free arm, he reaches out, tracing her forehead with two fingers. He moves to the bridge of her nose, with the back of his fingers he slides across her cheeks, where the skin is stretched taut.

Her eyes are closed now. He can see how long her lashes are and takes in their curve. With a finger, he traces her upper lip and then moves to the lower. She kisses the tip of the finger and eagerly accepts it, enclosing it with her mouth. He feels the warmth and wetness of her tongue. The sensation causes his breathing to increase, his stomach rising and falling.

She exhales a sound, one of pleasure, it encourages him. He can hear himself call her name. She responds with more intimate sounds that seem to come from a place deep within her, like a summons, urging him to continue.

Again there is a fluttering in his stomach, a warm glow.

They are now both lost to the world around them, alive only to their senses, the pleasure, and each other. He removes his finger, it shimmers with her saliva, he traces a wet path down the middle of her chin, and she presses and arches her head into the pillow while he continues down her neck, along the collarbone. He bends forward while she guides his head with her hand. He rests his hand on her hipbone, her skin is pale and smooth. It feels warm to the touch, inviting...

The tin mechanical drone of a moped ripped through the street outside, permeating his thoughts, seeping into him, like fluid from an injection. Louis became alert to the Light, the sheet entangled around his legs and the sounds of the morning.

He tried to influence the images, bring them back to life. Yet, the more he tried, shadows captured them moving further from him. Louis was left encrusted with familiar feelings that lay heavy on him, like enervating heat. He looked at his watch; he had been awake for an hour.

His nights were fractured events, occupied with dreams that had Louis questioning whether they were dreams or real life, and it was not until he swam to the surface and focused his mind, that his perception of reality returned.

That night, the landing at Athens airport was enveloped in darkness. When he arrived at the hotel, the early morning light was soft, and a pastel sky greeted the sun. He felt drained and exhausted and each step that drew him closer to his room brought a further ache to his complaining limbs. Once inside, he undressed and succumbed to sleep.

He threw open the shutters, an alien city sprawled out in front of him, a landscape that was foreign, yet the conventional volume of traffic, people and congestion were familiar; only the details were different. He was perspiring and sticky, an uncomfortable feeling, the sultry nature of the room did little to ease his discomfort. Its contents were sparse and basic but functional.

 A wooden wardrobe sat empty, apart from a few coat hangers that hung without clothes. Two small bedside cabinets sat at each side of the bed, one had a small lamp, the other a telephone. Louis wondered if the phone worked. Since his arrival, he switched his mobile off, a conscious act of abandonment and detachment; he did not want to be reminded of what he had left behind.

The walls of the room were white, a solitary painting hung at an odd and abandoned angle. It depicted the scene of a couple sitting at a table, eating a meal on a terrace, overlooking a whitewashed village, whose sun-drenched houses cascaded down a rocky hill that fell into a glass-like sea. The relaxed and contented postures of the couple reinforced what he had lost, yet he found solace in the quality of the resonant colour and tone. He felt as if he could touch the sky, smell the air and taste the food. It filled a deep gulf within him, his senses felt hypnotised by its magnetism. It dissolved any doubt that lingered in his mind that coming to Greece was an impetuous decision, for the picture made him feel alive and it was the discovery of such feelings that induced him to make this journey.

A newly bought book, 'Captain Corelli's Mandolin' by Louis de Bernieres, sat on a wooden dressing table that supported a mirror set flush against the wall. It was a book that Louis had considered reading for some time. While waiting for his flight at Edinburgh airport, he noticed a man holding a copy and, with the thought of four hours stretching out in front of him confined to the one seat, he considered it a good investment in money and time.

A large rucksack was propped against the wall. Louis decided to travel light, packing only the items he thought would be essential. He would buy whatever he required during his time here.

He showered and dressed. The therapeutic qualities of feeling fresh and clean were not only physical, as Louis detected a process of healing that gave birth to a positive outlook for the days ahead.

Athens was humid and living up to the stories Louis had heard about its congestion problem, although the hotel manager told him the city's traffic problem had improved. A cacophonous symphony of horns bellowed around him as he stepped from the hotel onto the broiling street.

Louis had chosen Athens for no particular reason other than it would make an appropriate starting point. He was unclear where this journey was going to take him. However even at this early stage; he knew it would be a mistake to stay in Athens for too long.

It was late afternoon; he wondered how the city would look and feel. It was then, he realised, this was the first time since his early days in Rome that he'd found himself alone, in an unfamiliar city.

It was a feeling he was unaccustomed to. He had always surrounded himself with people he knew. He was a creature of habit, eating and drinking in the same venues and, when he thought of them, Emma haunted these occasions, the restaurants, cafes and bars had become 'their' places.

He thought of the last gift Emma bought him. It was a shirt he admired and, at some point, he must have mentioned this to her. One evening, as he returned home from work, she presented the shirt to him with the instruction he was to wear it on the night of their fifth-anniversary meal.

It was still hanging in the wardrobe in the flat, untouched, and unworn. It occurred to him, like some posthumous postscript that that night was the last time they had made love.

He was resurrecting too much melancholy he told himself as he walked in no particular direction. Greece was to be the medium that would dissolve such thoughts. It was to be the medicine he prescribed, and it was to be his cure.

Such thoughts were still fresh in his mind as he sat drinking a coffee overlooking the pantiled dome of the Byzantine church of Agii Apostoli. He had stumbled upon the Plaka as he sought refuge from the noise and smell of the Athen's traffic. Marble pavements spilled with occupied tables under shading trees. The air resonated with the melodies of vociferous conversations and the addictive aroma of iced coffee frappe. Louis discovered that any thought of escaping the constant apparitions of cigarette smoke was viewed as an unfruitful task as it spread in epidemic proportions. And, as he finished his coffee, he wondered if the whole of Athens smoked?

Later, while ambling through the Plateia Monastiraki, he

sat at a table in a busy grill restaurant where waiters, like an army of ants, worked on automatic pilot, carrying plates of exotic smelling food, four at a time, a skill that impressed him.

He ate grilled chicken, tzatziki, and salad, complementing the food with an arctic bottle of Amstel beer. He walked his dinner off by climbing the path that ascended Mount Lykavittos. As the early evening sun grew closer to the horizon, it sprayed a soft light that painted the stone of the path a delicious tone of gold, like a stairway of celestial light leading to a sacred and heavenly secret. Louis laughed out loud at this impromptu thought and so it was, as he reached the plateau.

Smartly dressed couples and groups occupied tables, many wearing designer sunglasses, even though their backs were turned against the sun. Louis thought this amusing.

Louis walked to the far end and stood by a small wall, a vast expanse of the city spread out beneath him, like a labyrinthine and miniature toy Athens, crowned by the embroidery of a pastel embellished sky. He was fascinated by the white of the buildings, so many of them he smiled to himself. He found his spirits soaring. Yesterday felt a lifetime away. Louis had arrived.

The sky had turned velvet black when he pushed open the door of the small bar. He ordered a beer, and the barman acknowledged his request with a slight nod of the head.

He noticed numerous replica football shirts hanging from the walls, like wallpaper, he thought. Louis noted that the majority were Greek, English, and Spanish, teams such as AEK Athens, Panathinaikos, Olympiakos, Liverpool, Chelsea, Manchester United, Arsenal, Real Madrid and Barcelona. When Louis raised the subject, the barman explained in fluent English it had become the custom of patrons and visitors to donate a shirt of their chosen team to the bar.

'I will soon need to build an extension to accommodate them all.' He smiled. 'And what shirt would you give me to hang on my wall?'

The corners of Louis' mouth curled into a smile.

'Hibernian,' he replied, expecting a bemused response.

'Ah... the Hibees, they played well against AEK Athens... but not good enough, fortunately.'

He gestured to a television perched high in the corner of the bar.

'We watched the game, it was on live. We had a busy crowd that night.'

'I was at the game. They brought out a DVD of the match... I've got one actually.'

'Never,' the barman said, mystified. 'You mean they sold a DVD of their team getting beat on aggregate and knocked out of a major competition. That was never going to be a bestseller.'

Louis laughed. 'Yes, they did. I never thought about it like that.'

The barman shook his head, still trying to comprehend such logic. 'Imagine what they would have done if they had won the two legs and qualified for the next round.'

'I would have drunk a few more of these,' Louis said, lifting the bottle to his lips. The beer was cold and refreshing, its taste lingering in his mouth.

'The next time you come to my bar bring a Hibees top and I will put it on my wall.' He cleaned some glasses shaking his head in bemusement.

Louis sat at a table and watched him go about his work at a glacial pace, epitomising the reputation of that facet of the Greek personality. Louis smiled to himself, what a pity their footballers did not use the same work ethic.

'Excuse me.'

Louis was jolted out of his contemplation.

'I couldn't help but overhear your accent... you're Scottish?'

'I am, yes.'

'I thought so. A few years ago I studied in Edinburgh, beautiful city even though it was cold and rained most of the time.'

Louis took in the man's features. They were about the same age. Dark wavy hair and centre-parted brushed the fabric of his shirt. He grew a neatly trimmed goatee beard, exaggerated by an olive complexion. His pencil sharp features exhibited an elongated and handsome face. He drew heavily on a cigarette and, as he exhaled, he clicked his jaw where ringlets of smoke, like smoke signals from an old western movie, sailed from his lips.

'What did you study?' Louis asked, tapping the top of the beer bottle.

'Law... my father harboured grand expectations in his concern for my academic abilities. Five years, not all of it studying law mind you. I found the women more interesting, more of a challenge.'

'Where did you study?' Louis asked. A curious expression crossed his face.

'Edinburgh University.'

'So did I.'

'Really, ha ... small world, we both went to Edinburgh uni and now here we are in Athens drinking beer, I wonder what the odds would be on that?'

'Pretty slim, I'd imagine. By the way, your English is excellent.'

'Thank you, my father's legacy. He insisted that his children were fluent in more than one language.' He mimicked his father's voice. 'It's the only way to get on in life. It offers many opportunities that would otherwise be closed, he would say. I suppose he had a point.'

Louis sensed that there had been friction between father and son.

'He was right. We wouldn't be speaking now as I don't speak any Greek. I do however speak Italian. Coincidentally, my father also insisted; he was Italian you see.'

'Well, there's another thing we have in common; our fathers and their love of language.' He laughed. He took out another cigarette and lit it with the butt of the one he had been smoking. He offered one to Louis, who politely refused.

'My name is Demetrius... and yours?'

'Louis... Louis Satriani'

'Ah, after the American rock guitarist?' Demetrius

laughed heartily. 'Hey, you could tell potential girlfriends you're related to him, his brother even. Now that would be a good chat up line.'

The thought of instigating such a conversation that could lead to any kind of relationship instilled Louis with blind panic and fear, like a child starting a new school for the first time. The thought of having to get to know someone all over again felt daunting. He was not ready for such an experience. Could he reveal to another person his emotions, layer by layer, like an archaeological dig, until they were exposed to the surface? Could he bare his faults and his passions again to another person, could he share the things that made him feel alive... could he do that all over again unconditionally? Louis had a sudden image of Emma. The look on his face was one of panic. He drained the bottle. The urge for alcohol came upon him as an immediate source of release.

'I'm having another one of these. Do you want one?'

They had several more drinks in the bar. As the evening progressed, the bar began to fill, becoming increasingly smoky and noisy. Demetrius spoke of his time in Edinburgh and Louis asked about the best places to visit in Greece.

They spent the night drinking, moving from bar to bar. They were on their way to get something to eat when Louis saw them from the corner of his eye, dark shapes emerging from the shadows. There were no words spoken, vigorous gestures displayed their intentions. There had been no provocation to influence this encounter. No fiery looks or demonic eyes influenced by alcohol or drugs. This was a premeditated intention to attack and maim.

A silver object which was concealed was now exposed to the streetlights, a flash of incandescent metal slashed the air. Louis' heart thumped in his chest with such force he thought it would shatter his rib cage. His stomach churned, threatening to spill its contents onto the pavement. Demetrius lunged forward, spitting words in Greek. Louis did not see the blow. A velvety sigh, like deflating lungs emptying of air, escaped from Demetrius. His limp body slumped to the ground as his attackers made their escape.

An old man slid from the doorway of a shop. Louis stared at him before moving his gaze to the dark shape on the ground. Louis shook with involuntary spasms. A stream of dark fluid, twisting like the path of a river, stained the stone of the pavement. Louis stumbled, appalled and horrified.

The doctor at the hospital told Louis that by applying pressure to the wound, he had saved Demetrius' life.

Demetrius had no identification on him. Louis could only tell the hospital staff a name and that Demetrius was a lawyer. It was too dark to give any credible information about the attackers, other than their builds and how many there were. The doctor advised Louis to wait until the police arrived. Statements would be taken. He panicked and left the hospital.

He awoke the next morning with a furious storm raging in his head. Its momentum was so intense that Louis' remained planted on the pillow.

Mini earthquakes jolted his brain, where a hammer thumped, announcing itself in relentless and persistent waves. Louis' tongue stuck to the roof of his mouth as if glue had been applied to it during the night. His throat screamed for water. His insides clenched like a fist. Louis regretted his night of excess, as a dull debilitating ache travelled the length of his body, resisting every attempt he made to rise from the bed.

Images of the night before formed with a certain clarity. Like a television being switched on in his head, he remembered the events, recollecting each scene as if it were a movie. Louis reached for the bottle on the bedside cabinet; fumbling with the lid, he gulped the tepid water. His nerves were stretched. His mind was disarrayed with fear.

His first thought was of visiting the hospital, replaced by a strong desire to leave the city and the events of the previous night behind him. Louis didn't give a statement to the police? He reprimanded himself, trying to make sense of his actions, he was a witness to an assault, attempted murder, or worse still.

He did not even know if Demetrius was still alive. Why

did he panic and leave the hospital? A wave of nausea came over him. He didn't know Demetrius. There was no loyalty between them as it was with friends. His thoughts did not placate him in the comfort he sought. Instead, his conscience continued to tug at him, like a persistent child seeking attention. This was not how he had imagined his stay to be. It did not resonate with the images Louis had digested in his mind, which caused a lingering excitement, like water bubbling inside him.

    He needed to recapture those feelings and submit to the magnetic pull that had brought him this far, but before then he would return to the hospital.

Arcadia

A Meeting of Convenience

He is lying in a field. Above him, a clear blue ocean engulfs his view; a starched and creaseless sheet of the sky, vast and expansive. Blades of mustard corn caress his skin, like seductive feathers. The warmth of the sun seeps into his pores, massaging his skin with its radiant heat.

There are voices, drifting on the soft breeze, excitable and high-pitched, young voices not yet broken by maturity, familiar, conjuring faces he knows. Sounds of corn being flattened and bent by running feet caress his ears as laughter consumes and colours the air which smells of summer, clean and fresh to the taste, untouched.
A kite, the shape of a bird in flight, punctuates his view. Its outline is sharp against the bottomless contour of the sky. It floats on the currents, majestically turning and twisting, like the seagulls that are diving and hovering over an undulating sea.

He struggles to his feet, encouraged by the increasing volume of crunching corn and ebullient voices. He becomes caught up in their youthful stampede, contracting their euphoria and joins his sister and cousins, chasing the flight of the kite, dark and elegant. Behind them, a descending village of caravans is silhouetted against a slate grey sea that licks a long and white stretch of sand where the stone skeletal walls of a ruined cathedral, the witness to and victim of centuries of storms, dominates the skyline.

The noise of an old woman, discharging her cumbersome luggage on the rack above, snapped him from the world of thoughts and into the real world. The train was moving out of a station and building up speed. A brilliant white glare of light consumed the carriage with a luminous intensity. Louis squinted he dropped his head. He closed his eyes and immediately noticed small silver lights move across the black space, like a shower of shooting stars.

The rhythmic motion of the train carriage, played a

constant beat, like the rhythm section of a band, he thought. He listened to the pitch and tones of inaudible conversations, language that was alien and yet colourful and vibrant. The hangover from that morning had retreated to a permanent but dull heaviness.

The woman had now taken her seat opposite Louis. Her spectacles dominated her face, giving the impression the dimensions of her head were rather small. Her nose was sharp and long and her eyes were peculiar, offset to the side of her head, crowned with an obstreperous mass of hair.

Layers of leather and reptile skin folded in upon one other, bridging the chin and collar bone so that there was no discernible point where one began and the other ended. Her perfume was potent, convincing Louis that she must have bathed in the scent.

She read a newspaper, oblivious to Louis' studied observance, the occasional murmured commentary escaping her pencil lips.

Quite unexpectedly, he was drawn to a familiar image that ballooned from the page. Underneath bold and black Greek lettering, the distinctive and frozen face of Demetrius stared at him. A nervous disposition seized him, not for the first time that day. Only hours earlier, his conscience had pulled him to the hospital and, in doing so, he felt a great weight released from him. It was an exorcism of guilt that massaged his recognition of the right thing to do.

He could not leave Athens without restoring a sense of balance into recent events. However, he was unable to fulfill his intentions. As Louis made his way to the hospital entrance, a circus of cameras, reporters and police forced him to abandon his visit, just as a scuffle erupted between the police and a small but vociferous crowd that had gathered.

He returned to the hotel and hastily packed. As he checked out, the receptionist gave him an envelope. It was delivered that morning by hand. Instinctively Louis looked around him before opening the envelope. Written on a crisp piece of paper were the words - *Leave Athens now* - he knew then his anonymity had abandoned him.

He poured over the ramifications of the note. *They saw me; they know where I am and they must have followed me.* A new panic seized him. Within thirty minutes, he was on the first train out of Athens, without a thought towards its destination.

As he boarded, he received an occasional glance, but nothing out of the ordinary. He let most of the passengers embark before he chose a window seat. The view would help keep his mind off the note.

The old woman lifted her eyes from the page and glared at Louis, a look that permeated his skin. He asked if she spoke English? His stomach sank.

'Why yes, I do speak English,' she announced in an English accent.

'He's a lawyer, a clever one at that, if one is to believe what the papers are saying about him. It seems that he was instrumental in the conviction of a well-known criminal in Athens. However, as with all of these low lives, they have at their disposal undesirable associates, dangerous people, who, it would seem, have disposed of their revenge on the young lawyer. Seemingly the attack was witnessed, by an English man of all people. He has not come forward, although it says here, he arrived at the hospital with the lawyer. According to this article, he saved the lawyer's life.

'The police are asking for witnesses to come forward. They're especially interested in the English man, dreadful business. His wound is not life-threatening. He is expected to live.'

The woman's revelation bore the force of an articulated lorry ploughing into him. He imagined Demetrius in his hospital bed, attached to a myriad of bleeping machines and, within a few feet of this sterile bubble, the wolves stalked in their packs.

'I hope that meets with your satisfaction... and yes I'm English, although one feels more Greek than English. I've lived most of my adult life here. If you don't mind, I'd like to continue with my reading. You look pale, are you unwell?' She stared at him over the rim of her glasses. 'You need to drink lots of water in this weather.'

'I'm fine. I'm not a good traveller,' he lied.

'We should be in Corinth in less than an hour. Are you staying in the town?'

'I'm not sure, would you recommend it?'

'I would if you're feeling unwell. Your pallor has an unhealthy look about it. You could get something at a pharmacist to alleviate your complexion at least.'

'Do you live there? I mean, if you did you would be able to recommend a hotel?'

'No, I live in Nafplion. Another train journey away. I've lived there for many years. It's by the sea and I would recommend it if you are looking for somewhere to visit or even stay for a short duration. You'll find it agreeable to the eye. The architecture is a mixture of Greek, Venetian, and Turkish design. If you like history, there are three impressive fortresses and, on a day like this the sea is a temptress.'

'Are you sure you don't work for the Greek tourist board?'

She smiled for the first time. 'What about you? You're obviously not here on a business trip, pleasure maybe?' She inclined her head.

'I'm hoping to do some travelling around the country and see the Greece that's not in the travel brochures.'

'And you are travelling alone?'

'Yes.'

'What is a young man like you doing travelling without a companion? If I may say so, it's very unusual.'

Louis thought for a moment. 'I'm escaping the old to hopefully appreciate the new.'

'That sounds very mysterious. I like a touch of mystery. I find it tempting and unsettling at the same time. Are you escaping from somewhere or someone?' She looked at him interrogatively.

'Both I suppose.'

'Intriguing.' She removed her glasses. 'Now you have snared my interest Mr…?'

'Louis.'

'My name's Meredith. Well then Louis. Far from being

thought of as an intrusive old woman, but one does not need to be a detective to work out that the sight of that young lawyer had a somewhat adverse effect on your constitution.'

Louis smiled nervously. 'I don't know what you mean.'

'Come now, I may be old but I'm no fool. You nearly wet yourself when you saw that lawyer staring at you from the front page. I've never seen anyone's pallor go so white so quickly. Louis, my dear, don't worry. Your secret is safe with me.'

Louis felt uncomfortable with her line of enquiry. The still air magnified his unease. She is just an inquisitive old woman; Louis swallowed, and his pretense deserted him.

'I met him in Athens,' he said, immediately regretting the parting of information.

'Recently? Or had you known him for some time?'

'I met him yesterday.'

'I don't like Athens. It is too big, noisy and ghastly polluted. Did you stay long?'

He shrugged. 'Not really, just a day.'

'I see. Most visitors to Athens stay a while longer, appreciate the sights. Did you visit the Acropolis and see the Parthenon?'

'I'd planned to but didn't get around to it, unfortunately.'

'That's a pity. The view of the city is wonderfully panoramic. How did you meet this lawyer?'

'In a bar. It was my first night in Athens. He kindly kept my company and we drank in a few bars he recommended.'

'So you had no idea who he was or of his background?'

He paused. 'No, we spoke a little about our pasts. We studied at the same university as it turned out, so we had things in common.'

'I see. Fortunately, the police are looking for an English man. That's a Scottish accent I detect.'

'Yes.' He felt a slight relief. 'Yes, I'm from…'

'Edinburgh,' Meredith interrupted. 'That's not a west coast accent, certainly not the north, more an east coast accent. It's not an accent that belongs to Fife or Dundee but probably Edinburgh. Yes, Edinburgh it is,' she deduced with a conspiratorial smile.

'Well done,' Louis said, impressed.

'I lived in your fair city once. I was just married and my husband and I relocated due to work reasons. It was a long time ago now. You probably were not even born then.'

She gently rubbed a leg of her glasses between her thumb and forefinger, thinking for a second. 'So what's your plan? You must have a plan, an inkling about what you're going to do next?'

'Not really.'

'Well then Louis my dear, if you're looking for an opportunity to blend in and not be too conspicuous, I'd definitely recommend Nafplion. It's the ideal location to just merge into daily life. Many Athenians spend their weekends there and besides, it's also a delicious time of the year to visit. It also has lots of daily cruises. You could be on an island in a matter of hours. You'll need to decide as we'll be arriving at the station soon and you'll need to take another train. If you do decide to go, we can accompany each other. It's a bit of a rarity these days, speaking to someone in English. The opportunity doesn't present itself too often.'

Louis' thoughts raced, stumbling over one another. If an old woman could work out he was in some kind of trouble, how was he going to evade the police? Had he done the right thing, leaving Athens? Should he have spoken to the police? And what about Demetrius? Thank God he will recover, the news was a comfort and most importantly, no one had followed him onto the train. Was he the last to get into the carriage? He sank into his chair, deflated and exhausted. He leaned his head against the glass of the window and watched the countryside evolve every few minutes, like a film show.

From Athens, the train snaked a scenic path towards Corinth. He looked out of the window. White cotton wool clouds dominated the sky; he thought they looked like vast continents on a map. The sun's light skirted the tops of trees, like jewels, setting the leaves on fire in radiant light. For a moment, Demetrius, the hospital and his guilt ebbed from him. With such a view unfolding before him, it came easily to drift through his reflections, to float effortlessly through them, like a feather.

He found his thoughts visiting Emma. With clarity, he summoned the contours of her face, a pendulous shimmering earring, a strong coloured collar swirling in a low ruffle around her neck, cut low over her glossed skin, polished with scent, temptingly hinting at a shaded line.

There had been moments when, folded within his thoughts, he forced the colours and pictures from his mind, blocked them out in a mental tug of war. Yet, today, his thoughts were thirsty for her, they demanded her. He needed to erase the images and events of Athens. He was receiving a gift, experiencing the opening and discovery of it.

Around him, conversation swirled and floated, yet he was inhaling Emma's sweet and exotic fragrance, as they walked along a pulsating and vibrant Princes Street amongst a river of heads, flowing in colour and shimmering in the heat of summer. They held hands in a clasp. At the time it was an automatic form of behaviour, yet now as Louis considered this intimate act, he viewed it as an expression of celebrating their bond as a couple. And as they left Frederick Street, and moved along the imposing grandeur of George Street and its designer shops, Emma was duty bound to enter one.

They were met at the entrance by an assistant's smile, the name of the shop escaping him, although its white clinical interior remained implanted in his memory. It had always given Louis pleasure, observing Emma in her pursuit of a particular item of clothing. It had seemed to him that these moments were enveloped in a sense of erotic anticipation as Emma emerged from the changing cubicle, adorned and dressed in her chosen garment, hands on hips while scanning his face with upturned eyebrows and the hint of a subtle, 'What do you think?' smile.

He recalled the smell of lavender and the celebrated drink in some trendy bar to toast the purchase of her designer trophy, where the young and fashion conscious Saturday afternoon drinkers conversed in a socially coded language, where body language was an art and just as much a form of social interaction and communication as the spoken word.

He conceded that his life now comprised of a simpler and unattached level of existence. His old life, the one that Emma had belonged too, felt as far from him as a distant galaxy. He knew now he would never inhabit nor belong to that part of his life he now considered lost and unattainable.

He was a stranger to this country yet, comfortingly, he did not feel out of context with his surroundings. Athens was behind him now; the police were looking for an English man, not a Scotsman. He could sense a detachment from his former life, a liberation of a kind. He visualized himself at the horizon of new found possibilities and, as the train sped through the landscape, a timeless vault of discovery was waiting to be entered, and he held the key. His stomach turned in a symphony of bubbles as he digested the prospect that providence had placed him in.

Demetrius' face disappeared as Meredith folded her paper and placed it on her lap. Still elated by the thoughts that pulsed through him, he turned his attention to the view from the window.

Clothed in a patchwork of gentle brown, green and terracotta, the landscape was punctuated in an array of cypress, chestnut, cedars, and pine, as rolling hills scraped the ultramarine sky and tumbled into olive groves.

The sun pierced his eyes again as it surfed on the flat white roofs of a village. He turned from its glare, his eyes resting upon Meredith. She had been observing him, her bony fingers aimlessly curling around the gold chain of her glasses.

'Beautiful isn't she? Travelling by train is the best way to appreciate this jewel of a country. I came here fifty years ago with my husband. He was a diplomat stationed in Athens. He wasn't overly affectionate. We both had love affairs, his was with a government official's wife, and my weakness was that I fell in love with Greece. He had to leave Athens; the prospect of a diplomatic haemorrhage was not advantageous to the diplomatic service's cause in

Greece. I, on the other hand, have never left. We divorced soon after and from that moment until now I've been married to Greece.'

Then, to Louis' surprise, she looked at him how a person does when they have cultivated an intimate friendship.

'Just because I'm old and my body is stiff and doesn't move like it used to, that doesn't mean I've not lived a fulfilling life. I haven't always looked like this. I've ridden camels over the desert, looked into the edge of a volcano, loved another with passion and lust and seen a thousand sunsets. I will die in this country yet, since the day I arrived, my old self died, and I've been living in heaven ever since.'

He knew no detail of her life, had spoken only a few words to her, had tasted only a fragment of her life experience, yet her words had become like glue, he was now connected to this woman.

Was it a sign? Was there a force at work that brought them both together on this train? Did he mirror the old lady when she first arrived in this country? Did she see a part of herself in Louis?

He marvelled at how one's impression of a person could alter so suddenly, so dramatically. It was human instinct, he supposed, to judge a person and construct an image of them before a single word had been spoken. How animalistic, he concluded. He felt a stabbing of shame and, out of that shame, he wondered how Demetrious would judge him?

In his mind, he had developed the persona of a rambling old woman, self-centred and opinionated, whose perfume assaulted his senses. How differently he viewed her now. An icon of contentment, she radiated an inner peace. He yearned to bathe in her calm waters. Meredith was a comfort to him.

Heaven on earth... he heard himself say, it was an intoxicating concept and one which he found himself eager to explore. There was no other place more qualified, Louis reasoned, as Demetrius' words reverberated in his head, *'The cradle of Greece, Arcadia herself. You cannot travel through Greece and not appreciate its wonders. It would be nothing short of a crime Louis if you didn't travel through Arcadia. It's the place of my birth and upbringing.'*

He clothed the region in a mystical aura of ancient myth.

'Where mother earth cradled mankind to her bosom, kindling the words of poets and the thoughts of philosophers, inherent within the air and soil are qualities that expose one to the recognition of their very own Nirvana. It's the heart of Greece, Louis.' Demetrius enthused through the thick smog of his cigarette.

The image of Demetrius painting pictures with words and gesticulating extravagantly remained fresh in Louis' mind.

'How far is Arcadia from Nafplion?'

'You can see its mountains.'

Close enough, Louis thought, and the decision was made.

He watched as Meredith gazed out of the window at the moving countryside, her face illuminated in a glow of wonderment, as if she had been granted a vision of Christ himself. Her lower lip quivered in succession, but no sound emanated from her mouth. Louis pushed back into his seat, he scratched an irritating itch on his forehead and, once again, his vision travelled the landscape. The melody and hook line of a song he remembered reverberated around his head in a continuous loop, 'It feels like heaven'.

On the train journey south, Meredith described Nafplion as one of the prettiest towns in Greece, bursting with Athenians in the summer weekends and holidays.

'Don't let your first impressions taint your opinion. You go through the modern part of the town before you get to the old town of Nafplion. It's the most beautiful town. Every morning I wander down to the seafront cafes that look across the Argolic gulf towards the hazy mountains of Arcadia and it catches me every time.'

Gradually he explained the reason for his visit to Greece.

'Tell me about Emma,' Meredith said, and so he did, and to his surprise, he relaxed in her company.

Nafplion was all Meredith said it would be and its picturesque ambience seemed to contain his anxieties. Each day he met Meredith for lunch. They ate in her favourite eating haunts- a small café or taverna hidden in a warren of alleyways, a cafe along the waterfront or in Synatagma Square where the polished marble floor reflected the lights and images of restaurants and neo-classical buildings like a placid milky lake. After lunch, they viewed the sights or took in a museum. Meredith excelled in her unofficial role as a tour guide with polite enthusiasm. Louis thought it strange that Meredith attached herself to him. She insisted that he should not be alone, and he welcomed the company. Each day saw Demetrius and Athens recede further from his thoughts.

Louis stayed in a small guesthouse in the Psaromachalas area. He developed the habit of eating breakfast each morning at a small café, then taking a leisurely walk. He got lost frequently until the geography of the town became familiar to him. With confidence, he navigated steep steps and narrow lanes, where the bougainvilleas draped from balconies in deep purples and rich crimson. He sensed life becoming simple again. It was risk-free, and it helped him contemplate this change in pace; everything had changed, he was taking one day at a time.

One morning, with the sun warming his back, he ambled along a flat path that hugged the sea. Around the headland below Akronafplia he viewed a castle, perched above the town. He continued along the waterfront, peppered with restaurants and cafes whose tables spilled onto the promenade.

He was intrigued by the fortress of Bourtzi that rose from a shimmering Argolic gulf. One afternoon over lunch, Meredith explained that its walls had once been the home of executioners, a hotel, and even a restaurant. Louis thought it attractive, especially at night; it floated majestically upon the water, bathed in golden light from strategically placed lamps.

Continuing his walk, a young arresting woman in a tight fitting dress snared his attention. He observed these moments with an assiduous interest. She sat on the promenade, reading a book at one of the many cafes. Her hair fell in curls onto her shoulders, catching the sun and she flicked it from her face. A waiter arrived and set a cup on the table. She looked up at him, her head tilted, stressing the angle of her face, her olive skin polished like marble. Their familiar gestures spoke of occasional acquaintance. They spoke, and she smiled, absently placing the book on the surface of the table. Friends or lovers? The thought walked with him.

He paused by several small boats. There was a glare from the transparent water, a white sparkling light amongst shimmering reflections that floated upon its surface. Silver and gold fish glided and turned without urgency or purpose, in contrast to the smaller fish, curious and demented who explored each crevice in the seabed rocks with a frantic diligence. It was an unfamiliar scene and his mind turned to the known, the River Forth: dark, troublesome, oppressive, under a low opaque aluminium sky.

His days adopted familiar routines and he acclimatized to their predictable order. That morning, he awoke with a persistent thread of thought that graduated into an impetuous ache. It was time to move on. If he stayed much longer, he was sure he would never leave. It had been three weeks since his hurried departure from Athens. There had been no more reports in the papers and, more importantly, his anonymity prevailed. Meredith informed him she had paid particular attention to the national and local media and they had lost interest as Demetrious was expected to make a full recover from his injury, a fact that uplifted Louis' spirits.

An invigorating sweet scent tinged the warm air as he walked across Synatagma Square, smiling at the thought of meeting Meredith for lunch. He felt elated. The buildings absorbed the sun's light in golden tones that picked out the detail of the neo-classical facades.

'Do you mind if I smoke?' Meredith asked.

'No, not at all. Is it just me, or is it getting hotter each day?' He sat down and dabbed his forehead with a napkin.

Meredith opened a small silver case and took out a cigarette. 'I took the liberty of ordering. It was starting to get busy and I didn't want to wait too long for our food. I ordered the swordfish. I remembered you said you tried it once.'

Louis smiled. 'Yes that's right, in Rhodes; it was grilled. I've not had it since.'

Meredith waved away a fly. 'What's your plan for today?'

'I've been thinking about my long-term plans and the reasons why I came here. I promised myself that I wouldn't stay in one place for too long and look at me, it didn't take long to break that promise.' He smiled at the contradiction.

'I could quite happily stay here. I've not felt this happy for a long time. It's tempting and not just because of the town. You see, I wasn't expecting to find friendship.' Louis paused. 'You helped me when I was in a difficult situation. I can't thank you enough for that. I don't know what would have become of me if we hadn't met. I've valued our time together; it makes it all the harder to leave, but it's time. If I don't go now, I never will.'

'I see and have you any thoughts on where you'll go next?'

'Not really. This was never going to be an organized trip. I suppose I should have a schedule and plan a route at least. I might follow Demetrius' advice,' he said, a little embarrassed.

'I must admit I've enjoyed our time together.' Meredith smiled.

'I'm indebted to you. You've been very kind to me.'

'Nonsense. You've given me something to get up for each day, a purpose, and a reason. I now realise that is precisely what has been missing in my life lately. Even in such a place as this, old age can socially demobilise you, if you let it, but now I intend to fight back. I'm thinking of starting little tours around the town for those of a certain age. Short walking tours and such. I think I'll call it 'the senior walks.'

'That sounds great. You've got a talent there and a market,' Louis said, encouragingly.

Meredith extinguished her cigarette just as their food arrived.

'If you want to experience Arcadia, there's a lovely little place near Astros called Paralio Astros. It would be an ideal starting point to explore the area.'

'Well, you were right about Nafplion and I'm glad I took your advice. Since you have a proven track record, I'll take you at your word.' They both laughed.

'It takes half an hour by car to get there. In fact, you may be in luck. I know a taxi driver who lives in Paralio Astros. I could negotiate a reduced fare.'

'Your talents are endless Meredith. How am I going to travel through Greece without you?'

'If only. If I was twenty years younger then maybe, believe me, it would be an enticing offer.' She smiled sadly and then said, 'I hope you find what you're looking for and that it brings you happiness. Do one thing for me, Louis.' She looked at him seriously.

'What would that be?' He said, curiously.

'When you leave, and you're on your travels, remember that I've cherished our short time together. It's given me immense pleasure. Oh, and one last thing,' she added softly.

'Don't judge a person on the bad things they've done in this life. Instead, judge them on the good things they strive for and hope to achieve.'

'That's very philosophical.'

'Let's just say it's free advice from an old lady who has lived to regret many things.'

'I'll miss you, Meredith.' He reached out, took her hand and, raising it to his lips, he lightly kissed it.

A Small Matter Concerning a Light

The veil of night enclosed around him, unsuspectingly. The impenetrable darkness, absolute in its nature, magnified trees into blurred shapes that hovered in the stillness, like giant apparitions, emerging from the dense night. A beckoning silence held a forensic clarity as nature's osmosis permeated his pores. He succumbed to this prescription and inhaled her medicine, like a patient seeking the restoration of health.

The absence of electric light transformed the dark void of the night sky into a brilliant celestial canvas. Louis found that the longer he spent looking upwards, scores of sparkling stars, like small diamonds on black cloth, came into view.

Louis leant back in his chair and his thoughts fell back to Lindos, a village on the island of Rhodes, where he once spent a week with Emma. Lindos' white sugar-cube houses crept from a bay, up a rocky hill where an ancient acropolis crowned the summit. On one particular night, they made the most of a power cut. Under the shadow of the acropolis, they lay on the flat roof of their apartment and stared in awe as the sky became saturated in an expanse of far-away suns and shooting stars. Emma squealed in excitement, confessing that she had never seen so many stars. On that night, they surfed on a wave of wonderment. He remembered the acceleration in his eyes as they danced from cluster to cluster, until he found a group of stars he recognised.

Could he find the Plough again amongst this sea of suns? The pores of his emotions tingled as he scanned the heavens, straining his eyes until an ache radiated behind them. Eventually, there it was, as it had been since the first ever night. These were the stars Emma's eyes had fallen on and now they opened the door to precious moments that were locked and cocooned in some secure region of his memory, as images flooded him, like a dam bursting his defences. He felt alone.

Behind him, a small bar served the last remaining

customers, their conversations floating over him, melting into the dark void in front, where the only sound was the rush of gentle waves caressing the sand, like lovers.

Four days had passed since leaving Meredith and Nafplion. Meredith arranged the hire of a taxi. The driver introduced himself as Georgios. He informed Louis that, once they arrived in Paralio Astros, if he wished, Louis could stay with Georgios' parents, who rented rooms above their restaurant and bar.

Louis accepted the offer, a sentient calm settling upon him now that his accommodation needs were met. During the journey, Georgios translated the early evening news from the radio, an instructive commentary in perfect English, that Louis found illuminating, especially the revelation that the high temperatures were set to continue.

From the advantage point of the taxi, Louis' eye caught a soft pastel light transforming the red earth with growing shadows across sprawling olive groves, orchards of oranges and lemons, small clusters of houses and isolated farms.

As they approached Paralio Astro, Georgios announced that Louis would greet each morning by the sea and, if he desired, he could easily venture further inland and explore the countryside. The thought appealed to Louis, casting a smile upon his face, as he imagined being greeted each morning with the sound of waves.

They drove past groups of old men who sat, bent in huddled postures, outside cafes, like secret societies, smoking, playing cards and drinking dark coffee. He observed that those who weren't smoking, constantly flicked and manoeuvred chains of coloured beads through their creased and weather-beaten fingers.

He rented a room above the small bar and restaurant situated on the perimeter of the shore, where a narrow beach sloped gently into the sea. Tables were set neatly under the shade of several telescopic trees where meals were eaten under the protection of nature's natural umbrella. The view from his confined balcony encompassed the vast expanse of the sea and, to Louis' mind, such inspiration to the eye compensated for the sparse furnishings and basic amenities of his room.

Each morning, he rose early and acquired the routine of surveying the sea from the balcony. He often took an absorbing walk to the bakers, whose palatable aroma of freshly baked bread led a delectable path to its front door.

On each of these mornings he met the same scrawny, disengaged dog, who lay curled up on a stonewall with sad, dark eyes uninterested in the world around it. On his return, its indifferent demeanour transformed into an alerted state of excitement as it sniffed the air with a raised twitching nose. As it leaped from the wall, the dog dramatized its growing euphoria, by running around in circles, barking in anticipation. Louis indulged these humorous antics before eventually throwing a piece of bread. With smacking jaws, the dog devoured the offering and licked the earth with a glistening tongue, in case it had missed a morsel of food in its impulsive demolition. Then satisfied, it retreated to the safety of its wall, walked in a circle and slumped on the stone with an air of reticence waiting for its next charitable benefactor.

Louis ate breakfast, cooked by Georgios' mother. He sat overlooking steps that disappeared into the sand of the deserted beach. He had registered and accepted the inevitable subsidence into the somnolent pace of each day which, in such a short space of time, had become part of the fabric of his life now.

It became his custom to apply an attentive gaze and watch in awe as the sun composed another unique composition by painting the morning sky in rich light and glorious colour. Louis became addicted to each new creation; like nicotine, he craved its effect, and would marvel at the warm glow of orange, yellow and crimson which streaked the horizon, in a wealth of texture, infusing the clouds, like a priceless watercolour. Louis never tired of this vibrant and ever-changing cocktail of flush tones and soft pastels. He watched the sun stimulate and disperse small clusters of cloud, its proliferating warmth dissolving and melting them until all that was left was a striking canvas of blue, vast and infinite.

Louis moved in his chair and the wicker creaked with his weight. He reached for his beer and drained the last remnants of the bottle. He stared at the enveloping darkness looming like a black wall in front of him. It was now difficult to imagine, he thought, within a matter of hours this warm velvet night would be transformed into a delicate, yet, brilliant tapestry of light and colour.

As Louis sat contemplating this, he could feel the numbing of his mind soak his senses. He was drunk. He surveyed the row of bottles, standing like soldiers on parade, and reflected that he had drunk one too many. He hoped his intoxication would not prevent him from driving the next day.

The sound of tables being cleared announced the lateness of the hour. He rose, sleep pulling at his eyes and headed for his room. As Louis emerged unsteadily from the night, Mihlis (Giorgios' father) looked up from his work from behind the bar, 'Goodnight Louis, I'll see you for breakfast I hope?'

'I'll be down at seven as usual.' A perspicacious tone radiated in the timbre of his voice. Louis misjudged a marble step and stumbled, breaking his fall instinctively with outstretched arms.

'Are you ok?' Mihlis called.

'I'll live I think. By the way, you need to get that light fixed.'

Mihlis continued to clean his empty glasses; a smile suffused his face. 'What light?'

Heaven's Return

The next morning, Louis collected an open top jeep and bought a map from the village's only car hire company. He gradually acclimatized to the left-hand drive and became less clumsy when changing the gears. He felt exhilarated and light headed; the clarity of the air felt like a stimulant, as the open road shimmered ahead. As Louis drove, a hypnotic quality settled over him, pacifying his mind that became empty and still, like a crowded room that suddenly becomes serene after the exodus of its occupants.

Louis was surprised the roads are well maintained and, at times, it seemed his was the only vehicle for miles, apart from the occasional truck that swept past on the opposite lane.

At intervals, the jeep would skirt patchworks of burnt grass, speckled with wildflowers. Rolling hills rose majestically, where clouds, like trailing mist, crowned and draped their summits, casting dark shadows that moved over the land as if sedated, given the impression that the earth was being shaded and drawn by the hand of a giant.

The geography of the landscape captured him; it encapsulated an alluring appeal that drew him towards it. He drank his fill as if it were a tonic that celebrated life with its opulent decoration.

Further along, he came across a lemon orchard and felt compelled to stop the jeep in a cloud of dust and walk amongst the lemon trees, brushing their bark with his fingers and marvelling at the yellow of the fruit erupting against the green of the branches. It occurred to him that this was the first time he had seen a lemon orchard since his childhood holidays to his father's village in the Italian countryside.

He crouched under a tree, resting his elbows on his raised knees and even in the shade he could almost lean against the heat. He felt his breast pocket and fingered the outline of his mobile phone, wondering how many messages it harboured.

In his haste to leave Edinburgh, he had told only two

people of his intentions and destination, his mother and Jez. The mobile was turned off, yet he charged it nightly and kept it with him at all times.

Louis reached into the pocket and took out the phone. He sighed, hesitating before turning it on. It displayed twelve unread messages. His finger hovered over the button. Again he hesitated indecisively.

A distant mechanical drone distracted him from his quandary. He peered through the lemon trees, past the tufts of sunburnt grass and the clearing where the jeep sat. A tractor was pulling a large trailer and, from his seated position, Louis was unable to view its contents. A plume of blue tinged smoke rose above the cab, bellowing like the funnel of an old steam train. The driver was topless and covered in dark body hair. Louis could see the stub of a cigarette, clamped firmly between his lips. Two large dogs ran in front of the tractor, precariously crisscrossing its path, in an oblivious blind stupor, courting death from its wheels.

To his side, the cry of a donkey startled him. It stood close by and statuesque, one back leg bent at the knee where the tip of its hoof touched the baked earth as if nursing an injury. Strapped to its back, and protruding from each side of its matted body, a mass of twigs and small branches overburdened the creature. Wrapped in black from her headscarf to ankle length dust encrusted dress, an old woman emerged from the dark interior of a small rectangular and windowless stone building. She barked in a croaked voice, took the rope that hung from the donkey's snout and pulled on it, forcefully, causing the animal to follow her bent frame along a path that had been compacted by the feet of people and animals alike for generations.

Louis wanted to belong. He had witnessed the old and the new, both had tended the land for a lifetime; they were part of this landscape, this way of life with their ordered routine. What landscape did he belong to?

The rattle of pistons subsided as the tractor grew smaller, increasing the distance between them. The old woman and the donkey began to disappear over a slight rising in the land and Louis watched, as her body seemed to melt from her feet and then gradually to her head, as if the midday sun had dissolved her.

He glanced at the mobile and, for a moment, he was tempted to open the text messages but as he walked toward the jeep, he placed the mobile back in his breast pocket. He was not ready to let the life he had left behind intrude and disrupt these moments.

His journey took him through villages and towns. Each new corner unfolded another work of art, projecting incalculable richness, enlivening his senses as he imagined the effect of the enervating sun on his skin was like being massaged with warm oils.

The road curved and climbed a steep gradient, rising dramatically and precariously, skirting the edge of each vertiginous drop that sent a hot flurry through his stomach, a potent deterrent in reminding him to concentrate more on the road and less on his surroundings.

Small shrines ominously sprinkled the road. The thought crossed Louis that, by their existence, they could distract a driver's concentration and be invariably responsible for further accidents, not the purpose that proposed their construction. Determined not to become another victim or statistic, he employed a concerted effort and concentrated on each twist and turn of the road as it hugged each door like a precipice.

He was aware of a dull ache where his back stiffened against the seat. He gripped the steering wheel with a comforting firmness and, in doing so, spread a reassurance that soothed his anxiety.

Ahead, a sun-bleached sign advertised the prospect of *'Authentic Greek food and hospitality at Yorgo's taverna.'* Louis manoeuvered the jeep into a clearing. He studied the humbly built structure and his high spirits deflated, the flaking and bleached exterior seemed to succumb to the final stages of a fatal disease.

Louis' stomach groaned, and he hoped the dilapidated building did not reflect the quality of the food it served. He stepped from the jeep and walked towards the taverna reminding himself it was still not too late to engage in a hasty retreat.

Moving closer, his eye was snagged from the blistering paint by sloping terraces, overflowing with flourishing vegetation and crops that descended into a deep valley, like giant steps, leading to a mantle of ancient olive groves, each tree depicting its own character in shape and size. Behind the unkempt taverna, Louis had stumbled upon its secret garden. He gasped in awe at the incalculably rich colour that projected itself in a halo of glorious light. Walls of rock and stone, built by hand, separated land, like the border lines of small countries. Orange and lemon groves sprinkled the landscape. Cypress trees, shaped like emerald spears, pin pricked the land where vineyards sprung from the dusty earth, and flocks of goats searched for food to the music of their chiming bells that hung, like medallions, from their necks. He inhaled sage, oregano, thyme, and rosemary that rose towards him on warm rising currents. He felt drunk with their effect. Louis was transfixed; like reading a good book, he absorbed it all. So indulged in his discovery, he was unaware of the figure that appeared from the rear of the tavern, studying him with an expression, not unlike a hypnotist surveying the subject of his spell.

'It catches me like that too, every time.'

Startled, Louis turned.

A prodigious man, the size of a battleship, stood grinning at Louis. He wore a cook's apron, once the colour white but now covered in a map of stains. His bald crown reflected the sun, like a mirror, as abandoned wild wisps of silver hair licked his ears. A forest of silver and mouse whiskers covered his face, where a large curling moustache smiled at Louis. Thick caterpillar eyebrows sat like lips below a creased forehead. Louis noticed that the man's lips were almost lost within the great mass of facial hair.

'It's so intense, it almost speaks to you, don't you think?'

'It's incredible... truly amazing.'

'Amazing!' the cook boomed. 'Amazing is not a good enough word to describe it. If this was a painting it would be considered a masterpiece, if you could bottle such beauty you would make a fortune.'

Louis glanced at the object in the cook's hand. Dangling unceremoniously, a dead chicken, stripped of its feathers, hung by its clawed feet.

Noticing the stranger's apparent surprise, the cook held the chicken out in front of him. 'Lunch,' he stated. 'She's still warm; she'll probably yell with fright once she hits the pan.' He erupted in laughter, his whole body shaking. Gesturing with the sorrowful looking chicken, he beamed.

'Come and take a seat if you are eating. Otherwise, enjoy our little piece of heaven... it's the only thing that is free around here.'

Louis elected to take a seat in the shade of a fig tree that grew heavy with fruit. Several figs lay scattered on the hard ground, along with a carpet of pine needles that had been blown and uprooted from their branches. The same branches shaded the ground with their shadows and Louis was thankful that they would offer protection from the sun while he ate.

The sight of the tavern, the bulbous Yorgos, and his dangling chicken, left Louis feeling apprehensive at the prospect of consuming food prepared and cooked under less than desirable conditions. Relenting to his hunger and trepidation, he ordered stuffed aubergine, salad, bottled water, and coffee. The sound of singing birds, punctured the air, as the unread text messages crossed his mind, only to be replaced by feet crunching pine needles.

His lunch arrived, brought by a girl, not much older than fifteen, Louis guessed. She wore a Michael Jackson t-shirt, fading jeans and Adidas trainers. She placed his lunch on the table and smiled shyly. Louis returned her smile.

'Efcharisto.'

'Parakalo,' she replied. Then with a flicker of her lashes and a skip in her step, she returned to the kitchen.

Feeling pleased with himself, he surveyed his lunch. Like everything in this country, he thought, the potent effect of colour is startling, even emanating from his humble salad of feta, carrots, beef tomatoes, dark olives, lettuce and cucumber.

As he ate, the laboured drones of a coach swung into the parking area with an animal-like squeal of brakes and a whoosh of hydraulic doors that announced the mobilization of its passengers, disembarking in a wave of cameras and camcorders, descending upon Yorgos' taverna and its views, like an invading and conquering army.

To Louis' relief, his lunch was a palatable success that left him feeling contented and full. The young girl had now been joined by her older sister, as they struggled to satisfy the abandoned propriety of their customers. Even Yorgos appeared from the kitchen to serve drinks from behind the bar or to waiter at the tables. It occurred to Louis that, if there were no busloads of tourists, Yorgos could not sustain a living. Therefore a delicate balance had to be struck and observed if he was to continue to preserve his small piece of heaven.

Eventually, the tables emptied. The tour guide rounded everyone up, and the coach left in a plume of smoke and disappeared around a bend. The two girls collected the abandoned plates and glasses. Louis rose from his chair, as a soft breeze stimulated his nerve endings, moving across the surface of his skin, like the return of an old friend. He became aware of the returning birdsong that once again filled the air.

Yorgos appeared from the kitchen, wiping his brow with a towel.

'Can you hear it?' Yorgos asked.

'Hear what?'

'Heaven has returned,' he beamed.

That night, Louis finished reading Captain Correlli's Mandolin. It was a book that had occupied his time and mind, it had been a travelling companion and he had turned to it, just as one seeks the company of a friend. He felt the inevitable despondent pangs as he put the book down and digested its last few pages.

It was while he reflected upon the book's conclusion that the idea came to him. He would see for himself the island of Cephalonia. Such prospect brought a sense of expectation that welled up inside him. It was not unlike the wild anticipation he remembered feeling as a child on Christmas Eve.

This revelation had given him a concrete objective, a purpose to aim for. He would now not just amble away his days, he had a goal, something that was tangible and achievable. He felt invigorated.

The Beginning of Grief

On the morning of his journey to Cephalonia, an oil coloured sky sagged with the weight of rain, as if contemplating a downpour. Louis watched as the dark charcoal grey mass moved out to sea, like giant juggernauts and then, as if nature had cast a spell, the sky painted itself in strokes of watery blue and the sun, like a golden ball, dominated its territory, offering a radiant heat that warmed the ground below his feet.

After breakfast, he walked barefoot along the narrow strip of beach, wearing knee-length shorts and a t-shirt. The pervasive warmth of the sand under his feet swelled his optimism for his day of travel, like a sentient and luxuriating massage, relaxing and cleansing every cell in his body as he tasted the spray of salt upon his lips.

He listened to the murmur of the sea greeting the shore and it seemed to him as if the waves partook in a race, as they cascaded in upon themselves for the final sprint upon the wet sand where they faded away, only to be replaced by another continual rush of competing waves. He peeled off his t-shirt and discarded it.

The sea was a striking electric turquoise. Louis thought of it as alive and ever changing. In the days he had spent in this warm climate, he had not been tempted to seek the refuge it offered until now.

The sand became wet under his feet, like clay it moulded itself onto his skin and stuck between his toes. He made indentations in the soft sand, footprints stolen by the tide, as it retreated, like a thief, into the sea. The water was tepid, which surprised him; it licked his ankles and rose to his knees as he moved further into its depths.

The seabed rippled with ridged sand and, once again, he was taken aback by the pellucid and crystal water, as clear as bath water, he said out loud, as if the sound of his voice was a confirmation of what he saw. The sun reflected sheets of white glare on the surface and, below, tiny silver fish darted from his advancing feet at such speed it was impossible for the eye to follow them. When he reached waist level, he plunged into the sea, rolled onto his back and floated on the surface, like a small boat. The effect was exhilarating and brought with it a sense of freedom as he gently glided through the water with rhythmic strokes. The warm sea sloshing over his chest and legs dulled his senses into submission, the glare of the sun forced his eyes to squint, firing images that invited themselves. Pictures of memories, like a photo album, shared themselves, he floated between them... an icy North Sea... sand castles and ice cream... chasing a football on St. Andrews' beach with his father... his mother's gold crucifix reflecting the sun... a smiling Emma, eyes hidden behind designer sunglasses, lying on a grass verge in Princes Street Gardens, sunbathing away a lazy summer's afternoon...

A voice from the shore startled him. He turned in its direction and guided himself upright in the water. He opened his eyes and the sudden filtration of light blurred the figure on the beach. Gradually his eyes focused and dispelled the shimmering haze, as the waving arm of Georgios gestured him to come ashore.

Louis reached Georgios who, by now, had walked to the bar area of the restaurant. He handed a mobile phone to Louis, who recognized it as his own.

'It would not stop ringing. I thought it must be important, so I answered it. I saw you out in the water,' Georgios said.

I must have turned the mobile on when I charged it last night, Louis thought. He placed the mobile to his ear,

'Hello?' Small puddles had formed around his bare feet.

There was a deliberate silence, then a cough, the type that clears the throat in preparation to deliver an important speech.

'Hello?' Louis' tone was more insistent this time, a trace of annoyance discernible.

'At last, Louis, it's Jez... thank God I've found you... I've been trying to get in touch with you for days... Listen, you must prepare yourself for what I'm about to tell you.'

Louis could detect a tremor in Jez' voice. 'What is it Jez... are you ok?'

Jez sighed. 'There's been an accident, three weeks ago,

well, not really an accident. They think it was deliberate… they've arrested him.'

'Jez, slow down you're not making sense, what accident? Who's been arrested?' For a moment, Louis thought of Demetrius.

Louis sat down on one of the chairs. A film of fine sand coated its surface, travellers on the wind, he thought. He watched the sea. A large white boat, the size of a train carriage, sat graciously on the water. Again there was an elongated pause. Louis could sense Jez compose himself.

'Listen Louis is there someone with you? I need you to prepare yourself... it's Emma... she is... she's dead Louis.'

The voice sounded distant. A heavy sensation pushed on his chest. His abdomen tightened. He recalled when he last saw Emma in Amber's cafe.

'The police have arrested Paul.'

'I don't understand. How did it happen?' he blurted out, still wrestling with the reality of the words.

'From what we can gather, there seemed to be an argument between them that escalated and got out of hand. He hit Emma, and she struck her head on a worktop. They said she would've died almost instantly. The police have charged the bastard with attempted murder... God forgive my hatred... I'm struggling Louis. It's hard to feel anything but hatred, never mind forgiveness.'

'Paul killed her. I can't believe it. She can't be dead.'

'I wish there was another way of breaking this to you. Why didn't you answer my calls? I text every day. Its been weeks, I've been frantic and your mother too.'

'I'm sorry Jez. God, I should've answered them.'

'Louis,' Jez continued. 'I'm afraid there's more.'

A fire burnt in Louis' chest. The first waves of nausea swept over him.

'There's already been a funeral, we couldn't wait indefinitely. We had no idea where you were, you didn't reply to my messages; there was no way of contacting you. Paul confessed everything to the police and, after the autopsy, they released Emma's body.'

The text messages... if only he had read them, but then,

what good would it have done? He could not change what had happened. He could have gone back to Edinburgh and said goodbye properly at the funeral... they had argued and he had left her in Amber's. It was the last time he saw her, distressed and alone. He had not considered Emma's feelings; it had all been about him. He had abandoned her.

A rock lodged in his throat. His eyes stung, growing blotchy and red. He rubbed them with the palm of his hand. He heard his name several times, the voice was faint and then he became aware of Jez's voice, it jolted him.

'Jez, I can't believe it... oh God, we argued Jez, we argued about the baby.'

He realised two lives had ended. Why was he so angry with her? His guilt felt like a hurricane, pounding him in its wake.

'Louis, listen to me, I know this is hard for you and it's come as a great shock, but at a time like this you need people around you that you know. At least I've had time to come to terms with Emma's death, if one ever does... I think it would be best if you came home. I'll meet you at the airport if you want?'

'I've nothing to come home for now... She's gone, I've lost her for good and I wasn't there for her. If only I'd tried harder to get her back, this might never have happened.'

'Listen Louis.' Jez was more insistent. 'You cannot punish yourself; there was absolutely nothing you or I could do to change what has happened. This is not the time to cast blame. I know you're hurting right now; you need to come home Louis, heal that hurt inside you and celebrate Emma's life amongst the people who knew her. You shouldn't be on your own.'

Unnaturally, in the heat, Louis felt cold. He closed his eyes and, behind them, Emma appeared. He felt hollow inside, like a rotting tree trunk... and then it came, like a tidal wave crashing over him, enveloping him, as if grief had wrapped its arms around him. Louis felt suffocated. He tried to control each breath by drawing in large gulps of air and then slowly and deliberately exhaling. He thought his heart would burst from his chest at any moment.

Louis saw silhouetted figures sunbathing on the boat; a dark figure dived into the sea, disappearing for a few seconds before emerging a few meters from where it had entered the water.

He glanced at the boat which shone brilliant white against the azure of the calm sea. People were drinking and eating. How surreal, he thought, as the space between them acted as a spectrum of human emotion and behaviour.

'Jez I'm staying here. Edinburgh would just remind me of her.'

There was a silence. Jez understood his reasoning.

'Well look, keep that bloody phone on and promise me you'll phone. You're not alone in this, we're all hurting and it's good, in fact, healthy to share that hurt, even if we're thousands of miles apart.'

'I will Jez, I promise.'

Louis felt light headed and thankful he was seated. His shorts had started to dry in the clinging heat and the damp patches fading, the fabric returning to its natural colour. Louis heard a voice other than Jez on the phone, a female voice, possibly Carris, Louis imagined. The voice was muffled and distant. Jez answered and then addressed Louis.

'Louis, I've got to go now. If you haven't phoned within a few days I'll phone you, take care now and God bless. My thoughts and prayers are with you.'

Louis mumbled a goodbye and placed the mobile in his lap.

How fragile we are, he thought. Not the immortal beings we like to think we are in our busy lives. It can all come crashing down around us.

It came to him as an afterthought. For a second time that day, guilt engulfed him, fermenting a sense of shame. Jez had lost his sister, he was grieving, and Louis had been overwhelmed in an impulsive and inflexible grief of his own that he had omitted to ask after his friend. He felt the compulsion to phone Jez yet, a feeling rose within him, much stronger, smothering the urge. He could not, not just yet.

Georgios appeared. 'I heard your mobile ring, it would not stop... I thought it must have been important, so I took it from your bag. Your friend was very insistent that I should call you from the sea.'

'I'm glad you did Georgios. Thank you.'

'Did your friend bring sad news... you look upset... different.'

Louis looked at Georgios. iIt was a stare that did not see the man in front of him but, rather, a look that was fixed in the past.

'She has gone... forever.'

'Who?' Georgios said perplexed.

'My beautiful Emma.'

The Academic Exposed

Georgios persuaded Louis to postpone his journey to Cephalonia for a few days at least. Louis stayed in his room like a hermit, spending most of the day sitting on the balcony, staring at the sea. He ate his meals there, brought by Georgios' mother who viewed him with concern. When Georgios was not working, he would visit Louis and, although Louis only spoke about Emma, Georgios would listen and say very little. Louis looked forward to these visits, it was his therapy.

Louis felt as if he had fallen into a deep hole and he had neither the will nor strength to claw his way back out. He was building a protective shell around himself, like an oxygen tent that only he could inhabit. Louis would let no one penetrate its protective core, not even Georgios. It was his construction, his alienation from the outside world.

A veil of thoughts that concerned only Emma, consumed every hour, from the darkness of his dreams to the moment he opened his eyes to the light of the day.

She can't be dead. She was having a baby. People like her don't get murdered.

One night, he panicked and reached for his mobile. He punched in her number, before stopping; his fingers trembled uncontrollably.

Emma would have adored this view, he reminded himself; she loved the sea. He remembered holidays where she would spend almost their entire two weeks sitting on a beach, staring out to sea, lying sunbathing and falling asleep to the backdrop of waves crawling up the sands. If it had not been for Louis' insistence that it was an incredible waste not to explore the island's interior and countryside, she would have been content to stay there indefinitely, surrounded by sand, sea and the ubiquitous scent of suntan oil.

He lost recognition of the days of the week. One afternoon, as he stared at the sea, he remembered the hours of video he recorded on holiday and Emma chastising him for always recording too much. He recalled Emma's exasperated expression when he insisted on recording the contents of a meal or panning from her head to her feet when she was sunbathing. The videos were in the flat, sitting undisturbed in chronological rows, like books on a shelf. The thought occurred to him; he had her forever imprinted on these tapes. He could still see her, watch her vivacious smile, hear her voice and, in some strange way, she would always be alive. She would not leave him. His throat tightened at such a prospect, it ached and burned.

On the fourth day, Georgios entered Louis' room brandishing two bottles of wine, as if he had won them in the village raffle. Eventually, with some persistence, he persuaded Louis to accompany him to what he described as his special place.

They had travelled for fifteen minutes, when Georgios announced that they nearly were there. Louis wondered where being "there" was. They were surrounded by giant pine trees that straddled each side of the road, like green walls, before moving onto a road that was nothing more than a dirt track as the car's tyres crushed dry earth and small stones in a storm of dust.

They passed an old man riding a donkey, his clothes encrusted and grey with fine dust, as he spoke in an exuberant volume down a mobile phone.

'The old and the new living side by side in perfect harmony.' Georgios laughed, thrusting his head back into the headrest. Louis recalled the tractor in the field and the old woman and her donkey he had seen a few days previously. Spurred on by the old man's animated gestures, Louis laughed too and Georgios shook his head approvingly.

They drank the wine sitting on a cluster of rocks that acted as a natural veranda, overlooking a setting of vertiginous cliffs that plunged into a landscape of undulating emerald, olive, apple green and brown.

'I come here to escape, to be alone and clear my head. I find the wide open space helps me to think over my problems... work them out,' Georgios said.

The wine was warm as it wet Louis' lips yet, he drank it

as if it were water. Some of the wine trickled from the corner of his mouth, like blood. Louis wiped it with the back of his hand and studied the scene set out before him. He discovered that the colours of the landscape made shapes and, if he looked closely enough, he could just about make out a face. Louis traced its long hair; he found what looked like a beard.

He smiled and took another long drink from the warm bottle. The light was translucent and dry, hovering over trees and hills like a halo. Louis suddenly noticed the silence; it seemed to hum in his ears and fill his head, and he could feel it press against his skin, like a vice. And then, as if it had just started, he discerned the trickling sound of water, a stream maybe, or even a river. How strange; he had not heard it before. He bent forward and picked up a smooth stone. It reminded him of the pebbles he used to collect, as a child, on family holidays in St. Andrews. A picture of his father entered his head, unsuspectingly. He was overcome by a pining; it moved in him, like waves. He rubbed his eyes to suppress the tears that had welled up.

Louis had not cried over his father's death since the funeral. He had been the only person close to Louis that had died until now.

Louis turned to face Georgios, who was staring at the sky.

'Do you believe in life after death Georgios? When the body dies the spirit lives on?'

Georgios scratched his head. 'My friend and I would often come here in the summer; sometimes we would bring girlfriends and sit on these rocks, bring some drink and soak up the view. Anyway, he is dead now, an accident in Athens, a few years ago now. After that, I would come here on my own.' He shook his head. 'There were times, I swear Louis, he was sitting right there, where you are now. I could sense him, probably the effect of too much wine. Then, with each visit, the feeling faded.'

'I thought I would have felt something. Had some kind of feeling she was no longer alive, but there was nothing. I lived as normal. I thought and behaved as normal. Some people say they witnessed a sign, a smell like perfume or hear a voice. There was nothing. I dream about her. I am in the room with her, in their kitchen, but I can't do anything. I can't stop him.' He took a long gulp of wine, the bottle popped as it left his lips.

'If the dead could visit us, then I'm sure Emma would be sitting here right now and she would tell you to look forward, not back. She would urge you to reclaim your life and live it to the full. Nothing good can come out of shutting yourself away.'

Louis glanced at the view in front of him. 'Thank you Georgios... thank you for bringing me here.'

'Meredith wants you to know she is thinking about you. She feels your pain. She sends you her love.'

'You have spoken to her?'

Georgios looked at Louis without speaking for a while.

'Yes, listen to me Louis. Back in Athens, you were never in any danger. You just made the proceedings a little more... complicated. They wanted to intimidate and scare you. Meredith liked you very much. She told me to take care of you.'

'What are you talking about Georgios. How do you know about Athens?' He could not conceal his astonishment.

'The people who attacked Demetrius, not the thugs, but those who planned it and ordered it, are powerful; they get what they want. The intention was not to kill him but let him know, if they wanted to kill him, they could. They have been watching you ever since you stepped onto that train and left Athens.'

'But I was last on the train.'

'Yes, but Meredith was also on the train. She didn't get on at the next station as she said; she was already in the carriage behind. When you bought the ticket, she boarded the train then. They have eyes and ears everywhere, Louis. Even here.'

Louis looked at Georgios.

'I'm afraid so.'

'Why?' Louis replied perplexed.

'There is not a lot of money in the taxi business. I'm not

involved in the criminal side Louis; I collect information when required and report to Meredith. It's a little extra money that's all.'

'But how can that be, Meredith's an old lady, cultured and refined. It's ludicrous.'

'The perfect cover, is it not? You would never suspect an old lady. It became very obvious from early on that you were not involved with Demetrious. She genuinely wanted to help you. She cares about you very much Louis.'

'This is surreal. I feel angry with her and myself. Was she behind the stabbing?'

'God no. Let's call her semi-retired, she was never involved in that kind of thing. She was the brains. In her younger days, she had the nickname, *'the academic.'* She is not the biggest fish in the sea anymore and that suits her now. Did I say that correctly?'

'Yes, I get the idea. I don't know how to feel, worried or relieved. To think, all of this time, I've been under surveillance.'

'That was only at the beginning. Meredith was genuine in everything she did and said to you. She feels a responsibility towards you; she wants you to know that. Look at it this way, Louis, she protected you from the police. Her influence goes a long way, even to the top. She has many 'friends,' if you know what I mean.'

'And you, Georgios. You brought me here.'

Georgios smiled. 'Think of me as Meredith's babysitter. You're not a threat to their interests. I am to look after you, make sure you are safe before you continue on your travels. Meredith's orders.'

'And your parents, do they know about this?'

'No.' He looked at Louis pleadingly. 'I would like it if that continued. Is that ok with you Louis?'

He felt sorry for Georgios. 'Our secret then.'

Georgios squeezed his shoulder. 'Efcharisto.'

Olympia

Under Her Skin

She had taken this trip for two years now, every second Saturday. After a breakfast of toast and strong black coffee, Maria leisurely strolled down to the centre of town and sat outside the tour company's office. The office staff had not yet arrived to start work. The trip to Olympia had a notoriously early start.

This was her favourite hour of the day. The vivacious heartbeat of the capital left tamed by a somnolent veil of serene stillness. Maria felt shrouded in contentment. The drone of a passing car invaded the silence, reminding her that the calmness was not permanent, but an evolving ambience as the capital awoke from its sleep.

It had been Peter's turn to do the 'dawn shift' that morning. Early in the morning, the coach picked up its cargo of tourists from resorts such as Kalamaki and Argassi, skirted the coast and luminous sea and then swept into the capital, Zakynthos Town, before boarding the ferry to Kyllini, a coastal town in the Peloponnese, and an hour's drive from Olympia, the site of the ancient games.

The coach arrived. It stopped to collect Maria and then headed towards the far side of the harbour.

'Good morning Maria, I trust we are ready for our day of travel into antiquity,' Peter asked.

'As always.' Maria smiled, settling into her seat.

Peter leant towards his middle fifties, with straw tinged hair that fell from a Panama hat and hugged his shoulders. He resonated with a civilised Englishness. His voice was warm and educated and when he spoke, to capture a certain mood or illustration, he often produced a metaphor to colour his speech and emphasise his meaning, holding the attention of his audience.

Peter turned to face the expectant passengers. 'Before we leave the capital and let it rub the sleep from its eyes, may I draw your attention to my hat.' He touched the top of his hat. 'I would be grateful if you could all pay particular attention to it, as it will act as a beacon. When we reach Kellini and disembark from the ferry, I will raise my hat above my head and wave it for all to see. We can then all congregate, stay together, and hopefully all board the coach again safely. Kellini will be busy and especially crowded and we're ruled by the clock. Therefore, I would appreciate if we can all try to stick together. Thank you.'

Even at this early hour, the promenade danced to the varying rhythms of life, a striking contrast to the drowsiness they had just left in the centre of town. The coach crawled along the harbour towards a queue of rumbling vehicles and the throng of people on foot.

The ferry dwarfed its surroundings, like an opulent palace rising from the sea. Once on board, Maria climbed a flight of steps and emerged onto a spacious upper deck. She stood looking out over a placid sheet of water, a perfect impression of the capital and an azure sky capping steel grey hills, reflected upon its surface. Like a favourite painting, this view never failed to impress her. She could feel the sun growing warm on her skin, scattering its heat as the day rose from its slumber.

The ferry trickled out of the harbour through the silver morning light towards the vast panoramic expanse of the open sea. As it gathered speed, it cut through waves, as if they were ripples of melting butter and, gradually, Zakynthos Town shrank in size and Maria was struck, as she always had been, by the omnipresent sense of the sea.

She pushed her sunglasses onto the crown of her head and descended into the bowels of the ferry in search of coffee. A concourse of people queued for food and drinks, others sat at tables in loud conversations, while some lay on seats, catching up on lost sleep. In a corner, a television spurted out the familiar Saturday morning onslaught of cartoons.

Like an island in a stormy sea, Peter's hat hovered; he was waving her over and pointing to two newly acquired polystyrene cups.

He neatly folded The Times on the table as Maria sat down. To her right, two young women pampered a baby, and she wondered which one was the mother. She took a sip of coffee.

'That's better. Thank you, Peter.'

'You're welcome, my dear.' Peter studied her and detecting a melancholy air, asked, 'What is it? You look slightly troubled.'

She looked up from her coffee. 'Do you remember Angelini?'

'Yes I do. I remember that she worked as a tour guide before having a baby. You were friends. Do you still keep in touch?'

'Yes, I see her often. Those women with the baby reminded me of her. She's pregnant again.'

Peter looked surprised. 'My word. If I'm not mistaken, will this be her third child?'

'Yes, remember, she fell pregnant straight after her first was born?'

'That's right. I do recall that her intention was to return to work.'

'She loves being a mother, it suits her. It's her husband that is the problem. He works in a bar, at a disco in town; anyway, he has developed the habit of staying out most nights after work, the temptations on offer are obvious and a distraction he cannot refuse.'

'Ah, I see.'

Marie sighed. 'Angelini has given him chance after chance to change. Each time he tells her he is sorry and it will never happen again, but it does. Everyone knows what is going on. She threw him out last week and now she is on her own with two young children and a baby on its way.'

Maria cradled her coffee cup and glanced at the two women with the baby. A longing to touch the baby and smell it engulfed her. She suppressed the ache to cradle it in her arms. She turned away and caught Peter looking at her. Peter wondered, and not for the first time, why Maria had never found the right person.

'Angelini was making plans; she was doing things for herself, feeling like a woman again and not just a mother. She once told me she felt her life was just one endless roller coaster full of nappies, dirty dishes and housework.'

'We make our own choices Maria and those choices decide the direction we travel; they influence the aspects and details of our life. There are good choices and bad ones; every choice is a leap of faith. I hope Angelini's leap of faith brings her a happy reward.'

She fingered the rim of her cup. 'That sounds grand and philosophical, but I have a simpler outlook. Life can sometimes just be cruel and unfair, sadistic even.'

'It certainly doesn't distribute its riches equally.'

'What about you Peter? As long as I've known you, you've never settled down with anyone. Has that always been the case?' she asked.

'No, my dear, there have been a few but unfortunately, in those instances, I also made the wrong choices. At my time of life, the prospect of meeting that special person grows slimmer by the day. Anyway, I'm set in my ways. The thought of accommodating another man's routines and habits does not fill one with enthusiasm, although I do miss the companionship.'

'You should never say never, Peter.'

'I have the memories; they keep me warm at night.'

There was a pause between them.

'There's something else.'

'And what would that be my dear?'

'I've been offered a job. I went to Athens for the interview.'

'I didn't know you were looking for one.'

'I wasn't. It came out of the blue at the convention in Athens. I met an old friend who is doing really well. She owns her own tour company. It's expanding. She was very persuasive.'

'I see and is this what you want? I mean, if it is, then I am happy for you, of course.'

'The package is a generous one. I'll have my own place in Athens. I'd be a woman of independent means.' Maria laughed.

'And are you not now?' Peter asked.

Maria thought for a long moment. 'I am, but in Athens

there is opportunity.'

'Be more specific my dear.'

'I could never imagine life being any different. I love my life, but it's made me think of what my life could be like. If I want to, I can change the direction of my life. Athens will allow me to do that. Zakynthos will always be my home.'

'Well I won't lie, I would miss you terribly. You would have to promise to visit regularly.'

'I might not go. It's not decided yet.'

He placed his hat on his head. 'I think I'll stretch my legs. Are you coming?'

The Morea rose from the sea as the ferry sailed inexorably towards the coast. Maria witnessed this on the upper deck along with a growing crowd who, sensing the crossing was culminating, seemed eager to depart; willing Kyllini closer.

Two young boys accosted the attention of their parents; their impending excitement exploded, like fireworks, as the view of an ancient castle grew in size and detail with each passing minute.

Kyllini drew near and a reverberant wave of activity ensued amongst the passengers. Maria heard the distinctive tones of Peter's voice puncture the air, as he answered a couple's inquisitive question.

'Although small in size, its stature is of great importance in its relation to Zakynthos. You see, convoys of goods are daily transported by articulated vehicles that continually cross the water, as do smaller modes of transport, carrying provisions and other materials. Add to this, the hundreds of people who use the ferries, Kyllini could well be described as Zakynthos' umbilical cord. And indeed today, for our purpose, she could be described as the gateway to the Peloponnese and finally, Olympia itself.' Peter emphasised his words with sweeping gestures. The couple nodded in unison, absorbing every word as if they were children and had just been taught a lesson by their favourite teacher.

He performs best in front of an audience, Maria smiled to herself. She thought about the job offer. It sounded exciting, full of possibility, but unfamiliar. She sighed. She would miss Peter, her family, her friends and her island. Her feelings were intertwined; all this had done was unsettled her.

The ferry slowly cleaved a path into Kallini's small port. To the right, sunbathers speckled a beach as children played in the sea or made elaborate sand castles. Maria's attention was caught by a couple, husband and wife maybe, who precariously navigated a crop of rocks stretching out into the sea, like a finger. To gain balance, they raised their arms, like walking a tightrope, and tentatively they manoeuvered over black shiny rocks, slippery and wet from the spray of the waves.

As Maria observed them, the woman sat on a large slab of rock, resting her bare arms on her legs and clasping her hands together above her knees. The man walked further on, slipping once, before turning and raising a camera to his eye and, it was at that moment, that Maria noticed the woman was posing for a photograph. After a few seconds, the man turned from her and stared motionlessly into the sea, as white foamed waves crashed against rocks, leaving streams of seawater cascading over their surface, like miniature waterfalls. Maria rested her hands on the ferry's railing. The woman walked towards the man, precise in her movements, careful not to lose her balance. Strands of hair blew across her face. He handed her the camera and climbed down towards the lapping waves. The woman waited for him to find a suitable spot and then she crouched down, her t-shirt flapping against her back, like a sail in the wind and raised the camera.

Maria noted the colour of the sea. An electric blue shaded by patches of turquoise, shimmered and undulated before melting and evolving into a striking aqua green. Absorbed in the colour, a minute passed. Her eyes slid over to the rocks where she discovered that the couple had reached the safety of the flat sand.

He had wrapped an arm around the woman's waist, the camera dangling from his free hand. She, too, had placed her arm around his waist as if they were joined... inseparable even.

The quay became a sponge into which everything was absorbed. People and traffic choked the limited space available. Maria and Peter stood next to their coach, its engine purring like a contented cat. Peter waved his hat above the throng of activity, an island in a hostile sea, Maria thought. A head count established everyone was accounted for and the coach negotiated a maze of narrow streets, progressing at a crawling pace, until it finally tasted the open space of the main road.

Tomato and sweetcorn fields greeted them as the coach passed an army of sprinklers that sparkled in the sun. To their left, a range of mountains dominated the landscape, reaching towards the sky. Peter proclaimed that they were giant steps that the ancient Greek Gods used when visiting the world of mortals. He instructed his captive audience that, in Winter, the same mountains were coated in snow and ideal for skiing, as he commenced to paint a surreal image of men and women climbing to the summits with skiing equipment, while outside the coach the temperature steadily rose.

Maria stared out of the window, her eyes unable to acknowledge the passing landscape. She was deep within herself, under her skin, lost to the outside world of tourists, day trips and Greek families trudging up the snow-covered mountains. Maria had tried to bury the image of the baby, the attention the two women afforded it, the couple on the rocks and then their walk on the beach. She attempted to lay them aside like a finished meal, however, there was no waiter to take them away. Filling her time with work, family and friends allowed a reprieve from the pangs that now ate at her. She could go days, even weeks, when her thoughts would be free of the pull that seemed to turn her inside out and then suddenly, a word, a picture in a magazine, a T. V. programme would be the catalyst responsible for opening the floodgates of an outpouring of emotions that consumed her. It was not lost on her that she was not in a stable relationship. Maybe Athens would change all of that. At twenty-eight, should she be torturing herself about such things? She was young, in good shape, her figure attracted men, she was educated. My God, she concluded, at twenty-eight, she was in her prime.

Gradually, she floated back until the outside world and Peter's voice pierced her thoughts. 'As the centuries passed, the sands of time buried Olympia. However, the knowledge of its location survived. Archaeologists opened a window of history, an aperture tantalisingly full of possibilities, insight and discovery. The poverty of mankind's visual examples of the ancient world was to be presented with a gift of such magnitude it would forever enrich our perception of that time and civilisation.'

As always he held his audience spellbound, like a performer on stage; they hung on to his every word. Maria had given up long ago trying to match his rich and colourful descriptions, by accepting defeat gracefully and sticking to the more down to earth simplified language of your everyday tour guide.

By now, Peter was on a roll. 'In such places, one has to summon awareness and imagination to paint the splendour and grandeur that the vast site of Olympia undoubtedly was,' he waved his hat, like a conductor's baton. 'This is not to say that what remains today is a poor man's version, demeaning its authenticity as a spectacle of the ancient world,' he took out a white handkerchief from his trouser pocket and dabbed his forehead. 'On the contrary, a potent ambience encompasses Olympia, intensifying and haunting, indeed, it is almost spiritual, as if one has entered the holy and hallowed ground. From the moment one enters the site, the aura of culture is invigoratingly alive. It is palpable and everywhere. In fact, I can even go as far to say that one is assaulted by it.'

Peter handed the microphone to Maria. 'Your audience awaits my dear.'

She scolded him with a frown. 'And how do I follow that?'

Kyra

The notion of travelling to Olympia was planted by Mihlis, the night before Louis left Paralio Astros. Mihlis thought of himself as an amateur historian. With audible pleasure, his wife often reminded him that 'amateur' was the appropriate word, as he elaborated upon and stretched tales of Greece's historical and mythological past. After dinner, and fortified by several drinks, Mihlis spent several hours elaborating on stories and facts on the best historical sites and places to visit, adding that his only regret in life was being unable to visit all of Greece's historical jewels, to the pitiless look of his unsympathetic and long-suffering wife. Louis enjoyed these distractions; they offered a respite from his recent solitude and silence.

Instead of travelling directly to Cephalonia, Louis travelled through the towns and villages of Mihlis' rambling stories, staying in guesthouses or cheap hotels, until four weeks later he disembarked from a coach in the centre of Olympia.

As each day passed, the fist that remained lodged in his chest grew smaller and he was glad of its release. He told himself that it meant he was adjusting, he had an improved ability to cope, he had swum through the whirlpool of his grief and now he felt a need to reorganise and be in control once more. His anonymity suited him.

He kept the promise he made to Jez and phoned him several times. He phoned his mother, who was elated to hear his voice, and confessed she wanted him to return home, but reiterated several times she respected his decision to stay. However, the crackle in her voice, more evident than she intended, could not mask her incredulity.

One afternoon, he sat in a tavern. He had taken a seat underneath the protection of hanging vines and ordered an omelette. It arrived floating ominously in a sea of grease, like a struggling bird stranded in an oil slick. A confrontation with the chef had not been anticipated as part of his day's itinerary; it was not his manner either. He had always joked that he must have inherited the 'never cause a scene gene' from his mother. Louis wondered if the bread that accompanied the meal was to be used to soak up the offending grease. At this point, his stomach dictated that its need was greater than the palate's prejudice. He ate the omelette and was grateful for the chilled bottle of water that slid effortlessly down his throat. Several hours later, he spent the rest of the day and most of that night throwing up into the toilet or lying on his bed unable to move until another wave was heaved from him in an unstoppable rush.

The next morning, after enquiring, the hotel receptionist informed Louis that the site of Olympia was only a ten-minute walk out of town. He thought it a good idea to try to walk off his sensitive stomach.

Louis stopped at a small shop and bought a bottle of water. He sat on the steps of a church and eagerly poured generous amounts of the ice cold liquid over his throat. He absorbed the water and its quenching qualities. As he rested in the shade of the church, it reminded him that the orthodox faith cast its shadow upon all corners of Greek society, becoming part of the fabric that influenced the culture and traditions he had been continually reminded of during his stay.

The day's heat felt like a furnace upon his skin. His mouth filled with saliva, as nausea bit at his throat. He swallowed hard, but struggled to tame the feeling. The smell of coconut oil hovered in the air as he passed a huddle of tourists converging upon a trinket shop, like bees around a honey jar, Louis thought.

He strolled a little further and entered the air conditioned interior of a shop and the prospect of buying a gift for his mother's impending birthday presented itself. The cool interior was a welcome reprieve. The shop itself was spacious; a white tiled floor gave an aura of freshness and cleanliness, enhanced by a scent that reminded him of a garden in summer. In the middle of the floor space sat a heavy desk. Its stone legs curved under a marble slab. Upon its surface, a laptop, a telephone and a fax machine sat.

A young woman with short dark hair sat at the desk. His eyes were pulled towards her full and rounded lips; it was then he noticed her almond-shaped eyes, deep, dark and mysterious. She wore a light blue top, cut low to reveal her cleavage, where his eyes rested for a second. From where he stood, he could see she had on faded jeans and he noted that her legs were athletically long. Pushed back, high on her forehead, sat expensive-looking sunglasses. Like a statue, her face exhibited a flawless complexion. To his surprise, he imagined feeling her skin with the tip of his fingers and wondered if, like marble, it would exaggerate smoothness, delicate to the touch.

He watched as the tips of her fingers bounced on and off the keys of the laptop in a flurry. The constant clicking stopped as she broke her gaze from the screen and inquired, 'Can I help you?' Her accent threw him. American, he wasn't expecting that.

'I'm just browsing, thanks.'

She smiled. 'Ok, but let me know if anything catches your eye.'

She returned her attention to the screen and, like tap dancing, the rhythmic click of the keys began again.

His eye travelled the shelves and one display, in particular, caught his interest; sea blue vases and ornamental dishes with ancient Greeks brandishing swords and spears, some riding naked on horseback, while others showed athletes throwing javelins, jostling wrestlers and statuesque boxers.

He contemplated leaving, when his eye snagged a corner of the shop that displayed a small gallery of replica frescoes, portraits of Christ and the Virgin Mary looking down upon him, creating the impression he had just entered a church. He looked at the images in their gold leaf frames and a warm sensation radiated from his abdomen swelling inside of him. Perfect, he thought. He smiled and, as he did so, this simple act had a profound personal significance for it was the first time in weeks that a contented expression had suffused his face. He allowed himself to bathe in its glow. Finally, he took an image of Mary holding Christ as a child. His mother would like this one, he thought.

'I'll take this one,' Louis said, approaching the desk.

The young woman stood up. 'I'll wrap it over there for you.'

She moved over to a counter and he handed the picture to her.

She smiled. 'One of my favourites, good choice. The colours are so vibrant.'

She wrapped the picture in brown paper and string.

'I didn't expect to hear an American accent in Olympia,' Louis said, reaching for his wallet.

'Not many people do.'

'How long have you stayed here?'

She continued to work on the wrapping as she spoke. 'It all started with my grandparents, who moved from Greece to the US after the Second World War. At that time, there were many others, just like them, in search of a better life. My father was just a baby when they left. Anyway, to get to the point, when he was older he started his own business specialising in Greek holidays. The business prospered and, as time passed, he wanted to return to his roots. After all, he'd spent his working life sending people to Greece and, I suppose the pull became too strong for him so he uprooted us all; four children, a wife, and my grandmother, who returned home.

'I was devastated; the only Greece I'd seen was the one in the travel brochures on the shelves of his shop. But hey, here I am. Oh and I got over my devastation. I feel more Greek than American now.' She laughed.

'Is this the family business?'

'Oh no, dad retired to the village he was born in. We still have relatives living there. This pretty little thing is all mine.'

She recited the same story several times a day, like a learnt verse. However, with the parting of the well-worn words, she did not tire in reciting her story this time. There was something about him, something different when he entered her shop. He had an unmistakable air of sadness about him, unlike most of her customers.

'It sounds like a movie,' Louis said.

He pulled some notes from his wallet, counted them and handed them to her. He noticed that her fingers were long.

'I've wire and hooks for hanging the picture,' she said, handing Louis the package.

'It's ok. It's actually a present for my mum, and it's her birthday soon. That reminds me, if I use the post, how long will it take to arrive in Scotland?'

She tilted her head. 'That depends. Remember, this is Greece,' she smiled, placing the picture into a plastic carrier bag.

'I'll post it today then.'

'That would be a good idea. The post office is next to the church,' she smiled. 'Are you with one of the tours visiting the Olympic site?'

'No I'm on my own but I intend to go there today in fact. I'm staying at...' he struggled to remember the name of the hotel, 'It's not too far, just around the corner.'

'The Neda?'

'Yes, that's it. I'm shocking with names.'

'Don't worry. As long as you know how to find your way bac,k that's the important thing. My name is Kyra.'

'I'm Louis. Your name sounds Greek.'

'It is, it means, *'like the sun.'*

'Ah, I see.'

'I know, it means I'm hot,' she said, a conspiratorial smile crossed her lips. 'I'm sorry I didn't mean to embarrass you. I'm American after all. I'm just kidding. I couldn't resist the pun.' Kyra chuckled.

Louis laughed. 'You didn't. I like humour and self-confidence. The world would be a poorer place without the two.'

'I couldn't agree more. I hope you enjoy your visit to the Olympic site. By the way, it can get really hot so put on lots of sun cream and drink plenty of water, most of the site is in the open.'

'Thanks for the advice.'

'Oh, I almost forgot, the post office closes early today, you'd better hurry. I hope your mum likes the picture.' Kyra smiled warmly.

'She will. It was nice talking to you.'

'Likewise, and remember to drink lots of water or you'll dehydrate.'

A Fortuitous Incident in the Temple of Zeus

As was their custom, Peter and Maria split their party into two groups. Maria took one to the Olympic site while Peter took the other to the museum, then vice versa before they would all meet up again in the coach park. She stood in front of her expectant group, like a teacher at the head of her class. Around them, white sandy paths cleaved zigzagged patterns, connecting each important aspect of Olympia. Through the shade of her sunglasses, Maria tilted her head towards the vast ocean of blue where a ship of the sky, a small wispy cloud, sailed.

She was reminded why she does this job, for it is in such places as Olympia, where the ancient world penetrates the present, that history becomes a living museum.

She ushered her party towards a large tree, which she chose as it offered a refuge and canopy of shade from the broiling sun. 'Ladies and Gentlemen,' she began, attracting their attention. 'As you know, Greece enjoys a hot climate but, even by her standards, the heat inside the Olympic site can become exceptional, as it is today. Therefore, I will conduct our tour from the vantage point of the shade of the various trees populated at intervals around the site whenever possible.' Her words were met with appreciative smiles and nodding heads.

She continued, 'The Olympic games were sacred festivals and held in honour of the God Zeus. The games were held at the time of the second or third summer solstice. The athletes would prepare for the games at Elis, a town nearby, for thirty days. A two-day procession occurred before the start of the games. The athletes would compete naked, covered in oil, white dust and powder.'

This revelation stirred the party into small groups of animated conversations. Maria grasped their attention once again with the disclosure that the games were exclusively male-dominated affairs.

'In those days, before any notion of feminism was conceived, this public showing and parading of masculinity and sexism were absolute, apart from one woman, the priestess of Demetre. Being the only woman amongst forty thousand males would have had its advantages.' Maria smirked.

She introduced the group to the athlete's gymnasium, where two rows of vertical pillars stood in the classical Greek style. Here, she told them, the athletes trained, limbered up and used weights. The colonnade would have supported a roof, shielding the athletes from the fierce sun. After training, the athletes would go to the bathhouse where oil and sweat were scraped from their bodies, before they relaxed in the hot and cold baths.

She took a drink of water, and encouraged the others to do likewise as they moved across the plain of Olympia.

Louis posted his mother's present, along with a birthday card he bought at the post office just as it was about to close for the day. He had taken Kyra's advice, but had drained his bottle empty by the time he came across a museum, opposite the main site.

To reach the museum, Louis walked along a tree-lined avenue, appreciating the shade it offered. In the entrance hall, he squeezed through a crowd clustered around several postcards and bookstalls and a small scaled-down model of the original Olympic site.

'The resonating opulence and grandeur of the prolific buildings are amplified by the sheer scale and magnitude of the Olympic site, itself a monument of intelligence, achievement and craftsmanship,' said a man in a Panama hat.

The educated delivery of the voice tugged at Louis to linger longer. He paced the periphery of the group, trying to catch the commentary, until he came across a large hall. He wandered in and found that time was bridged in one single moment. The past transformed into a visual banquet that could satisfy any hungry eye.

He discovered the relics of a lost civilisation staring at him through marble eyes, demanding his attention. He digested their detail and felt in awe at their animated presence. Louis found the statues to emanate a lifelike quality, as alive as the craftsman whose hand first moulded and styled the marble with precision. He imagined the sculptor's eyes roaming the lines, scanning the curves of his creation, just as Louis had eagerly done. He thought, in that instant, they shared a sense of mutual satisfaction and pleasure. The sculptor created a seed of life that gave birth to the emotions that erupted within Louis. His senses tingled with wonderment he touched the passion that surely burned within the men who had created and then frozen a moment in time. Was this not the purpose of art, he thought, to make the recipient feel alive and vibrant?

He ambled in the foyer, scanning postcards and bookstalls, before leaving and finding the shade of a roofed courtyard. A large party of vociferous Italian schoolchildren filed past him, supervised by several adults, one engaged in a concentrated head count. He abandoned his shelter from the heat and, walking through an avenue of tall trees, he wondered if the statues would grasp the children's fledgling imagination.

Once in the Olympic site proper, he pottered around the ruins. Eventually, he negotiated a construction of flimsy wooden steps that led to the floor of the Temple of Zeus. He had left his sunglasses in the hotel and cursed this oversight, as the white glare from the fierce sun reflected like a shield underfoot.

He shaded his eyes, as they swept across massive fluted columns that lay on the dusted white earth like giant dominoes that had once been pushed over by a giant hand. Each column consisted of ten symmetrical blocks of stone, three feet tall and six foot in diameter. Louis noticed a small aperture in the centre of each block and he imagined that once standing vertically, a column would stand thirty feet tall. In appearance, the Temple of Zeus would have mirrored the Parthenon, the Temple of Athene and even the Acropolis in Athens itself.

Louis levitated inside; his nerve ends tingled, motoring into overdrive, as he realised that he stood on the spot that was the epicentre of a religion practised thousands of years before the conception of Christianity. He imagined what the columns must have seen and witnessed and, if they could talk, how they would unfold the centuries with their revelations. He could feel history upon his skin and he shivered as a tingling ran down the centre of his back.

Suddenly something snagged his eye; a pebble lay upon the film of white dusted sand, not unlike the type he collected from beaches as a boy.

Louis crouched down and picked it up. The pebble was oval and smooth. He ran his fingers over it and, to his satisfaction, it felt like glass. Thin lines ran along its surface as if drawn by a pencil. He studied the lines and exuded an appreciation that stretched back to his childhood.

Louis placed the pebble in his trouser pocket and, as if returning from a trance, he was aware of the pressing crowds that had descended upon the temple and an image of Edinburgh in rush hour flashed through him. He looked up at the canopy of unblemished blue sky and the hint of a perceptible smile curled his lips.

He stood out like a teetotaller at a beer festival, a lone individual amongst the couples, families and organised tour groups.

Maria observed him walking idly amongst a section of pillars, hands dug deep into his pockets and then he crouched and picked up something, a stone maybe, she couldn't see. He was looking at it closely, intently even. It must have appealed to him, she thought, as he placed it in his pocket.

'This is the temple of Zeus then?' A small rounded man asked pedantically.

'Yes, it is,' she snapped, and then wished she could remove the irritation in her voice.

She gazed once more, with intent, but it was as if he had melted into the stone. He seemed lost amongst a swarm of people and to her surprise, a pang of regret washed over her as expectancy dissolved.

She turned to her group, informing them to take extra care when climbing the wooden steps. 'Zeus was the chief God of the ancient Greeks and ruler of the heavens. His statue by Phidias is said to be one of the Seven Wonders of the World.'

He was about to leave the environs of the Temple, when a voice, carried on the sultry air, floated over the ancient rock and stone before sweeping over him, like an incoming tide. He spun round and again, to his frustration, he had to shield his eyes.
   The voice leaked into him like liquid.
   'Upon the great columns, an entablature would sit and then, horizontally, we would find an architrave upon which would be the frieze. It was here that the temple was ornamented with statues, depicting Gods, horses, and soldiers. A cornice would sit on the uppermost division of the entablature. Unfortunately, the crowning entablature hasn't survived. The statues, on the other hand, have and today they are to be found in an excellent condition, which we'll see later once we visit the museum.'
   He scanned the area, intent on finding a face to match to the voice. Already an image was forming, just as when one speaks on the telephone to a total stranger; the timbre of the voice announces an age, and the features of a face evolve. An impulse compelled him to advance further into the crowd, now strewed across the temple floor. A warm delicious feeling radiated through his stomach. His eyes strained as they peeled off people, a young couple with a camcorder, a man consulting a guidebook and a group of elderly people shading from the sun under assortments of hats. A collage of colour fluttered in the heat haze. He could feel a tug of irritation and a sense of panic soak into him.
   Like peeling bells, the voice lifted above bobbing heads. He turned to the right; she was slightly obscured by a semi-circled huddle. She spoke slowly and warmth levitated from her delivery, almost glowing, Louis considered. And then, like a lamp being turned on in a darkened room, she appeared.
   A wash of light illuminated the profile of her face, as he scanned her features as if studying a portrait for the first

time. He noted that the texture of her skin was soft and smooth. He watched how her mouth moved when she spoke, following the curve of her lips and, like a fly in a web, his eyes were snagged there.

    She gestured with her hand and he noticed that her elaborate movement carried a presence of elegance within its simple deliverance. He observed her neck and the curve of her bare shoulders that fell upon arms where olive skin covered smooth muscle. He traced the pronounced bones of her clavicle and followed the fabric of her dress. Her frame was small, yet he knew she emanated an influential aura amongst her party. Louis abandoned caution and ventured closer, impelled, as if in a dream. He detected an ambience of contentment in the way she stood.

    The air was flushed with heat, his eyes squinted, as a debilitating sense of wanting to be sick tugged at his throat and then the feeling became alarmingly overwhelming. He felt dizzy, his head light. He made a concentrated effort to look at the ground, his eyes blurred and the white sand of the earth began to move of its own accord. A slurred thought fought its way through his brain. He needed to sit down, and then like a felled tree, the ground was moving towards him.

He appeared in the corner of her eye and it seemed he had walked from the very stones she was describing. Maria was aware she felt a flutter of relief and that his reappearance pleased her. Then, quite unexpectedly she was astonished to hear instantaneous shouts, accompanied by a clamour. It felt as if her heart had jumped from her chest. She did not see him thud against the ground for, as he fell, her view was obscured by two large sisters.

    She ran towards him, her first aid training kicking in, as she felt his wrist for a pulse. A curious crowd had gathered, and one of the sisters was pushing a path towards Maria.

    Panting heavily she gasped, 'Is he alright, dear? Can you feel a pulse? I was a nurse before I retired, a sister actually, so I'm more than happy to assist you if required. Should we put him in the recovery position?'

He lay still as if asleep. She noted his hair was dark, almost blue. His skin, no longer the pallor of wet cement now had a natural copper glow. She was drawn to his eyes, they remained stubbornly closed.

He dived into a vast blue lake and began to swim under the surface. Something smooth brushed his skin, long hair flowed down a slender and naked back; a woman swam next to him. Her skin exuding a creamy white complexion, she smiled as she turned to face him and, in an indistinct murmur, she said something. In a rush of blinding light, he broke the surface.

His eyes blinked several times before fully opening and she was struck by how deep and impenetrable they seemed. On closer examination, she noted subtle silver flecks speckled them.

Louis' head spun and felt like something had exploded inside it. He made an attempt to focus on a nearby pillar but it seemed to sway as if caught by a great wind. He took deep gulps of air to quench the tidal wave of nausea that broke over him, sending a hot flush creeping over his skin. With the back of his hand, he wiped beads of perspiration that had dripped onto his eyebrows.

Louis felt a palpable embarrassment at his predicament, which intensified when he became aware of a woman leaning over him.

'Are you all right?' Maria asked soothingly.

'I think so.' He rubbed his head where a lump began to emerge, like a newborn island rising from the sea.

He could smell her perfume and, despite his tender disposition, he fought a compulsion to draw closer to her. With a slender hand, she brushed strands of hair from her face and offered him water.

'Take a drink, it's unopened... I've another bottle, anyway.'

Although overwhelmed by his unfortunate disposition, he noted her hair fell onto each side of her face, like fine silk sheets emanating a polished glaze. The sun's warmth splayed across his face and he became aware of others pressing down, peering at him curiously. She offered him the water, and he attempted to stand and test his balance. He sat on a small section of wall.

'Thanks, I feel better now and a little embarrassed. I should've had something to eat this morning.'

'Never go out on an empty stomach, that's what I always say. It's served me well. I've never felt sick before lunch,' offered a small man, to no one in particular. He was the same man who Maria had snapped at earlier. He was struggling with the heat and wiped the back of his neck with a discoloured handkerchief. He continued to irritate Maria.

A slight breeze lifted, and it felt as if someone, maybe even the ancient Gods themselves, had breathed across Louis' skin. He drank the water and was grateful for it, wishing now that he had bought another bottle.

'You should really get yourself checked by a doctor. There'll be one in the town. Until then, you're welcome to join our tour,' Maria offered. 'I'm sure no one will object.'

A consensus of approval rose from her party.

'Good idea,' said the perspiring man.

'We'll look after you, my dear,' said one of the large sisters.

'You're best to tag along with us just in case you take another funny turn,' said the other sister.

The smooth oval of Maria's face broke into a smile. The replenishing water seemed to revive Louis' senses, as he thanked her for the invitation and hoped he had preserved his dignity. His head still floated, leaving a light stubborn sensation. However, the imminent release of his stomach's contents no longer threatened to spill over onto the ancient dust. He felt a lot better.

He made an effort to scoop himself from the wall and onto his feet.

'You can walk with us. I'm Dorothy and this is my sister Lucinda.'

Lucinda smiled. 'Pleased to meet you...'

'Louis.'

'Pleased to meet you, Louis, you are in good hands.'

'Well, that's a comfort to know,' Louis said, glancing at Maria.

'I'll leave you in their safe hands... Louis.' Maria smiled, pleased to know his name.

'She is our guide,' Dorothy whispered. 'Maria is a lovely girl, very knowledgeable on Greek culture and history.'

'Of course, she is. It's her job to know such things,' Lucinda retorted incredulously.

'Now Lucinda, let's not give this fine young man a bad impression of ourselves.'

'Oh, you're right dear. Come on Louis, we don't want to be left behind now, do we?'

Dorothy laughed a high-pitched cackle. 'That would be nice. Imagine two old ladies alone in an exotic country with a nice looking young man. Don't worry Louis; we'll be gentle with you.' They both laughed this time and Dorothy gestured for him to follow them.

The Greek Zola Bud

Within the hour that followed, Louis learnt that the sound of her voice painted pictures within his mind. It conjured from the dust alluring images, history transported to the present day, where he could almost touch, smell and hear its presence.

Louis stood and gazed at the site where the Olympic flame is born, given life every four years by the heat of the sun onto glass. Maria informed the group it was from here that the flame begins its traditional journey in a tribute to the original forefathers of the original Games that comprised of foot races, chariot races, boxing, wrestling, pankration–a combination of boxing and wrestling, long jump, discus and javelin, all contested by men and boys. The winners of these events, were given olive branches cut from the sacred grove of Zeus by a boy whose parents had to be still alive. The winning athletes were given large pensions. They became heroes in their villages, towns, and cities and had statues erected in their honour to celebrate their achievement and, by their very nature, bestowing on the athletes, immortality.

They walked a dusty track that led to the stadium entrance. It was here, on either side of this path that the athletes' statues stood. On one side, the statues of the winners of the Games were erected and to Louis' surprise, the stone plinths and bases had survived the ravages of time. The athlete's name and that of their town or village were imprinted for eternity on stone. Louis noticed that, although the statues no longer stood in victory, he saw the imprint of their feet.

Maria explained that, on the opposite side, another column of statues lined the entrance to the stadium. However, unlike their counterparts, who faced them in jubilation, these statues were the stone images of those athletes exposed as cheats. Their humiliation, a doubled-edged sword for not only had they to suffer this public spectacle of shame, the name of the town or village from which they came was also carved into the stone. Then finally, to the echoes of murmured approval from the group, the last indignant act bestowed upon the cheat was that he had to pay for the statue to get made.

The stadium itself lay just beyond this symbol of human achievement and failing. To gain access, they walked under the remains of an archway that spanned the entrance between two intact walls that led into the stadium proper. Once through the entrance, Louis stood on the sandy white earth of the original track. His first impression was tinged with wonderment, yet flavoured by a dash of disappointment. He had envisaged a stone construction but, as Maria explained, the stadium was built on banked areas; the spectators would have been seated on the sloping side. It was constructed with one curved end, long enough to accommodate the running track where the contestants ran up and down and not around the track. The track would be found in the middle, where boxing, wrestling and field events took place.

'Can you imagine,' Dorothy speculated. 'Forty thousand people attended these events. It must have been one of the wonders of the world for its time.'

Maria drew their attention to a line of stone sills thought to have been starting blocks. They spanned the full width of the track, each sill about four feet.

'It's become the custom to have a race along the track, for those who are able of course.'

A small band eagerly stood in line, the temptation to stand at the archaic starting blocks, and then follow in the footsteps of the world's first athletes, was an irresistible invitation.

Dorothy and Lucinda opted to count down the race and declined to partake. 'It would not do to fall and bare one's mortification for the world to see,' Lucinda sighed, 'and besides, we are no spring chickens. In my younger years... well, that would have been a different matter.'

Maria stood next to Louis; she was a head shorter. He felt her arm softly brush his skin.

'Are you sure you're feeling ok to run?' she asked.

'I feel fine now thanks.' He raised his eyebrows. 'You

wouldn't be trying to deplete the competition I hope?'

'What competition?' She smiled.

'On your marks... get set... Go,' Dorothy yelled in anticipation.

They ran in a straight line, before the leaders staked their claim leaving the others behind. Some already struggling, slowed to a walk but shouted encouragement to the remaining runners... Maria, Louis, and a young couple recently married and on honeymoon.

Maria wiped strands of hair from her face as she edged into the lead. Her dress flapped around her knees, like clothes on a washing line, and it was then that Louis noticed she was running barefooted.

The warm air brushed his ears, he tried to swing his arms faster and with more effort, yet the more deliberate his action, the distance between himself and Maria continued to open up. From the corner of his eye, an image appeared. The newly wed had left his wife trailing behind; he was now at Louis' side, both men breathing heavily, willing air into their protesting lungs.

Then, as suddenly as it had started the race was won, Maria throwing her arms into the air in victory, to the vociferous remarks of encouragement and clapping. She turned to face the others, hands on hips, head tilted to one side as if to say..., *"and what competition was that then?"*

Louis bent forward, resting his hands on his knees. 'You run fast Maria... very fast,' he spluttered in between breaths.

'I know... I was my college champion for the one hundred metres. I've not lost a race yet,' she said, sliding past him. 'And you were first to come last,' she smirked, turning back to him, 'by coming second.'

'You lost your shoes,' he panted.

She looked over her shoulder at him and smiled. 'I run quicker without them... oh, but of course, you noticed that.'

Louis straightened himself and flapped his t-shirt to fan air around his upper body. He smiled to himself. 'The Greek Zola Bud.'

Maria hung back and waited for Louis to catch her up and the thought occurred to her she was flirting with him, this man she had only just met, yet she couldn't deny the definite and palpable appeal of it.

'We're going to the museum now. You're welcome to join us,' Maria suggested.

'I went earlier this morning,' Louis said, before regretting his words.

They walked towards the others.

'Did you enjoy the museum? There are so many beautiful pieces there,' she added, attempting to hide her disappointment.

He wanted to say, 'but none as beautiful as you,' but held back. 'I was impressed by the statues. Does your tour finish once you've visited the museum?'

'We have lunch in the village. We use the same taverna each time, it's part of the tour, and then we leave at three o'clock to go back to Killini.'

'Killini, where's that?'

'It's about an hour's drive by coach; we then get a ferry back to Zakynthos.'

'Oh, so you don't stay in Olympia?'

'Oh no, I live in Zakynthos, we're here on a day trip. I work for a tour company based on the island.'

'I see. I just assumed you lived locally.' His disappointment crushed him.

Maria looked at him and smiled. 'No, I prefer to wake up to the sight of the sea in the morning.'

Louis' thoughts reclined back to the sunrises.

'Before I came to Greece, I never really appreciated the sunrise or sunset. I'd be aware of the sky changing colour but it's different here, the light has a certain quality I hadn't noticed back home. The most striking ones are over the sea.'

'My father use to say that the best sunsets could only be found on Zakynthos. I think he was slightly biased. As a girl we'd watch the sunset together. He described the colours to me as if we were in a gallery looking at a painting and he'd use words like intense and vibrant. He always said that, apart from his family, the sunsets were perfect creations on God's earth.'

Louis smiled and caught her eye. She looked away towards the tourists filing into the stadium.

'Are the sunsets on Cephalonia the same as the ones on Zakynthos?'

The question hung in the air like a plume of smoke.

'Why do you ask?' she replied, puzzled.

'It's where I was going next. There's no point in going if the sky can't produce an inspiring sunset. I'm following the sunsets, you see.' He grinned.

'Then Zakynthos would suit you fine.' She smiled. Maria's eyes drank him in as she asked, 'So you're not on holiday?'

'No... I've been travelling through the mainland for a while, just visiting places that appealed to me so I suppose I'm not your typical tourist. I'm booked into a hotel in the town for a week.' A concentrated look crossed his face. 'Do you visit again, with a tour, I mean?'

'I'm back next Saturday, filling in for someone who is sick. Why?'

'Let me buy you lunch.' He surprised himself with his opportunism.

'I don't think so,' Maria said abruptly, rebuking him.

Louis' heart sank; he had moved too quickly. He had offended her. Louis frowned and fought to conceal his frustration. 'That's ok, I understand,' he fumbled.

She raised an eyebrow. 'I'll make a deal with you. If you let me pay for my half, I'll let you pay for your half,' she said mockingly, enjoying the moment.

A slow, perceptible smile spread across Maria's face and an expectant expression danced in her eyes. Louis scratched his forehead and returned her smile. She has been playing with me, he contemplated; considerable warmth emanated from his abdomen.

The Crossing

A Decision is Made

They agreed to meet the following Saturday in a taverna Maria recommended. The next few days passed slowly and, although Louis had planned to stay for a week, the thought of meeting Maria again was the only reason that kept him from leaving Olympia.

Louis spent his days by the hotel pool bar under the shade of a large canopy. He took long walks in the early evening as the day's heat subsided. Louis chose a different restaurant to eat in each night. On one of these nights, he met Kyra who was out with a group of friends. She invited him to join them and so he did, welcoming the distraction.

Eventually, Saturday arrived, and he went to the taverna early, eager to meet her again. He chose a table that offered an unobstructed view of the street which had descended into a muted murmur, depleted of shoppers who, having dabbled with the trinket and jewellery shops, were now, with the onset of lunch, benefiting the livelihoods of the taverna and restaurant owners. He ordered a coffee as the vines weaved above his head, like coiling snakes, shading him from the inexorable sun that bathed the street in its white glare.

A black cat with white socked feet arched its back and purred contentedly, as it rubbed against Louis' leg in anticipation of dropped scraps of food.

'Hello White Socks,' Louis said and clapped the cat's back, which arched even further.

Louis had not felt such contentment since the last weekend he shared with Emma. He remembered they had gone out for a meal to Bar Napoli, their favourite Italian restaurant and, in retrospect, when he thinks of that night, Emma seemed preoccupied. Louis asked her if she was feeling all right and she replied that she was fine, just a little tired, before taking a fortified sip of her drink. Her veil of secrecy remained drawn that evening, and he brushed it aside, as she made a concerted effort to indulge in conversation and enjoy the experience of their meal. The devastation that would soon be unleashed remained caged, biding its time to unleash its strike.

Sipping his coffee, the irony of the situation tugged at him. It had been Emma's affair that inevitably led him to be sitting in the shade under a Greek sky, anticipating with apprehension his meeting with a woman he had met only a week ago.

He watched White Socks sniff the air enquiringly, following an invisible trail of cooked food, as its tail snaked around Louis' leg. He found the sensation soothing, and he reached down to stroke the bony back again.

Louis sat back up and there she was, walking towards him. Maria had tied her hair back from her face; she wore sunglasses and held the strap of a small bag that hung from her shoulder. Something jumped inside his stomach, and as she drew closer, it began to do somersaults. He shifted in his chair and rose to greet her. White Socks scurried away, in search of another set of legs and lunch. Until that point, Louis wasn't even sure if he would ever see her again. He was entering new territory, like an explorer yet, unlike an explorer, he lacked the experience. He thought he would never find himself in the situation of meeting someone again. In fact, he had never even contemplated such a reality.

Should he kiss her cheek in greeting or be more formal and shake her hand?

'Just be you,' he told himself. Small beads of perspiration escaped the pores of his forehead, a combination of the furnace heat and his forthcoming encounter. A feeling of guilt walked over him, should he be doing this? Doubt entered him like a spear.

Emma would want this, Louis scrutinised. He permitted himself to bathe in her reaction. She would not have wanted him to remain alone, without female companionship. Emma had always remonstrated, usually in wine-soaked nights, that if anything ever happened to her, she would want him to be happy and experience love with another.

'Have you ordered yet?' Maria asked, as she reached the

chair.

'Not yet, I've just had a coffee.' Louis leant towards her and, for a moment, he hoped his breath did not smell of stale coffe,e but Maria sat down and placed her sunglasses high on her forehead.

'You should try the chicken, it's lovely.'

Her voice entered him, melting his self-reproach, and he felt vindicated; it moved within him, like liquid. She has amazing eyes, he thought. Maria placed her bag on the ground.

He hesitated, as a nervous current tingled within him. She seems so confident, he thought.

'Oh, and the wine,' she added. 'We should try that too. Although not too much, especially in this heat.'

Maria looked at Louis and smiled. I hope he doesn't think I do this all the time, she thought. She had hoped to project an air of confidence about her but, within the moment of meeting him, she regretted that decision, denting her assertiveness with the image it conjured.

She looked down at the table and then met his eyes again, still smiling and it felt to Louis as if he had been wrapped in that smile, like a warm coat.

'I wasn't sure if you would come.'

'I nearly didn't. The coach broke down on our way here but luckily one of our passengers is a mechanic. It was nothing serious just a blocked filter.'

'That was lucky. How has your day been?'

'Oh, it's been fine. It's very hot today, but no one has fainted... so far.' She smiled.

'That was embarrassing. I've been drinking lots of water since then.'

'Good. Shall we order?'

A waiter approached them. Maria ordered their lunch in Greek. Louis noticed patches of sweat stained the waiter's white shirt and Louis wondered if he longed to be free of the clinging material. He watched Maria's polished skin, the dress straps that followed the curve of her shoulder and to his surprise, for an unguarded second he imagined kissing her there. This was the first time he'd heard her speak in her own language. The pitch, and tone of her voice was different, the intonation slightly exaggerated, her words delivered in a flowing rhythm, animated with exotic tones and colourful textures that danced before him, as if he were in a trance.

They ate lunch, gradually relaxing into each other's company. Half an hour passed, soaked in conversation. It surprised Louis how freely he could talk to her; his inhibitions and natural defences melted, like thawing snow.

Under the blanket of the hanging vines, White Socks scanned the ground and around table legs for morsels of fallen food, flirting with each customer, rubbing itself against legs, purring exorbitantly and standing on hind legs to be met by a piece of chicken offered by a hesitant hand.

Maria enquired about the circumstances that led Louis to Greece. She seemed curious, what events had engineered such a decision? He found it easy to divulge his story. It was like being in the confessional booth but, instead of the faceless voice exuding penance, Maria's perceptible appearance of empathy swelled his willingness to immerse himself in the telling of his raw and recent past.

He told Maria of his unexpected find, Emma with Paul, the initial storm that broke and the aftermath. Living alone in the flat as Emma moved out to stay with Paul. Emma's disclosure that she was pregnant, his chance meeting with the traveller whose lifestyle formed the idea of travelling to Greece. Louis told her of Demetrius, Meredith, Georgios, the taverna by the sea, the weeks of travel through villages and towns until, eventually, arriving in Olympia. He almost fell short of telling Maria about Emma's death, like someone who hesitates before a jump, but he continued illustrating his need. Louis referred to a map of the world that draped a wall in the foyer of his hotel. That morning he stood and studied it for the first time to the background of two male voices in conversation, the more prominent of the two being American; the other, in his broken but clear English was Greek. The American was furthering his companion's command of the English language and, by his competent display, he had already grasped it quite adequately. The subject under discussion was the planets of the solar system. As their voices stole the silence, Louis studied his present position on the earth's surface. Whilst the two men marvelled at the infinite structure and nature of the skies, Louis told Maria how he noticed the vast expanse that lay before him and Edinburgh, the tens of millions of people who filled and lived their lives in that landscape and how the sudden realization crept upon him that Emma no longer belonged to that space. He explained to her that since his arrival in Greece it was the first time he had felt homesick, but that there was nothing at home to draw him to return. He had his family, his close friends, but the space that Emma filled was an indescribable void and he had nothing in Edinburgh to fill it. As he spoke, he realized, that, by chance, he had stumbled upon someone who could finally complete his healing. He felt the pit of his stomach stir. He wanted to know how it would feel to touch her skin, to brush his fingers through her hair and feel her breath upon him. She asked if he still loved Emma. Her question unsettled him; he had not expected her line of enquiry. An awkward silence filled the space between them.

He shifted uncomfortably and spoke quietly. 'She devastated me, tore my world apart... It's like losing an arm, you'd still miss it and feel a need for it because it was a vital part of you, but the need changes as you eventually heal and reclaim your life back... I'm learning to pick up the pieces.'

He drained the last of the wine from his glass. He had never spoken like this to anyone but he felt good and a weight that had borne down on him was lifting, gradually.

'I suppose I've changed or have I just accommodated a new way of living?' Louis shrugged, unable to answer his own question. He placed his glass on the table and looked at her.

She smiled, recalling when she first looked into his eyes as he lay on the sand of Olympia and like a swimming pool she wanted to dive into them.

'That must have been difficult for you; I can't imagine how that must feel.' Maria thought about the decision she had still to make, one that could inevitably change her life; at least she had that choice to make.

Louis hesitated. 'I'm sorry. It's a wonder you're still here. If I were you, I'd have run a mile by now.'

'Nonsense,' Maria dismissed him. 'Sometimes it's good just to listen. I know that's hard for us women, we do like to talk, but you can learn a lot more about someone by just listening to their story.'

'I'd like to hear your story,'

'Where will I begin,' Maria said, rhetorically. She looked at her watch. 'We'll be leaving for Kyllini soon.' She paused, as if a thought had just entered her head. 'What are you going to do now?'

He shrugged. 'I've already booked out of the hotel. I thought about going to Cephalonia.'

'We would virtually be neighbours.'

'What do you mean?'

'On a clear day, you can see Cephalonia from Zakynthos.'

'I could pop over, we could have lunch again and you can tell me your story then.' They both laughed.

'How have the sunsets been?' Louis asked.

'They're getting better by the day.'

'I'd like to see them. Seriously, I would. There's no reason why I can't visit Zakynthos.'

She placed her wine glass delicately on the table. 'Are you sure about going to Zakynthos?'

He shrugged. 'I'd planned to start visiting the islands, eventually. I've just finished reading a book about Cephalonia and it seemed like a good one to start with.'

'Then why don't you come with us? There are a few empty seats on the coach. I'm sure the others won't mind.'

'Are you sure? Are you allowed to do that?'

'I don't know. I haven't asked anyone before but it makes sense. You'll have to buy a ticket for the ferry once we get to Kyllini.'

Louis could not conceal his elation. He grinned widely. 'You're certain about this? I wouldn't want to get you into trouble.'

'I won't tell if you don't.'

'I'd better get my things then.'

'That's settled.' She looked at her watch. 'We leave in half an hour.'

The Gambler and his Greek Tragedy

The coach roared into life, the engine offering its heat to the sultry air. Louis was surprised to see Dorothy and Lucinda again. The two sisters were ecstatic in discovering Louis would accompany them to Zakynthos, fussing around him with incredulous delight. Lucinda explained that they had enjoyed the tour so much, they booked again for the following week. Dorothy insisted that he sit in the empty seat across the aisle from them.

Peter, however, viewed Louis with suspicion, born out of a protective instinct for Maria, almost fatherly in its nature; yet, he relented to the unusual request and reservedly agreed to it. He did not trust the man's motives, he told her stubbornly.

Maria had explained to Louis that they could not sit next to each other as it was against company policy. She took her seat at the front of the coach beside Peter. Louis wondered if his presence had caused a rift between them. He felt nervous. He had watched them talk and Peter's body language eluded stiffness; he seemed agitated, disappointed even, and at odds with his usual graceful manners. Maria's thrusting hand gestures charged the air. Louis felt an uncomfortable guilt; after all, he was the source of this disharmony between them.

He sank into his seat, inducing a feeling of wanting to sleep as it took his weight. Dorothy leant over and offered him a mint, which he kindly refused. As the coach progressed, and the last buildings of Olympia gave way to countryside, Louis tried to concentrate on the passing villages, olive groves and farmhouses that dotted the landscape. It reminded him of a holiday programme he had watched on television.

It was Peter's habit to entertain his passengers with stories while they journeyed to Kyllini and, by now, he was in full flow painting, with his customary detailed and coloured vocabulary, pictures of myth and legend, using landmarks of passing towns and the landscape as his canvas.

To Louis' relief, the sisters had succumbed to sleep. Dorothy slept with her mouth open; her top denture slid slightly out of its fitting and was resting on her lower lip giving the impression she had a mouth full of prodigious teeth.

Louis craned his head, but was unable to see Maria; he wondered what she might be thinking, what did she think of him? She had shown an interest in the events that led him to Greece, and he had obliged, by talking quite openly. She made him feel like an opened book, while she listened intently. It now occurred to him he had been like a spinning top; once he had started he could not finish until it felt like he had run out of words.

He immersed himself in images of her. A week ago, her face was unfamiliar to him but today it seemed as if he had known the features and symmetrical curvatures of her face all of his life; like a negative it was imprinted on his mind. When he floated to the surface, he would catch sections of Peter's narrative-a bell tower that punctured the skyline, exploits of a young sex-starved Greek God who met with a premature end, as he endeavoured to enjoy the charms of a young female God. Peter pointed out of the window, where they viewed skeletal trees sprinkled hauntingly in a black film of ash. Large reefs straddled the road, skirting part of their route and a tale was weaved, around why they grew to be so tall. Louis lost the thread of the story as the hypnotic tone of Peter's voice, the constant rhythm, and vibration of the coach intoxicated him like a potent drug and he slid and submerged into sleep and Peter's voice trailed off, like mist.

Maria was furious with Peter; he had called into question her judgement of character. How dare he, she thought accusingly. 'You have just met him, you do not know him.' Peter had said. The first part was true, but she felt as if she knew him. 'I know he has loved and lost and suffered. I know where he comes from, what has consumed the last few months of his life... God, I know him better than the people who have paid to come on this trip.' She warned in a raised voice.

Peter accepted her argument gracefully, knowing it

would be futile to persist with a disapproving line of enquiry; he placed his Panama on his head. 'Then who am I to judge, my dear. It seems that you have sorted it out in your head already.' Maria looked at him sternly. 'I would say,' Peter continued, 'He is a very lucky young man,' and with that parting shot, he headed for the coach, leaving her to stew.

Maria massaged her temple, the beginnings of a headache tugged at her, like a child seeking attention. *Maybe Peter was right,* she reflected, as her irritation with him subsided. *Peter always has my interests at heart, was it foolish to invite this man on the coach?* It was the first impulsive thing she had done in a long time. *What harm could it do… I hope the sisters are not too over powering… poor Louis.* She concluded.

Out of the window, she saw a large tomato processing plant. During the picking season, Peter encouraged everyone to count the number of trucks systematically lined up outside the processing plant. She remembered that the last count came to over one hundred. A lot of tomatoes, she thought.

Nearing Kyllini Maria saw, as she always did, the fortified walls of a castle that imposed itself on the landscape. She rubbed her eyes, reached into her bag and produced a pocket mirror. She looked at her face staring back at her as if it belonged to someone else. There was something about him, she reminded herself; she felt it the very first time she laid eyes on him. It was a sensation unlike any other. It made her happy, a warm tingling feeling spread and fanned out from her stomach. She remembered the way the sun reflected off his hair, the rising and falling of his Adam's apple as he drank his wine at lunch, the pronounced curve of his chin, chiselled and strong, like a statue; those eyes with their intent look. She had listened to him speak, finding his Scottish accent pleasant and distinctive and it sounded as if he was singing.

And she imagined his life as if watching a movie: images appeared, his words influencing the story line and he was the main character, its focus and he held her attention like all good movies do. She observed how he lowered his eyes when he mentioned Emma's name, circling the rim of his wine glass with his middle finger, subdued by the memory.

The dull ache in her head subsided, which was just as well, as she had nothing to take to ease the pain, although she now considered, she was almost sure that one of the sisters would have come to her aid and produced some form of medication. She would soon be comforted by the sight of the sea. She lowered her sunglasses over her eyes and smoothed the light fabric of her dress, as the coach snaked its way through narrow streets and finally rested to a stop.

An oil grey sea laps at dark rocks; white foam runs through black clumps of seaweed. A boy clumsily throws a fishing line into the water. Louis notices a man and his dog, a Labrador, walk over the white sand of a beach. He catches sight of a jogger and then a woman sitting on a rock speaking into a mobile phone, a green bag at her feet. Children explore a crop of rocks that harbour a small pool that the incoming tide will later claim. A tug slices through the water and a sailing boat with a white mast ominously disappears behind the green headland, as if it has been gradually rubbed out. Fast moving clouds skirt a wooden hill; a white plane climbs into the sky, emitting a sound like distant thunder. The setting sun illuminates the rustic red Forth Rail Bridge as a rumbling train, like a stick insect, crosses the dark and undulating waters of the River Forth. A couple shares a cigarette; above them, seagulls catch rides on pockets of air and the skyline of Edinburgh becomes sucked into a haunting and trailing mist.

He opened his eyes to a flurry of activity, the coach now motionless amongst a perpetual stream of traffic and noise. He heard Peter's voice announcing that it was customary to place a generous tip into his hat, which would then be presented to their driver. Each passenger was to depart the coach with an appreciative 'efcharisto.' Louis was alarmed to find that Maria had already left the coach, but then the rock in his chest dissolved as he overheard someone say she had to change the boarding passes as Peter had unwittingly issued the wrong ones.

He stepped onto the quayside and into a throng of humanity, diesel fumes and heat, pressing against him. He made his way to the ticket booth at a steady pace and stood in a well-ordered queue that seemed at odds with the busy crowd around him; he felt both exhilarated and exasperated. Eventually, he bought a ticket; his eyes stung from the scanning of so many faces. He must have passed Maria at some point. He imagined her handing out boarding tickets. In his efforts to secure a passage on the ferry, he had lost his bearings. He studied the sea of bobbing heads and the fleet of coaches in the foreground. They all looked similar and it was impossible to discern one from the other.

Ten minutes had elapsed since he left the coach and he was increasingly aware of vehicles and people filing onto the ferry, like a focused army of hyperactive ants. Louis felt shipwrecked in an ocean of unfamiliar faces. His mind felt exhausted, a hot surge of panic set in. Then to his relief, he snagged a straw-coloured hat hovering above the crowds.

He made his way to the upper deck with its rows of wooden benches and as he sat down the smell of fresh paint and ammonia surrounded him. The sparsely populated beach of that morning was now a pulsating and shimmering tapestry of colour and flesh. Around him, parents monitored exuberant children who had just discovered a new playground, a source of exploration and adventure. Couples entwined in affectionate embraces. A group of young men flexed their masculinity in a drunken performance, as an old man and his unsteady wife welcomed the solace of a comfortable seat, as they tended to ache muscles. A backpacker studied a map with an intensive urgency that seemed to betray the laid back, almost vertical casual manner with which his partner rearranged with meticulous tidiness the contents of their rucksacks.

Louis noticed a fatigue that once again seeped through his body; even the potent sun could not lift this feeling of heaviness and alleviate the lethargic ache that lingered in him. He had entertained the thought of attempting to walk around the ferry in search of Maria, when he heard her now familiar voice.

'There you are. I was beginning to think you'd changed your mind.'

Louis gazed over his shoulder, glad to see her again.

'I thought I was back in Princes Street on a Saturday afternoon, there are so many people trying to get on the ferry.' A tangible evidence of relief was now fortified by her presence. 'I was looking at that beach. I haven't seen a beach that busy in a long time.'

'It's very busy; the weekends are always like this.' Maria held two polystyrene cups of coffee. She recalled seeing the couple on the rocks that morning.

'I bought one for Peter.' She gestured towards the cups with her head. 'He's had to attend to a woman who has sprained her ankle.' She sat next to him.

'Well then, Peter's misfortune is my gain.' Louis smiled.

She handed him the coffee. He suppressed a need to touch her hand as he took the cup and raised it to his lips.

'I was getting worried back there. I thought I'd lost everyone until I saw Peter's hat,' he confessed.

'Ah yes, the famous hat.' Maria smiled. A gust of warm air blew stray hairs over her face.

'To be honest,' He looked down at the cup, avoiding her eyes. 'I feel a bit guilty. I spent most of our lunch speaking about myself and asked very little about you. I didn't mean to seem rude. I'm sorry.'

'No, not at all. You don't need to apologise. It must have felt good to talk. You needed someone to listen, and I was glad to be that person. It's obviously been a hard time for you.'

He realised the ferry was moving. A castle on a hill held Louis' attention, and he thought it looked crafted from the very rock it sat on.

He blew on his coffee cup as the evening sun lacquered her face in soft light. A plume of cigarette smoke hung around them, an unwanted intrusion that impelled Louis to suggest that they walk to the railings at the edge of the deck. A sudden realisation engulfed his chest. He wanted to open her up, read her like a book and absorb every page that was revealed to him. They dropped their cups in a waste bin. He asked about her.

'I live with my mother and twin brother just outside Zakynthos Town; the house has beautiful views of the sea. My father built the house when we were young; it's now the heart of our family. I have an older brother who is married. He has two children, my mother adores them, family is very important. My father would always tell us that there were only two things in life that mattered, God and family.'

'Wise words. He sounds like a good man.'

'He's dead now,' Maria said, looking at the diminishing coastline.

'I'm sorry,' offered Louis.

She looked at him. 'We both know what it feels like to lose someone special.' Maria paused. Louis sensed a sadness about her. His hand lay a few inches from hers, resting on the railings. In that moment, the desire to hold it felt right, it demanded it, but then she continued.

'I've worked in the tour industry, well, since I was old enough to work. I studied on the mainland, in Athens, received my diploma in tourism and then came home... and I've been a tour guide ever since.'

The moment had passed, slipping from his grasp, like an animal disappearing into a forest.

'Do you enjoy it?'

'It's all I've ever wanted to do. I love history. Being able to inform people from other countries about our history and culture is a passion of mine. It's not just a job, it's more of a vocation.'

'And you're good at it, a natural.'

'I wouldn't go that far,' she said self-consciously.

'You can tell how much it means to you. Your audience is drawn into the whole experience because you snare their interest with your enthusiasm; it's quite infectious.'

'I'm just the same as the rest of my colleagues. I'm not that special,' she said with a self-deprecating smile.

Louis hesitated. 'Is there anyone special in your life?' he

said, abandoning all decorum.
'No... Not for a long time,' she said honestly.
'Is that good or bad?' he wondered.
'That depends.'
'On what?'
She paused. 'It depends on what I want out of life.'
'And what do you want?' he asked gently.
She gazed at the sea. White foamed waves rippled out from the ferry, like a tractor ploughing through a field. Her fingers wrapped around the rail, she could feel the spray of sea salt coating her skin, her face, shoulders, and arms and ,for a moment, she panicked.
'I would like to run my own business that promotes the ecology of Zakynthos. Ecology tourism. It's not a new idea, but it's something I'm passionate about, especially the loggerhead turtles; they're endangered and use the beaches on Zakynthos to lay their eggs. We need to protect them but, at the same time, we can educate a wider audience; it's a subtle balance. I've lots of ideas, but at the moment that's a long way off. I need experience, that's what I lack. I need to know how to run my own business and learn from others.' She thought of the job offer in Athens before continuing, 'It would be nice to think one day I will meet the right person and have a family of my own and a house that's a home.' Maria turned her head from him, 'Is that too much to ask? What do you think Louis?' She looked at him. 'Am I being too idealistic?'
Louis was surprised at the intimacy and honesty of her answer.
'I think it sounds beautiful. It's what most of us aspire to.'
'Is that what you wanted with Emma?'
Louis nodded.
'You need time to come to terms with it all. I can't imagine how it must have felt.'
'When Emma became pregnant, it knocked a hole in me, I became infested with anger. It felt like a betrayal and at the same time her death didn't feel real. It was like she was still alive. I just wanted to hide away.' He mustered a smile.

'And I ended up running away to Greece.'

Peter's words of caution floated to the surface of Maria's thoughts.

'Are you still running?'

'I've stopped running, ghosts can't chase me anymore.'

'So what are you hoping to find in Zakynthos. Why there and not Cephalonia?'

'I want to see as much of Greece as my wallet will allow. I got off to a shaky start, but since then I've been to some incredible places and met the most accommodating and welcoming people. It feels surreal at times, life changing even. Because of it, I'm not the person I was.' He smiled vaguely. 'I would rather be here with you. That's more exciting than being alone in some hotel room or guest house in Cephalonia. I'm a bit of a risk taker; I feel I have got lucky. The moment I saw you, I knew my life was going to change.'

Maria looked at him steadily. 'You are a fool. You don't know me. I'm a stranger to you. You only know the job I do. That doesn't define who I am.'

'I know that,' Louis said awkwardly. 'I'd like to get to know you better, if you'll let me. That's all I meant and if not, then I'll head off to Cephalonia with my tail between my legs.' He grinned.

'You've lost the person you loved; how do you know your own mind at this time? You think you want to get to know me, but what you need is time Louis,' Maria's voice rose. 'You're in a different country, you don't have the responsibilities you had at home, you can travel where you want when you want. The business of normal life doesn't apply to you, you have no emotional ties here.' Her lips set in a fine line. For a moment Louis was lost for words.

She looked away from him out towards the sea. She watched large white birds glide above the water, like kites, surfing the invisible currents of the air. Even though she felt irritated by him, she said finally, 'I'm pleased that you are here.' Her gaze was fixed on the sea as she spoke.

Louis registered an acceptance. It encouraged him. He imagined brushing her lips with his fingertips. She removed the band that held her hair from her face, and it fell, like a veil, concealing her left eye, licking at the rounded curve of her upper lip. Louis noticed the shiny texture of a subtle scar, just discernable, which created a small indentation on her skin. He moved his hand and hesitated before brushing a stray hair from her left eye. She turned to him; his touch was unexpected and pleasingly disorientating. Louis cupped Maria's hair in his hand and inhaled its scent as if smelling washed sheets. Maria felt as if she had been touched by an angel, the sentient effect was tranquillizing. Peter's words of warning trailed off inside her head, like evaporating steam. He breathed deeply, as if the essence of it was imperative to nourish body and soul. He moved closer and brushed her cheek with his lips, seeking her mouth. A small sigh escaped her as their lips met for the first time. She tasted of strawberries and he wanted to go on exploring her mouth forever. Her skin felt warm as it pressed against him and the sensation of a roller coaster, as it plunges the curve of the track raced through him. The intensity was electric. Their lips parted, they held each other's stare in the knowledge that something sacred had passed through them and galvanized them in the warmth it created. An invigorating pulse streamed through Maria's veins as she composed herself. She felt her cheeks flush.

'That was unexpected,' she said.

'It just happened... I'm glad it did. I'm cementing my emotional ties.' He smiled coyly. 'It could've gone dreadfully wrong, though.'

'What do you mean?'

'I was half expecting a slap or something worse, maybe.'

'I didn't take you for a gambler.'

'I'm not but, if that is the rewards, I think I've become addicted.'

'Very amusing.' Maria smiled.

They sat on wooden seats still on the upper deck. He regarded her with a contemplative look and then asked her to describe to him Zakynthos as she would to a group of tourists. She glanced at him suspiciously as he leant back, crossed his legs and waited.

'Very well.'

Maria spoke as if reciting a poem. 'Zakynthos is a member of the Ionian group of islands and is the most southerly, with a population of 35,000. Zakynthos Town, the capital, is home to 9,500 people and easily the largest town on the island.'

Louis nodded, impressed by her introduction and gestured, like a king, for her to continue. She crossed her arms and glared at him.

'You're enjoying this.'

He grinned. 'Most definitely... carry on. Good introduction by the way.'

She played along with him. 'Its nearest neighbour is the island of Cephalonia, over 12 km to the north.'

'Ah, my friend Captain Corelli,' Louis interrupted. Maria's eyes threw invisible knives and she continued,

'Being a relatively small island, 106km square, by car the island can be explored quite easily. Olives, cypress and citrus groves are typical and familiar to the scenery of the island, which also farms and yields crops such as the current and grape. These vineyards can be found on fertile and flat plains, situated at the foot of the Vrachonian Mountains.'

'Impressive,' Louis said with a playful smile and folding his arms behind his head.

Maria ignored him, now determined and fuelled by intent she continued, 'The darkest and most tragic period of the island's history occurred on the 12th and 13th August 1953. An earthquake devastated and engulfed the entire region and left only a few buildings untouched. As well as the tragic loss of life, the architectural splendour and richness that decorated the island were destroyed in the devastating impact. When the regeneration of the capital began, most of the buildings were rebuilt and restored to their formal grandeur and beauty.'

'You are beautiful,' Louis interrupted. 'I should have mentioned that earlier.'

She frowned and, for a second time, his gamble paid off.

'Shh,' Maria remonstrated playfully. She paused.

'Although many buildings have been restored, one would have to visit the Solomos museum to become aware of and grasp the true nature of the tragedy.'

'The only tragedy I can see is that I've been in Greece all this time without knowing you. It's my very own Greek tragedy.'

'Louis.' Maria laughed. She pointed with an outstretched finger. 'Look, Cephalonia.'

The island hovered placidly, as her truculent mountains, dark and undulating, sat silhouetted against a pastel and salmon sky.

'Captain Correlli will just have to wait.' Louis smiled.

Soon they were nearing Zakynthos, as if it had just risen like a submarine from the sea. The sight of the island increased Louis' intoxicating mood. The intimacy of their kiss encouraged him to lightly touch her shoulder in view of a group of men, glazed eyed and boisterous who had spent the crossing in the bar.

He bent to her ear. 'I know how they feel, I'm drunk with you.'

Zakynthos

A Room with a View

Louis sat in the back of a taxi, rolled down the window, and breathed the tepid air. He crossed a bridge over a small stream, the colour of coffee it scarred the view, and Louis thought this was one part of Zakynthos that would fail to find its way inside travel brochures and newspaper supplements.

An ebullition of traffic claimed the road as its own. Screaming mopeds, driven by half-naked young men and women, dangerously weaved in and out of the briefest spaces between the moving traffic. He caught sight of an old woman, draped in black; she shuffled at a glacial pace, her curved back supported by two rickety walking sticks. He observed men sitting at pavement cafes, deep in conversation and animated in expansive gestures. Others played cards, smoking as if it were an epidemic or a celebrated national pastime. Maybe it was both, as they sipped their Greek coffees under the hanging smog of cigarette smoke. He wondered why Greek men spent so much time in each other's company while the women, as far as he could tell, were the most industrious, the workhorses of Greek society.

The sea and a narrow strip of sand hugged the coastal road, like a slithering snake; it linked Zakynthos town with the nearest village, Argassi. Behind him, where the capital nestled, the sun slid behind a hill, casting long shadows, painting the dusk sky with dramatic brushstrokes of purple, orange and scarlet red.

He tried to secure a room in Zakynthos town without success. Maria, who felt responsible for his predicament, made a phone call to a friend of her mother who once ran small holiday apartments in the neighbouring village of Argassi, but was now retired. Eventually, a reluctant deal was won.

The radio emitted traditional Greek music, interspersed by the crackles of a radio controller. The taxi driver, an older man with a weather-beaten complexion, delighted in enlightening Louis that Argassi started life as a small fishing village. Through his broken English he informed Louis that today, tourism is the only industry that flows richly through her veins, concluding with a smile, the only fish seen these days were the ones on menus and dinner plates.

He told Louis, in a proud spirit, that his brother had emigrated to America and now drove a yellow cab in New York. He reached into the glove compartment, causing the taxi to swerve, and produced a photograph of his brother standing beside his cab, like a married couple.

Nothing seemed complicated now; Louis' spirit soared, floating effortlessly. Maria remained a constant presence in his thoughts, in his head; he could reach out and touch her. When he stepped into her company, nothing else mattered. He felt like a mountaineer who has just reached the summit of a climb. He felt like he had stumbled upon a new religion and, exulted and transfixed, he had become a devoted follower. A warm glow spread over his chest, feeding his desire and eagerness to be with her, to touch her skin and see her face, now superimposed on his thoughts. He responded to these thoughts with the realisation she was the last piece in his jigsaw, yet alone and without her, the jigsaw sat incomplete, imperfect.

Entering the environs of Argassi, Louis was pleased to find the village had grown and scattered in an uncluttered manner, creating an ambience of space that lacked the ominous monstrosities that masqueraded as hotels and apartment blocks. These he viewed as nasty scars that left crusty scabs on the surface of the even most picturesque village. He found a complementary demeanour existed as a uniformed look of primrose yellow exteriors supported terracotta tiled roofs, the tallest of these buildings being only three levels high.

He passed a fusion of restaurants, shops, and hotels that straddled the main street, thronging the nucleus of the village. They drove in silence. A stillness settled into the village: waiters set tables, dusted empty seats, rearranged menus, and unfolded and pressed white tablecloths in preparation to welcome early diners.

Louis imagined this somnolence replaced by music, conversation and the civilised clicking and chiming of cutlery, the pastel light replaced by its electric counterpart.

He noticed a blackboard that rubbed against a stone wall. Its author advertised in white chalk, '*Souvlaki, lamb chops, pork chops, fillet steak, mix grill, shrimps, fish fingers, meatballs all served with salad, rice and lots of chips.*' He wouldn't go hungry, he thought. Instead of remaining in the taxi, Louis had a notion to walk through the village.

From the boot, the driver gathered Louis' small assortment of luggage that had served him sufficiently. Louis noted the fading sunlight glint off the terracotta tiled roof of a house, attractive against the dusk sky, it was a reminder it would soon be dark.

Louis paid the driver and asked directions to the guesthouse. He passed a street vendor who had set up a primitive small table covered in black cloth. Louis scanned the objects she had placed on the cloth, an assortment of jewellery, bracelets, rings, necklaces and pendants. The young woman leant over and lit a small lantern. She looked up at Louis and smiled. Her eyes were set deep into her head and brown hair fell about her face in shiny curls. A large bump swelled her stomach and Louis could see that she was heavily pregnant. He returned her smile and continued in his search of the address Maria had given him.

He passed a gauntlet of waiters, each with their own strategy encouraging him to enter their restaurant, '*The best souvlaki in all of Zakynthos.*' '*Happy hour every hour.*' Although their efforts were convincing, the nearing prospect of a shower urged Louis to refuse their offers. He found their ingenuity of persistence comical. He had just arrived, laden with a travelling bag and still to find where he was staying, yet, he was being invited in non-abrupt and non-truculent manners to dine out.

'*You come back later, we are the best restaurant in all of Argassi,*' each parting remark resonated in his head.

The dusty road wound gently to the rear of the village.

On each side, stone built walls bordered its rising gradient. It curved around a hotel, with a primrose yellow exterior and marble steps that led to dark wooden doors. He rose higher above the village, where the wall gave way to patches of vegetation, thick bushes and shrubs. A sudden feeling of being lost swept over Louis. He considered retracing his steps back to the village when, to his left, he came across large iron gates supported by a six-foot whitewashed wall.

He consulted the address Maria had given him. This had to be it, he thought. The gates opened with a creak. The exterior of the house projected a refined quality, the house was large, and a veranda wrapped around the ground floor immediately snagged his eye. Ceramic pots burst with brilliant purples, whites, yellows and mauve-blue flowers, where an aromatic and exotic orgy of perfumes collided with one another. He traced the flight of two swallows and detected a nest under the eaves of the veranda. He would not even have noticed such things back home.

His eyes followed a stone path that led to a circle of olive trees and a solitary wooden bench. Behind him, white and red roses clambered up the whitewashed wall. Lemons and oranges hung from branches, like decorations on a Christmas tree. He imagined spending early evenings soaking up the perfection that exploded in colour and sitting in the many shaded corners the garden afforded the visitor.

'You must be Louis. My name is Anna,' a wavering voice announced as a woman stepped from the shade of the veranda.

'Eh yes, pleased to meet you,' Louis stammered, startled at the sudden sound of her voice.

She cautiously navigated the steps onto the flat ground of the garden.

'It is this way.'

He guessed her age to be somewhere in her late sixties. As he followed her, she shuffled along, every small-step an effort. She placed a hand on her padded hip and turned to face him.

'It is two weeks rent in advance, no loud music or

parties... Is this fine with you?' She turned from him not waiting for an answer and continued to shuffle, like an injured animal.

'Eh yes... that's fine.' The impression crept upon him that his presence was not welcome.

'Are you busy at this time of year?' Maria had told him his host was retired. However he felt the need to make conversation.

'No... We are closed now. I am what you say...' She paused, searching for the appropriate word.

'Retired?' Louis said.

'What is this word?' She grunted.

'You no longer work.'

'Yes. Yes, for a long time, since my husband died. I do this as a favour. Maria is a nice girl, she phoned and was concerned. I offer you a room, you are a friend of Maria, you are welcome... the rooms are nice, you will see.'

What Anna lacked in height, she made up for in size, she was as wide as she was tall. She wore a lilac sleeveless dress that fell below arthritic knees. Behind her upper arms, loose skin swayed as she walked and her swollen ankles reminded Louis of elephants' feet. Her hair was black, apart from a long silver streak. It was her habit to tie it back from her face.

In front of the house, a second building stood. The exterior was plain and whitewashed with a balcony at each room.

'Would you like a room at the bottom or top? The view is better up there.'

She pointed a small sausage-like finger towards the stairs.

'The room with a view it is then.' Louis smiled.

'You stay long?' Anna asked, leaning a dimpled arm on the white wall, as she considered each marble step with an asthmatic wheeze.

'As long as I am welcome. I don't want to be a burden.'

'You pay me, you are welcome, I clean sheets for you once a week. I do not cook, that is not in the price. You will have to eat in the village.'

'Of course. That will be fine,' Louis said.

She turned the key in the lock and the door creaked as she opened it. The room was shrouded in darkness. They entered, and Louis waited for his eyes to adjust to the sudden change in light. Anna pulled open the wooden shutters and heaved the glass sliding doors with considerable effort.

The sound of birds welcoming the falling dusk and a dog's bark floated around them. Walls became washed in a soft pale glow, highlighting small dark stains of splattered mosquito. The scents of the garden penetrated the air, like a feather floating into the room, dissolving the musky atmosphere that haunted the unlived in space.

In the confined space of the room, Anna's cheeks looked rounder, her eyes smaller, lost inside wrinkling folds and stretched skin.

She brushed past him. 'You pay me two weeks money today; you unpack and pay me later.'

A warm breeze moved through the room, like a ghost, roaming over the bed where white sheets lay creased and folded. The room was sparse and bare, comprising of a wooden cupboard, a bed, a bedside table and a lamp without a shade. He opened the drawer of the table and found the previous occupants had left candles. The only other feature was a small room consisting of a shower, a toilet and wash-hand basin.

He walked onto the balcony, where he found two chairs and a table. He considered the view and, even in the fading light, the wash of colour caught his breath; he found it striking, transcendent, and exhilarating. Below him, terracotta roofs the colour of baked earth, sloped towards the sea, like giant stepping-stones, he thought. He noticed that many of the roofs were equipped with solar panels. An emerald foliage of shrubs, bushes and trees were sprinkled with vibrant blues and brown, and the yellow and pink of wildflowers. Where the swell of waves met the beach, it became saturated in electric turquoise and, as the evening claimed the day as its own, a fading ice blue sky trailed out towards the horizon.

To his left, the capital lay under the protection of a wooded hill, its white buildings, from such a distance, reminded Louis of children's building blocks. The fading glare of the setting sun sheared off the white caps on the sea, as contentment settled upon him like a blanket. An insect buzzed past his ear. He flicked it with his hand and decided that he would greet each new morning in front of this view with the thought that something wonderful had entered his life.

An Embarrassing Incident on the Balcony

A soft light threw a shadow across the wall, catching his attention and, like an alarm clock, it forced him from the bed. He remembered the alluring view now concealed by the shutters. Louis moved across the room, scratching an irritant itch on his head and yawned. He peered through the slats of the shutters, smacking his lips as the sultry air pressed against him. The moment he stepped onto the balcony, Louis was transfixed as he scanned the rooftops and sea, inhaling the scent the morning air offered. A collage of crimson and orange light swept across and infused the sky, bursting and fanning over the horizon, like celestial highways. Louis leaned on the edge of the balcony and clasped his hands contentedly. To his left, the small capital sheltered in a bay amongst a hierarchy of yachts and boats. He was surprised to see two naval vessels, minesweepers, he thought, resting next to the harbour wall. He caught sight of a ferry, not unlike the one he had travelled on, entering the harbour, its white complexion in stark contrast to the blue of the sea.

With a long appreciative scan, he took in the garden. A swallow darted from its nest and he followed its glide over the garden in majestic arched waves. And it was then that his attention fell upon Anna, her small round eyes now wide in horror, the countenance of her round face suffused in a disbelieving shock, as if a ghost had walked right through her garden. In that moment, a sudden realisation coursed through Louis; he was naked. He waved, a sheepish gesture as his other hand concealed the area Anna's eyes burned into.

'Good morning,' Louis blurted out, failing to conceal his debilitating embarrassment.

'Kalimera. So this is what a Scotsman has under his kilt, very little,' Anna cackled.

Louis willed the room to swallow him in its concealment. He fell onto the bed and covered his face in disbelief.

'Well, that has broken the ice between us,' he groaned.

The night before, once Anna had left him to settle into

the room, Louis unpacked and showered. He ate his first meal in the village, at a rooftop restaurant, taming his hunger with mushroom soup, goulash, potatoes and salad. He ate under a sense of feeling exposed, as if a large sign hovered above him, advertising he was on his own, amongst the couples and families that occupied the near to capacity restaurant.

After his meal, Louis wandered along the main street. The sights and smells of restaurants and the intertwining rhythms and mingling beats of the music bars fought with the calmness of the small supermarkets, trinket shops and the tranquil marble interiors of jewellery and perfume shops.

He stumbled upon the pregnant street merchant, who sat, reading a book under a lamp. Louis stood for some time considering and studying the rows of rings, necklaces, bracelets, earrings and a row of watches that weren't displayed before. The young woman occasionally broke her gaze from the page to find out if Louis had made a choice. He picked up a silver bracelet woven together like rope.

'I will have this one thanks.'

'A good choice, I have one myself,' the vendor said, in perfect English. 'It is not for yourself, it is too small. Is it a gift for someone?'

'Yes, for a special friend.' He indulged himself that he was no longer alone.

'Ah, I see.' She nodded, placing the bracelet in a small black box.

'Have you sold many? These are really good quality.'

'Later on, maybe. Once people have eaten and had a few drinks they are more inclined to stop and browse.'

Louis paid her and she thanked him with a flash of milk coloured teeth.

He walked further, pleased with his purchase, and noticed the satiety of colour and illuminating lights of the bars and restaurants give way to the subtle orange glow of windows from quiet houses whose occupants were concealed. It was here that Louis noticed the thump of the bass drum softened to a distant beat.

He discovered a path of marble blue and dusty pink slabs, where clay pots stood like chimneys on a small wall and disappeared into a vale of blackness. Continuing further, he walked down a slight slope and passed a huge copper vase, to the sound of waves lapping gently and the hypnotic pulse of a cricket. His shoes sank into the soft sand; above him, the moon hung like an illuminant bulb in a curtain of black sky. He could see the small shimmering lights of the capital, like distant stars, and he wondered what Maria would be doing at this moment.

That night an undisturbed sleep eluded him as he tossed and turned impatient for hours to pass until he saw her again.

A Bond in Silver

After the incident on the balcony, Louis showered and changed, finding it hard to replace the image of a transfixed Anna now burrowed into his mind. On his way to the village, he walked around Anna's house with an air of determination around him and purposefulness in his stride he hoped would deflect the prospect of another humiliating encounter with his landlady. It was not until he passed through the iron gates that he allowed himself to relax.

The early hour of the morning saw Argassi enshrined in a sleepy stillness. Louis glanced at the hill behind him. Somewhere up there stood his room, the prodigious Anna and the beautiful garden, hidden like a secret treasure chest. Louis noticed that the hill dominated the foreground and, in the subtle morning light, it seemed serene, undisturbed and majestic even. He inhaled dry, sweet air, confidently striding into the village.

The Green Frog had begun serving breakfast, as he sat at a table and consulted the menu. Louis looked at his watch. He had half an hour to spare. He ordered toast, scrambled egg and coffee. From his seat, he could see the main road where several people gathered. In thirty minutes, he would see her again; an accelerating rush passed through him, like a thunderous stream after a heavy torrent of rain.

Yesterday, as the ferry entered the harbour, he had asked Maria when he would see her again. Maria commented that she would be working the following day, taking a group around the island. It was then that the thought occurred to him, there was nothing to stop him going on the excursion as a paying customer. He could spend the entire day in her company.

He felt pleased with himself. His satisfaction was short-lived; the excursion may be full? To his relief Maria smiled at the suggestion. She thought it a wonderful idea as she told him the coach had its first pick up in Argassi.

He finished his breakfast. The Green Frog filled up at a steady rate. Other people no longer intruded upon his vulnerabilities as they did the night before. He contemplated his day ahead and then the grumbling of changing gears summoned an urgency to pay his bill.

It was understood between them that, while in the company of the tour party it would be inappropriate to display a familiarity or affection towards each other. They would meet during breaks for refreshments and lunch, yet Louis asked himself, how could he deny or bleach from his mind the feelings that had sustained him, that had given life to the arid desert that had lived within him? She had entered that hostile place, like a flower pushing through the sand. Could his desire, the intensity of wanting her, be dispensed with?

As he mounted the steps of the coach, such inner anxieties were dispelled, as the softness of her skin reached out to him and bored into his eyes, eradicating any trace of denial. He was a fly caught in her web and it was unimaginable to be anywhere else. The erosion was complete.

He smiled at her as he reached the aisle, enticing a returned acknowledgment. He wanted to be near her and relished the possibility of being in proximity. However, a German couple took the seat he had eyed, forcing him to be content with two seats behind where she sat. He settled into the mould of the seat as the coach moved at an exorbitant pace, leaving Argassi to wake and bask in another new morning.

They collected a large group in Zakynthos Town. No one sat next to Louis, so he sank into the anonymity the seat afforded. They passed the outskirts and surrounding countryside of the capital and then turned inland over flat plains, passing vineyards and the Vrachonian Mountains that rose and towered towards the heavens, like ancient guardians, patiently watching the centuries fold and pass.

An elegant house snagged his eye and, like a child to falling snow, he was captivated by the natural wealth and beauty that emanated from the stimulating colours and conciliating textures of the landscape. It reminded him of a vast garden expanding and exploding with life and growth. They passed a pickup truck with a goat standing in the back. It stared at the passing countryside as if it was the most natural thing for a goat to do and maybe in Greece it was, Louis thought.

Maria instructed the tour party on the island's history. He concentrated on her voice. It floated over him and he focused on the sound, the intonation of the words, the ascent and descent of her pitch and delivery; the oscillating tone licked over him, like undulating waves.

'It is here,' Maria said. 'On the flat plains where the vineyards prosper in the rich and fertile soil that currants are grown, becoming the island's main export. Grapes are also harvested and left to dry in the warm months of August. The local wine produced from these vineyards is sold all over the island and we will have time to sample it on our scheduled stops.' She concluded on a satisfied note.

They passed through several villages and, although not immune to the tourist industry, they snared Louis' attention, their character still preserved and evident within the buildings and churches, where the seekers of the old untouched Greece could bathe in their authenticity. It occurred to him that the simplistic qualities of these villages needed to be protected from an industry that was all too often guilty of saturating and suffocating the essence its livelihood depended on. More debilitating visions impaled him, depressing warning signs that if ignored, an onslaught of development and cannibalism of the natural resources would cause the scenario like many parts of Spain through decades of unrestricted expansion. Such a vivid image was at odds with the Greece he had come to know.

Maria announced that they would soon enter the village of Macherado, their arrival casually observed by a group of men, sitting in the shade of a café. The prospect of another coach load of tourists visiting their church was not an event to either stir their curiosity or prise them from their game of cards.

They left the coach and walked across a square towards a church. In their hurried intent to view the inside of the church, a section of the group had whisked Maria to the entrance. He wanted Maria to himself and the others irritated him with the demands they put on her time.

A pang of agitation pulled at him. This would not be the trip he imagined. He entered the church through two dark wooden doors. Above him, an inscription with the date 1873 caught his attention. A further sign proclaimed in English, 'Please enter the church respectfully dressed.'

A redolent fragrance of yellow flamed candles and burning incense reminded him of the palatial churches in Rome, transforming him to another time, another life.

The tour party converged around the icon of the Saint Agia Mavara. It stood encased in a golden cabinet; at its pinnacle Louis noticed a beautiful dome. Gold coloured wooden leaves framed the icon and, on each side, infused within this decoration, stood a young angel.

Maria explained that the Agia Mavara had become renowned for her deep-set dark eyes and, more interestingly a reputation for answering the prayers of those seeking to heal from affliction or recovery from illness. Her audience was intrigued to learn that it had become the custom to offer the saint jewellery or small wax figurines depicting the body part that was in need of her divine intervention. Louis wondered if a cottage industry had sprung up to attend to the needs of the miracle seekers. As yet, he had not been offered a wax arm or leg, a potential gap in the local religious market, he smiled to himself.

Above him, he viewed a pictorial library of Old Testament stories. On each wall, paintings radiated more biblical scenes, and it seemed he had entered a religious art gallery whose colours were infectious to the eye.

The group ambled through the church. Once outside, Maria drew their attention to a tower that loomed dominantly above the roofs of Macherado. The tower was one of the few buildings to miraculously survive the earthquake of 1953 intact, its bells still ringing out on a daily basis.

Their stay in Macherado was short. They were shepherded onto the coach and soon ascended a narrow and steep road, rising through olive and cypress trees. Louis noticed the occasional small shrine by the side of the road as a whitewashed monastery, fortified by a wall and bell towers came into view.

Before long, they stopped at a taverna and disembarked. Louis followed the other passengers and, to his delight, the rear of the taverna opened onto a large veranda, sprinkled with tables and chairs. He walked over to a small stone wall and observed the view with immense satisfaction. A flat plain stretched out towards the headlands and shimmering sea. Olive groves, acorn and cypress trees punctured the landscape like strokes from an artist's brush. Terracotta roofs floated on the haze of the sun, and the tower of the church of the Agia Mavara rose above the roofs of Macherado, like a beacon. To his right, Louis spotted the monastery they had passed, sitting in a clearance. At the periphery, a range of steel grey hills lined the sky.

He felt her touch on his arm. 'So what do you think of my island?' She smiled confidently.

He turned to look at her. 'It's perfect, just like you.' He couldn't help himself.

Maria smiled and tilted her head towards him. 'Unlike Zakynthos, I have my imperfections.' Her hand left his arm.

'How are you coping with the tour?'

'Fine... it's... interesting.'

'You didn't come here to be a tourist then.' Maria mocked him.

'Well, I'm a different kind of tourist.'

'And what would that be?' she asked.

'I've come just to see one particular sight... I'm very fussy you see.' He laughed, enjoying the game they played.

'And what sight would that be?'

'I'm looking at her.'

'Ah, I see and was she worth it? I mean some tourist sights don't live up to their reputation.'

'And what reputation do you have?' Louis quizzed her through curled lips.

'That would be telling. A woman likes to keep a veil of secrecy around her... that's her attraction,' Maria teased.

'Well, I look forward to peeling back the layers.'

The air was warm, a sweet scent floated up from the

valley. A warm feeling levitated in his stomach, a sensation that pronounced itself every time she was close to him. He pictured being alone with her, feeling her skin against his. He remembered their kiss on the ferry.

'Coffee?' she asked.

The suggestion catapulted him back to the veranda. He nodded; a coffee would sober his thoughts.

They sat under a large parasol. She pushed her sunglasses onto the crown of her head and crossed a leg, her dress riding above her knee. She flicked a strand of hair from her face.

'How have you found your accommodation?'

'It's fine. Basic, but clean. I'm just glad that I have somewhere to stay.'

'Good, I hope Anna has been nice to you?'

'She has been… kind. I feel I'm a burden. She didn't have to take me in. It feels odd being the only person there. Are you sure Anna doesn't mind?'

Maria flicked away his concern with a gesture of her hand.

'Being retired doesn't suit her, it was forced upon her. Her husband died unexpectedly, and she struggled to keep the apartments going on her own. Anna employed a young girl to do the cleaning, but it didn't work out. She's alone now. Anna liked it when her apartments were busy, full of people.'

'I'm not sure if she wants me there.'

'Nonsense, it will give her a sense of purpose again. She is always telling my mother she needs something to do with her time. Wait and see, she'll be like a mother hen all over you in no time.'

Louis cringed at the thought.

'I hear Anna has already been getting to know you better. She phoned my mother this morning.'

'Ah, the balcony. God, that was embarrassing. I'll never be able to look her in the face again without thinking about it.'

'Don't worry, she found it hilarious, once she got over the shock.'

He took a sip of coffee enjoying its bitter taste. 'When I woke this morning, I couldn't believe the view from the balcony.' He gestured with the cup towards the valley. 'Like most views on this island.'

'Maybe I should see for myself.'

'I would like that, but I don't think Anna would approve.'

'No you're probably right... you would have to sneak me in.' Maria laughed. 'I've known her all of my life, she is my mother's best friend. In fact, Anna is my Godmother.'

'Almost family then.'

Maria looked at her watch.

'Is it time to go?' Louis asked, a hint of anxiety in his voice.

'Not yet, we'll have time to finish our coffee.'

'Good, I've only had five minutes with you all day.'

'I know. It's not perfect, but at least this way we can still spend time together.'

He closed his eyes, and shifted in his chair to place his hand in his pocket. He took out a small black box and laid it on the table. Maria watched him curiously.

'What is this?'

'Open it and find out.'

She did as he asked and peeled away the white tissue paper.

'It's beautiful.'

He took her hand and placed the silver bracelet on her wrist. It was a gesture that cemented a bond, simplistic in its nature, yet profound in its symbolism.

'Louis you shouldn't have... you have embarrassed me... I've nothing to give you.' She blushed, rubbing the bracelet with the tip of her finger.

'It fits,' Louis exclaimed, relieved and satisfied. 'I didn't buy it to embarrass you. I wanted you to have something that would remind you of me, so that when we're not together, I would still be close.'

'Yesterday I told you you were a fool and you haven't changed, you're still one today. A romantic fool. You have only known me for two days.'

'I know, but it feels as if I've known you longer. Have

you ever had that feeling when you meet someone for the first time, and it's like you've known them most of your life? Even their voice is familiar to you.'

'No, I can't say I have.'

'Well, anyway, that's how it was when I first saw you in Olympia. I felt I already knew you. It sounds bizarre, but that's how it is. When you think about it, we were drawn to Olympia on the same day and at a very precise point in time. Amongst all of those people in that vast site, we shared the same space and found each other.'

'And now you're a daydreaming fool,' Maria whispered, allowing a slight smile to cross her lips. Her hand still rested on his. She brought it to her face and gently traced his skin with the tip of her finger. He submerged himself in her touch and leaned forward. The weight of his elbows lifted the table, like a child's seesaw. Instinctively, he grabbed the table's edge. With a clatter, their cups shattered into jagged pieces onto the floor, evoking the unwanted attention of several turned heads. He looked at them apologetically, before inspecting the aftermath that his graceless action had incurred.

'Shit,' Louis spluttered. 'I was meant to be discreet.' He retrieved the remnants of the cups.

'Are you wet?' Maria smirked, covering her mouth.

'Luckily no, are you?'

Maria attempted to suppress her surmounting amusement.

'Obviously not.' He grinned. 'That's what I would call a passion killer.'

'It certainly went downwards.' The humour in her voice widened Louis' grin as he eased himself into his chair. The sight of the coach driver gesticulating enthusiastically towards his watch caught Louis' eye. He nodded in his direction. 'I think he's trying to tell us it's time to go.'

Maria raised her eyebrows. 'Well don't lean on the table when you get up.' She chastised him jocularly, sliding back her chair and standing up. 'There will be another coach load arriving soon and the taverna will need every spare cup.'

Louis smirked, scraping his chair off the floor and

moving backwards in an exaggerated manner. 'Do you think this is far enough?'

She slanted her eyes. 'Is this what you call... let me see... taking the piss?'

The Girl in the Photograph

They travelled for twenty minutes, the driver negotiating each bend with practiced skill, to Louis' relief. Soon they reached the monastery Anophonitria, where the island's patron saint, St. Dionysios, the then Bishop Dionysios Sigouros, had been Abbot.

They passed a tower that stood at the entrance to the monastery. Maria said it had been used as a refuge from attacks for hundreds of years and was another building to remain intact after the earthquake of 1953.

Theirs was not the only party to descend upon the dust of the monastery and, in the courtyard, clusters of people aimed cameras and camcorders towards a small church and the monks' renovated living quarters, which Louis noted did nothing to lift the otherwise charmless surrounding of the unremarkable buildings.

Watching the others, Louis became excited by the idea of buying a camera. He now nursed a regret at the missed opportunities of capturing the images of the people he had met and the places he had experienced. Maria would be his first subject.

Louis did not join the others instead; he sat on a small wall. He noticed that Maria had already gained the habit of rubbing the bracelet with her forefinger and thumb; it brought a well of satisfaction. Louis had surprised himself at how unguarded he felt when he spoke with her. He also felt a surge of panic. Louis had grieved for Emma, and had been consumed in the loneliness that had brought, until now. He felt exhilaration when in Maria's company and delirious when she touched him. Louis tried to rationalise it, but it made no sense to him. He was also reminded that such feelings could be supplemented by agitation. He heard Maria's voice and turned, as she and her party evacuated St. Dionysios' house and headed towards the church before stopping at the entrance. Not for the first time that day, he envied the attention she afforded them.

'Within the small church, we will view what is a source of pilgrimage, a pair of shoes said to be worn by the saint himself. When we enter, we will come across the shoes, encased in a glass case, as well as viewing the icon of Panagia, which was discovered on a shipwreck that had set sail for Byzantium after it fell to the Turks in 1453. During droughts, the icon is taken on a tour of the island in the hope that it will bring rain.' With these words, they disappeared into the dark interior and Louis drew a line in the dust with his foot, enduring his own drought.

Louis noticed a graveyard that adjoined the monastery. He walked idly, unable to make sense of the Greek lettering, but feeling strangely invigorated and alive amongst such symbols of loss and death. Louis felt the sun upon his face as he moved indiscriminately amongst the headstones.

Occasionally he stopped and bent to look at a photograph of the deceased enshrined within a sliding glass case, flanked by burnt candles cascaded into frozen shapes of wax. The faces in each photograph, also frozen in time, gazed out into the living world holding Louis' stare. He came across a black and white photograph of a young girl that had faded and turn yellow at the corners. He pressed his fingers against the glass, as if reaching out to touch her. His fingers smudged the glass with their imprint and, in that moment, he felt a rush of pity for her.

He wondered when the photograph was taken. What may have caused her death? Did she know what it felt like to love and be loved, to touch and to embrace another, to be engulfed by the presence of a lover? Did her family still visit the grave? And keep her memory alive in conversation and thought? Bring flowers and tell her of their lives, the lives that had once stopped in grief, but now continued without her, an evolution of the living.

'Here you are,' Maria said. 'I was wondering if you had got bored with the tour and left us.'

Louis turned. 'She looks so happy... animated even.' He rose to his feet, relieved to see Maria.

'Who?'

'The girl in the photograph.'

She touched his arm, running her fingers the length of his

forearm. She had pushed her sunglasses onto the top of her head. He noticed the sun glint off her bracelet.

'You look sad, Louis.'

He tried to smile and turned towards the grave.

'I wonder what she died of. The photograph looks like it was taken a long time ago.'

He looked at the gravestone. 'What does it say?'

'Her name was Katerina. She died on the 3rd of February 1979. She was fourteen.'

'A life full of promise and opportunity stolen,' he mused. 'Does it say how she died?'

'No, only that she was taken from them too soon.'

A silence fell upon them, a respectful lull in their conversation.

He shook his head and smiled. His voice slid into a relaxed tone. 'When we get back to Zakynthos Town, I'm going to buy a camera and take lots of photographs of you, your island, its sunrises, and sunsets, and maybe even Anna.'

Maria smiled.

He was aware how close they stood. They stopped short of touching, their eyes fixed on each other's stare and then their lips hovered, millimetres apart, he could feel her breath upon him. He placed his palm against the nape of her neck and guided her towards him. Snaking his arm around her waist, he was pleasantly surprised at the intimacy of their kiss, the hunger of it.

She pulled away. 'We need to be careful,' she whispered in his ear.

The revelation about the young girl and her short life made Louis want to seize each moment with a newfound urgency.

An envious impatience grabbed him. 'I hate this pretence. I want to walk beside you and hold your hand. I want to feel your touch on my skin.' He sighed heavily. 'I want them all to disappear and leave us alone, together.'

She covered his cheek in feathered kisses. 'Remember, I am working. You don't want me to get into trouble, do you?'

'I'm sorry,' he mused. 'I didn't think it would be as hard as this.'

'There's only one more stop. It's nice, actually. You will like it, I think. It involves a boat.'

The Boatman, the Cave, and a Profound Feeling of Coming Home

To reach Ormos Skinari the coach descended a steep road. As they drew closer, it became evident that Ormos Skinari comprised of a cluster of buildings that hugged the beach. Amongst them, several restaurants catered for a throng of day-trippers who had descended upon the village in search of lunch. Several yachts had berthed alongside a wooden jetty, while smaller, less majestic boats, bobbed gently, closer to the beach.

Their route had taken them from the east coast of Argassi to the flat plains further inland and then north. They had now travelled towards the coast, where the ever-changing colours of the Ionian awaited them. Maria had coloured their journey with stories of the island's culture and traditions, elaborating on a traditional wedding, where guests pin money to the bride's wedding gown to the christening ceremony of the Greek Orthodox Church and colourful Easter parades.

As the day progressed, Louis had become fascinated by Maria's composed demeanour and knowledge. She was good at her job. It occurred to him he was seeing a different Maria to the one he knew when they were alone together. Even those married for years may never see their spouse perform the roles their job entails. Louis felt privileged and relaxed, consoled by this realization; his irritation with his fellow passengers ebbed from him.

Louis thought back to the graveyard and their kiss. He wanted to reestablish his feelings; they were volcanic, yearning sensations, a sexual quickening that could not be tamed. They implored his attention and he dived into their waters, unashamed and invigorated.

Maria stepped from the coach and took a deep intake of breath. The walk to the narrow beach was short and Maria informed Louis they would have time together after the visit to the blue caves of Ormos Skinari. Louis assumed their mode of transport would be one of the larger boats or even, he considered with a lick of excitement, one of the impressive yachts. They were directed to a corner of the bay where a fleet of small boats bobbed upon the calm surface of the water. His enthusiasm deflated; compared to the other boats, these were toys.

Louis judged that the capacity of each boat could comfortably accommodate twelve people; any more would worry him. They split into two groups and he was relieved to discover Maria accompanying him, as a hesitant queue formed on the shore. He positioned himself behind her as they stepped onto a wooden brow. Once on the boat, he attempted to maintain his balance by spreading his feet and shuffling forward; worryingly its dimensions felt diminished. Louis tried to mimic the boat's motion as he sat on one of four wooden benches that spanned its width.

He was pleased. Louis had claimed the space beside Maria. She lowered her eyes and smiled. Her shoulder brushed his upper arm and he could feel the heat of her skin radiate against him. He dared himself to touch her hand, but just then a man bumped into him, apologising. Louis nodded recognition, trying to seem unconcerned, but the incident left a trace of agitation about him.

He caught her eye and smiled, not too excessive as to invite speculation from others, but a gesture that was polite. A concoction of emotions uncoiled inside him. Again, he found himself remonstrate that he did not enjoy this pretence, even though he understood it was necessary. To compensate, part of him was excited by the sexual energy that moved within him. Not for the first time that day all he desired was to be alone with her, engulfed in her presence.

The tingling on Maria's shoulder when she brushed his skin confirmed that today was set apart from the normal visit to the caves. He had smiled, and it infused a current that trickled deep inside her, like electricity.

Having taken this trip many times, Maria was no stranger to the boatman. They spoke to each other in their own language. He had not introduced himself to his passengers but smiled and nodded politely as each individual boarded his boat; occasionally he offered a steady hand to a woman or child. His face was lined and weather-beaten-an occupational hazard Louis thought. His white shirt flapped in the welcome breeze, opened to the chest; it displayed a crop of curly grey hair and a gold crucifix. Although Louis could not understand Maria's conversation, the boatman's body language did not convey signs of distress at the number of passengers he was allocated. Louis took this to be a good sign, immediately consoling his nerves as the engine spluttered into life and the small craft negotiated the water with ease. An image of his father and grandfather taking him fishing when he was a boy on a glass-like lake in Italy entered his thoughts. He could not remember the location and the images that sprung to mind did not offer him a visual clue. It left a melancholy ache.

Above the drone of the engine and lapping waves, the boatman shouted greetings towards similar boats entering the bay, returning from the caves with their freshly bronzed cargo. With each passing minute, Louis eased into the boat ride, as it moved with swiftness, speed, and alacrity.

The boat stayed close to mountainous cliffs that rose above them like vertical walls. Louis was drawn towards the austerity of the rock, its harshness, and severity of character yet, he was aware of a subtlety that emancipated the fierce contours in an emanating aura of grandeur and beauty. The sea lapped at the cliff and its deep blue sapphire surface looked forbidding and mysterious.

It soon became apparent that theirs was not the only boat heading for the caves. A flotilla of all shapes and sizes bobbed up and down upon the waves of the Aegean.

There they were, cut into the cliff, their dark interior looming. The caves of Ormos Skinari beckoned them to enter and the small boat obeyed their command.

Maria turned to Louis. 'You'll enjoy the caves.' She smiled. Daringly she placed her hand on his. Surprised at the physical touch, Louis welcomed it as he cupped his fingers between hers.

Once inside, the caves were not devoid of light as he had expected, an unnatural glow made it possible to view the entire interior. Louis noticed that this was aided in part by the extraordinary quality of the water as a striking array of turquoise blue emanated from the surface in an exorbitant flurry of brilliance and intensity, as if projected by underwater lights.

Spontaneous gasps reverberated around the cave, amplified by the sensitive acoustics.

'It's the water that's blue, not the caves,' exclaimed Louis, as if he had just uncovered a magician's trick.

Maria grinned. 'But it's lovely. I never tire of it.'

The boatman displayed considerable skill and judgement as he carefully guided them through the caves, using an oar against the rock wall to manoeuvre the boat around several corners towards the exit. Maria's fingers had remained interlinked in Louis' the whole time they were in the caves. Louis dwelt upon the curve of her mouth and the fullness of her lips which summoned an impulse to kiss her. He knew this was the feeling he had thought would never reveal itself to him again and yet here he was experiencing the beginning of something he recognized as being real. He feared that, if it evaporated, he would no longer touch and be connected to such moments again.

The boat effortlessly worked its passage through the water, which graduated into a calm and gentle surface as they neared the shore.

They ate lunch, peppers stuffed with rice, baked potato, and salad, accompanied by cold bottled water in the welcoming shade of a small restaurant. Their return to Argassi saw them journey down the coastline. Like a lover's charm, he found himself intoxicated within a second love affair.

A suffuse flush of turquoise populated vast areas of the sea hugging the headlands of the twisting coast. He gazed, fascinated, at the pockets of vegetation that painted dark patches beneath the brilliantly clear water. Beyond this, he was drawn to the horizon that drew a straight line below an azure sky. Further inland, olive groves shared a brown and emerald carpet of shrubs with sunburnt grass, an excessive ornament of Mother Nature's tablecloth, he mused. He picked out the evergreen cypress tree that sporadically pin pricked the plain, slender and tall, a giant within the landscape, its overlapping green leaves reminding him of fish scales. White snowy sand and rock emitted a radiant glow while to the south, set against a backdrop of lavishly fertile hills, Louis saw the seaside resort of Alykes where once salt lakes supplied the island with a constant supply of salt. The beauty of the region touched a deep part of him; the effect was profound. He felt spellbound, caught within a web of splendour.

They travelled further, down the backbone of the island, through somnolent villages, whose only inhabitants seemed to be emaciated cats and languorous dogs. Passing through one particular village, Maria drew their attention to a vacant space between two houses and a visible brown tide-mark imprinted upon the walls of the buildings. She explained that Zakynthos can be prone to torrential downpours. It was this village's unfortunate locality, perched on the side of a hill, that caused the usual baked and dry earth to transform into a steadily flowing river, like volcanic lava. An exorbitant avalanche of sliding mud consumed the streets and buildings, its force and energy engulfing and destroying an entire building, as if it were a child's doll house.

Soon the hotels and apartments of Kalamaki became prominent features as the coach neared the outskirts of the resort. They crossed the island to the east, skirting Zakynthos town, the short drive along the coast bringing their day of travel to an end.

As they neared the periphery of Argassi, Louis was astonished to find a sense of coming home surge through him. He had barely set foot on the soil, yet here, in what was once a small and irrelevant fishing village, he knew it would always remain within him, like a tattoo ingrained upon his skin. Such a connection was immense and immeasurable and Louis knew that, now he had tasted the root of this attraction, whenever the time came to leave, he would be forever homesick.

Revelations Part 1

Two 'Gentlemen'

The weeks passed quickly. Louis did not go on another trip with Maria. Instead, he fell into the routine of exploring the now familiar streets and lanes of the capital, eating lunch at a taverna, or reading a newspaper or book on the balcony of his room. Louis bought a Nikon camera, one with a zoom lens. He hired a car and travelled the island, capturing the landscape, the ever-evolving sea and rustic villages. Louis took portraits of the locals, young and old, their stories imprinted on their features and reflected in the light of their eyes. Wherever he went, the face of the young girl in the fading photograph at the cemetery accompanied him. In a strange way, he felt that in his photographs he was showing her the world as it was now, the island she had left.

When Maria was not working, they submerged themselves in each other's company, eating lunch at a sea-front restaurant and taking long walks in the afternoon sun. During these times his camera knew only her face, her gesture, her image. He told Maria of the places he discovered, the people he met and the extraordinary light reflected from the landscape.

He felt a contentment descend upon him. It first unfolded when he took photographs of the newborn sky or the sun melting into the sea, engulfed by the horizon. It was at its strongest when Marie was framed in his lens. He found an immense pleasure in capturing a specific light or draping shadow. He even managed a few clandestine shots of Anna tending to her garden.

One night, as Louis was dining alone at The Green Frog, an old man asked, in broken English, if he and his friend could join him. As there were still a few vacant tables, Louis thought the approach unconventional however, not wanting to seem inhospitable, he accepted the request.

'My name is Denis, my friend is Marios, he not speak English very well. I have a farm, lots of land, I grow olives and grapes. Lots of wine. This is Marios' shop.' He pointed to the mini supermarket next to the restaurant. 'He has many more,' Marios smiled shyly at the mention of his name.

'My name is Louis.'

They all smiled in unison.

A waitress came and took their order. 'They eat here every Friday night and always invite themselves to the table of a family or a couple.'

'They must have taken pity on me then.'

'Denis told me you looked lonely, and he thought you needed the company.'

'Good food.' Denis gestured to the other tables. 'To enjoy, you need to have the company of others and... oh what is the word.'

'Good conversation?'

Denis looked puzzled.

'To talk.'

'Ah yes, with people, like Marios and me.' Denis smiled, animated by a radiance that defied his years. Silver wild hair swept over his forehead, a thick correspondent moustache and deep-set eyes complemented the grandfather-like presence he emitted. Marios was smaller, timid and content to let Denis speak for them both.

Their respective meals arrived and, as the plates were laid on the table Louis discovered that Denis had bought him a beer.

'I'll buy the next one,' Louis offered.

Denis smiled. 'And I the next.'

During the meal, Denis produced a small writing pad from his breast pocket.

'Louis, you write your name and where you stay in my book. I have many names in my book.'

Denis handed the small pad and a pen to Louis, who wrote his name and address below the previous entry which he noted was from Stockholm.

'You come to my farm and try my wine Louis, very nice. You stay as long as you want. I cook lamb with garlic, you like?'

'It sounds delicious.'

Marios continued to smile. It was a routine he had witnessed on countless occasions.

Louis warmed to the gentle and genuine companionship he shared with the two gentlemen and then Denis' veritable qualities were elevated even further when, translated through the waitress, he proclaimed that it would please him if Louis accepted a small gift. His humble and sincere gesture left Louis feeling that he wished he could converse with Denis in Greek and express his gratitude in reciprocal conversation. The opportunity had shown itself and he was incapable of sharing fully its offer of communion. All around him people spoke English to various degrees, yet he was a visitor to this country and he was ignorant of its language.

In the mini market next to the restaurant, Denis bought Louis delicatessens. Denis smiled through his prominent moustache; his eyes sparkled and danced like the golden sun's rays as they skirt the Ionian. Louis thanked Denis and added that he wished he could speak Greek to convey the sentiments properly. Denis listened intently before affectionately patting Louis on the back. Returning to their table, Louis repaid Denis' gesture by buying another round of drinks.

'I teach you Greek Louis, 'Stin igia mas.'

'Stin igia mas, what does it mean?'

'To our health.' Denis beamed.

'Stin igia mas.' Louis smiled, raising his glass.

Denis and Marios raised their glasses, just as another round of drinks arrived accompanied by a portion of garlic mushrooms. Denis gestured with his hand. 'For you.' he grinned.

'You shouldn't have. I'm full.' Louis sighed.

Louis forced a few mushrooms into his mouth, then pushed the plate towards Denis.

'We can share.' Although politeness left him obliged to offer them his plate, he was more than glad to do so as his stomach groaned and stretched. There was no hint of hesitation as Marios and Denis polished off the rest of the mushrooms with a feverish gusto, dipping slabs of crusty bread into the residue of the garlic oil, soaking it up like sponges. Denis wiped his chin with a napkin and tipped the last of his beer over his throat.

'It is time for us to go Louis.' Denis took out a bundle of notes from his wallet. 'This will pay for the meal.'

'No, no, you don't have to do that.'

'Thank you for your company Louis, the money is nothing.' He waved his hand dismissively. 'You have made Marios and me happy.' They both stood slowly, Denis more stiffly than Marios. Louis shook their hands.

'You learn some Greek Louis for the next time.'

'I will.' Louis smiled apologetically and obliged him. Denis ushered Marios onto the pavement. They walked off into the night, Denis turned and waved and, through his thick moustache, Louis saw a broad smile. Back in his room, he thought about Denis and Marios, the meal they had shared and how surreal the experience now felt. He had dined with two people he had never met before, yet it felt natural. Even in the silences that often fell over the table it did not feel awkward, there was no rush to fill the gap with inarticulate conversation. Denis filled the space between them with his lingering smile.

He fell into bed. A thought travelled through him. 'You don't know a country until you can speak its language.'

The moon cast a silver light over a horizontal crack in the wall and he fell asleep instantly.

Disclosures

A Tradition

An administration of light seeped into the garden as Louis surveyed the copious amount of food that covered the table. Chicken baked with herbs, potatoes, thyme and sage meatballs and courgettes sprinkled with olive oil. A giant salad bowl erupted in colour, bread, fruit and bottles of wine complemented what seemed to Louis a banquet, rather than a Sunday lunch.

He had met Maria's mother, Clare, in the kitchen. Maria introduced him to her and he was amazed to hear her speak in unbroken English, her voice centred and grounded.

'Your English is really good,' Louis said.

'Thank you. That's because I'm not Greek.'

Louis' eyebrows rose, he felt embarrassed. 'Oh, Maria kept that quiet. I just assumed you would be.'

Maria laughed lightly. 'I wanted to see your reaction.'

'I've lived most of my life in Greece,' Clare said. 'My father worked for a shipping company that was based in Athens. I did all of my schooling in Athens. My mother and father were Irish.'

'Ah, that explains the accent, although it is soft.'

'Yes, it's not entirely left me.'

Louis helped Maria, her brother Stelios and his wife, Katrina, manoeuvre the heavy wooden table from the kitchen to the garden. Clare surveyed the removal, like a foreman, instructing them to be careful not to mark the walls, as they tipped the table onto its side and cautiously glided it through the doorway.

'We need a smaller table,' Stelios grunted. 'In fact, you should buy a garden table. I'll even give you the money for it.'

'Stelios!' Clare scolded him as if she was addressing a child. 'This table seeps with your family's history. As you know very well, it's been a family tradition to eat out in the garden on this table since your father was a child. Did you hear your father or grandfather complain when they took it out into the garden? Well?'

'They never suffered from a back complaint,' Stelios muttered.

'They were real Greek men.' Katrina laughed.

'I didn't hear you complain last night.' Stelios grinned.

'Stelios,' Katrina protested, rolling her eyes.

'You'll be giving Louis a bad impression of us all. Keep that talk in the bedroom... and watch that wall,' Clare remonstrated.

'But he can't speak Greek. He doesn't know what I've just said,' Stelios said indignantly.

'In that case, we'll all speak English. Louis is our guest, let us show him some manners.' Clare scooped up one of her grandchildren in her arms. 'Your daddy needs his mouth washed out with soap.' She smiled.

Michalis surveyed Louis in a shy, yet, determined manner. Louis smiled in return. Stelios filled the glasses with wine. Katrina clapped her hands and distracted the persistent cats that were bowled over into a frenzied stupor by the tempting aromas that consumed the air.

Clare lowered herself into her chair. 'Let's eat before it all gets cold.' She flapped her napkin and pressed it onto her lap.

The children, Isabella and Nicos, stared at Louis, Katrina had told them that Maria had invited her special friend to lunch and they were to be nice to him. They spoke to each other in mumbled voices, absorbing the fact that a foreign stranger sat at the table. Louis raised his eyebrows, meeting their gaze, enjoying their attention as it deflected his otherwise nervous disposition.

'A toast,' Stelios pronounced, raising his glass towards Louis. 'May your time in Zakynthos bring you all that your heart desires.' Stelios grinned widely. 'May you find what you are looking for and, if you have found it already, cherish it forever.'

Louis flushed at the unsuspecting attention directed towards him. He moved nervously in his chair and then under the table out of view he felt Maria's hand upon his, she squeezed it lightly for fortification.

They all raised their glasses and sipped the wine, except Stelios who drained half his glass. The children shuffled in their seats, their eyes alert, confronted with so much food they wrestled with the temptation to eat. Katrina caught their longing gaze; she nodded and curled her lips. With permission granted, they scooped up their forks and knives and ate, purposefully swallowing the food as if each mouthful was their last.

'Maria tells me you are from Edinburgh,' Clare enquired, raising a glass to her lips.

'Yes.' Louis wiped his mouth with a napkin. 'I am.'

He found it odd, hearing the soft Irish tint emanate from her voice, his mind's eye had not visualized that image but rather the one Clare projected when she spoke Greek. Louis was conscious that, in a strange way, this made him perceive her as two different people.

'A beautiful city I'm told. Does your family still live there?'

'Yes, they do.'

'The Athens of the North,' she suggested.

'It certainly has some beautiful buildings.'

'Maria also told me your mother is Irish too, how extraordinary. Which part of Ireland does she belong to?' Clare asked curiously.

'County Mayo.'

'Ah, my parents were originally from Dublin but, because of my father's work, we moved around a lot. I was seven when we came to Athen. I don't remember much before that.'

'Have you been back to Dublin?' Louis asked.

'No. I've been too busy with this lot. Maybe someday but, to tell you the truth, I've never really considered it. I've lived here most of my life. The memories I have of my childhood are all about growing up in Athens, not Dublin. I'm as Greek as my children.' Clare smiled directly at him and then a silence fell as they concentrated on eating.

Louis could hear a bird, somewhere in the garden, as the soft whisper of a breeze brushed the tree above them. He poured himself a glass of water and asked Maria if she would like some. He was grateful for the parasol that offered a refuge from the sun, although he found the heat a comfort, almost therapeutic.

Clare looked up from her lunch. 'How did you find the mainland? I hear you've been travelling a lot.'

'It was beautiful, but I preferred to be away from the cities. Athens was noisy and impersonal. It has the history and monuments, but I felt an attraction to the countryside, the villages, and the sea. This is the first island I've been to. I initially intended to visit Cephalonia, but here I am.'

'There are hundreds of islands all over Greece each with their own personality and character. I'm sure you will find that with Zakynthos too.'

'Do you plan to visit any more islands?' Stelios asked.

'I don't know. Maybe.' He faltered. He was thrown for a moment. The way he chose to answer was important. 'I'm sure Maria has not shown me all that there is to see in Zakynthos.'

Maria smiled encouragingly. 'The beaches are next.'

Michalis signed with his hands, the corners of his mouth lifting.

'You can only come if you keep your fishing rod at home,' Maria replied.

Michalis frowned. His hands moved again forming shapes and flicked gestures.

'What did he say?' Louis asked.

'I think it's safe to say he'll not be coming with us.' Maria grinned.

'The reason you have found yourself in Greece is a sad one Louis.' There was a short pause. Maria must have told Clare but then again why shouldn't she? Louis' mind stumbled from word to word but none were forthcoming.

Clare added, 'I'm sorry to hear of your loss. The worst thing about living is losing those we have loved, even those who have hurt us.' There was a genuine sense of affection in her words.

Louis swallowed. He nodded in acknowledgment and, for the second time, he felt uncomfortable, yet, he knew this was not Clare's intention. He felt droplets of perspiration seeping from his brow.

'The food is lovely.'

A smile dressed Clare's face. 'I don't mean to cause you any distress. It's hard enough coming to a strange country and finding yourself at the table of a family you've never met before.' She said this as if contemplating a distant memory and then she remarked reassuringly. 'I know how that feels Louis. I sat at this very table many years ago in similar circumstances. Just relax and be you.' Her words wrapped around him like a warm coat.

He caught Maria's gaze and her warm smile. As Clare had instructed, they all spoke in English for the remainder of the meal, except the children. Once their appetites were diminished and satisfied, they threw pieces of chicken to the cats that devoured these gifts with conviction.

Isabella turned to her mother, her face lit up. 'When I went to bed last night I prayed for the sun to shine all day on a cloudless sky so we could have lunch in the garden and my prayer has been answered.'

Katrina smiled at her daughter, placing a hand on her head.

'That was stupid, it's always sunny in the summer. Any way you also said you hoped Maria's boyfriend looked like David Beckham.' Nicos laughed, his eyes alight with mischief as if he had just disclosed some guarded secret.

The adults broke into spontaneous laughter. A triumphant look crossed Nicos' face.

'I did not,' Isabella yelled, affronted by the unwelcome attention. She pushed her brother in the chest, toppling him from his chair onto the cats who dispersed with shrieks of alarm. It was Isabella turn to look triumphant as Nicos glared and pleaded with his mother to reprimand his sister.

'What's going on?' Louis asked as he surveyed the solemn Nicos.

'It seems that Isabella was expecting David Beckham for lunch.' Maria laughed.

'Ah, I see. I take it she's disappointed in me.' He supplemented the thought with another. He leaned towards her. 'I hope your mother's not.'

Maria touched his arm. 'Of course, she is not, she likes you,' she whispered reassuringly close to his ear, sensing consternation blossoming in his voice.

'More wine?' Stelios boomed.

Maria eyed him suspiciously. 'Are you trying to get Louis drunk?'

'He's from Scotland; surely another glass won't do him any harm.'

'Don't let my nationality fool you; we can't all hold our drink.'

'Not unlike some of us,' Maria imparted sarcastically, frowning at Stelios.

Louis lifted his glass. 'One more won't harm me,' he said, appeasing the moment.

When lunch was over, Stelios invited Louis to sit with him under the shade of a large tree that dominated the garden. Sitting on a wooden bench they observed the women clear the table. In an industrious flurry of activity, they disappeared into the kitchen with crockery and cutlery only to return again, like a human production line.

Whilst watching their labour, Louis could not help but feel guilty as he had not offered to help in the clearing up, yet, he was aware of the relaxed and contented Stelios who seemed oblivious to the women's work. Maybe Greek women were indeed the backbone of society, while their men drank coffee and smoked all day, he considered.

Stelios offered Louis a cigarette, confirming his theory. Louis politely refused.

'It's good you don't smoke, Louis, I've been trying to give it up for years and, as you can see, without much success.' Stelios leaned against the tree and blew smoke above their heads. House sparrows swooped through the air, darting down into the garden, like feathered missiles.

'How do you earn your living Louis?' Stelios asked.

'I'm an architect.'

'Ah, a good profession. Will you have to return home soon?' he asked sceptically.

'Maybe.' Louis shrugged. 'I'd love to stay indefinitely, especially now.'

'You must have an understanding boss.'

'We have an arrangement.'

Stelios nodded. The thought of returning to Edinburgh made Louis' stomach sink.

'An architect,' Stelios repeated, drawing on his cigarette. 'We have several of them on the island. I know most of them personally. I'm a building contractor you see, so if you are ever looking for a job I could put in a good word for you. In fact, these days, business could not be better. My company specialises in traditional houses. We build in the traditional Greek style and there are many people from Britain who come here to buy or have their houses built for them.'

Louis watched as the women continued to clear the table. He noticed how they talked continually without drawing breath, their words punctuated by animated gestures, behaviour he had now become used too, since his arrival in Greece. He considered it be as natural as the blues of the sky, the aquamarine of the sea and the verdant rich trees. He noticed that his pangs of guilt had abandoned him, subsiding as these thoughts presented themselves.

'I've seen a change in Maria in the short time that she has known you Louis... you're making her happy.' It was spoken as an observation, rather than a question.

Louis sipped the tepid wine. 'And I have never felt happier,' he said frankly, taken aback by his forthright acknowledgement.

Stelios patted him on the shoulder. 'That my friend is the easy part. Staying happy, now that's a different matter. We must all work at that.'

Stelios reached for the bottle of wine he had brought from the table and added. 'Let me fill your glass. You see Louis, family is everything. If we have disagreements or fall out we get together, we eat a meal, drink some wine, drink some more wine, eat some more until we are full and talk, always talking, until we have reached an agreement or come to a compromise and then everyone is happy again. Who needs therapists?' He drank from his glass, pleased with himself.

'You like the wine, Louis?'

'Yes, it has a fruity dark taste. I like that.'

'It's made here in Zakynthos. Does that surprise you, Louis? I love this wine and do you know why? Because it's part of my island, grown from the very soil we stand upon. I love this island. I will never leave here. You have left your country Louis under unimaginable circumstances, I know, but there will be a time when you will have to return and I am worried what the implication might be for Maria. You understand Louis?'

In the distance, Louis was conscious of a plume of smoke that curved towards the sky.

'I know at some point whenever that will be, I'll have to return to Edinburgh, but the person I love does not live there.' Louis eased himself back against the bench, a flowering of emotion flickered in his stomach. 'I love your sister Stelios,' he said boldly, satisfied that he had eventually told someone.

Inside, he felt liberated. His disclosure had come as a welcome release.

Stelios offered a smile. 'Your words confirm what everyone can see my friend.'

A Dying Man in the Garden

The kitchen offered a refuge from the heat of the boiling sun. The table had been moved back to its commanding position on the rustic tiled floor. A powder blue vase exploded in coloured flowers, picked from the garden by Clare and placed on the table the moment it arrived back in the kitchen. A ceramic bowl containing oranges and lemons, freshly plucked from the small orchard at the bottom of the garden, was placed at the other end of the table.

'Some coffee I think,' Clare said.

Louis hoped the caffeine would dull the lethargic effect of the wine. Clare poured the coffee into five cups, where steam rose, like smoke from chimney rows. Maria lifted two cups and offered one to Louis. He smiled, his eyes searching her face, its features now branded and burned into his memory.

They sat at the table, the three of them. Louis rubbed a finger over the patterned grain.

Stelios, Katrina, Michalis and the children remained in the garden. Louis could hear their voices radiate into the kitchen and, within their laughter and resonance of play he detected tones of security, familiarity. Quite suddenly, he ached to hear his mother's voice again.

Clare brought the cup to her lips and blew on the surface of the coffee. Her hair fell onto her shoulders in thick natural waves. Louis noted her skin emanated a polished shine defying her years. Upon the wall behind her, a gold leaf frame encased an inscription written in English that read, '*This is my house, This is my home, This is where I raised my family, This is where I belong.*'

'I hope your time here will be a happy one.'

'I'm sure it will be. The island is beautiful, just like your daughter.'

'Louis,' Maria protested.

'Leave him be, Maria,' Clare said dismissively. 'I admire a man who is not afraid to speak his mind... I hear you once trained for the priesthood.'

'Yes, that's true, a long time ago. It feels as if it were in another life.'

'I can relate to that,' Clare said, flicking a strand of hair behind her ear. 'Before I met Maria's father, I was just another young girl in Athens and look at me now.' She gestured with opened palms. 'I am more Greek than most of the young men and women who were born here, they all want to leave. I adopted the religion and now my children only go to church at Christmas or Easter, or at a friend's Christening or wedding.' She paused. 'There are more empty churches than full ones.'

'It's the same in Scotland.' Louis shrugged.

He drank from the cup, warming to Clare and her coffee which tasted strong and bitter.

'When I was younger, it was different.'

'Mum I don't think Louis wants to hear about that,' Maria remonstrated.

'No it's fine, honestly, I'd love to hear about it.' Louis leaned forward.

'In those days, we didn't have mobile phones and not everyone had a television. We had to make conversation with one another, we communicated with the person standing next to us. Our entertainment was a night out at the local dance hall, dancing to a big band, real music. We girls never got drunk; for one thing, we didn't have the money.'

Maria smiled at Louis who was smiling broadly, enjoying the moment.

'When I met Peiros, Maria's father, he was a young man in the Greek merchant navy. We met on a Friday night at the dancing. Peiros and some of the younger lads from his ship were on shore leave. He was the most courteous man I had met, not like the young men from Athens who were usually drunk by the time they got to the dance hall. We talked most of the night and did very little dancing. He spoke good English too, but we spoke in Greek. I found out later he had two left feet, so it suited him to talk. He offered to walk me home. I wasn't happy with that as it would take him out of his way, so we came to a compromise which was, he hailed me a taxi and insisted on paying my fare. I learnt the next day he had been beaten up by drunken Dockers and landed up in the hospital. In those days, I was a nurse and next morning I was on an early shift. Well, you can imagine my surprise, when I saw Peiros lying in bed in the ward. Whenever I was on shift, he would tell me stories about Zakynthos; it was a million miles away from busy and crowded Athens. He was in the hospital for four weeks and, on the day he was due to leave he asked me to marry him, after only four weeks, could you believe it? He was different, dark and handsome and easy to talk to. Each day, I hurried into work and asked to work longer hours just so I could be near him. The others were jealous, but I didn't care. Even the matron eventually had words with me. I told Peiros I would only marry him if he gave up his job sailing around the world and settled down in Zakynthos. I had fallen in love with him and his stories of Zakynthos. My parents didn't approve, but they were returning to Ireland as by that time, my father was about to retire. Athens was my home, and I had a reason to stay. We married in Zakynthos, three months after our first meeting. I never saw my parents again; they returned to Ireland and died in a car crash a year later.'

Louis visualised the young bride on her wedding day on an island she had never seen, but had fallen in love with through the stories of her new husband.

The sound of laughter and play stopped abruptly as a commotion filtered into the kitchen from the garden. Stelios' voice was heard, it was insistent and commanding. Clare gazed at Maria, the contours of her face hinting at the panic in her voice as her expression froze and she muttered, 'Michalis.'

When they reached the garden Michalis was sprawled on the ground his arms and legs curved into a shape like a letter 'C.' Michalis' eyes stared, unseeing, as if focused on an empty void, the life and sparkle sucked from them. Louis was aware that both arms and legs were rigid, as muscles extended. Michalis' body jerked in a riot of spasms, rapidly contracting and relaxing in unrelenting waves that overwhelmed every living tissue and cell in his body. A

deep inhuman moan escaped him where a slither of saliva dripped from the corner of his mouth and a small stream glistened and curved onto his chin.
Stelios knelt and supported Michalis' head with his arms.

'He will be fine,' he said.

Louis stood hesitantly. 'What's happened?'

'He's had a seizure,' Maria said, as she knelt beside Michalis and gently stroked his hair.

Louis was shocked by the undignified sight of Michalis convulsing as he lay in the garden. A profound calmness echoed from those around Michalis, as if there was something of routine about the unsystematic jerking of the body.

Maria glanced at Louis and recognised his cloud of incomprehension. 'Michalis has had an epileptic seizure, it will pass soon, don't worry. He'll be fine, a little tired but fine.'

Louis could do nothing but nod his head and he was amazed at how accepting the children were in their detachment of the situation. Louis thought Michalis looked like a dying man in the garden.

The seizure lasted a minute, but it seemed an eternity to Louis. A dark ominous stain covered Michalis' groin.

'Michalis has had epilepsy since he was a young child,' Maria explained.

'I've never seen anything like that before,' Louis said, swallowing hard.

Maria got up from her kneeling position. 'Help us take Michalis to his room. He'll be tired and need to rest.'

'Yes of course,' Louis said, relieved that finally, he could be of some use, instead of an onlooker dwelling upon his own anxiety. They gently guided the limp and relaxed Michalis to his room and laid him on the bed.

Louis felt the weight of guilt and shame roll over him.

'There was nothing you could do. We've lived with this most of Michalis' life. When he experienced his first seizure, I remember being scared and the feeling of being useless was overwhelming. All we can do is make sure he's comfortable until he comes out of the seizure. His medication keeps him stable but there are times, like today for example, when it makes no difference.'

They moved through the house in silence. In the kitchen, Clare sat at the table, in between the children who were drawing with crayons on white sheets of paper. She smiled as they entered the room.

'He's sleeping now,' Maria said.

'Good,' Clare said, satisfied. 'Now Louis come and sit down and tell me about yourself.'

'What would you like me to tell you?' Louis asked apprehensively.

'As much as you like really, whatever makes you comfortable.'

He slid a chair across the tiled floor to allow Maria to sit before he did so himself. Clare had tied her hair back from her face and, for the first time that day, Louis noticed that she wore very little makeup. Her cheeks were peppered with tiny flecks of freckles.

'Well.' Louis cleared his throat feeling nervous at the sudden attention afforded him. 'My father was Italian, he is dead now and my mother, as you know, is Irish. I have two brothers and a sister. My father owned a cafe and ice cream parlour in a part of Edinburgh called Cannonmill. I had a typical Scottish upbringing. During the school holidays, we went to Italy, to the village my father's family came from. I went to Edinburgh University and then, after gaining my degree, I started working as an architect. Out of the blue, I suddenly experienced yearnings to become a priest. I carried this around with me until, one day, it just felt like the right decision to make. When I finally made the decision, a great weight seemed to lift from me as if I had been rehabilitated; suddenly I was happy. I went to Rome, I was content with life. It had a purpose and meaning and then I met Emma and that all changed. The calmness that consumed me unexpectedly turned into a turbulent storm and ,as a result, after a lot of deliberation, I left the priesthood and began a new life in Edinburgh with Emma. I returned to architecture, finding a good job. Life was good. We had a close group of friends and I thought we loved each other. That's unfair, we did, but it changed. She loved me, but she was not in love with me and well, you know how it ended. It is what it is. If I am to be honest, I came to Greece to escape it all and I suppose I thought by coming here I would at some point make sense of what had happened. I wanted to escape the bubble and not be eaten up by bitterness or hate. It was easy to hate, but not to forgive. I have a lot of regrets.'

Maria lowered her eyes and stirred in her chair. Louis took a deep breath. Clare had held his gaze throughout. He smiled nervously. He had said too much, he thought, but it had come easily to him. His mouth felt dry and he could taste stale coffee on his breath. Maria's eyes were fixed on Louis. Regret tugged at him.

'It must have been hard for you Louis. I admire your strength of character and compassion.'

'Compassion,' Louis said puzzled.

'Why, of course, it colours your words, you could have spoken of your hurt, of resentment, of vengeance even, but you mentioned neither. There's a sense of reconciliation about you when you speak. It's hard to forgive a person who has turned your world upside down. We're not all capable of that.'

'I'm not sure if forgiveness is the right word. Time helps. It makes it easier, somehow.'

Louis now realised that his mind's constant occupation with Emma was receding. She did not accompany him throughout his day like before. He was aware her image was not always possible to sustain. Sometimes he had to concentrate to summon her face with the vivid clarity he once found easy. Like a weakening light, her mouth and eyes were no longer permanent features that his mind's eye pored over. He had not abandoned her; she had been a physical presence in his life that was now taking its place in his past. There was a new awakening in him; its birth had dominated him. He felt alive again by its existence. It was a flower that had still to bloom and he felt contented to be a part of its growth and rapture.

'We're going for a walk.'

Maria surprised Louis with her statement. She touched his arm as she always did and rose from her chair. Clare watched them and smiled, before turning her attention to the children.

Doubt and Affirmation

Louis walked with Maria through the garden and was reminded of the disturbing image of Michalis sprawled upon the ground, jerking as if his arms and legs were dislocated from his body, his marbled eyes not belonging to the living. As Louis walked his ears were still infected by the inhuman and low growling sound that emanated from Michalis' throat, like an angry dog. He looked upwards to the trees towering towards the lacquered blue sky.

    Maria was telling him how, as a child; she would play amongst these trees. She would imagine that she was a princess in an enchanted forest, being held prisoner by an evil king, and she would always be rescued by a handsome prince. It was here that she cut herself above her lip, leaving the small scar. She was taken to the doctor and her mother had to persuade her to come out from under the table with the promise of sweets, so that the doctor could administer stitches.

    Louis asked about the age gap between Maria and Stelios. Maria explained that after Stelios was born, Clare had many miscarriages and it was viewed as a blessing when five years later, two came along at once.

    Louis focused on her voice and noticed how it amplified as they walked amongst the trees that stood, like onlookers in a crowd. When there were silences between them, the calls of birds travelled around them, a therapeutic melody that filtered through the air and settled upon him, like falling soft snow. Their feet disturbed a fine thin carpet of pine needles and from this covering, a sweet odour rose around them, perfume from nature's larder he thought, as the cicadas' rhythmic pulse followed their progress.

    Louis was struck by the trees, crowned with dark green leaves, shimmering silver in the sun, imposing a striking contrast upon a limitless blue sky. A lizard scurried under his foot and disappeared over the crest of a rock.

    Maria allowed Louis' hand to rest on the base of her back. An uplifting burst of pleasure emerged inside him, a hot flickering sensation in his chest that dislocated him from time whenever he touched her.

Their walk took them to a small clearing. By now it was late afternoon. They sat on a flat rock and rested, a soft breeze washed in the trees behind them, like whispers. Maria pulled her knees to her chest and wrapped her arms around them. They looked out towards the sea. The sun broke the covering of a watery cloud and splayed shafts of light that flashed turquoise and azure from the sea below them. The sky burst in crimson and orange, like flames licking solitary clouds from a fire that scorched the horizon.

'Look over there. That's Mount Skopos and down there is Argassi,' Maria said as if making light conversation but behind her words, there was edginess, a slight rasp. Louis could hear it.

He turned and looked at her as she stared out to sea, her face now a pensive mask. Maria placed a finger on her lip, biting the bottom one as if considering a decision. He detected an uneasiness about her, an impatience that manifested in her pulling at her dress and fingering her bracelet.

He brushed a few stray strands of hair from her face.

'Are you all right? Tell me what you're thinking?'

He put his hand in hers and pressed it slightly. She hesitated.

'What's going to become of us Louis? Are we just indulging ourselves, like some holiday romance. How can this last? Your time here has its limits.'

'What do you mean?' he murmured solicitously.

'How long can this last between us, Louis?' She sighed, turning to face him her eyes wide, like a deer in glaring headlights.

'As long as we both want it to.'

She brushed her fingers through her hair. 'But you've another life, a life I know nothing of. It's not a part of me... of us... it's a life you can return to.'

'Stop Maria,' he said, he brushed her cheek with the back of his finger, an attempt to deflect this unwelcomed inquisition.

'Yes I had a life before I met you, as you had, but our

meeting has changed that... forever.' His voice rose. She withdrew her hand.

There was a long silence between them, an ocean of time that burned into Louis.

'Today when you spoke about your life with Emma, I felt vulnerable... afraid. You had no choice in the decision that was made, you had no idea what was going on. Emma was the one who ended it, not you. You loved her. When I was living away from home, I was the one who ended that relationship, I was in control of that decision. If Emma hadn't had an affair, you would still be with her in Edinburgh, she would be alive and you would still be in love with her. Today, in the kitchen, when you spoke about Emma, I doubted you Louis, your intentions, concerning us, this arrangement we have, how can it be permanent?This is not your home.' She looked at the sea again. 'You'll soon return to your job, your family and friends.' She turned from the sea and glared at him, her eyes wide and fearful. 'And if Emma was still alive,' she said, slicing the air between them. 'Tell me the truth Louis, Would you feel different about us? Would there even be an us? Why is it so difficult? Why does it have to be so complicated? You still love her Louis.'

'Maria.' He sighed in exasperation, his mouth dry with anxiety. Emma's name emanating from Maria burned his chest; intrusively it seized him, like an unsuspecting mugger. A heavy dull weight encroached upon him; the feeling shrouded him, clouding his mind. Maria stared at Louis, her eyes scanned his face, searching for an answer and, when it came, he took her hand, the physical contact eradicating Emma from his mind.

'When I left Scotland, I thought she was still alive and I could have gone back at any time, but I had nothing to go back to. Then, when I learnt of her death, yes I mourned the loss of what could have been. Yes, I loved her but that was seized from me, it died long before she did. I was alone.' He brushed his hands through his hair. 'I was alone,' he repeated defensively. 'Her death only increased that loneliness. It was sometime after that that I decided I wasn't going to feel sorry for myself any longer. This is what matters to me Maria, being here with you, right now, seeing you laugh, and seeing you smile. Today meant so much to me, being with your family and knowing that they accept me for who I am. I don't feel alone anymore. When I awake in the morning, you're the first person who enters my thoughts. In such a short time, you've become so much a part of my life it scares me, but I want to feel scared and do you know why? Because you're the cause and I love you more than I have ever loved anything or anyone...'

Louis words were a declaration, easing a great weight from him. His eyes stung, glazed with the surge of tears; his throat ached. Louis' composure collapsed, folding in on itself; he had no control over his senses as an involuntary moan escaped him, so alien that he did not recognise it as his own.

Louis leant forward and they embraced, Maria buried her face into his neck and, as she inhaled, she thought of his scent seeping into her pores. She felt impaled by shame for her incongruous thoughts. Her defiance slipped from her.

'I'm so sorry Louis, please forgive me.' She sighed, her lips touching his skin.

'There are no barriers between us now,' he whispered.

Maria had not anticipated this reaction. She should not have pushed so far yet, she needed to satisfy any lingering doubt concerning his feelings for her. Her uncertainty had magnified her fears and an emotional investment as its foundation needed to be based on knowledge of trust and openness. Above all, she craved that security, even now to her shame. Maria had behaved selfishly, allowing her doubt to boil over. She needed to gain an insight into his feelings. Maria needed to know if those feelings collided with those that he may have harboured for Emma. And now, she felt none of the pangs of elation that came with his disclosure; she had intruded too far, she knew now. Maria loathed her actions, she would no longer accommodate any thoughts of Emma, she decided.

He pressed her against his body and it felt as if they had melted into each other. A rippling current spread deep within him, flowing through him, like the blood in his veins, even to the tips of his fingers. He pressed her harder, and the current became an ache. Something in his chest jumped inside him. She shrunk into him, now unwilling to venture or enquire any further on the matter of Emma. Louis' hand stroked her hair, and she was overwhelmed. Maria gulped air to fortify her resilience. A ball of emotion wrapped itself around her throat, like roots, as an audible sob jerked her shoulders. He placed his hand behind her head and pushed her towards him. Louis could taste the salt of her tears on his lips; a catalyst that awoke a passion within him that demanded more; a sense of unleashing gripped him. Locks of her hair curled between his fingers and he felt that if she were an ocean, he would dive into her and never break the surface.

A Thaw in Relations

Eventually, Anna's indifference towards Louis began a process of melting. Her thaw materialised in a neighbourly gesture, when she offered Louis an old refrigerator that had gathered dust during its forced exile and retirement in a lower floor apartment. Louis was grateful for this unsuspecting gift, imagining the luxury of commanding at his disposal cold beer, water, cheese and milk. He could buy a kettle, he thought, as he struggled up the steps with the refrigerator's awkward bulk, progressing towards his room.

Further evidence of Anna's softening displayed itself when one particular morning she invited Louis to join her for breakfast on the veranda. Anna justified this offer by stating there was no benefit to be gained from Louis descending into the village each morning to buy breakfast when she always made enough for two, and anyhow, it was a sin to waste so much food, she told him.

Whatever her reason, Louis was appreciative as it allowed him to save money each day whilst heightening his spirits knowing that Anna's hard edge towards him was subsiding, like an ebbing tide. It became apparent that during these meetings, Anna was glad of the company and Louis was content to carry out this morning ritual which joined them favourably together whilst serving both agendas.

One morning, Anna indulged Louis in a full English breakfast before she confessed that it was good to have a man around the house once more. Louis delighted in her revelation, as it coated him with a sense of purpose and usefulness. The void that had been mined into the deepest recess of his being was beginning to fill each day he spent on the island.

There existed an element of symbolic dependency in the manner Anna laid out the table each morning and Louis too noticed a surge of responsibility he was unwilling to suppress. It made his attendance inevitable for, within its nature, it brought him a sense of security, a contented calmness that prepared him for each new day.

Initially, they conversed in minor details and fragments, gliding upon the surface of politeness, without extracting their inner thoughts. These were sealed within the vaults of their minds and guarded until the layers of self-consciousness were peeled back with the onset of familiarity, whereupon, their level of communication slid into a natural flow, where thoughts and feelings were unwrapped and divulged.

Anna spoke of her desire to visit her son. He had left several years previously to take up a post of teaching at a college in Athens. His return visits were infrequent and although he telephoned once a week, it had been six months since she last looked upon him in the flesh. This lack of physical contact perforated Anna with a great sadness that infected her, like an open wound upon her skin.

Instinctively, she offered excuses for her son's lack of urgency in his need to visit her by suggesting that he led a hectic life full of timetables, students and teaching. After all, he is the head of his department, she justified, injecting a final piece of evidence to seek solace in and support her son's long established investment in his new life, that seemed to Louis to be detrimental to a mother's longing.

The wash of Anna's heavy heart provoked a stinging guilt within Louis. He was reminded of his promise to keep in touch with Jez. When did Louis last phone his own mother? As Anna spoke, Louis noted an inextinguishable sound of melancholy in the deliberation of her words, reflecting the derelict composition of her small eyes that sat heavy in their sockets upon her rounded and flushed face.

At other times, Anna would glow with enthusiasm as she engaged in talking about her passion for her garden. She would describe each type of flower to the best of her broken English in animated vocabulary, like an art critic depicting the virtues of a painting. She pointed out, named and described for Louis' benefit Citrus, pink and white flowers, a creeping jungle that claimed the garden wall as their own, Marigold, hyacinth and roses that filled the garden with colour and intoxicating scents.

Her forehead crinkled into a frown as she recalled the splintered wood and flaking skin of varnish on the old bench in the centre of the olive trees. Louis smiled and offered to sand and varnish the wood and then, anticipating this transformation, Anna's expression became uplifted in the comforting curl of a smile.

Anna spoke with enthusiasm when recalling the family business that had seen each busy day merge effortlessly into another. When six months of the year brought an endless succession of holidaymakers to her apartments and how she finally struggled to maintain its day-to-day running after the death of her husband. She was now content with her quiet and solitary life, religiously tending to her garden, visiting friends such as Maria's mother, Clare or, on occasions, inviting them to her house. Anna was uncompromising in her refusal to sell the apartments, even though the offers would have left her well provided for. However, she was unable to detach herself from the memories they summoned. Two decades of work and routine were entrenched and soaked into their walls. Each metre of space held a precious memory of her husband and so, for Anna, it was a sacred place and to sell would defile his memory, something she could not bring herself to do.

Summer nights found her in the garden, reading in the glow of white pinpoints of light from a cluster of glass Moroccan lanterns that splayed a white brilliance amongst the branches of the olive trees, keeping at bay the impenetrable blackness. Under this illumination, Anna sat on the old bench immersed in a book, sipping an endless flow of coffee supplied from a silver flask.

On his part, Louis depicted the world he had once inhabited. Anna held on to every word and pored over each new image his voice formed for her, as if she had glimpsed a view of another world whose inhabitants intrigued her and whose landscapes captured and impressed themselves upon her, like a discovered oil painting.

She listened with intent to the events that led to his journey to Greece, from his days in Rome to his contentment in Edinburgh. She learnt of the deception, the pregnancy and Emma's death. His voice lightened when he spoke of his travels and a soft effervescence laced his words when he depicted his final day in Olympia as a sacred moment, an impulsive intuition which led him to Zakynthos.

Louis settled into a routine that accommodated his needs. Occasionally he took a trip to the village to buy food, provisions for Anna and, on these small excursions he became familiar with the shopkeepers and waiters and struck up casual conversations that were cordial and well-mannered affairs. He even took photographs of the waiters, who posed like male models and the shopkeepers, who were more stiffly reserved in their approach. His days on these occasions were satisfying, and each moment brought an intrinsic glow, the unfamiliar became the known and warmed him inside.

Revelations Part 2

Theology and the Socialist

Intricate shades covered the surface of the sea, a pulsating patchwork that moved and merged, constantly reinventing itself; alive and always in motion, a living mass.

 Louis observed this metamorphose from the taxi he hired in Argassi's main street, taking him along the coastal road towards the capital. A salmon tinge impregnated the early evening sky, as his eyes paused upon a white yacht becalmed. He, too ,surfed upon a wave of contentment. He accommodated thoughts of the view from his balcony, where every morning the sea took hold of him as he gazed, fascinated, as if seeing it for the first time. That morning ,the sun cast a silver brilliance along the sea's surface, where brush stroked waves added a splash of white amongst the distinguished company of a ferry, white yachts and a cruise ship hovering placidly on the pencilled line of the horizon. Clusters of wildflowers broke through an assorted green carpet of trees that dropped steadily into the arms of Argassi, whose terracotta roofs stretched towards the aquamarine sea, like giant stepping stones. The white sugar cubed appearance of Zakynthos town shimmered in the rising heat. Gliding further, his eyes rested upon the mountainous peaks of Cephalonia, steel slate against an azure sky and beyond, towards the coastline of the Peloponnese. Each new morning, Louis would contemplate that a part of heaven had fallen from the sky and blessed this part of the Ionian.

 He sat in the rear of the light blue Mercedes, brushing splayed cracks in the leather of the seat with a fingertip. Louis had paid little attention to the driver, but now noticed he was middle-aged and grey-haired with deep creases fanning from the back of his neck that descended behind the collar of his white shirt. A cross hung from the rearview mirror gently swaying like a lethargic pendulum.

 Louis asked if he could roll down the window.

 'Of course, my friend, it is a lovely evening,' the driver

grinned.

Tepid air immediately washed over Louis' face, like expelled breath and he sank into the seat, his body feeling heavy.

The driver regarded him through the rear mirror. 'You are Scottish. I can tell by your accent. It is softer, easier to understand than some of the Scottish people I have had in my taxi. Some are difficult to understand, they speak too fast. Nice people, very friendly.'

'Your English is good.'

'Thank you. I have Scottish friends. A family, they visited for many years. Before I drove taxis, I was a tourist guide, then, the big companies took over. I was too old for them; they want younger people. My Scottish friends, Stan and Isla, visited my family many times, then Stan had a stroke and could no longer travel, very sad. I have not seen them for many years.' He sighed. 'I planned to visit them in Scotland, my first time in your country, but my mother was ill. She was old so I could not go, just in case something happened to her. And she died in hospital, ninety years old.'

'I see. I suppose you were glad you didn't go.'

'It took her six weeks to die. I could have travelled to Scotland, but I am glad I did not go. This was a few years ago. I am saving up to take my wife on holiday to Manchester. I have a cousin there who has a restaurant. We are going to visit Edinburgh.'

'When are you going?'

'December.'

'Well, all I can say is, take lots of jumpers. You'll never have felt cold like it.'

'I am looking forward to seeing some snow. It can snow here too, but only in the mountains. It is very rare.'

'Do you get much time off?'

'I work six days a week, from seven in the morning to seven at night. I go home, have something to eat, drink a few beers and spend time with my family. I have four grandchildren.'

'It must be a long day, driving a taxi for twelve hours?'

'It is not too bad. I meet a lot of people, most are nice but not everyone. Yesterday I picked up three people. I did not recognise their language. One spoke a little English. Very bad man, nasty,' he screwed up his face. 'They had the windows rolled down and then he told me to roll down my window and turn my radio off.'

'What did you do?'

'I said this was my taxi, not his. I made them take their luggage out of the boot while I watched. Nasty people.'

Louis listened in fascination and soon they were entering the capital, passing a tall bell tower and a large church.

The driver pointed. 'That is the most important church in Zakynthos, dedicated to our patron saint, Dionysios. Is this your first time to Zakynthos?'

'Yes.'

'I hope you like it here.'

'I'm sure I will. It seems popular.'

'Yes, it is good for us. It brings jobs.'

'You must feel you are being invaded, especially in the summer.'

'It is a delicate balance, but a necessity.' He shrugged.

'The tourists are just part of a long line of invaders that Zakynthos has had. Her history is full of them, Spartans, Macedonians, Romans, and Venetians who built many fine buildings. We were known as the flower of Levant and the Florence of Greece. The French have invaded, even the British have tried to have a say and, of course, the Italians and Germans in the Second World War. So, you see, we are used to it, although most holiday makers are a lot friendlier.' He grinned.

Along a promenade, Louis' attention was snagged by bustling shops, cafes, and restaurants. He glimpsed early evening diners being waited on by attentive waiters. He caught their relaxed passive gestures and felt intrigued at the prospect of meeting Maria and the evening ahead. He saw fishing boats and two small naval vessels, one Greek, the other Italian, hugging the harbour wall. They stopped opposite Solomos Square, a large colonial square. Louis paid his fare and reminded the taxi driver to take lots of warm clothes when visiting Edinburgh.

He patted Louis on the shoulder. 'I won't forget, my friend. My wife will remind me a thousand times. I think she has packed a suitcase full of them already.'

The earthquake of 1953 destroyed and devastated virtually every building on the island, leaving the capital and villages resembling a war zone. Buildings and houses were reduced to rubble and shells. A programme of regeneration restored the capital too much of its Venetian splendor, and it was in the square, that Louis absorbed the grandeur and elegance of the opulent buildings. Louis discovered a museum and art gallery but, disappointingly, they were both closed. He consciously noted that the statue in the square was that of Dionysios Solomos, Zakynthos' famous poet, for it was there that Maria instructed him to meet her. Louis looked at his watch. He had an hour to spare. He found himself in St. Marcos square amongst early diners and those taking an evening stroll, contemplating the assortment of menus on display.

A simple looking church with a muted cream facade attracted his eye. Sandwiched between two buildings, a plaque announced it as the Roman Catholic Church of St. Marcos. Through the open wooden door, a tall man appeared, middle aged with a sweep of silver hair, combed back from his forehead, which he dabbed with a white handkerchief.

'Come on in and look around if you want, it's a bit cooler in here. It's getting warmer every day.' He smiled broadly, gesturing for Louis to enter. 'Did you know there are fourteen churches in the capital and you have just walked into the only Catholic Church on the island?'

The fact was surpassed by Louis' astonishment at hearing a distinctive southern Irish accent. Clare entered his mind.

He moved, as directed, into a small entrance where a large dark wooden cross dominated an otherwise sparse wall.

'Well then,' the man continued, placing his handkerchief into his trouser pocket. 'What do they call you then when you are home?'

'I'm Louis.'

'Well Louis, I'm John, and you are welcome to look around this humble little church of ours,' he gestured in a swaying motion with his hand. John wore a white short sleeved shirt and black trousers. His face was bleached red from the sun and beads of perspiration dotted his forehead, replacing those he had just dabbed. He drew Louis' attention to a notepad he held.

'I'm working on my sermon for this evening's mass. Mark's gospel… definitely my favourite. Did you know, Louis, that Mark was the first gospel to be written. The others came after him, second hand if you like. It's almost a firsthand account... it's the closest we will get to one.'

'I was surprised to see the sign outside. I didn't think there would a Catholic church in Zakynthos.'

'The original was destroyed in the earthquake and subsequent fire that ravaged the homes of the islanders. Many of the islanders went to the mainland and never returned. You can't blame them, I suppose. The church was rebuilt. Today, there are lots of people from the Philippines working in the hotels and restaurants. They make up the bulk of the congregation, along with the occasional tourist. There isn't a parish priest as such, one comes every month from the mainland and, since I was here on holiday with some friends, I offered to celebrate mass for the duration of my stay.'

They moved into the main body of the church. There was a silence between them as Louis took in the interior. The priest sensed his disappointment.

'I'm afraid she comes a poor second compared to the Orthodox churches in the town.'

Louis felt odd. In a country whose people exclusively follow the Greek Orthodox faith, he stood in a miniature microcosm of the Roman church, sharing the company of another archetypical image of Catholicism, an Irish priest. No one would believe me, he thought.

'Tell me, Louis,' John said, narrowing his eyes inquisitively. 'When you're back in Scotland what football team do you support: the blue and white or the green and white?' He curled his lips into a smile, an expression that caught Louis' eye. Louis grinned, acknowledging the tactful delivery. The question placed before Louis referred to his religious persuasion. Was he a Catholic or a Protestant?

'That would be the green and white.' Louis paused, 'but of the Edinburgh variety.'

'Really?' the priest exclaimed, smiling broadly. 'I had a great uncle who had a trial for Hibernian; he ended up playing for Dublin City before a badly broken leg ended his career. A big man he was, he played centre back, Well then, Louis, isn't that a coincidence?'

John took a box of matches from his pocket, lit one and floated the flame over a large candle until the wick burst into a yellow flicker. He lifted the candle from its holder and, with the flame, he lit another.

John rubbed the short silver bristles on his chin. 'You're welcome to attend mass if you'd like Louis, the more the merrier.'

'It's been a while since I've been to church. I'm actually meeting someone for dinner later.'

John dismissed his invitation with a flippant gesture. 'Oh, I see, and where are you eating?'

'I don't know exactly.'

'Well, you're indeed spoilt for choice. There are some good restaurants especially outside in the square.'

Louis glanced at his watch, he still had forty minutes to spare. A tension in his body relaxed, dispelling any urgency to leave.

'Well then, there's no point in me trying to tempt you to join our little celebration, if you are having dinner with a friend. I'll be eating in the square myself tonight with some friends.'

'As I said, I don't go to church that often now. To tell you the truth, we don't often speak the same language anymore.'

'Ah, and what language might that be? Let's say, if we were talking about a political perspective, where would you sit Louis?' John's eyes glistened, he indicated for Louis to sit on a pew.

'I suppose I tend to lean towards the left. That would be a fair analogy, possibly the far left, but that depends on the issue. I suppose I could be best described as a religious socialist.' He laughed at the thought.

'Well, then Louis, would you care to elaborate on your form of religious socialism? It sounds very intriguing.' John smiled.

'I wouldn't want to offend you.'

'Nonsense, when I was studying to be a priest we had a debating society, you know the kind of thing, the universe was made by God or the universe just popped into existence or the universe is infinite and goes on forever. Huh, we live in a miraculous world, Louis. I love a debate. I might even surprise you.'

'I'm pretty sure my views are not on the margins, they're probably part of the mainstream, the silent majority. I'd be excommunicated by now if I'd become a priest.'

'Become a priest?' John said curiously.

'Yes, I trained for several years, but left before I was ordained,' Louis explained.

'Fancy that. It happens to the best of us. Better to find out sooner rather than later that it's not for you, eh?' He dampened his forehead with the handkerchief. 'So you had a conflict of interests then?'

'It was more complicated than that.'

'I see. So then Louis, you don't like sitting on the fence?' John's smile broadened.

'No, you tend to get splinters.'

'Exactly.' John laughed. He sat in the pew opposite Louis. 'It's a good thing to be opinionated I like that; people know where you stand, where you're coming from. Don't worry Louis; I'm not going to try to convert you back to the fold. So tell me, what language does your conscience speak? I'm interested that's all.'

Louis discerned an expectant quality in John's question. He coughed to clear his throat.

'A modern language I suppose, one that the church definitely doesn't speak today, unfortunately.'

'And that disappoints you?'

'It frustrates me. I think today many people are now practising their faith in conflict with the church's teachings on certain issues, as I said, the silent majority.'

'Now that sounds mysterious. Tell me about this silent majority.'

Louis felt uneasy. 'Are you sure, you invited me into your church. The last thing I want to do is offend you.'

'Theological discussion should never offend, it should inspire reflection.'

'Ok then. Personally, I've always thought the church should allow priests to marry. There's a shortage of men entering the priesthood. So if a man was considering becoming a priest and he knew he could marry then surely if and when he married, such a commitment would enrich that priest's ministry. And, if a married man could become a priest, well then, that would open the priesthood to many individuals who feel that calling, but currently are denied what they may feel to be their vocation in life. It would go a long way to combating, let's face it, a situation that is unsustainable, the decreasing numbers of men entering the priesthood.'

'So you think there are a lot of married men who feel a calling to the priesthood?' John asked.

'I know the issue of marriage and celibacy turns a lot of men away from the idea. How can a man who's led a celibate life be qualified to counsel a married couple. Only a man, or a woman for that matter, who is married can offer that kind of support; they'd be in a position that allows them to empathise. You don't go to a baker to get your car fixed; you go to the mechanic.'

'That's a logical point.' John nodded.

'Another justification that the church puts forward in support of celibacy and non-married priests is that a priest that's married would not have the same level of unconditional commitment and time for his parishioners than one who isn't married. Yet, other Christian denominations don't suffer because they allow their priests to marry, even some of the apostles were married and the early popes. It's quite hypocritical.'

John's face took on a serious expression. He sighed leaning his elbow on the backrest of the pew.

'The numbers of priests being ordained from the western world is alarmingly falling. It's a problem that won't disappear, yet the church is slow to change. Will the church ever address the issue? I'm not sure. I think it would need a dramatic shift in doctrine and that could only come from those in authority, from the main man himself. I'm afraid we are a long way off from that.'

'Then does it have a future? If there's no blood to work the heart, it will simply die.'

'Precisely,' John said.

'The church is forcing millions of people to abandon the faith they were born into simply by denying the right of free choice and being dictatorial on issues like contraception, sex before marriage, homosexuality, forcing millions to die of aids because it does not condone the use of condoms. Where in such a belief system is there room for tolerance, unconditional love and acceptance when it will not allow a married couple to use birth control even if one of them has AIDS or is HIV positive?' The words poured from Louis. He avoided John's eyes. Louis had not thought of or spoken about such things in a long time, not since his days in Rome. He felt weirdly uncomfortable. Louis had not anticipated imparting his thoughts on Catholicism to a stranger when he walked into the church. He wondered if he had been too vehement. John smiled warmly, immediately dispelling Louis' awkwardness.

'Very potent arguments Louis. I can see you feel passionate about these things.'

Once again he avoided John's eyes. 'This is awful. I've done nothing but criticise you.'

'Nonsense. You've not spoken to me personally,' John waved the assertion away. 'I've not told you what I think yet. I have a feeling you're just getting started.' Although John's voice was soft, it resonated around the church.

'This is bizarre. I just came in to look around.'

'Ah, God indeed works in mysterious ways.' John shrugged.

'It's strange speaking like this in a church, especially to a priest.'

John did not seem to be perturbed. He raised an eyebrow. 'Pretend you are in the confessional, although there is no need for me to offer absolution.' He smiled and nodded encouragement. The church was encased in a quietness and the softness encouraged Louis to venture further. He felt an urge to exorcise his thoughts from the recesses of his mind.

'You're enjoying this aren't you? Ok then.' He thought for a second. 'When I was younger I'd a strong spiritual affinity towards Mary, the mother of God, but now as an adult, I've questioned many of the church's teachings and their authenticity regarding her. She's not often in the gospels and the veneration that the church bestows upon her is not because there's evidence in the written word, it's more a matter of faith.' He gave a resigned smile. 'I believe Mary was a virgin when she gave birth to Jesus, that's fundamental to my beliefs. However, I do struggle with the church's insistence that Jesus was her only child. Why shouldn't she have had more children? There are instances in the gospels where James is mentioned as the brother of Jesus. There are very prominent figures who subscribe to the view it's possible that Jesus had brothers and sisters.' John nodded. Louis wondered if it was a confirmation of the agreement. He continued.

'I struggle with the immaculate conception. It has no biblical foundation or scriptural support. The argument that if Mary was able to sin when she conceived then Jesus would also inherit the ability to sin. So it goes without saying the theory is flawed because wouldn't Mary's mother then also need to be without sin. Again, there's no evidence to suggest that the assumption of Mary into heaven ever happened; it's not recorded. As you know, it was Pope Pius X11 who proclaimed this doctrine, the bible doesn't even mention Mary's death. I don't think such beliefs demean the concept of Mary as being a holy person but after saying all that, I'd be totally opposed to any theory that suggested Jesus had experienced sexual relationships... simply because of his status as the son of god.'

Like the church, John sat still in silence; he had listened intently. He scratched his chin. Louis wondered, and not for the first time, if he had ventured too far.

John stooped forward as if to give weight to his words.

'My word, you needed to get a lot of your chest Louis. Every one of your arguments has surfaced many times and been debated and written about by theologians throughout the church's history and they'll continue to do so. It's healthy to have such thoughts. We must question our faith. We also must reflect upon our faith. You're not alone in your beliefs. It brings to mind a book I read a few years ago, *"The Best Sermons of 1996"*. It described a poll that was taken amongst 31 diocesan bishops of the Anglican church, and between one-third of them questioned the Virgin Birth, Christ's miracles, and his resurrection. Now, that was controversial. To accept Christ as our Lord and walk with him in an intimate relationship demands a forensic inquiry of our hearts. I believe that it makes faith stronger.' He wiped his brow and continued. 'I have the view that it's not just the words that come out of a person's mouth that are important, but rather, what that person feels in their heart and if there is unselfishness there and a compassion for humanity, then, in my opinion that person is a religious being. Yes, I've contemplated the views you express and personally I don't have a problem with most of them, for you speak of the human side of living. There would be those in the church who would be horrified at such suggestions, for this is not the catholic faith they profess. Then again, others would say that such opinions are enlightening. I feel that to take part in such debates is healthy, it encourages one to explore their faith and their concept of God.' John shifted his weight. 'The virgin birth is not at the centre of my faith. The sermon on the mount defines my faith. It's the greatest speech that was ever spoken. From it, all the great men that have shaped our thinking and changed our world in one way or another, either unknowingly or purposely, borrowed from those great words. Jesus speaking about justice, poverty, forgiveness, charity, faith and love inspired people to change the way they lived their lives. His death and resurrection are at the centre of my faith, for without them I have no faith. So it's not whether Mary was a virgin when Jesus was born, nor that she wasn't stained with sin or that she ascended body and soul into heaven but rather, and this is fundamental, am I inspired to live the life that Jesus' words reveal to me?'

He sat back, a satisfied smile crossed his lips. He looked around the church fondly. 'Religion is not about how grand and opulent our places of worship are, or about the rituals and ceremonies that take place in them. Real religion is concerned with our relationship with our world, with the people in it. It's about being able to love unconditionally and to be able to forgive. It's difficult, it's a struggle for all of us but fundamentally, it's about trying to be Christ-like.'

'I'm disappointed I'm going to miss your sermon now.' Louis could feel a confident surge return to him, encouraged by John's words. 'Since I've spent time in Greece, I've felt a spiritual presence in its people, its landscapes and certainly the churches. I think it's because, in this country, its people and society are ingrained in their religion in such a way it filters into every fabric of life. You cannot go anywhere in Greece without finding a church in the most unsuspecting places.'

Louis noted that one wall was ablaze in sunlight, splaying light on the dark wooden carved images of the Stations of the Cross.

John glanced at his watch. 'I'm afraid time is running away from us. I would like to have had the luxury to talk more, but I must begin to prepare for this evening's mass.' They both rose to their feet.

'Of course, I'm glad we met, John. I enjoyed it.'

'You're a good ma,n Louis and I thank God for allowing us this time together. Now, you enjoy your evening with your friend.'

'Thank you, I will.'

John extended his hand, Louis accepted it and was surprised at how strong and firm his grip felt.

'A female perhaps? Your friend, that is.'

'Yes, her name is Maria.'

'Well then Louis, make her happy. God bless now.' John smiled.

'Goodbye and thank you.' Louis left the church with the thought he would probably never see John again, but the experience would always stay with him. The majority of the people he had met while in Greece would forever be encapsulated in his memory but they would play no part in shaping his future. It was a comforting feeling that followed him out of the church to know Maria did not belong to that process.

A Curious Kind of Healing

Louis walked without purpose, vitalized with each step. He wandered along Metropoleos, a narrow lane. He came across a street named, Alexando Roma, flanked on both sides by cosmopolitan shops. His thoughts turned to his conversation with the priest who had remained friendly and polite as Louis expressed his theological misgivings on the faith the priest had dedicated his life to. Louis doubted if he could have shown such restraint.

He walked further and came across the familiar setting of the promenade. The traffic became heavier, the intimate features of Alexando Roma left behind him. He inhaled the scents of cooking and strong coffee and he was gratified that such simple pleasures had been revealed to him.

He faced the church of St. Dionysios. An old priest sat on a wooden stool at the entrance, his silver beard cascading onto his chest. Thin and vein lined hands lay on his lap, resting on the folds of his ankle hugging black robe. Several people climbed the steps to the church and, with an Olympian effort, the old priest stood up and greeted them warmly.

Louis approached the entrance. The old priest had rested his body on the creaking stool. He did not greet Louis with the warm affection he had displayed previously, but simply regarded him with a light nod. Louis smiled. His attention was snagged by the flicker of gold, the scent of burning candles and the audible intonations and hypnotic tones of a melody, a prayer that ventured outside and caressed his ears with a gentle, low voice, amplified by the acoustics of the building.

There were many people inside the church, some lighting candles, others deep in meditation and prayer, amongst an ornamentation of gold that illuminated the interior, like emanating rays of sunlight.

A vast wealth of colour adorned the ceiling and walls, a pulsating and vibrant spectacle that Louis found addictive. Layer by layer, his senses became alive with wonderment. He sucked in a breath and the curtain of his memory blew back, as images presented themselves; a thread of another life enfolded upon him. Pictures and voices filled his head as real as the old priest in his black robe; each contained clarity of detail that shocked Louis, as they surfaced one after the other, shedding memories.

Louis stepped into this world as a silent witness. He watched Jez ride a scooter, for the first time, cumbersomely along a narrow lane in the heart of Rome. He encountered the contentment on Emma's face as they scanned the distinguished Edinburgh skyline from the advantageous height of the observatory. Louis could feel Emma's voice soak into him as they drank coffee in 'Ryan's Bar' and shared a scone with jam and cream. Emma touched his cheek and kissed his forehead, he could sense her lips upon his skin as the familiarity of her perfume surrounded him.

Louis saw her walk into a glorious light and turn, with a baby cradled in her arms, before her body melted into that brilliant source. And then his eyes were clouded in a glaze; he dropped his head and covered his face with his hands and began to sob.

Eventually, he adjusted himself and wiped the wetness from his face. Startled, he heard a tentative but reassuring voice. 'Let it pass, it is part of the healing,' Louis turned to find the old priest standing next to him, his thick beard falling like a curtain.

'I have seen this reaction many times; some are overcome with happiness, others with a profound sense of grief. St. Dionysios enters and touches the lives of many people who come to this church.'

Louis was astounded. It seemed inconceivable and unbearable that such a reaction could overcome him with such intensity he had no control over it. It emanated from his stomach, tightening in his chest, before lodging in his throat and escaping through the convulsing sobs that paralysed every nerve ending. Louis could not disengage himself from it. He felt anaesthetized by emotion, plunged into a deep ravine of embarrassment, of pity and of guilt.

Louis attempted to compose himself, but the sensation had not yet completely left him. He sniffed the gathering mucus from his nose, involuntary spasms jerked the muscles of his shoulders and a look of agonised shock and bewilderment suffused his face.

Louis was in no doubt that time had exorcised the ghost of Emma from his mind, yet, each living cell and fibre in his body was now traumatised by the realisation of the life Emma could have had. He understood that his grieving had been a self-centred, selfish cycle. Emma had occupied the centre most part of his mind and he had only been concerned with what had been taken from him, not what had been lost to Emma. Louis now knew the enormity of the unveiling. The promise of motherhood, of nurturing an innocent life full of possibilities, the prospect of marriage, Emma sharing her life with another human being, thoughts, emotions, senses, discovering together the unfolding of new chapters that could have shaped new directions and become impressed upon her life; these things he now conceded would never be hers to experience.

As he thought of these things he walked to the entrance of the church and stepped outside, into the soft evening sunshine. The old priest shuffled alongside and laid a skeletal hand on Louis' shoulder. Two swallows cleaved through the still air gliding and turning in an articulate display of artistry that resembled the proficient precision of an eloquent dance.

The priest pointed a crooked finger. 'Some people say returning swallows are the souls of dead friends visiting their loved ones; that is why they return year after year to the same houses and buildings.'

The thought presented itself that if Emma was a swallow, she would visit him and make sure he was well. A warm sensation erupted within Louis abdomen; he nodded and smiled at the priest.

'Yes, I'm sure she would,' he whispered.

St. Marco's Square

He breathed deeply and a tight pulling grabbed his chest. The thought of spending the evening with Maria submerged him in an apparent nervous flurry, a discomfort he attributed to the resurrected emotions for Emma that had shattered his bubble of contentment that the last few weeks had afforded him. And now he had confronted the veiled emergence of his submerged grief with the understanding it was unavoidable, he felt relieved it had been exposed and was now over with. He could now channel his emotions with renewed vigour towards the profound and pleasurable feelings he cradled for Maria.

The indiscriminate clinking of the fishing boats accompanied him as he strode with confident strides towards Solomos Square. Running parallel, voices and traffic reached him as he eagerly considered feasting his eyes upon her once again.

Prompted by the gripping need to unfold himself within her presence, he craved the immediate details of her features. He crossed the road and jogged towards the square. The sound of impatient car horns cursed the air as Louis noted a lengthening number of vehicles ground to an inconvenient halt. Several drivers had left their cars and approach the vehicle in front, whose owner lay slumped over the steering wheel. Louis did not see the man who looked as if he had succumbed to a deep sleep, but instead, he was drawn to a woman with an orange and yellow tattoo imprinted upon her arm. His jog became a quick walk, as the sultry air threatened to stain his top with sweat. Once he reached Solomos Square he looked around anxiously. To his surprise, he found scores of children had converged upon the square with bicycles, tricycles, and scooters, like an army of purposeful ants, watched by the protective glances of parents on the sidelines. Louis scanned the crowd and noticed a cumbersome, yet intent infant wandering around the square in search of something to detain his curiosity. Unsteady on his feet, the infant stumbled several times, though each time he regained his balance. A panic passed across a woman's face announcing the mother's parental attachment, amongst the swell of curious faces that inspected the child with varying degrees of weighted detachment. And then, amongst this concoctive concerto of blissful excitement radiating from the square, Louis heard his name being called.

They sat at a table in St. Marco's Square. Louis contemplated the construction of Maria's face, and without taking his eyes from her he glided a finger upon the skin of her arm. Louis withdrew his hand; her face was exquisite to him.

'Are you feeling ok?' Maria asked.

'Yes, I've never felt better.'

She stared at him. 'It's just that you seem... How should I say this... over indulged in your affection.'

He placed his hand on hers and leant towards her.

'I can't help myself.'

Maria smiled. 'I've thought of nothing else but tonight.' Maria had spent the day willing the hours to pass, a languorous waiting that felt as if her watch had stopped and time refused to pass, as the day stretched out before her and uncoiled itself in a slow lethargic motion.

'I feel like I did when I was a child on Christmas Eve, filled with excitement and expectation.'

Louis smiled and thought about this. 'What fills you with excitement and expectation now?'

She paused for a moment. 'I've always wanted to start my own tour guide business. That would be exciting; maybe one day.'

Louis was reminded of Meredith and her proposed walking tours for senior citizens. 'Have you thought of your market and your client group, would you specialise or be broad in your approach?'

'I would promote the beauty of the island, its ecology and the loggerhead turtle, its history and how that has built the Zakynthos we see today,' Maria said, thoughtfully.

'So why don't you?'

'It's one thing thinking about it and actually having the resources to make it a reality. I've spoken to Peter about it.

He hasn't dismissed the idea. In fact, he thinks it's a good one but he's right when he said I need to research the business side of things, work on my business plan.'

'Would he be interested in joining you?'

'Possibly, he likes his job, sometimes I think he was born to it. I'm not sure if he'd be willing to take such a risk and neither am I. It never used to but risk unsettles me, it frightens me.'

'What do you mean?'

She hesitated. 'I've been offered a job.'

'That's great. I didn't know you were looking for one.'

'That's just it, I wasn't. The more I thought about it I became excited by the prospect and, at the same time, I felt this sinking sensation. The choice was difficult. I was unprepared and confused.'

'But why would you think like that?'

'The job is in Athens,' she said quietly.

'Ah, I see.' A panic rose in him.

'The week before we met, I went to Athens for the job interview. I needed to go, it felt urgent. I needed to be convinced that if I was offered the job it would be the right thing to do. I had to ask myself, could I leave my mother and Michalis? Was Zakynthos holding me back? Athens promised another life; what was wrong with the one I already had? And then, meeting you only complicated the matter.' She smiled warmly. 'In the end, the decision came easily. Sometimes we need to have the things we take for granted taken from us, to really appreciate their value, to realise how precious they are, even if that is just imagined in our thoughts and in our mind. I realised then there are things in life that are irreplaceable.

'Like your island?' he said with relief.

'Exactly, we can't choose the bonds that make us who we are; maybe they choose us.'

She scanned the menu.

'What about you,? Since you came here what excites you, present company excluded of course?' Maria looked at him inquisitively.

Louis thought for a moment.

'It has to be photography. I've become addicted to it since I've started to take photographs. It's not just about taking the photograph, I try to look deeper than the surface and then the beauty of the landscape is revealed in detail, colour and texture; it's an intimate experience. I didn't realise how personal it could be.'

'It sounds as if you have connected with Zakynthos.'

Maria pushed her hair back off her face.

'I'm fascinated by the play of light and colour in the trees, buildings, a face, and the sea and then, in an instant, the intensity can change and it suggests something completely different. The camera catches that moment, it never lies; the angle of light influences shadows and colour. It's a beautiful thing, Maria.'

She lifted his hand and kissed it. 'You have changed Louis Satriani.'

'I have.'

'Yes I think so, you're becoming contented. Zakynthos is wrapping her arms around you.'

'I could get used to the feeling.' He smiled. 'Oh, how is Michalis?' Louis asked.

'He is fine, no more seizures.'

'I'm glad ... and your mother?'

'You must have made a good impression, she wants to know when you're coming for lunch again... a well-mannered man she said and I was not to let you go.'

'It's nice to know that I'm welcome. You have a lovely family, Maria.'

'In fact, she was asking about you today and wondering when I was seeing you next.'

Louis watched Maria as she spoke. Her dark eyes sparkled, like the sun skimming water, he thought. The revelations in the Church of St Dionysus tugged at him. He pushed them away. He felt a confident swell build inside him, a feeling that emerged with a fulfilled sense of acceptance. It encouraged him.

'You have a beautiful face.'

She lowered her head shyly. He reached out with his hand and lifted her chin. 'I find it unbelievable that I'm here with you on this island.'

Maria wrapped her fingers around his hand, brought it to her lips and kissed his skin softly. 'What did you do today?'

Louis tried to gather his thoughts. She replaced his hand with a glass of wine. He watched as she brought the glass to her lips and, for the first time in his life he found himself envious of a drinking vessel.

'Well, I had my usual breakfast with Anna on the porch. She's finally decided that she is fed up waiting for her son to visit her. She's taken the matter into her own hands and invited herself to his apartment in Athens.'

'Really?'

'Yes, in fact, she's leaving tomorrow morning.'

'Good for her.' A pleased disposition laced her voice.

'She plans to be away for at least a week. She said she hasn't been to Athens since she was a young woman, so she's going to take advantage of her free lodgings. She's asked me to watch over the house for her.'

'Anna must think highly of you, entrusting you with her house.' Maria raised her eyebrows as she watched Louis' face.

'Yes, I suppose she does.'

'In fact, Anna told my mother she has grown fond of you.'

Louis smiled. 'And I of her. I think I fill a void in her life. She's even let me take her photograph…. more than once.'

A waiter arrived, disturbing their conversation as plates of fried aubergine and Horiatiki (Greek Salad) were placed on the table, the silence between them punctuated by the occasional courteous 'efcharisto' as the waiter arranged the table with a courteous smile. For their main meal, Louis ordered a Stifado - beef cooked in onion and a tomato sauce and Maria a Kokkinosto - stewed beef in a tomato sauce.

Louis saw several people coming out of St. Marco's Church. He thought back to the conversation he had with John. 'I spoke with an Irish priest today in the church over there. It was quite surreal, an Irish priest in a Catholic church in Zakynthos. We tried to put Catholicism to right.'

'And did you succeed?'

'Unfortunately not. We were up against two thousand years of rights and wrongs.'

'Couples come from all over to get married in St Marco's, especially the Irish.'

'Really, wedding tourism, what next? In fact, it was a day for visiting churches, I also went to St. Dionysios church.' He hesitated and felt the sensation of falling. His mouth felt dry. And then he saw John with a group of people walking towards a restaurant and recovered his composure. 'That's the priest I spoke to over there.'

Maria looked up from her food and turned to look. To Louis' relief, she had not registered his discomfort. He leant back in his chair and drank some wine.

'This wine is good, Italian?' he asked.

'It's made here in Zakynthos at the Solomos winery, it is an Akratos red. Most of the grapes are grown in the east of the island, mostly by family vineyards.'

Louis put his nose to the glass. 'Red berry and a hint of cinnamon.' He took another drink.

'This is one of my favourite wines,' Maria said.

'It's becoming one of mine too.'

Waiters progressed from table to table, lighting candles whose flickering flames reminded Louis of the rows of wavering luminous candles in the Church of St. Dionysios. At this time of the evening, the facades in the square transformed into luminescent backdrops as if daytime refused to yield against the night sky.

'Are you working tomorrow?' Louis asked.

'No, it's my day off.' She drank some wine. Louis watched the movement of her Adam's apple.

'And have you any plans?'

'I thought we might go to the beach, if you want to that is.'

'The beach,' Louis repeated. 'What a wonderful idea.' He constructed a sudden picture of a golden beach uninhibited but for Maria and himself.

'Agios Nicolaos is very popular. I often go there with friends. The water is lovely and clear, we could go there.'

'Perfect.' He fermented with excitement.

'In fact, Zakynthos has a lot of beautiful beaches. Some of my favourites are Porto Zoro, Ionia and Geraks beach, where I swam with a Loggerhead Turtle once.'

'Really? what was it like?'

'Incredible, she was about two metres long, beautiful. I tried to follow her for some time. It felt so serene, magical even. When I was swimming alongside her, I gave her a name.'

'What did you call it?'

'I called her Charisma, it means, *"Given Grace"*. She was the most amazing creature I'd ever seen. When I started to return to the shore, I was a few hundred metres out. Every muscle ached when I got back onto the beach, but I would have turned back and done it again just to get another glimpse of her. We won't see any at Agios Nicolaos, I'm staying close to the beach.'

'I'd like that. We can see Charisma another time.'

'A few years ago, a crowd of us would go to a different beach most weekends. It's funny how life has a habit of getting busy, changing things and people for that matter; most of us drifted apart.

'One of my best friends went to Athens, to study Egyptology; she became a tour guide at the pyramids. She loved it. We stayed in touch as much as we could and nearly always ended up talking about our work. She was very serious about her work. I remember once she'd been all day with a certain group and it was her style to ask her group questions about the places they had visited and its history, like a quiz. One of the questions was who married Cleopatra? Someone replied Richard Burton, well, she was not impressed... I laughed when she told me. I thought it was funny, but she wasn't amused. I can imagine her reaction. She had a lack of ability for humour, but that was always part of her charm; it was a standing joke amongst us all.'

'Does she still work in Egypt?' Louis grinned, appreciating the pun.

'No, not anymore, she's dead.'

'Oh, I'm sorry.'

'She overdosed on heroin, it came as a shock. She managed to hide it, until it started to physically affect her. She fell into a bad crowd, it was sad. In the end, she lost her job, by that time it was too late. She died in Egypt and her body was brought back to Zakynthos. She's buried beside her mother.' Maria looked away, her face immersed in a tangible sadness.

'That's terrible. I'm sorry Maria.'

'It drained her, squeezed the life out of her. The last time I saw her she came home for a friend's wedding. A few weeks later, she was dead. She'd become a different person.'

'In Edinburgh amongst some of my friends, cocaine was viewed like it was a fashion accessory, especially at dinner parties. It was the dessert instead of pudding. It was widespread. They would spend all day working in the office and then unwind with a line of coke sniffed through twenty-pound notes. Most of my friends started taking it during university; it was part of the lifestyle, the social scene. I tried it once or twice just because everyone else was. And then, at weekends, at friend's houses, it was handed out, like cups of coffee. There was such an acceptance. A few were getting the stuff delivered to their offices in envelopes by couriers. After the weekend they'd be looking for their next hit by Wednesday. These people were feeding a serious habit, they were addicted.'

Maria listened, her eyes transfixed, not leaving Louis face. Louis drew in a deep breath, he felt compelled to tell her. He wanted Maria to know about his life, the naked ugliness and the good parts.

'My only experience with drugs was some hesitant puffs on a joint, it made me feel sick, so I never tried it again.'

'Well, as I said, some people had a problem, I never let it get that far... I hate the smell of cigarette smoke; my only indulgence is alcohol.'

Maria raised her wine glass to her lips.

'Mine too,' she said smiling.

'Although,' Louis said, curling his lips. 'I could easily

find another indulgence.'

'Oh, tell me, what that would be?' she said curiously.

'Well.' Louis teasingly stretched the word. 'I could get addicted to your mother's cooking.'

'Louis.' Maria laughed.

The distant sound of hooves tugged his attention and as he turned he saw an open top carriage, pulled by a magnificent black horse that snorted as it explored the ground with its twitching nose. Its body shone in the glow of lights from the square and restaurants.

'Venice has its gondolas, but here in Zakynthos we have our horse drawn carriages.'

'Why don't we try one? I haven't seen the town at night; you can give me a running commentary.'

'That sounds very romantic,' Maria said, running her finger over her bracelet.

They spent the rest of the night moving from bar to bar and, as they did, they held hands. At quarter past midnight, they strolled in the shadow of the church of St. Dionysos. They sat on the steps that led to the church. Louis thought about the priest who had spoken to him and he wondered what he would be doing now. He fiercely regretted not telling Maria about that day's experience in the church, it left him tense, it still felt raw. It felt like a betrayal. He hated himself for that, but he wanted to protect Maria. He did not want to compromise the place they were now both in. How could he explain it to her? Some things were best left unsaid. Some things were best buried. He pushed it away again but it would not leave him.

Maria looked at him for a moment, uncertain. 'Are you ok?' She pressed his hand.

'I'm fine.' he shrugged.

'Let's get a taxi.'

He floundered slightly. 'To where?'

'I'd like to see the view from your balcony.'

A Table Set for Two

The bellowing voice of Anna filtered into the room; its sudden intensity hijacked his sleep and dragged him into the awakened world. Louis forced his eyes open and, still heavy with sleep, he focused on the whitewashed ceiling. At his side, he could detect a slight movement; the serene face of Maria brought forward the images and palpable feelings of the night before. He slid from the sheet and dressed into a t-shirt and shorts, before opening the door and seeking the portly frame of Anna. He did not have to look far, as Anna stood at the bottom of the steps.

'There you are. You have slept late.'

'Er... I had a late night,' Louis muttered

'My flight is at eleven, the taxi will be here soon.' She gestured to the veranda. 'I have made some breakfast, but I do not have time to eat with you. Take this key, it is for the house. I want you to make breakfast and eat on the veranda every morning when I am in Athens.' Anna looked at Louis sternly. 'You are not to sleep in my house.'

Louis nodded sheepishly.

'Good. Come, take the key. It will take me all day to get up there.'

Louis descended the stairs, took the key from her sausage like fingers and placed it in his pocket. A car horn sounded from behind the garden wall.

'That will be your taxi, I'll help with the luggage.'

Louis loaded the suitcase into the boot as Anna lowered herself into the back seat; she shut the door and rolled down the window.

'Now, you are not to eat all of that breakfast by yourself. I have made enough for two.... leave some for Maria.'

Louis' jaw loosened, Anna winked at him and smiled.

'You saw us,' he stuttered, consternation licking his voice.

'Why yes, I see everything.' Anna laughed, falling back into the seat as the taxi moved off, the wheels disturbing the dry earth in a cloud of rising dust.

Louis stood and watched the taxi disappear down the

gradient of the hill and round a bend. A smile curled the edges of his mouth, as he shook his head in disbelief. He turned and walked towards the house, a bubbling sensation tickling his abdomen. By now, the sun had crept over the terracotta roof of the apartment block, forcing him to shield his eyes as he stood and surveyed the breakfast Anna had prepared. His eyes glazed over the contents of the table. He noticed that it was set for two. He grinned, a sign of her approval, he told himself.

Back in his room, he took care not to wake Maria. She was lying on her side, the draping sheet exposing her back. His eyes traced the button curvature of her spine, as it protruded against her tight olive skin. Subtle shadows shaded various areas of her body, like the sun's light moving across a landscape. Louis studied suggestions of lean muscle, moving over her hipbone and thigh. He considered the texture and angles, the smoothness bringing to mind the sculptured image of a statue.

I share you with so many people, I want to lie here and breathe you in, he thought yearningly. He dismissed the temptation to brush his fingers over her skin, in case he disturbed her; instead, he indulged himself with the details of the night before, playing the layered images over in his mind.

They had taken a taxi to Argassi, drank in a few bars, before walking the dimly lit road that led to Anna's house. A solitary light in the house suppressed their anticipation and brought an alertness upon them.

Avoiding the unwanted attention of Anna was of paramount importance, so to evade a conspicuous confrontation they moved silently amongst the protection of the shadows. Above them, a luminous moon carved a subtle path of light leading them through the dark to the small two storey apartment block.

Louis' room was bathed in a soft illumination that covered an entire wall. Abandoning caution, their lips met in a frenzied hunger. He cradled her head in both hands, running his fingers through her hair. Their lips parted, they stared searchingly into each other's eyes, and a delicate purpose seized them with its intimate revelation. There remained a silence in the space between them, the spoken word inadequate, redundant even, and the sensitivity of touch prioritised itself. He could feel her warm breath on his lips and it encouraged him to draw closer. A controlled tenderness established itself as their lips met, a venturesome urge producing an assertiveness that found a moist and warm return. Louis attributed this exultant contact as an unguarded sign of encouragement that sent salacious currents pulsing through his chest. He peppered her cheeks with kisses and sought the skin of her neck with his lips, which she accommodated by raising her head, submissively.

   Louis ran his hand over her slender back, which arched to the touch. His lips caressed her collarbone, then, brushed the exposed flesh of her shoulder. Instinctively he immersed his face in her hair, inhaling deeply, filling his senses with its scent, as if the essence of it was imperative to sustaining life itself. His hand moved to her shoulder, it slipped under the strap of her dress and let it fall from its support.

   Louis sensed her breathing grow more rapid as she settled a hand on the nape of his neck. An arousal seized him, excitement and passion gripped him in its clasp. His hands glided over the soft fabric of her dress, descending the curvature of her back and delighting his senses. Louis did not remove his hands as he lowered himself into a sitting position on the bed, which submitted to his weight with a tired creak. He looked upwards, over the curves of her body and, fixing his gaze on her face, he slid the remaining strap from its support. Maria assisted its progress, by easing it over her skin until it fell from her body effortlessly. Louis struggled to breathe as he gazed upon this most intimate of gestures, which the moonlight tantalizingly shaded. His enraptured eyes traced the round curve of her breasts and rib cage that heaved with the rhythmical movement of her breathing.

   He laid his hands over the curvature of her hips and drew

his face towards her skin, kissing her abdomen with light, quick teasing motions. Below her belly button, he discovered a small birthmark, dark in colour. Louis traced its shape with the tip of his finger and brushed it with his lips. Maria gripped his hair, she closed her eyes and parted her lips as the light from the hanging moon reflected and seductively outlined their fullness.

Louis grazed her inner thigh with a delicate touch. Maria bit her bottom lip. She threw her head backwards and whispered his name, the sound of her voice driving a feeling through him, like hot melting liquid as he kissed and licked her glistening skin.

They were cocooned in their world of touching, sensing, tasting and exploring; the physical world around them ceased to exist. The only relevance was the meeting of skin on skin and the stroking of hair and flesh. They had become insulated in a union that their passions fused together with every new and profound sensation that they instinctively submitted to, imploring to be bathed in its intimacy and its reassurance of unselfish giving and acceptance.

Maria shuddered, feeling his warm breath upon her, as a small spasm crackled deep inside her stomach. She lowered her head to his and consumed his warm lips. She kissed him deeply, gently stroking his hair. Maria reached down and stroked the front of his trousers with her palm. Louis responded with a soft whispering moan. Their lips parted and she moved so that she knelt between his thighs. She fanned her hands over his chest, a perceptible look of intent glazing her eyes. Louis found himself astonished by their depths and, when she fumbled with his trouser button, a determination passed over her face that transpired into a smile, as the button was eventually released.

They both stood and slipped from the rest of their burdensome clothes and, once naked, they instinctively embraced. Louis became enthralled with the sensation that their closeness induced. He was inflamed by the delicious pleasure that every curve gave, he shuddered with the sliding feeling of skin on skin, the softness of her breasts against him. His hands roamed her shoulders, seeking the firmness of her back and the roundness of her thighs. The sweetest scent rose from her skin, surrounding him, like a burst of petals.

    Effortlessly, they lay on the bed. The moon accentuated their bodies in a silver halo of light. Maria glided her hands over Louis' body, touching him with delicate strokes that induced slight moans from his lips. She rested her head against his chest and brushed his skin with light kisses and suggestive flicks of her tongue. Louis ran his fingers down her back with a feather light touch, and with his free hand he clutched the sheet and, in his mind, he absorbed the heat from her body as it brushed against his.

    Instantaneously, she rolled over and straddled him, guiding him inside her. Galvanised by this intimacy, Louis felt as if an intangible transaction had passed between them; entranced, they remained motionless, immersed in their closeness. She leaned towards him; he lifted his head and accepted her breast with his mouth, as she moved her weight upon him. She could feel him pulse inside her, as she submitted to the contracting that swelled within her. She pressed herself against him; he drew his lips over her mouth and became overwhelmed. He swelled inside her, causing undulating warmth that proliferated, like crashing waves deep within him. Maria's muscles tensed, she shuddered, as the heat rose through her body.

    She pulled her mouth to his as a flow of spasms surged through her. She cried out, a muffled sound against his lips. He could no longer suppress the surge that demanded to be released, a sigh exhaled from his mouth as his body shuddered against her skin. She cried out again, submissively, and collapsed into his arms that folded around her. She felt his heart pound with dull thuds inside his chest, it rose and fell against her cheek, and she closed her eyes and slept without dreaming.

A Secret Disposition

Jez stood with his hands rooted in his pockets, staring out of the bay window. Lost in thought, he did not register the rhythmical tapping of rain against the glass nor the approaching car and its loan occupant.

He was drawn to the last time Carris could have a lucid conversation with him.

'They took me to a place called Bestburgh House in Cork, a dark forbidden looking building. It was cold and it seemed to rain for weeks.' She paused to gather her resolve and, for the first time, he witnessed Carris' fortitude dissolve. 'I was told, "*Nobody wants you.*" She put her hand to her mouth, and it was then she exhaled as if she had been punched in the stomach. "*Nobody cares about you.*" Her eyes glistened with tears, her words cracked and fought with her sobs. "*You have sinned.*" Jez regarded her in disbelief; he had never heard her speak this way before. He was stunned by the bluntness and cruelty of the statements.

'She was born on the 13th of October at five o'clock in the morning. She weighed 6 pounds and she was beautiful.' Carris paused and whispered, 'I never saw her again.'

The resonant ringing of the doorbell broke his dazed glaze, tearing him from his bubble. Forced to abandon his insular world of thought and confront the world of the physical, Jez recovered himself and opened the door. She introduced herself as the MacMillan nurse who had phoned earlier that morning.

Jez invited the nurse indoors and offered to take her jacket. It occurred to him she looked too young to be a specialist nurse, and he found himself amused at the image of an older woman, bulky and matron-like, that had formed in his head during their conversation over the phone; a portrayal, that he now considered, had been constructed on the tone and delivery of her voice.

As they climbed the staircase, he noted a determined overture occupy her stride. He put this down to her confident and assertive manner. As they reached the landing, Jez knocked on the bedroom door and entered the room. The drawn curtains shaded the room in a dull light. It took a second or two for his eyes to adjust and, like a gust of air, he breathed the fragrance of lavender.

He crossed the room and a vivid image of an industrious Carris revealed itself and then just as suddenly dissolved as he looked upon her vulnerable and skeletal face. He laid his hand on her forehead and brushed a few strands of damp hair from her cheek. She opened her eyes, slowly registering his face and, with a struggle, she curled her cracked lips into a smile.

'Carris, there is someone here to see you. She is a nurse and she will be look after you from now on.'

'Hello, my name is Yvonne.' The nurse stepped towards the bed.

Carris's eyes moved from Jez and fixed upon the silhouetted frame of the young woman. Carris made to speak, but no sound resonated from her throat. She swallowed, and the labour drained her. With a herculean effort, Carris whispered in a dry and crackled voice, 'Please don't take my baby from me.' Her eyes rolled, submitting to sleep.

Yvonne glanced at Jez expectantly. He looked at her, defeated. 'I'll explain later.'

'If you don't mind, I'd like to get started.' She was eager to begin, and crossing the room, she laid her bag on a chair.

'Of course.' Jez retreated to the door. 'If you should need anything, I'll be downstairs.'

She did not answer, but instead lowered her eyes and instinctively concentrated on the repetitions of Carris' rapidly rising and falling chest.

Jez stood at the bay window. He had no recollection of time. He heard the voice of Carris and turned, but the empty doorway deflated him, like rushing air from a balloon. A blanket of cloud consumed the sky as the sun announced its presence through a crack in the grey, with yellow and salmon pink light. He watched as the sky evolved, influencing light and tone, reinventing itself in shades and colour, chasing shadows over the Fife landscape. The ringing telephone snared his attention.

'Louis! How are you and where are you?' It was a comfort to hear his friend's voice.

'I'm good Jez. I'm on an island called Zakynthos, I've been here for some time now. In fact, I won't be going anywhere else.'

'You sound happy, Louis, that's good.'

'I've met someone. Her name is Maria, I never thought I'd feel this way again Jez.'

'That's excellent, Louis, if anyone deserves some happiness it's you. It's good to hear your voice.'

'And how are you?' Louis asked.

There was a pause. 'To tell you the truth, not too well. Do you remember Carris my housekeeper? Well, she is staying with me in the manse. She has…' His voice wavered. 'She has cancer Louis, cancer of the esophagus. Carris only told me about it eight weeks ago; it's well established and basically,' he paused, before regaining his composure. 'She's dying Louis. She wouldn't entertain hospital and since she lives alone and has no family, I insisted she stay in the manse. I fear she'll not be with us for long. She doesn't seem to be in pain, the drugs are strong thank God. She has her lucid moments but not often. Her memory hasn't deserted her entirely and the Carris we know appears but she can be very incoherent at times, well most of the time to be honest.' He paused again. It felt good to talk to someone. Many of the older parishioners asked about her, mainly after the daily morning Mass, but their enquiries were polite, well-mannered and short, as if referring to that day's weather. Jez closed his eyes, he felt exhausted. He rubbed his forehead.

'She speaks a lot about her past and the baby. Do you remember I told you about that?'

'Yes, it sounded shocking.'

Jez's voice was flat and unleavened. Louis felt awkward. His news had been extinguished by Jez' weighted revelation. He hated listening to a voice and not being able to read a facial expression or gesture.

'And are you ok?' Louis asked.

There was a moment's silence. 'Oh, I'm fine.' He spoke

with a crack in his voice. 'It came out of the blue, so suddenly. I suppose one can never prepare for such news. If there's any comfort to be taken from this, it's that Carris seems to be unaware of her condition. Even when she is making sense, she asks why she is in bed, in this room and not at home. She's no comprehension of the situation, really. I sometimes feel that the woman I use to know is no longer present in her body. In a strange way, cancer has also eaten away at her mind. I look upon that as a blessing; she would be mortified at the thought of being incapable of looking after herself. The nurse is taking care of that side of things. Carris is definitely moulded from a different era, proud and dignified, but also bloody stubborn at times.' Jez smiled wearily.

Louis remembered the air of impeccable composure that surrounded Carris.

'Yes, I remember her like that too.'

'I feel responsible for her now. She has no family in the village.' Jez hesitated. 'I regret I took her for granted. She has become like a mother to me.'

'She sounds a remarkable woman.'

'Yes she is.' Jez sighed almost inaudibly. 'Do you remember the day you visited, I told you about Carris' baby and how she was forced to give it away?'

'Yes, I remember.'

'Recently she's spoken a lot about that time and what happened.' Jez described to Louis what Carris had told him and then he said, 'I thought it strange at the time; she had never spoken like that before. Carris was always guarded about her past. I know now she knew she was dying and only had a short time left. Robert was her first love, the love of her life. She described him as her soul mate. She not only lost her baby, she lost the person she loved to the war; he never returned home. It comforts her he knew she was pregnant before he left for France. She spoke of the baby being taken from her, the nuns… the cruelty. God, they dehumanized those girls. There were lots of them, just children themselves. They were failed by the church, it sinned against them and it continues to fail them. She carried this unbearable grief around with her; she has been tormented all these years... that has been her secret. It was time to release her anguish. She said she was now tired carrying such an emotional weight all of her life... I think it was a comfort really. To finally tell someone what really happened. Her emotions were still raw.'

'It obviously didn't comfort you. Are you coping ok?' Louis asked firmly.

'I can't come to terms with the immense sadness that obviously lurked behind a woman that projected such an ability to be in control. She told me she thinks about her daughter every day. Dwelling upon what she might look like, what colour her eyes might be? She often wondered if her daughter looked like her. She felt guilty for not trying to find her and fears what her daughter might think of her. The worst part is not knowing if she has grandchildren. She often daydreamed and constructed images in her mind of the things they would have all done together, like a proper family... she said she lit a candle every day in the church for a child who is now a woman and who will probably have a family of her own... it must be unbearable.

'A few years ago she left her name with an adoption agency in the hope they might trace her... she lived every day, hoping for the miracle of seeing her child again.'

'And now she is dying, God ,that is awful Jez,' Louis sympathized.

'It's stretched my faith I can tell you that, although it seemed Carris' faith was the one thing that sustained her and yes, eventually, she got her miracle. A nun from the order managed to get in touch with Carris. She told Carris it was wrong what had happened; it had plagued the nun for years, all those babies being forcefully taken from their natural mothers. She wanted to make some kind of contrition and although she couldn't tell Carris in great detail, she said her daughter was adopted by a respectable couple. It was a great comfort to Carris to know her daughter was brought up in a loving family. Even after all these years, the nun didn't tell Carris the name they gave her daughter... seemingly the mothers had no part in that.

Can you imagine not knowing your child's name? Bastards! I'm so angry Louis; I'm sorry for burdening you with all this.'

'Not at all,' Louis insisted. 'It sounds like you needed to talk to someone as well.'

'I've spoken enough... tell me all about this girl you have met.'

***

Louis phoned Jez on the eve of Anna's return from Athens. On that first day, they had eaten the breakfast Anna prepared. Louis considered Anna's approval and the knowing smile on her lips as the taxi moved off. Maria felt embarrassed and flushed when he told her. Anna was practically family; she had always felt protective towards Maria. Louis calmed her anxiety by reminding Maria that Anna was not annoyed and the breakfast was her way of giving her blessing.

Maria looked perplexed before finally agreeing with him. After breakfast, Maria showered in Louis' room before returning home. She collected Louis later that morning in her blue Corsa.

They travelled along the coast and left the flat and gentle shoreline for a road that climbed, twisting and turning, fringing the coast in parts, like a giant coiled snake. They passed lush emerald coves that painted a voluptuous sea of green on an azure canvas. Perched precariously on steep ridges, large houses, tavernas and hotels offered rooms to let as they periodically appeared by the roadside hiding amongst the opulent camouflage of pine trees. They veered off the main route and ventured along a dusty track, straddled by olive trees, wild flowers and where the sun burnt the grass.

Louis sat with an indulgent expression across his face as they parked alongside dust caked cars and coaches. Maria smiled and kissed him on the cheek. 'I hope it's not too busy.'

The beach's silken sands slid into a shallow sea. Louis

noted two restaurants. One in particular caught his eye, its hanging vines offering shade from the broiling sun, perfect at lunchtime he thought. They were spoilt for choice, as vacant sunbeds studded the beach in an uncluttered and orderly fashion.

They spent the morning sunbathing, swimming and walking in the crystal clear water of Agios Nicolaos, where small silver fish darted between their feet like hyperactive torpedoes. These activities summoned a palatable pleasure that, as the day progressed, surrounded Louis with a tranquil serenity. He feared he would wake from a dream at any second.

A rocky headland stretched like a pointing finger, where a yacht slid through the calm contented water mooring fifty yards from the shore, its brilliant white contours commanding a striking contrast against the azure shades of the sea and sky.

They spoke about their pasts, filling in the spaces each of them did not know.

'I'd love to go to Italy,' Maria said. 'Especially Rome and visit the museums, the ancient monuments and, of course, the food. It would be wonderful.' Her face lit up at the thought.

'Maybe we could go sometime. It's a great city for just wandering from square to square, there's so much to see. We could visit the village my dad is from, some of his family still live there.'

As they talked, Louis wondered about the trajectory of their future. The thought of visiting Rome with Maria excited him but in the past, such excursions and small breaks were accompanied by the familiarity of life's routines, structure, work and friends. His life had been full of such things, they were his identity. What did he identify with now? Life's pattern had still to establish itself.

'The day we had lunch in the garden, my mother called Edinburgh, The Athens of the North.'

'That's right she did.'

'And is it?'

'When you live there, I suppose you take it for granted.

You don't always see it as others might; your mind can become blind to it. The buildings are there obviously, but sometimes they just become part of life's background.'

'Do you think it is the same with people? You can love someone, but also take them for granted. Become blind to them. Emma did not see you as I do.'

'I suppose there's a difference between loving someone and being in love. Emma loved me, but she wasn't in love with me. Do you understand?' Louis asked.

She nodded.

He thought for a moment. 'We all set down roots, but if they are to grow, we need to nourish them and that's the problem. We may neglect them, even when we've invested so much of ourselves in those roots, we may forget to feed them, and eventually, we become use to living that way, we become immune to the weeds growing around us. It becomes part of normality, until inevitably the roots are strangled by the weeds. In a way, I think Emma and I were both guilty.'

'You have a strange way of saying things, Louis. I hope you're a good gardener.' They both laughed. It pleased Louis that they could talk about Emma in such a way.

They ate lunch underneath hanging vines, shading them from the sun. The owner of the restaurant, Nikolaos, was married to Sarah, an English woman. Louis and Maria overheard her talking to a couple at a table. Sarah first met her future husband as she ate in his restaurant while on holiday with friends. After that, they met each other almost every day and, once she returned to England, they kept in constant contact. Nikolaos visited her in England. She returned to Zakynthos and worked with him for six months. They married soon afterwards, their two-year-old son Andreas, was born a year later. She continued that it was not uncommon for some visitors to Zakynthos to establish lasting relationships with their hosts.

Louis sat with a hint of reticence visible on his face.

Maria smiled at him. 'Listen, we have just become a statistic.'

As Sarah spoke, Andreas unwittingly entertained his

parents' costumers. Clothed in only a t-shirt that almost kept his modesty intact, Andreas licked an ice cream cone. Clamped between his small fingers, it gradually decorated the eager features of his angelic face. Spurred on by his enquiring mind, he explored the burnt out remains of a barbecue with growing enthusiasm and an inquisitive curiosity.

The barbecue materialized into a playground of endless proportions. To the amusement of his captive audience, he reshaped his features. The charred remains and melting streams of ice cream caked his eager hands, inevitably graduating to his elated and contented face.

'Barbecue ice cream. Mmm I can't see it catching on.' Louis grimaced.

Returning to Argassi, Maria swerved a stationary truck, abandoned by the side of the road. A short distance ahead, they stopped to pick up the driver who explained with exorbitant gesturing that he had now broken down three times in that week. 'That piece of shit is as reliable as a nun in a brothel,' he spat exasperated. Louis floated upon the hypnotic wave of the two Greek voices flavouring the air and he thought their words danced with the rhythm of the car.

His eyelids grew heavy, induced by sun and heat, he drifted in and out of sleep and then vivacious colours and sounds punctured the view from the car as familiarity painted the scene - Argassi.

Mount Skopos

It pleased Louis that Argassi had developed in a way that was agreeable to the eye, not unlike many of the faceless monoliths that had sprung up over the Mediterranean like a contagious rash. It reassured him to see hotels did not fight for space, side by side, like ugly and obtrusive gigantic slabs of concrete. One would have to look hard to find buildings taller than three levels. This was the Greece he had come to know. The simplicity of life was infectious, the light, a revelation, transforming the land and sea into living entities and in such witnessed moments, Louis found words a redundant medium, only the fluidity of cognitive responses captured it entirely.

He tried to make sense of these thoughts one afternoon as he walked with Maria along a dusty vestige that carved its passage behind Anna's house. The afternoon light washed their route in shaded shadows and opulent tones, like a watercolour painting coming to life. The enervating sun complemented their progress and, as they climbed higher, below them a mantle of olives, citrus and cypress trees, flame-coloured wildflowers, yellow stucco and whitewashed houses stretched towards the sea like a carpet decorating the red earth. As they progressed, Louis was aware of a palatable silence and distant softness that complemented aromatic scents floating upon the warm currents of the Ionian air like some magic potion exhilarating his mind. The business of living could be put into perspective, he thought. the medium was available to meditate on what was important, significant and of value to one's personal existence. It would be difficult to attain such tranquility and serenity in the realms of built up areas in towns and cities, where the exorbitant level of noise and pollution were a constant irritation.

They came across a sign advertising a taverna several metres along a path that branched off the main route. They ordered coffee and bought some bottled water for the remainder of their walk; they were grateful to rest for a while. The coffee was fetched. Louis noted a sign advertising the taverna's specialty 'Greek nights'; to attract potential customers they offered transport from the centre of Argassi to the taverna.

They continued their ascent, as the late afternoon sun watched their progress, warming the earth below their feet. The dusty track veered to the left, zigzagging upwards. To their surprise, they came across a solitary house. In the shade of a veranda, an old woman sat with a boy, of no more than three, perched upon her lap. The woman had cut up cloves of garlic into a decorative bowl and was now allowing the boy to suck her fingers, his eyes wide and delirious, bathed in joy. 'Kalispera,' Maria called out.

The old woman lifted her gaze and squinted into the afternoon light. She returned the greeting in a hoarse voice. Louis noticed a group of goats gnawing at a patch of sun burnt grass. They were tied to a solitary post and, as they turned their heads to inspect the newcomers with inquisitive glances, the indiscriminate peeling of bells rang around their necks.

One goat broke wind, a baritone explosion that brought a smile to Louis.

'They weren't born with manners and you can't teach them any.' The old woman sighed, irritated.

Her fingers now barren, the boy slid from her lap. He ran towards the goats, waving his arms in wide arcs. The startled animals made frantic efforts to escape the strained ropes. The boy ran amongst them slapping their backs and pulling their ears.

The old woman frowned. 'Thomas,' she croaked. She glared intently at the boy, her patience running thin. Pleased with his efforts, Thomas ran around the side of the house and disappeared from view.

'Wait till I get you, you little shit.' The old woman groaned, rising stiffly from the chair. She placed a wrinkled hand on the base of her back, scooped up the bowl of garlic and shuffled into the darkness of the house.

Louis watched the silhouetted figure disappear. He asked Maria what she had said.

'It looks like there's more than one old goat dispelling

hot air.' Maria smiled, she took his hand and curled her fingers around his, luxuriating in the touch.

They walked further. Maria had not felt this content for as long as she could remember. She had taken the week off work, since Anna's absence afforded them the opportunity to be alone together in the apartment. They retreated into a world of their creation. She felt like a goddess, omnipotent within the surging cyclone of her senses.

Ahead of them, the ground shimmered in the heat. Their feet disturbed dry earth in small clouds with dust as they navigated the curve of the track which finally brought them to a small clearing.

They sat under the shade of an acorn tree. Louis suggested, it felt like sitting on a high wall.

Below them, they overlooked a rich and flourishing garden.

Verdant wild flowers, cypress trees, olive, and lemon groves congregated in decorative clusters. Louis gazed upon them and noticed there was no uniformed pattern, no orderly structure, just natural formations, enriched by the whitewashed and primrose-coloured buildings of Argassi. Crowned in terracotta tiles, the biuldings roofs wove their passage towards the Ionian, like inland rivers finding the sea.

It reminded him of his morning ritual. He now had the rudimentary appliance of a kettle and fresh milk from the old fridge Anna gave him and, each morning, before breakfast, he drank a coffee on the balcony, absorbing the character and satiety of colour the sea afforded him. He never found it static; the sea greeted him on each occasion reborn, fresh and unpredictable. From his current advantage point, the sea did not disappoint either, as the waves undulated gently, the white surf bearing a striking contrast against the sapphire quality of the water. Towards Zakynthos Town, the deep nature of its colour subsided as a tame and palpable turquoise saturated the bay. The sprawl of houses, restaurants, churches, shops and museums that constituted the small capital completed a fusion of natural and manmade beauty.

Louis felt exhilarated. He could easily spend a lifetime here. It was an attraction that had welded onto his heart; he felt emancipated, transfigured even, as if a sacred light had reached and illuminated the darkest recesses of his being. Such a perfect moment was not lost on him, as he had felt its potent effect many times during his stay on the island.

Unexpectedly, a sudden surge of panic crept over him, how long could this last? Then, as soon as it came, the feeling receded as Maria spoke, commanding his attention.

'I wish moments like these could last forever; it just feels so perfect. When I am with you, the world could stop spinning and I wouldn't notice.' Her words struck him forcibly. He felt an acute and serene love for her, as a soft breeze licked the skin of his forearm. He brushed a strand of hair from her face.

A reflective look crossed his face. 'I don't think I've ever felt like this before. It feels like my life is being shaped by the movements of an unseen hand so no matter where I went in Greece I was always going to end up here with you.'

Maria looked at him curiously. 'Do you mean our lives are already mapped out, and we are destined to follow that path or that it's up to us to make choices that will lead us along that path? They are two different things.'

He thought for a moment. 'Don't you think some people are just destined to meet? Everything they do leads them to that single moment in time. That's how it feels to me. Every day that passed, every place I visited, drew me closer to you, leading me towards that very spot in Olympia where we finally met.'

Maria leaned back against the tree. 'It was a coincidence. We just happened to be in the same place at the right time. I've always been concerned with the here and now, living for the moment, planning for the future. I believe we make our own path.'

'Whatever happens in your life does so for a reason. We just need to work out why it happens.'

'No you're complicating it, it doesn't work like that.'

'Then how does it work?' he asked, raising his eyebrows.

'We instigate things by our words and actions, maybe there are no rules. What if life just carries on and whatever happens in it does so because of circumstance?' Maria smiled, content with her analysis.

'No,' he said insistently. 'You weren't just an accident. What we've got is more precious than that. We were destined to be together, every second we lived, every breath we took, every experience was drawing us closer to that moment.' He looked at her steadily, the conviction in his words still hanging in the air.

'So, if I've understood you correctly, what you're saying is our whole lives are mapped out for you - us, it's just a means to an end. So your relationship with Emma and her death were part of some master plan so that we could eventually meet.'

A dismissive expression crossed Louis' face. 'No, I'm not inferring that at all. Of course, if Emma and I hadn't separated, then I would never have met you but we're not responsible for her death.'

'Good. I'm glad. Such a thought would be inconceivable and tarnish what we have together.'

Louis detected a whisper of emotion in Maria's voice. He also considered his theory lacked serious substance and was fuelled by emotion.

'It would be ridiculous to even consider it.' A smile hovered on his face, a gesture that offered a truce.

Louis waited for her to say something, anything. She nodded and returned his smile. A truce was struck. Louis touched her chin and lifted her face to him. He drew a finger across her cheekbone and traced the outline of her lips. Louis cupped her face in his hands and, permeated by an effervescence that flowed through him, their lips met in a protracted kiss.

She pulled away from him. 'Did you feel that?'

'Yes.'

'The ground moved, just a little.'

'Like an earthquake?' he muttered.

'It was just a small tremor. We experience little ones quite often.'

'That's a bit scary.'

'Only if you're not used to it. Fortunately, we've not had a big one for a long time. It's not like the one in 1953. Then, none of the buildings could take the force of an earthquake that powerful; that's why it was so devastating. It's different now; all the buildings and houses are built to withstand earthquakes.' She paused and suppressed a smile.

'Don't worry, they say Greece is hit every fifty years by a big one. That gives us another year, at least.'

'Thank goodness for optimism.' Louis smiled.

Maria's eyes sparkled; glittering jewels that looked at him and then something else caught her attention.

'I wonder what that is.'

Louis followed her gaze and turned to discover a small building in amongst a clearing of trees.

'It looks like a church,' Maria suggested.

'If it is, then it's the smallest one I've seen.'

'Who would come here?' Louis thought out loud. For a moment, they sat and observed the flaking white paint of the walls.

'Come on, let's take a closer look.'

They rose to their feet and walked towards it. Louis felt a perceptible knot tie in his stomach. He peered through the only window, ingrained with dirt and dust; he was unable to see inside the small building. They moved around to the front of the building and discovered a wooden door. Maria pushed it and, to her surprise, it creaked open. Intrigued by what may lie beyond, they entered the diminutive building.

It took a second to acclimatize to the change in light. The air was stale and still, inhabiting a musky aroma that had not been inhaled by another human for months. They found a depletion of character; the walls were bare, cracks in its surface spread out like veins and tailed off into smaller trench like capillaries.

Mustard coloured paint bubbled in areas, protruding sores that peeled, like the shredding of diseased skin. A shadow of disappointment shaded them, yet Louis felt a compelling intimacy evident in the confined space. In a corner, he noted a small table arranged with two wooden chairs dusted in a coat of grime. Upon the table, an empty wine bottle sat, crowned with a candle where solidified wax had moulded into lava-like formations.

'It's certainly not a church?' Louis said. The image of the burnt candle unsettled him; he considered their presence as an intrusion.

'There's been no one here for a long time,' Maria said.

Under the table, cigarette butts littered the floor, ground underfoot. Bread and cheese, the evidence of a meal, lay undisturbed under a skin of mould that colonized the abandoned food.

The percussion of their voices peeled off the walls, amplifying their confinement in the small building. They stood, transfixed within the silence that enveloped them. His abdomen fluttered as if a flock of birds had been released inside him. Louis felt an urge to abandon himself to the rawness of his senses.

He could smell the perfumed scent of her hair, a sweet, invigorating fragrance that rose around him, seducing him, the temptation was too strong. Louis ran his fingers through the shining strands of her hair and bent forward, inhaling them as they fell and rippled from his fingers, like pages of a book caught in a breeze. He held her face in his hands, transfixed by the curling lashes and deep effervescent eyes.

'Louis.' Her lips widened into a smile. 'You shouldn't be doing this?'

'Why not?'

'Someone might come.'

'That's the whole point.' He smiled and drew her close to him kissing her longingly. She could feel the bulge of his trousers. She drew back from his lips and released him from his confines. He felt a warm rush of breath as she lowered herself onto him. A feathery sensation tickled deep inside him, he felt himself swell as his knees buckled slightly.

'Not yet.'

He turned her so that her back was against the wall. He pressed his weight against her body and slipped his hands under her dress, sliding along smooth skin. They eagerly sought each other's welcoming mouths and, still kissing, he lifted her. Maria wrapped her legs around him and, after a few attempts, eased herself upon him. His hand moved over the fabric of her dress. She arched her back and he could see the tilt of her throat and the curve of her chin. Louis kissed her there, covering her in light kisses until he found her mouth. His thighs ached and burned, protesting, as lactic acid rushed through muscle fibre, like a raging torrent. He moved towards the table, and as he gently laid her onto its surface, he swept the table with his hand, sending the wine bottle tumbling to the ground, in continuous arcs. He held on to her, moving deeper as her dress lay in folds across her body.

Maria felt the rush of heat build and the contractions came in waves. Louis lowered his mouth onto her lips, muffling her soft sounds. She clung to his back, and they both moved to a place where time became suspended. A bond wrapped itself around their hearts and there was no reluctance between them to become untangled from it; the abandonment was complete.

***

The voices seeped into him, floating around his head, like light feathers, until he opened his eyes and the voices continued to reverberate. Maria continued to sleep undisturbed; her only movement was that of her long eyelashes that flickered and for a second Louis wondered if she was dreaming. He rose and a surge of panic made Louis shake her.

'Maria, wake up. There's someone outside.'

Maria awoke, startled, until the familiarity of her surroundings became bathed in recognition and the implications of his words sunk into her. She got to her feet and straightened her dress, swaying in the hot and airless room. Maria breathed deeply, trying to keep at bay a wave of nausea. Louis looked at the window and the fading light, the sun was low in the sky and he wondered how long they had slept. A dark shape pressed against the glass and then moved away.

'There was someone at the window,' Maria whispered, a panic in her voice. Her head began to spin, the voices on the other side of the door now more audible.

'What should we do?' Maria asked, feeling vulnerable, her eyes wide and childlike. An irrepressible urge to protect her gripped him. It was an astonishing feeling, and he knew its presence had smothered his own fear.

'I'll go out and see who it is,' he said confidently.

'Maybe we should just wait, they might go away,' Maria suggested, staring at the door already persuading herself that such a course of action was unlikely. Louis leaned towards her and brushed the skin of her arm reassuringly.

'It's probably just someone out for a walk, children maybe?' he said gently.

'What if it's the people who were here before, smoking these cigarettes and eating this food?' She gestured to the remains scattered on the ground.

'There's only one way to find out.'

There was a silence, a moment of tension. Maria stood still, staring at the door, her heart pounding in her chest. Louis placed a finger to his lips and leaned an ear towards the wood of the door in concentration. His face strained with alertness, he listened, almost frowning. Maria shuffled towards him, as if reducing the space between them offered a reprieve from her agony of apprehension. A muffled sound could be heard just behind the door. Louis went to place his hand on the handle; he then turned to look at Maria and was about to speak, when from the other side a forcible push sprung the door open. It struck him on the forehead; its movement projected him backwards, stumbling awkwardly towards Maria who screamed and covered her mouth with a shaking hand. Louis grunted a curse as he massaged the pain in his head.

He glanced at two men who stood in the doorway. He rose to his feet, deep rapid breathing escaping his lungs. An uncomfortable silence permeated the air, as a perplexed expression froze across the stubble face of the man who had forcefully opened the door. He was middle aged; cracked leather skin suffused his face. Matted hair stuck to his scalp, thinning and unkempt. A coating of dust and grime caked his shirt and he had tucked his trousers into black boots, where a layer of dried mud clung to dull leather. Alarmingly, Louis' eyes traced a rusted rifle that loosely swung in dirt-ingrained fingers.

Standing behind him and peering over his shoulder a younger man stood, a baseball cap crowned his head with Nike blazoned on the front. He carried a rucksack on his back and from his belt tied with a length of rope, three rabbits swung from their bound legs, patches of deep red smudging the grey of their fur.

'Now this is a surprise,' the older man said, smiling through tobacco-stained teeth. His companion tipped a flask to his lips and swallowed, wiping his mouth with a sleeve. He laughed a deep cackle resonated in his throat, like a growling dog.

'Well then, if I had known we were having company, I'd have tidied the place up.' He threw his head back and laughed. 'Now you have used the facilities, I'm sure you wouldn't mind paying us a small fee. You'd be paying for our sense of generosity, you see, my friend here is particular about who he invites to our little place.'

Maria glanced at Louis. 'I'm frightened Louis,' she said. The man had spoken in Greek. Louis had no idea what he had said, however, their intimidating mannerism was enough to persuade him of the danger they were placed in; it became urgently clear that drastic action was needed. The only exit was blocked. Louis felt cornered, like a frightened animal. He grabbed Maria by the wrist and pulled her towards the door. He lurched towards the intruder, his shoulder crashing into his face. The older man's expression changed from amusement to confusion, as he fell against his companion who let out a surprised scream, as they both crumpled helplessly to the ground.

They ran until they could hardly breathe. Eventually, they sat against a low stone wall. Louis' heart pounded and, through a burning pain, his lungs screamed for air. Like a hammer, a pulse knocked against his temple. He massaged his forehead, nursing the bump. It felt tender and bruised.

Louis strained, listening desperately for any sound that might indicate they had been followed. Only a stillness met his ears, punctuated by the pulse of a cricket in the shrubs. Maria laughed. Louis turned to look at her.

She rested her fingers on him and stroked the bruise that coloured his skin.

'Did you see his face when you knocked him over?'

'I'm glad he fell into the other one. I don't know what I'd have done if he'd stood in front of me. Did you see how big he was?'

'You were so brave. My hero.' She smiled at him and he blushed. Louis recalled the look of surprise on the older man's face and he began to grin, recollecting his relief as the two men crashed to the ground in an undignified heap. He brushed her hand and a spark, like electricity, ran through him. Louis entwined his fingers around hers. She brought his hand to her lips and kissed it. He felt the familiar rush of excitement at the delicacy of her touch against his skin.

'I'm hungry. After all that excitement, I need to eat.' She smiled, rising to her feet.

A Sanctuary Invaded

They returned to Louis' apartment, where he made coffee, and ate small pastries on the balcony. That night, they went out for dinner in Zakynthos Town.

There was a menacing figure leering unscrupulously from the pavement. He pressed a crumpled bag to his face peering with demonic glassed eyes. He volleyed words in their direction, spat through a row of yellow stalagmite teeth. The diners could not to hear their meaning. However, his defiant demeanour and threatening posture enabled them to appreciate that they were not conducive to pleasantries, but rather delivered with a provocative sting.

'Today must be the Zakynthos' national convention for dodgy characters.' Louis tried to make light of the situation and continued to eat. He considered what he would do if the dishevelled figure entered the restaurant and continued his hostility towards them. An image formed of the two of them rolling between the tables and chairs and a depiction of American wrestlers presented itself. The comic illustration was replaced by an uneasy anxiety, laced with an urgent protectiveness towards Maria.

Either bored or craving another stimulant the unsavoury figure moved on, monitored by the curious glances of a few waiters. Louis watched him cross to the opposite side of the street and he shared Maria's relief, eradicating the prospect of an unwelcome confrontation.

'Has he gone?' consternation blossomed in her voice.

'Yes, I watched his reflection in those windows across the street,' he said, assuring her. 'He has moved off.'

'Are you sure?'

'Yes, of course, I am. Don't worry,' he said amiably.

As they ate, Louis noticed a small golden cross that hung from a fine delicate chain around Maria's neck.

'I've not seen you wear that necklace before.'

'It was a birthday gift from my mother. I've had it for years. I used to wear it all the time but the chain is fragile now and I only put it on for special occasions... like tonight, it's our last night together before Anna comes home.' She smiled, fingering the cross and guided it through the chain several times.

'Are you staying tonight? Anna won't be back until tomorrow morning; you might feel awkward.'

Maria looked at him. There had been a reticence about him, a delicate change from his usual self. 'Is there something wrong?' she asked softly. 'You've been in a strange mood since we came out.'

'I'm sorry,' he said. 'I phoned Jez earlier. I was just thinking about him, that's all. In fact, your necklace reminded me of something he said.'

He noticed a skinny cat stretch luxuriously under a table, its anonymity evident amongst the diners. Maria's necklace flickered, catching the nighttime lights of the restaurant.

'Do you remember I told you about a woman called Carris, Jez' housekeeper?'

Marie nodded.

'She's dying. Jez is devastated.'

'Louis, that's so sad. What is wrong with her?'

He told Maria the details of the call. Once he had finished, he took a drink of wine.

'That's awful, poor woman. I can't imagine how that must feel. It must have been dreadful. Imagine living a lifetime knowing nothing about your own child. She could be a grandmother by now.' Maria ran her fingers through a curtain of hair.

'And now it seems she'll never know. The sad part is time has moved on and attitudes changed. She's watched society accept teenage pregnancies. Today's children grow up in single-parent families; the state even provides for them. She's lived with the shame of abandoning her child, who can get over that? The gravity of it has remained with her to this day. Carris is not expected to live long, to the end of the month at the most.'

'That's only two weeks away.'

'I know.' Louis shifted in his chair. Maria thought there was still something playing on his mind.

'There's something else isn't there?'

Louis felt a nervous apprehension tickle him, he

hesitated. 'Jez asked if I'd consider coming home... just for a short while.'

She sat still; a rush of panic ran through her. 'And what did you say?' She swallowed, poised for his answer.

'I said I'd think about it. He's a close friend, what else could I say? I wanted to tell you first. I've known Jez a long time; he's like a brother to me. I feel I've abandoned him.' She looked away from him.

'He's just lost his sister Maria; he doesn't need to go through that again on his own.'

'Do you have to go?'

'No, but I feel I should.'

'People change, you might feel different about us.'

'I won't.'

'How do you know? You could be just caught up in this whole experience and, when you step out of it, I may not be an important part of your life.'

'I know my own mind, that won't happen. It doesn't mean I won't be coming back. I won't be gone for long, a week or two, maybe three, it depends. I won't know until I get there. The thought of leaving you, leaving all of this isn't something I would choose to do.'

She saw the agony of the decision he had to make, it crawled over him, and for a moment it calmed her storm. She reached out and took his hand across the table.

'Then you must go,' she said, quite matter of fact, and, once she had spoken the words, she fought to control the conflicting emotions that clawed at her. Maria lowered her eyes and stared at the food on the table; it seemed insignificant and unappealing. Louis detected her sadness, perceptible in the delivery of her words.

'It would only be for a short time, a couple of weeks at the most,' he said, answering his own indecision.

Maria swallowed. 'When will you go?' Her throat burned, as if a hot poker had been thrust into it.

'Within the next few days, I suppose. If I can't get a flight from here, then I'd have to book a flight to Athens and then to Edinburgh or Glasgow.'

The thought of this emphasized the distance that would

be between them. Louis lifted her chin and stroked her face.

'I'll only go if I know you want me to,' he said, soothingly. Although she tried not to, her eyes sparkled with tears. She looked at him and bit her lip.

'You'll be going back to your other life and I'll be here waiting for you, not knowing what you're doing, where you're going, what you're thinking. You might even meet someone else, a Scottish girl; you'll be attracted to her and forget all about me,' she said.

He smiled reassuringly. 'I'll think about you every second of every day and I'll phone in the morning, afternoon and at night and there's no one that could ever come close to how you make me feel.'

His heart raced. He gulped the sultry air, now flavoured with an aroma of cooked food and animated conversations that rose and fell in low murmurs around them. His sanctuary had been invaded; fragments of another life had cascaded over its walls. He contemplated saying he would phone Jez this very minute and say he could not go but he knew such an instinctive reaction would only make matters worse between them. He felt as if he had been punched in the stomach, but most of all he felt he was betraying her.

Shit, he screamed to himself. Could anything be worse than this. He waited until their eyes met.

'The last thing I want to do is hurt you, Maria. I couldn't bear it if this came between us. You must believe me; I love you more than anything in this world.' He paused to let the inference of his words sink in.

Maria composed herself, she hesitated. 'I'm being silly and selfish. Of course, you must go. Your friend needs you at this time. I'll be working, time will pass quickly. I know you'll come back.'

'My life's here Maria. Everything I want is here with you.' He tried to smile.

His thoughts somersaulted. The thought of not seeing her face for several weeks left him hollow. He could not have gone without her approval, he was sure of that; even though it felt as if it was forced upon her, she had no choice. Did she feel duty bound? The thought alarmed him; it engulfed him and flooded him, like torrential rain.

'Come with me.' He heard himself say as if someone else had spoken the words. 'Yes that is it, Maria. We'll both go.'

The idea of Maria accompanying him to Scotland made him instantly undisturbed. His face lit up. Why had he not thought of this? It seemed so simple.

'Jez would love to meet you.' His voice rose in a blinding certainty.

'I'm not sure Louis. Maybe under different circumstances.' She felt an uneasiness stab her.

'No, it's perfect Maria, can't you see? I won't be expected to be with Jez all the time. I could take you to visit my mother. You could see Edinburgh. We could stay at my place. There is no one staying in the flat now. The arrangement I had with John from work has expired. He has his own place now. What do you think?' He looked at her intently.

'I'm not sure Louis. One minute we are eating, then you are going to Scotland on your own, now you want me to come with you, all during a meal,' she said, exasperated.

'What am I to do?' The thought of being in the rooms that Louis shared with Emma, the place they called home unsettled her.

'It's perfect Maria, can't you see?' He touched her face as if to strengthen his argument. 'It is the perfect solution.'

'For you maybe, but not for me. You would have to ask Jez. I wouldn't want to intrude on someone else's grief. And then there's my work, and the money involved. I don't even know if my passport is still in date. I've not travelled abroad for years.'

He took her hand. 'When did you last go abroad?'

'When I was studying in Athens, some of my friends and I went to Spain for a holiday. It was renewed then.'

'Then it will still be in date. I want you to come with me... I'm not going without you.'

She smiled. 'You're so persuasive, but I've already had a week off work. I was lucky to get that. We're busy this time of year. I won't get any more time off.'

'Then tell them you're sick or you have to visit a dying

relative,' Louis insisted.

'No. I can't do that. Too many people know me, it would feel wrong.'

His elation evaporated. The more he tried to persuade her, the further his argument receded. Concern washed over him.

She sighed and lifted a glass of wine to her lips for fortification. Louis watched as a wet circular mark stained the tablecloth. The temptation to agree with him was a compelling thought, yet the logistics left Maria uncertain, and the prospects frightened her.

Louis was in turmoil. He had not wished for this. Louis sensed an insurgence of frustration. Regret was a painful thing. A smiling waiter asked if the food was to their satisfaction and Louis envied his cheerfulness as they made a polite comment. Louis tried to fight off his sense of betrayal, now that guilt ebbed at his reluctance to support his friend without Maria accompanying him. He could hardly speak. Louis gulped the remainder of wine that lurked in his glass; under the circumstances getting drunk seemed an appealing prospect.

Long silences punctuated the remaining fragments of their conversation and a sullen air hung over them to the detriment of their meal, which they both left uneaten. Anna would be back in the morning from Athens, their week alone had come to an end, like the inevitability of a sunset. Its culmination was now flat, subdued by the act of making a telephone call that left questions unanswered. How different tonight could have been, he told himself, frowning at the unwelcome predicament they were both faced with.

After their meal, they drank in a few bars and it was not long before their appetite for alcohol deserted them. Maria's glow of anticipation for the evening ahead had dulled and the consummation of the week at Anna's faded. Eventually, Louis walked Maria home, stopping a short distance from the house. They both hesitated, and when their eyes finally met, Louis leaned towards her and kissed her gently, tasting the scent of wine on her breath.

'This doesn't change anything.' He sighed.

'It already has Louis.' Heaviness filled her chest, like the turning on of a tap. Louis sensed a tightening in her voice.

'I'd better go now.' She sighed.

Maria freed herself from his embrace and turned to walk away. Desperately, Louis reached out and grasped her arm. She turned towards him.

'I belong here with you Maria. I've never been so sure of that. I want to be with you and share my life with you.' His voice strained, aching with tiredness.

'You are needed by your friend. We cannot change that.'

She released her arm and walked towards the house, her head bent forward in resignation. Louis sensed she was crying and nausea knotted in his stomach. He could not detach his gaze from her and even as Maria entered the house, without turning, he stared at the closed door. He knew she would not emerge and the door's stubborn stillness portrayed an air of finality around its frame. The temptation to run towards it intensified as each anxious moment slipped passed.

This is not right; an angry voice reverberated in his head.

Reluctantly he took a taxi to Argassi. A full moon hung in a black satin sky, like a luminous bulb, cascading silver light onto a contented sea. Louis hardly noticed the triangle of shimmering light that soaked the water. Instead, he recycled the turmoil of recent events and pondered the uncertainty that lay ahead of him.

Argassi greeted him with the bombastic ambience of a resort in the full flow of the tourist season. He stumbled into a bar and jostled for space, ordering a drink above the crashing sound of a pulsating bass drum. When his drink arrived, he swallowed the contents as if curing a ravishing thirst. He moved from bar to bar in a similar fashion, not stopping long enough to warm a seat, but draining the beer from each bottle with long siphoning swallows. Gusts of anxiety blew through him incessantly.

Eventually, he staggered out onto the dusty street. The lights of restaurants and bars seemed to possess a life of their own; they danced erratically before his bleary eyes. The inextricable dulling of his senses was at an advanced stage as he passed the pregnant street vendor. She looked up at him from her stool. A bulb from a solitary lamp splayed a soft light over her goods, which lay in uncluttered rows on a small wooden table that would be folded in half at the end of the night. She smiled as Louis passed and then her eyes clouded with concern at his intemperate appearance. She continued to watch his progress as he inevitably stumbled into a group of boisterous and drunken young women. She raised a hand to her mouth, as Louis tripped, his trajectory only broken by an impulsive outstretched hand that cushioned his fall against a stationary car. A middle-aged couple passed him with disapproving looks. An inward panic seized her, a desperate concern for the safety of the pleasant-mannered man, who had once bought a bracelet from her stall.

Finally, Louis approached the track that led to Anna's house; with the absence of electric light, he found he had to rely on the light of the moon. A thin covering of cloud periodically smudged the moonlight, forcing him to negotiate his way through a wall of thick blackness with the assiduous pulse of a cricket as his only companion.

The house was devoid of light, shrouded in a slumbering darkness. Anna would be home in the morning; he had missed her and their morning ritual. He walked towards the whitewashed block of small apartments he now called home, recalled with fondness the unsuccessful attempt to evade the attentions of Anna and the nights that followed with Maria. With such recollections, a profound ache bored into him with all the force of a pneumatic drill.

That night he could hear the wind rise, like an approaching train. The trees rustled in whispers, moving majestically as he watched the leaves dance against the black veil of the night sky. Dark stains coated the ground, slowly at first, forming patches that appeared more frequently, indiscriminately and without prejudice upon where they landed. The rain came in heavy sheets, falling at an angle; it created its own rhythm, the sound rising in the air, until it crashed all around, vibrating, a waterfall of rain. It was the first time it had rained since he had arrived in

Greece. It seemed that the sky had been saving its torrential onslaught for this moment. He stood at the edge of the balcony. Resting his hands on the peeling white paint, he raised his head. The droplets of moisture fell onto his face, feeling cool across his skin. Rivulets of rain trickled down his forehead spreading across his cheeks, small rivers traversing their path along his skin, like roads on an atlas. The water tickled his scalp; he opened his mouth, allowing the droplets to stroke his tongue, refreshing him, like the soothing touch of a masseur's hand. He felt as if the rain had baptized him in a new faith, as a renewed source of optimism wrapped its arms around him. It felt rejuvenating, and he was inspired with this newfound strength of confidence, for he told himself that he would persuade Maria to accompany him to Scotland. Somehow she will come with me, he convinced himself.

A Necklace's Secrets Revealed

'Ah, Kalimera Louis, I see my house is still in one piece.' Anna waved a bread knife as she spoke.

Louis' eyes squinted in the morning light as he walked with tender steps towards the shade of the veranda.

'Lucky for me.' he replied, a dull ache spread through his head. He gestured to the knife. Anna laughed. She finished slicing a loaf of bread and offered Louis a freshly poured cup of coffee.

He sat down, trying to avoid aggravating the throbbing pulse in his temple.

'You had a good night I see.'

He shrugged. 'How was Athens?' he asked, avoiding her question.

'Hot and noisy, we did not have breakfast like this; it is good to be home. I have missed our mornings together.'

'Me too. How was your son?'

'Oh, he is fine.' She waved a hand as if brushing away an irritation. 'He spends his time teaching and when he is not in his classroom, he is out with his new girlfriend,' she said disapprovingly.

'Oh, I see.' Louis noted a disappointed sternness in her voice. He allowed himself a slight smile.

'We had lunch and dinner only once together. All I wanted was some time alone with my son... oh and they are planning to be engaged.'

'It must be serious then. Before you know it, you could be a grandmother.'

Anna frowned. 'I would never see my grandchild. My son has forgotten where he came from. We have both changed. He is a man now, and I was still looking for the boy. It is hard for me to let go of that.'

'You're still his mother. You just have a different role now.'

'That is my problem. Anyway, enough about me, what about you, have you had a good week?' Anna sat back in her chair that creaked, as she folded her arms expectantly across her prodigious breasts.

Louis recalled the events of the past week and the phone call from Jez. Finally, he said, 'She knew her baby would be taken from her and the nuns would name the baby. Can you imagine, they didn't even allow her the dignity to name her baby? Somehow before the birth, she managed to persuade the doctor who delivered the baby to agree to take her necklace. Her own mother gave it to Carris when she was a child. It had her name and date of birth inscribed on it with the Virgin Mary carved on the pendant. She pleaded with the doctor to promise he would make sure the necklace was given to those that adopted her baby. She never found out if her wishes were carried out. The doctor left after that and she never saw him again. The thought that her child may have her necklace, something that belonged to Carris, that she valued, gave her great comfort throughout her life. In her lucid moments, she's told Jez more detail about that time. I think he's struggling. The fact that the church is responsible for hideous crimes against these women some of them just children themselves is playing with his conscience.'

Describing the phone call and its subsequent drama, Louis' voice became heavy with remorse and he settled on honesty. 'I hate myself for how I have made Maria feel.'

Anna listened, occasionally she would nod and sip her coffee but mostly she gazed at him thoughtfully. She reached for a plate of toast. 'Take some; you have not eaten since you sat down.'

'I seem to have lost my appetite.'

'Well then,' Anna said, replacing the plate on the table.

'This means you will be returning home.'

The words hung like particles of dust.

'The funny thing is Anna, I feel I am home. If anything good can come out of the things that have happened, then I am living it right now.'

'I am old Louis, but sometimes it is good to be old. I have had a long time to think about things and work things out. Some people say things happen for a reason. We do not understand why time goes on and we make some sense of it. We see it differently. We make our choices Louis, but if we want something good to come out of our choices, we need to make the right ones.' Anna smiled. 'So Louis, convince Maria you have made the right choice.'

'I think she knows.' He paused. 'I hope she does.'

A thoughtful expression crossed Anna's face.

'Clare had a necklace just like you described. She has had it as long as I have known her.'

'She has?' Louis drew in his breath.

'When she first came to Zakynthos, she wore it like it was part of her body. She tried to get one just like it for Maria's first communion day, but she decided to get one with a cross instead.'

'Really?' Louis leant forward in his chair.

'I have not seen it for a long time, she was afraid that she might break the chain.'

Louis stared at her and his look surprised Anna.

'What is it, Louis?'

'Was there anything written on the back of the pendant?'

She considered his words and her hesitation installed an impatience that pressed upon him.

'Try to think Anna, this is important,' he urged.

'I try Louis. She never told me about a name.'

Louis stood up and walked to the end of the veranda. He looked up to the sky taking in its vast expanse. He turned towards Anna.

'What is it, Louis?'

'Can't you see what this could mean? My God, the similarities are striking, it's so obvious now.'

'What?' Anna sighed, perturbed.

'But it doesn't all fit.' He scratched his head.

'You are not making sense, Louis.'

'Clare was born in Ireland and lived there. Am I right?'

'Yes, when she was very young.'

'Then she moved to Athens with her parents.'

'Yes, we know all of this. Everyone does.'

'The baby was born in an orphanage and would not have known her real parents.' He sighed. 'Clare knew her parents. The necklace is just coincidental. Lots of people have them. What am I thinking.'

He took a slice of toast, but then dropped it on his plate, at this moment eating felt like a distraction from his thoughts.

'Why did I not think of this before? I am an old fool, Louis,' Anna said apologetically.

'What?'

'Clare did not know her real parents.'

'What do you mean, Of course, she did'

'No Louis, she was adopted… is this what you say?'

Louis stood, as if paralysed.

'Clare never speaks of it. Her parents were her family, she knew nothing else. Clare's memories are of growing up in Athens. Her necklace is the only connection to her past. She has always known she was… adopted; her parents wanted her to know. They did not hide it from her. They told her that they chose her.'

A thought struck him. 'Clare has a necklace that originates from her childhood. If there is the name 'Carris' written on it and the dates of birth match then, my God, it's not impossible, unlikely, but still, things like this have happened, I suppose.' He rubbed his head.

Anna looked at Louis in astonishment. 'Louis, the name you have just said is Clare's middle name.'

'You're joking.'

'Why would I make a joke?' Anna looked puzzled.

'It's just a figure of speech.'

He approached the table. The enormity of such a possibility impressed upon him and as the seconds passed his stomach fluttered uncontrollably, like a butterfly entrapped within him. He sat down, trying to make sense of it all.

'Clare and Carris' baby could be the same person.' He paused to let it sink in. 'The name on the necklace is Clare's middle name…… Clare Carris.' The name rang in his ears.

Anna reached out and held Louis' hand. She pressed it tightly.

'I know Clare's date of birth.' Anna grinned.

Louis' stomach leaped as if he had just run off a cliff

edge.

'We celebrate our birthdays by going out for a meal. It has become a tradition.'

Louis could feel his excitement grow, it blossomed inside him.

'I have to phone Jez, we need to know if the dates match. Anna, this is incredible.'

She smiled. 'We may have just solved your problem.' Louis looked at her blankly.

'If this woman is Clare's mother, then Maria will go with Clare to Scotland; this woman will be Marie's grandmother.'

He imagined Maria's reaction and, with such thoughts, visualized the deep ocean of her eyes.

Anna continued, 'This will be the first and last time Clare will see her real mother.'

'If Clare is Carris' daughter, then her mother is dying.'

The realization disarrayed his thoughts, a disturbance that highlighted a new urgency.

'We don't have long, Anna.' He looked at her and smiled vaguely. 'If we've just discovered what I think we have, then we have one man to thank for this.'

'Who?'

'The doctor. Out of a sense of shame or kindness, by giving the necklace to Clare's parents, he may have just brought Clare and Carris together again.'

The Homecoming

Life's Full Circle

The interior of the taxi was refreshingly cool. Through the open window, the breeze licked his skin, like a trailing finger across his forearm. Spontaneous thoughts presented themselves, replaying his conversation with Jez. Louis smiled, recalling his friend's ecstatic reaction as the filtering of information made its impact over the crackling phone line, confirming Clare was indeed Carris' daughter. In quick succession, Jez thanked Jesus, sucked on his cigarette, tilted a whisky to his lips and whispered, 'Fucking hell Louis, what have you been up to over there?'

Louis recalled the irrepressible somersault in his stomach and it once again moved inside him as his thoughts turned to Maria. He smiled, replaying their conversation, and he laughed as her increasingly hysterical voice failed to quench the upsurge of naked emotion, as Louis relayed his discovery.

Louis turned to look at the sea, its calm and glass composition in stark contrast to the swirling and knotting of his stomach. He would soon be at the house; everything had been arranged in a flurry of activity. Stelios had insisted that he would pay the plane fares to Edinburgh, stating with satisfaction that, after all, what was the value of money if you could not spend it at a time like this? Stelios viewed it as his responsibility, he informed the family.

Clare had called to her and, as Maria climbed the stairs to her mother's bedroom, she recalled a house rule that even as a child she had never broken. The sanctuary of her mother's bedroom could only be entered by an invitation. She stood in the doorway and examined the room. Her eyes fell upon the extravagant dressing table, its surface impeccably neat and arranged with bottles of perfume, a silver brush and a hand-painted makeup box which sat before a mirror set in a dark wooden frame. The air was rich with the fragrance of lavender. A large rug covered the floor and opposite the bed, whose sheets were pristinely pressed, a prodigious chest of drawers dominated the room.

It had been constructed by local carpenters for Clare's wedding, a present from her soon to be husband. When it arrived a few days after the festivities, Clare was sceptical whether it would ever see the inside of the bedroom. Her fears were proved unfounded, as the persistence of her husband, two carpenters, and a neighbour saw them precariously move the cumbersome load up the stairs. Once the chest had reached the entrance, one carpenter had to remove the bedroom door from its hinges to allow its entrance to the room where it stood ever since.

Maria's eyes travelled the room. She remembered, as a teenager, sitting at the dressing table, applying her mother's makeup, whilst her amateurish attempts brought a radiant smile to Clare's lips.

The wooden slatted doors were opened to the veranda, allowing the light drapes to sway in the soft breeze as if someone had momentarily brushed passed them.

Maria walked over to Clare, who stood in front of the dressing table, passing a gold chain through her fingers. As she crossed the room, Maria noticed the familiar feeling of protection. A safe and secure sensation that washed over her as it had done on countless occasions, when as a child and a nightmare had stolen her sleep, she stood at the doorway and a protective hand guided her to the warmth of her parents' bed. She moved closer and stood by her mother's side and, in doing, so she caught the familiar scent of her perfume. She looked at the necklace and noted Clare's fingers lightly brush the inscription.

'I've had this necklace all my life. I was told that my birth mother gave it to me before we were separated and now this same necklace will have brought us together.'

Maria touched her mother's hand. She knew her eyes glistened with tears.

'It has taken so long, a lifetime; it may be too late now. I have found my mother, an old woman who is dying.'

'You've been given this wonderful chance. You'll be able to be with her you have an amazing opportunity to tell her of your life. She'll finally know she has a daughter, a daughter she can be proud of. You can give her this special gift. She has also been waiting a lifetime.' As she spoke Maria could feel the heavy irony in her words.

'Before she dies,' Clare said softly. She hesitated. 'I'll never know her. She'll always be a stranger to me.'

'But you do know her. She's part of you, you'll have her eyes and you'll laugh like her. You've been the mother she would have given anything to be. She's in your heart and you have been in hers all these years.'

Maria's throat tightened.

Clare raised her eyes from the necklace and smiled.

'Help me put it on.'

Maria brushed her mother's hair to the side and fastened the clasp.

'When you and your brothers were born, I realised then what it must have been like for her. I couldn't imagine the pain of having the most precious thing in your life taken from you. I've thought about her every single day and, as the years passed, well, life has a habit of moving on and I've almost become numb to such thoughts.'

'It has a habit of coming full circle as well.' Maria smiled.

Stelios was the first to greet Louis, as he led him to the kitchen and hugged him, like a long lost brother. Maria entered the kitchen with Clare close behind and, around them, a flurry of expectation and excitement fused the air, like an electrical storm.

Maria walked over to Louis, smiling. She laid her hand on his shoulder and kissed him on the cheek and, in doing so, she looked into his eyes for reassurance.

'Jez will pick us up at the airport and then take us straight to the manse.'

Louis words confirmed she was not living in a dream; their meaning indicated a tangible reality that washed over her. A smile of gratitude crossed Clare's face as she walked towards him.

'Let me embrace the man who has made today possible.'

Clare's arms enveloped Louis. He felt uncomfortable with the intimate attention. Hesitantly he placed his hands on her back. He was as astonished by his discovery as Maria's family was, and his reaction clarified he had not been given the fullness of time to appreciate the effect and significance recent events had imparted upon all of them.

She sensed an awkwardness about him, like a child unable to answer a teacher's question in front of a class.

'I'll never forget what you have done for us Louis; you will always be a part of my family.' The sincerity that laced Clare's voice relaxed him, even as her hair tickled his skin.

'My journey will be a homecoming.'

A Family Tradition

There was a sense of achievement in Louis' posture as he walked into the heat of the garden. Maria followed him, her face transparent with wonder, an expression significant to the revealing proceedings of the last few days. They settled themselves on the bench, within the shade of the large tree that dominated the garden.

'You look incredibly happy,' Louis said, his lips curled at the edges, into an approving smile.

'I am, I want to express my happiness. How can I conceal what I'm feeling on a day like today? That is the difference between men and women. We are more intense. We express how we are feeling through our facial expressions and body language. We communicate our feelings, it's a natural thing for us to do. I will never understand men. It's alien for a woman to behave like a man. Men hide their feelings with silence, you control them, where women, especially Greek woman, we're like erupting volcanoes; our words are like lava pouring from us.' She smiled at the association.

Louis looked away awkwardly.

'See,' Maria accused.

'What?' Louis looked at her defensively.

'You're concealing your emotions through your behaviour.'

'And when did you become a psychologist?' Louis grinned.

'All women are psychologists; it's a biological thing, part of our makeup actually.'

'Especially the Greek ones.' A playful tone laced his voice.

'Another thing; men can only do one thing at a time, useless.' She shook her head. 'We women can do many things. I could be stopped at traffic lights in my car watching the traffic, while at the same time I could be looking in my bag for lipstick and talking on my mobile.'

'I've no doubt you speak from experience,' he teased.

She bent forward to flatten a crease in her dress and her hair fell like a curtain across her cheek. Something stirred in him, an animalistic pang. He pushed it away.

He cleared his throat and held her hand. 'I'm going to be serious now. I've thought a lot in the last few days. It's made me feel a sense of urgency about us. It's made me reflect on what I really want. I can see that very clearly now. I don't want to regret not making the decisions that need to be made.'

'And what decisions would they be?' She lightly squeezed his hand.

He took a deep breath. 'Remember when we were on the ferry and I asked you what you wanted out of life? Well, I'm going to answer that question now. I belong here. I want to spend my life here in Zakynthos. I want to find a job and buy a house and maybe someday have children who can grow up in the warmth of an extended family. At the centre of this, there is one person, you Maria. I'm asking you to marry me.' He felt a glow of satisfaction.

Maria looked surprised; she turned her gaze to the ground. Louis reached out and lifted her chin, turning her face towards him. He looked into her gaze and, as always, he found himself being drawn into her large glistening eyes.

'Now who is concealing their feelings with behaviour?'

'Do you?' She floundered. 'I mean, are you sure this is what you want?'

'Maria, apart from getting on one knee, I'm asking you to marry me. I can't be more explicit than that.'

'No, I suppose not.'

'Well then.' He looked hesitant.

'Well, what?' She teased with a smile.

Louis moved closer to her. He swallowed.

'Will you be my wife?' he said softly, almost whispering the words.

'Did you know my father proposed to my mother under this tree?'

He lowered his lips closer to her mouth.

'And will you make it a family tradition?'

'Yes, yes.'

He kissed her, smothering her words of acceptance.

***

The afternoon sky looked relentless, dark and menacing. In an instant, a deluge of rain, like thousands of rapid tiny sparks, flashed off the pavement forming an impetuous flow that engulfed already swollen drains. They huddled outside the airport terminal, cowering under umbrellas that offered little protection as they hurriedly endeavoured to seek the shelter of Jez's car.

Once inside the vehicle, their clothes stuck to them, like a second layer of skin.

'I see you've been having another typical summer.'

Louis wiped the spreading condensation from the windscreen. Jez turned the fan on to its maximum point and raised his voice over the blowing drone.

'One thing for sure, it's been consistent.' He smiled at Louis. 'Consistently bloody wet… welcome back Louis.'

Maria's mouth gaped open, an expression that amused Louis.

'You'll get used to him.' He smiled.

'I've never heard a priest swear.' The words sounded awkward in her mouth.

'That's nothing. You should hear him on a Saturday afternoon at Easter Road, especially a derby game.'

'Now Louis, I wouldn't want these lovely ladies to get the wrong impression of me.'

'You're doing a good job of that on your own,' Louis smirked.

A damp heat circulated in the car, as Jez put it into gear and moved slowly from his parking space. Looking in the rear mirror, he observed Clare's fixed and glazed expression and he knew her thoughts were consumed with only one person. He turned and smiled at her and, in doing so, he noticed that she sat with her fingers tightly entwined. Clare stared at the sky with its promise of more rain.

'It's time to take you to your mother,' Jez said, with a sense of urgency.

Reunion

They entered the warmth of the manse, their clothes still damp. In the hallway, Jez placed their luggage at the foot of the stairs.

'Let me take your coat.' He motioned with his hand.

Clare released herself from her jacket and looked at the top of the stairs.

'Is her room upstairs?' It was the first words she had spoken since they had left the airport.

'Yes, it is. The nurse will be with her. Would you like something hot to drink, tea or coffee perhaps?'

Clare shook her head and offered Jez her jacket.

'This is where she worked,' Clare said as if speaking her thoughts out loud.

She looked around the hallway, an intimate stare that consumed every inch. She traced her finger over the polished surface of the banister; a pleasing smile crossing her lips. Meticulously, she studied each detail of her surroundings, walking through the ground floor, from room to room, in a slow but purposeful manner. She paused and stared, grazing each surface with a trailing finger or attentively looking out of a window. She found herself in the hallway again. She noticed a crucifix on the wall and touched the feet of the crucified Christ. In a whispery voice, she said, 'Efcharisto.'

Jez lowered his head towards Louis. 'What did she say?'

'Thank you,' Louis whispered.

'I'm ready now.' Clare drew a deep breath. 'Will you take me to her?'

'Yes, of course. Do you want to be alone?' Jez asked.

'No. We've all come a long way for this moment. We can go together.'

They climbed the stairs in solemn silence, the creak of a floorboard, the only audible sound. They reached the landing, where the light became dull shading the walls with elongated shadows. Maria rested her hand on her mother's arm, a gesture to fortify them both. Jez paused and knocked lightly on the wooden door panel, before entering the room.

The nurse slid passed them, smiling awkwardly, and then descended the stairs.

Clare hesitated at the entrance as Jez crossed the room and opened the heavy drawn curtains, and in a grey light, the interior revealed itself. Jez gestured subtly with his hand, prompting Clare into the bedroom. She edged through the doorway, her eyes instinctively drawn to the bed, infiltrating in her a burning sense of anticipation. The room was large and spacious; again, she hesitated before moving closer to the side of the bed and the motionless Carris.

Clare found herself surprised, but relieved, as her eyes fell upon the calm and gracious composition of Carris' face and upon that face, the recognition of an extraordinary woman was instant. Carris was unresponsive to the solemn procession that filed into her room, the outside world no longer existing.

She moves as if floating through the field of grass. The breeze bends the stalks and they look like undulating waves on an angry sea. She is wearing a blue sleeveless dress that falls to her ankles. Her feet are bare and she can feel the ground under them, hard and compact as she walks. The sun is hot; it warms the skin of her forehead and arms. She can hear birds singing, their song rising in the air, like heat. It reminds her of long summer walks in the countryside when she was younger and like that time she does not feel alone. A rabbit scurries ahead of her and darts into a burrow. Up ahead, shimmering in the heat, as if hovering above the ground, she can see a two-story house, sitting on its own. As she draws closer, she can see it is constructed of fine stone. On the porch and in the shade, an old man and woman sit on wooden chairs. They rise stiffly from their seated positions and wave. The man leans against a wooden post. A dog, a long haired Retriever, wags its tail and barks excitedly, the man leans forward and pats the dog.

Clare sat on a chair, next to the bed. Carris' hair rippled out onto the pillow, falling over her shoulders. Clare reached out and held Carris' hand.

'It's me, mother. I have come home.'

Clare bent forward, her forehead resting on Carris' hand and it was then that her fortitude abandoned her in irrepressible sobs. The expanse of a lifetime folded in on her, as time tapered to this one defining moment.

She lifted her head and placed Carris' hand to her mouth and, ever so lightly her lips brushed her mother's skin. She combed the tumbling hair with her fingers. So much hair for her age, she thought.

Clare recorded and stored her mother's features, every detail, putting them in a safe place in her mind, which would be revisited, replayed and pored over in the years to come. She rested her finger on Carris' face and gently grazed her milky skin. She traced her mother's lips, where faint lines fanned from the edges of her mouth. Clare watched the long eyelashes that curled at the ends. They reminded her of Maria. She longed to gaze upon Carris' absent eyes and submerge herself in their depths and colour. Clare ached to hear the sound of her voice, to watch the movement of her lips and catch the words spilling from them. She craved to recapture the years they were denied, a lifetime. The loss crawled within her, like a prowling animal, a loss defined by years of absence and the unknown.

The grass is long, and she brushes it with the tips of her fingers. The woman is speaking to her, gesturing with her hand. Because of the distance between them, she is unable to hear the words or the sound of the voice. An irresistible urge is pulling her towards the house. She is singing a song, its beginnings stretching back to her childhood. She can smell the sea, a hint of salt in the air. The sky is like an ocean, its colours unbroken and vast. She can feel dust between her toes; her toenails are painted red, glittering in the sunlight.

The potent fragrance of lilies hovered in the air and it was then that Clare noticed a glass vase erupting with white petals and emerald leaves on the bedside cabinet.

'They're her favourite flowers,' Jez said solemnly.

Clare breathed in deeply. 'And mine too.'

'We should leave you alone,' Jez pronounced, glancing to the door.

Maria moved towards Clare and kissed her on the cheek. They left the room in silence, relieved that their intrusion was at an end.

'You're a grandmother; your grandchildren are Maria, Stelios, and Michalis. You're also a great grandmother to two lovely children. We live in a place called Zakynthos. It is an island in Greece. I left the orphanage when I was a baby. One day a couple arrived, and they took me to a house in Dublin. When I was seven, we moved to Athens, and I grew up with my new family. I became a nurse. I met my husband, Peiros, in Athens; you would have liked him. He took me to his home in Zakynthos, where we were married. My mother and father returned to Ireland, and I was adopted for the second time in my life as Peiros' family became my family. It was not long before I had children of my own and I raised my family as best as I could. I thought about you every day. I wondered what you looked like if, you had married and started your own family. Then when I became a mother, I was finally able to understand what you must have gone through. I don't blame you, I've never hated you. I know you were made to give me away... I have always loved you. It was the necklace you gave me as a baby that led us here. It was the only connection to my past I owned. It's strange how things can turn out. It's as if I was meant to keep the necklace because it would lead me to you.'

The old man and woman descend the wooden steps, steadying each other. Behind them, a young man in an army uniform follows. They walk towards her, smiling as they near her. Other people too, have appeared, their voices filling the air, like a choir of a church. She is surrounded by many people, faces that are now familiar to her. They are smiling and happy and she is filled with the most wondrous elation as her mother and father embrace her.

Clare bent forward and kissed her mother on the cheek and, in doing so, she noticed Carris' eyelashes flicker, like the movement when someone is sleeping and, to her wonderment, a hint of a smile appeared on Carris' lips before she exhaled a deep breath and her chest no longer rose.

Louis blew on the hot coffee, as steam rose from the cup like an apparition. Underfoot, the grass was heavy and wet, squelching with each step, leaving the stems of grass flat with traces of footprints as he walked. The air around him harboured an earthly odour as he looked out upon the patch worked Fife countryside. The architecture of the clouds reminded him of giant cotton wool shapes pursuing each other over the pale blue sky. He marvelled at how suddenly the weather could change and he remembered days where it felt like the four seasons had visited.

Jez stood on the patio, portraying an anxious figure as he spoke to Maria. Louis noted a stiffness in his posture and then it occurred to him that Jez was not just anticipating the loss of a housekeeper, but someone whose continuous presence in the fabric of his life had become like a mother to him. He walked over to them.

'Are you ok?'

Images of Carris swam in Jez' head. 'I'm fine,' he lied.

'I've had time to prepare myself for the inevitable.' His face betrayed the lack of emotion in his voice, as his eyes welled up with tears. 'She is a remarkable woman.'

'I know.' Louis placed his hand on Jez' shoulder, offering the physical support his words failed to convey.

Clare stood in the doorway. A pensive statue. Each sensing her presence, looked at her, intently reading her body language, like the pages of a book.

The cigarette fell from Jez' hand. Maria's fingers tightened around Louis' arm and the tight skin across her collarbone heaved as panic swept through her, like a storm.

'She has left us,' Clare said simply.

The screeching wail of two seagulls broke the silence.

Clare walked across the lawn and lifted her gaze towards the sky. The two birds glided upon the air currents, circling above them as their wing tips almost touched. They moved in fluent motions as smooth sweeping curves dictated their direction, like a dance gracefully performed with the stillness of the sky as their audience. The sun caught their wings in silver light and it seemed as if they were waiting in anticipation for some specific event. A third seagull appeared and joined their dance as a palpable excitement radiated from their cries, intensifying as they flew in a great circle and then as a group they headed in an eastward direction. Clare watched as their wingspans grew smaller, becoming blurred as the distance grew between them. A smile crossed her face.

The sound of a choir accompanied by a gravelly organ floated from the church and across the lawn, like a trailing mist.

'Incredible.' Jez said.

'What is?' Louis asked.

'That's Carris' favourite hymn. She sang it almost every day.'

'How Great Thou Art,' Louis said.

'Yes, the sound of it filled the air in every room. She would sing as she cleaned or cooked,' there was a tremor in his voice before he gained his composure. 'I will miss her terribly.' He felt Maria's hand on his elbow.

'Come inside and I'll make us all a coffee.'

'I need something stronger,' Jez said. 'I'm sure Carris would approve, just this once.'

Maria walked over to Clare and hugged her. Her mother's eyes glistened with tears.

'It's ok Maria. She has gone to be with those that love her. There's no sadness in that, only great joy.' Clare touched Maria's arm. 'There's no death for those that believe. We must celebrate her life and not mourn our loss.'

'I couldn't have said that any better myself. You're right Clare. I'll pour the drinks and we'll toast the woman who has touched all of our lives in so many different ways.' Jez ushered them inside, as the choir fell silent.

Athens of the North

She reluctantly emerged into the awakened world. It took an effort to open her eyes but, in doing so, her attempt gave witness to silver shafts of light that speared the dim bedroom like an electric storm. She felt disorientated, unable to gather her thoughts into a coherent sequence, until the progress of recollection revealed itself, like the awakening sun outside, rising above the Edinburgh skyline. This was the fourth morning since Carris' funeral. Jez had insisted Clare stay at the manse, an invitation she eagerly accepted to spend time in the surroundings where her mother's life had been decorated in meaning and purpose and it was here also that she hoped to discover a closeness, a reassuring bond that would remain with her when her time to return home came.

At the funeral, it seemed the entire village had assembled to pay their respects. The news of Carris' daughter returning from Greece had filtered into every corner of village life, like an epidemic. Clare had been met with friendly smiles and courteous nodding of heads. She felt uncomfortable with the attention, but accepted with a resigned grace, she would be the source of inspiration for conversations, exchanges and glances that felt like an inquisition . In her hurry to travel, she had neglected to pack suitable clothing for a funeral. Although her mother's death was imminent, it had not occurred to her she would attend her funeral so soon. Jez had seen to the practicalities of arranging the funeral, which left Clare and Maria to go shopping for suitable outfits.

Throughout the day of the funeral, which Jez conducted with a graceful duty, Clare felt tired and exhausted. She endured ripples of panic, as she prised her mouth open to acknowledge another stranger who emerged from her mother's world. The same sentences and phrases spilled from her mouth, like the recited lines from an actor's performance. The words became stripped of their meaning in reply to the seamless parade of sympathetic voices and curious glances. She felt ashamed that her instincts demanded she escape their good intentions and empathetic utterances, but mostly she was overwhelmed by their sincere compassion and stories that concerned her mother's life.

After seeking Clare's approval, Louis and Maria used his flat as a base. Louis insisted that this was the best time of year to be in Edinburgh, during the festival, where the streets pulsed with a vibrant concoction of nationalities, colour and cultures. Maria smiled at the elation in his voice as he described his home city with vivid and descriptive accounts which left her thinking, if she did not accept his invitation, he would be in a constant state of bewilderment. After spending a few hours in the festival bubble herself, she felt ablaze with excitement and exhilaration.

They visited Louis' mother, who prepared a lunch of homemade vegetable soup and slabs of crusty bread, which Maria ate feeling uncomfortable under his mother's gaze, whose eyes examined her as if she was surveying a mannequin in a shop window. Later, and to Maria's surprise, Louis remarked that she had met with his mother's approval, an observation that dulled the spiral of knots in her stomach.

She pulled the duvet to her chin. She could hear the murmur of activity in the kitchen, the clinking of crockery and a kettle bubbling with hot water. The sounds of domestic mediocrity soothed her senses that were fraught with a feeling of being watched every time she found herself alone in a room.

She had detected a dragging in her stomach that pronounced itself when she lay in bed at night. Although there was no residual evidence of what had taken place, and Louis had never spoken of it since they arrived, this was the bed that wove the roots of deceit and lust. Entwined in its sheets was the deception that spiralled two lives apart and ended in the death of Emma and her unborn child. A loss that entered Louis life, wrenching him from the world he knew, he identified with and which eventually evaporated, like steam on glass. Yet, without such tragedy, Maria contemplated, Louis would not have met her on that sultry day in Olympia. He would not have touched her life with such galvanising clarity; his hands would not have traced her skin and left her bewildered in its rapture. She had been exhilarated and found herself in the wake of elation. She had come out of the shadows and he had stirred in her the flicker of a flame. The contradiction was not lost on her.

She endured instinctive reservations when Louis suggested spending a few days at the flat. Between the two of them, a tangible uneasiness was evident. On the first day, Maria sensed an air of reticence around Louis, which he tried to suppress unconvincingly. Emma's adultery had covered each room and hallway, like ugly wallpaper. Its corrosive effect was endured by both of them; even in her absence, death could not remove Emma's imprint on each room.

That night she asked him what side of the bed Emma slept? She elected to sleep on the opposite side, eventually falling asleep in Louis' arms. On the third night, they made love. Louis' enthusiasm for the intimacies of their passion was felt by both of them as a disclosure. Their cravings for each other evaporated the uncomfortable atmosphere and gave way to an outpouring of relief.

As she lay in bed, drifting in and out of a shallow sleep, she felt a comforting warmth when recalling the scintillating pleasure of the night before.

'Good morning,' Louis said brightly, entering the bedroom in a crumpled t-shirt and pants and holding two mugs of coffee.

'I was hoping to wake you with a kiss.'

'Are you sure that was all you were going to wake me with? Someone looks happy to see me.' Maria smirked.

'Oops.' He looked at her intently, 'I'm afraid that's the effect you have on me.'

'Coffee will do just fine,' she said, sitting up and reaching for the mug. Louis sat on the edge of the bed.

'I thought we could go out for breakfast and do some shopping before lunch. There's a nice little place not far from here. They make the most amazing scrambled egg, toast, and bacon.'

'That would be nice.' The thought of breakfast made her realise how hungry she was. She reached out and touched his arm.

'Last night,' she said. 'In a way, it made it easier being here.'

'I know.' He smiled, gazing warmly into her eyes. 'I felt it too.'

She kissed him affectionately on the lips and sensed that something had lifted between them. 'I'm going to take a shower now,' she said, an optimistic tone colouring her voice.

They emerged into the golden sunlight where elongated shadows cast the pavement in charcoal patches, like seeping oil spillages. The opulent grandeur of St. Mary's cathedral provoked an outpouring of feverish appreciation from Maria and it was only the intractable wave of hunger that restrained her desire to take in an excursion into its shadowy interior.

They made their way along William Street, passing Amber's café and a smiling Carla who waved at them. Louis had introduced Maria to Carla the day before and a satisfied feeling encased him as the two women warmed to each other and conversed as if they had been best friends for years. They passed decorative shop windows that specialized in clothes distinctive in look and appeal. The streets opened into an expanse of space, bordered on each side by a sequence of symmetrical and palatial facades. As they turned into Queensferry Street, lined with sandwich bars, delicatessens, bars and restaurants, an incessant flow of traffic and pedestrians cumulated a wall of noise that absorbed them.

'Here we are,' said Louis, opening the glass fronted door to Ristorante Anti Pasti.

There were few diners, which offered them the luxury of the pick of tables. They elected to sit at the windows; the floor to ceiling glass fronts afforded them an unrestricted view of the confluent throng of people hurrying to offices and shops. A young waitress, with a white shirt and hospitable smile, took their order and relayed it in Italian through a wide kitchen hatch. The walls were stripped to the original stonework, supporting shelves where rows of wine bottles stood, like soldiers on parade. Several walls were adorned with original paintings that used the stonework as their canvas, depicting Italian cities and squares with ornate fountains. The waitress returned with two plates of toast, bacon, scrambled egg, two cups of coffee and a bottle of water. As they ate, Maria felt relieved, sensing a semblance of normality descend upon them, in contrast to the protracted amalgam of emotions the previous few days had induced. With the funeral over, her thoughts now concentrated on home.

After breakfast, they walked to Charlotte Square, dominated by symmetrical buildings, clean lined and mirror imaged. They strolled hand in hand along George Street. Maria stopped every few yards to inspect a window display, sometimes entering the shop and asking Louis' opinion on an item of clothing, 'Do you like the colour? I should try it on, what do you think?' He felt exhausted just answering her. They spent the morning walking around the shops of the new town area of the city. At lunchtime, they turned into Hanover Street and strolled towards Bar Napoli. They ordered their starters accompanied by a bottle of house red. Maria was invigorated and spoke with excitement about their return to Zakynthos and the planning and preparation that would need to take place. Her mood was buoyant as she suggested they would need to consider a date for the wedding; his mother would need to know also those members of his family he was thinking of inviting. Of course, not all of them could come to Zakynthos, so it was important to get numbers sooner rather than later, she said. She spoke in an intense flurry, her words coming to life as she spoke. He rolled tagliatelle around his fork and speared some asparagus. Maria had ordered a Bolognese ravioli.

'I need to make arrangements, put the flat on the market, that sort of thing. I've got an appointment with the estate agent tomorrow and there're a few things I need to tie up at work.'

'That's good.' Maria smiled at him. 'It's really

happening.'

'By tomorrow we'll have started the process. We've come so far in such a short time.'

'It's a big step, Louis.'

'It is, but it's the right one to take. The flat is only bricks and mortar. I've never been surer of anything in my life.'

'And I too.'

'I was thinking this morning, most of us were born out of love stories; we're all the product of our parent's love stories essentially. Look at Clare and your father, for instance. What they did all those years ago is no different to what we're doing now.'

'I never thought about it like that. I suppose we are.'

'I need to ask Anna if I can stay at the apartments for the time being.'

'I wouldn't worry about that. She'll be glad to hear you're staying longer. She's fond of you.' Maria smiled.

Louis thought of Anna, his small room in her apartment block and his morning habit of taking breakfast with her. He realised he missed these routine connections to Anna and Zakynthos.

'It's strange. I sometimes feel that Greece didn't happen, it was a dream somehow, but having you here with me in Edinburgh is a constant reminder it's real. I can't believe you're here with me.'

'It's strange for me too. I never expected to be here.'

There was a moment's silence between them. Maria could sense him thinking.

'With the money from the sale of the flat we could buy a house anywhere on the island, you decide, probably near your mother. There's nothing stopping us building our own house. We'd have enough money and some left over. You can design the house and I'll draw up the plans. In fact, we could get Stelios to build it. It could be ready for when we get married.'

Maria felt she was standing on the edge of a cliff with her stomach in her mouth. Yet, hers was not a reaction to some imminent proposition of dread or one that appalled her. On the contrary, it was a life-changing prospect, the possibilities of which had been blurred by so much uncertainty and the convoluted details of their relationship, the debris of which had now been washed away, a cleansing that had left them both renewed and replenished. These adjustments to her life suffused her in a feeling of incredible warmth.

After lunch, they strolled, arm in arm through Princes Street Gardens. Ahead of them Louis saw a young boy running after a ball; the boy stumbled and, unable to keep his balance, fell against the concrete pavement. A group of his friends had caught up with him and, as Louis and Maria passed, his friends were studiously inspecting a grazed knee, at which point Louis heard the boy report, 'If you rub your spit onto the graze it helps it to heal.' They all craned forward, examining the wound like doctors on a ward round.

Around them several children rode on bicycles, weaving in and out of small groups of adults who supervised children swarming over climbing frames and roped walkways, like an army of industrious ants. A girl threw a ball up into the branches of a conker tree. Louis watched as her expectant look gradually faded with each failed attempt and her enthusiasm drained from her, until eventually, disinterested, she ran off, throwing the ball at intervals and expertly catching it.

Further along, they sat on a bench, several pigeons congregated at their feet, pecking the ground feverishly. Maria teased Louis' visible unease, as he squirmed in their company.

'It's the flapping of their wings I don't like. It's an involuntary reaction, I can't help it,' he protested. 'It's like a phobia. When I was about five I saw a film by Alfred Hitchcock, what was it called again? *The Birds*, that was it, it scared the shit out of me and, ever since then, I hate being close to birds when they flap their wings. '

Maria clapped her hands and the pigeons took off in an instant. Louis instinctively ducked, covering his head.

Maria laughed. 'Don't worry, I'll protect you from those nasty creatures.' She mocked him, wrapping her arm around him.

'See, I can't help myself. You'd better be on your guard now. I'm going to get you back for that.' He playfully pushed her from him.

'Oh no, a bird has come between us,' Maria said, over dramatizing the pronunciation of the word 'bird.'

Louis touched her face; she took his hand and lightly kissed his fingers. 'I love you, Louis Satriani, and don't you ever forget that.'

Her mobile rang. The conversation that followed was in Greek. Louis loved to hear Maria speak her own language. Her pronunciation was laced with rich textures and tones, rising and falling in a pitch that was not apparent when she spoke English. The prosody of her voice exaggerated words with deep tones, rising and falling like waves. He noted her hands moved in flicks and circles, flowing effortlessly, like her very own and unique sign language. As he watched, an almost hypnotic state encased him, like a drug-fuelled syringe.

'It was my mother,' Maria said, placing the mobile in her handbag. There was a resigned look on her face. 'She's ready to go home now. We'll be leaving in a few days.'

'I have to show you something,' Louis said, rising from the bench and taking her hand.

'Where are we going?' She looked at him puzzled.

'It won't take long, but you can't leave Edinburgh without seeing this.'

'See what Louis?'

'The Athens of the North.'

The taxi weaved its way down the Royal Mile and deposited them at the foot of Arthur's Seat. The sun's light diluted the pastel sky, now washed in crystal blue. It was busy, people peppered the parkland, sunbathing during their lunch hour, sitting on grass verges reading books and magazines, eating pre-packed sandwiches and drinking piping hot coffee and tea out of polystyrene cups. As they walked, Louis felt like a spectator witnessing life's evolution. Life was evolving, nothing stayed permanent;

there was no detachment from this state, no influencing its relentless progress. He felt exhilarated, the blood in his veins coursed through him.

'Where are we going? I hate secrets,' Maria asked again as they crossed a road.

'It's not a secret.' Louis pointed. 'Look up there.' He gave a flicker of a smile.

'All the way to the top?' Maria gasped incredulously.

He leaned towards her. 'Well no, not exactly but that depends. Once we get up there, you might want to go all the way. It's eight hundred and twenty-three feet tall. It's called Arthur's Seat.'

'Oh I see and where exactly did Arthur sit? Just in case I need a rest.'

'It was a volcano you know.'

'You did mean was, it is extinct?' She craned her head towards the steep incline.

Louis looked at her with a teasing smile. 'Do you think a city would have been built next to it if it wasn't'?'

'Pompeii springs to mind.' She looked at him sheepishly and then narrowed her eyes. 'I presume this is the only way up there.' She nodded to the path that snaked its way upwards, like an artery.

There was a sense of urgency about him. 'Come on.' He pulled her arm. 'Every step is worth it just for the views alone.'

The shingled path, uneven under foot, rose in a steep and precarious ascent, skirting the edge that fell, like a draped curtain, where blocks of flats huddled in its shadow. Above them, wisps of bone-coloured clouds hung in an ice blue sky. In the foreground, separating the sky from the River Forth, the Kingdom of Fife emerged from its encasement through a silver haze. They had been walking for several minutes and Maria was surprised at how high they had climbed. Edinburgh stretched out before them, like a contented cat.

They held hands, climbing steadily higher and, as they did, the buildings and streets gradually shrunk in size, transformed. Cars and buses resembled miniature children's toys and the metamorphosis of people into blurred stickmen accentuated their progress. Louis drew Maria's attention to Easter Road Stadium, Holyrood Palace, and the Scottish Parliament building, which he described as an architectural scar, a hideous disfigurement on the body of the city.

From the Observatory, the city subtly inclined where each building and spire sat in a uniformed manner; a masonry path, building blocks that led to Edinburgh castle, dominant in the skyline, like a crown sitting on top of the city where roofs glistened in the sunlight, as if layered in slates of diamonds. Above Louis and Maria, precipitous cliff faces, ancient and volcanic, gazed over the city, like primordial guardians and protectors of all they surveyed.

Gradually, they came to a flat shelf, where several people were scattered, sitting on large rocks; a respite for tired legs.

'The views are amazing,' Maria gasped, her eyes sweeping over the panoramic expanse.

'There's no other way to see Edinburgh. I knew you'd love it. Now you can see why it is called the Athens of the North?'

Maria nodded, entranced.

'Listen, I need to tell you. Don't worry but I've met Emma's mother. She heard I was back and asked to meet me.'

'What did she want?'

'Just to talk.'

'About Emma.'

'Yes.'

'When was this?'

'Yesterday. She called when you were out with Clare. We went for a coffee at Amber's. Carla was there.'

'Why didn't you tell me this?'

'I wanted to find the right moment. There's nothing to worry about.'

'So what did you talk about?' A panic asserted itself.

'She wanted me to know that what Emma did came as a shock to her. She was really upset by it, she always thought of me as a son in law.'

'I see.'

'She spoke about Emma's death, the funeral and how she wished I could have been there.'

He turned away from her.

'There is something you are not telling me. Louis, look at me.'

'Before her death, Emma told her mum she didn't know who the father was. The only thing she knew with any certainty was that it could have only been Paul or me.'

'My God, Louis, it might have been your baby.' Her mouth went dry.

'I don't feel angry or sad. I can't change what has happened. I want to feel angry, but I feel nothing. I wanted to tell you, but I needed time. The last time I saw Emma she could have said something but, for whatever reason, she chose not to. It would only have made a bad situation worse. She chose Paul over me. I'll never know why. There's no point, anyway. I've decided to let it go.'

'And can you do that?' She tried to keep calm.

'I already have,' he said flatly.

They sat for a while on a large rock staring out towards the city.

'I like it here,' Maria finally said. 'It reminds me of the Acropolis. You can see the whole of Athens spread out in front of you. Someday we'll bring our children to this place and show them where their father once lived, worked and loved and where their mother pledged her undying love.'

A long sigh escaped him, an exhaustive relief, as he buried his face into her neck, choking with emotion. She held his head there, running her fingers through his hair. An older couple walked passed them. The man looked at them discreetly and then turned his gaze away. The woman removed her sunglasses, her lips curled into a smile. Her eyes, warm and thoughtful, met Maria. Around them, the world spun in slow motion and, in the seconds it took for the couple to pass, Maria felt the woman had seen a fragment of her own past, a sequence, and frame that had shaped and determined the trajectory of her life. Of course, Maria did not know this for sure but in considering it, a reassuring emotion fortified her. Maria watched as the woman gently took her husband's arm; he smiled at her and kissed his wife's forehead affectionately.

Zakynthos 2004

Louis stood staring at the sea as he had done so on each new day. The subtlety of light that influenced the colour of the water's surface never ceased to draw a breath of wonder from him. The odour of the earth's garden surfed on warm currents and surrounded him with a burst of herbs and flowers. He had found contentment, and it was expressed each morning with a smile, influenced by the gratitude of breathing the warm air of Zakynthos.

Maria and Louis were married almost a year to the day after their return from Edinburgh. The wedding took place in the small church where Clare had been married and each of her children had been baptised. The reception took place under the vast ocean of blue sky in the garden where every family celebration took place.

To Louis' left the apartments stood, doubled in size from when he first set eyes on them and the not too welcoming Anna who had put up with his intrusion as a favour for an old friend's daughter. The old accommodation block still stood, but where there was once one there were now two, one with four, two bed-roomed apartments and the other with two, three bed-roomed apartments. Each had a living room, fully fitted kitchen, en-suite, further bathroom, sofa beds and satellite TV. It had taken a year to plan and complete the renovation work. It was a project that was galvanized with Anna's blessing and Louis and Maria's vision of cultivating a life of fulfilment.

The apartments now stood unrecognizable from the neglected specimens they had become from their years of forced disuse. The whitewashed walls reflected the ever-present sun, and each window was framed by a sky blue border where above the roof tiles crowned the buildings in earthy terracotta. Louis had wanted a pool, an attraction that would profit the holiday experience of families. However, Anna was having none of that, preferring to entice the older tourist with sunbeds, tranquil balconies, and colourful vegetation. They came to a compromise; instead of a pool Louis had installed a luxuriant Jacuzzi, shaded by timber framed covers, where vines wrapped around the wood like coiling snakes.

The work was financed by the capital Louis raised after selling the flat in Edinburgh. Louis had found part-time work at a local architect office. His less than adequate income influenced their decision to postpone their plans to build their own house. They deliberated on setting up their own business a prospect that excited them both. With Maria's knowledge of the local tourist industry and the financial investment Louis provided, it seemed the perfect arrangement to earn a living on the island. The rejuvenation of the apartments was Louis' incarnation. He drew the plans, Stelios took control of the legal and contractual obligations, and his team of builders, undertook the work. Maria busied herself with the interior design, and furnishings and fittings. An industrious fever had infected the project with the ever present culmination of the approaching tourist season.

The work began in the winter months, when the climate was more palatable to such an undertaking, and the final touches were completed as the first wave of tourists descended from the skies and caressed the tarmac of the airport.

Louis felt a presence by his side. Maria touched his arm. He turned and smiled.

'How are you this morning?'

'I feel a lot better now. It seems to be easing since I took the tablets the doctor gave me for the sickness.'

Louis bent to her stomach. 'I hope this doesn't mean you are going to cause us trouble, little man.'

'I still don't like the smell of coffee. Anna brought you a cup out onto the veranda and the smell of it was awful.'

He turned his attention to the sea.

'Just think, Maria. One day soon there'll be three of us looking at this view each day.'

'Eh, four.' Maria smiled, a trace of amusement in her voice. For a moment, the significance of her words was lost on him and then his jaw loosened.

'Twins. I don't understand. There was only one at the

scan.'

'Ah yes, the scan. It was faulty, but the mistake wasn't picked up until we left. Dr. Samaras took another scan when I went to see him this morning about the morning sickness and there they were, four little feet and hands.'

He felt compelled to smother her in an embrace.

'Maria, twins!' he gasped, before smiling expansively.

'We'll need the four bedrooms now. The house won't feel as big.'

Anna's house now had a recently built extension that comprised of a small kitchen, bedroom, living room and bathroom. During the renovation of the apartments, Anna announced that she had visited her solicitors in Zakynthos Town and subsequently amended her will after lengthy deliberation. She now accepted the inevitable that her son would not return to the island. Athens was his home now. She wanted her house to be a place where roots could be planted and lives evolve. It was her wish that the house was to be called a family home once again. Therefore she declared that, after her death, the recipients of the property were to be Maria and Louis. Until then, Anna insisted they should decorate and furnish the house to their taste and live in it as if it were their own, allowing them to move out of their rented accommodation in Zakynthos Town. There was one condition, however Anna was adamant she would not live in the house but insisted on living quarters to be provided for her. And so, as the apartments were modernised, so it was that the small extension gradually took shape, supervised by a tempestuous Anna, who instructed the tradesmen, like a dictatorial foreman, and who, in turn, anticipated her arrival each morning with trepidation.

The rumblings of an engine and the hiss of hydraulic doors announced the imminent arrival of their first paying customers. Anna appeared from the shade of the veranda carrying a tray of glasses filled with iced lemonade. They both walked towards her, each step filling Louis with exhilaration.

'She looks twenty years younger.' Maria smiled, as Anna

straightened her posture, welcoming the new arrivals with her thirst quenching offering.

'Welcome to the first day of our new life,' Louis said, wrapping his arm around Maria.

THE END

A note from the author

Thank you for taking the time to read The Homecoming. If you enjoyed it, please consider telling your friends or posting a short review. As an author, I love getting feedback from readers. Thank you for your kind consideration.

If you'd like to be first to know about any of my books, please visit me on my website and sign up for occasional updates about new releases and book promotions. I'd love to hear from you:

http://www.dougiemchale.com

**Like me on Facebook:

https://www.facebook.com/www.dougiemchale

**Follow me on Twitter:

https://twitter.com/dougiemchale

The Boy Who Hugs Trees

A novel by Dougie McHale

Everyone has secrets but some can change your world forever.

Emily has a secret; 30 years ago the choices she made changed her world forever. And now, it resonates in the present, threatening to reveal its truth.

When Georgia removes her son, Dylan, from a prominent Edinburgh school, she relocates to the family home on the Greek island of Corfu. The discovery of her late mother's diary immerses Georgia in her parent's troubled marriage, a story of love and tragedy.

Adam's life has become predictable, something is missing, and it has to change. When he answers an advert to home teach a boy with autism, he hopes his life will take on a new direction and meaning. But he hasn't bargained on falling in love.

Can Georgia and Adam continue to resist the profound attraction that draws them closer? Nothing will prepare Georgia for the diaries final revelation which will force her to question everything she knew about her mother and everything she knows about herself.

The Boy Who Hugs Trees is an intimate, compelling and intensely moving love story that unfolds and reveals the profound impact of impossible choices.

Buy From: Kindle UK * Kindle USA

Excerpt from The Boy Who Hugs Trees

Prologue

1994

Her movements are slow, but deliberate, as she places the teapot on the kitchen table. The low sun washes the room in an autumnal light. A soft illumination rejuvenates the floor tiles with a white shine that her years of monotonous cleaning have failed to produce. She moves a wisp of hair behind her ear; a weariness lodged in her chest escapes with a sigh.
As she positions the vase of flowers into the centre of the table, she touches the yellow petals between her forefinger and thumb, as an eruption of colour and perfumed scent declares its simplistic beauty before her pale and drawn face.
She stares out of the window. Unwashed weather-marks stain the glass. A creased smile curls the edge of her lips, as she feels a distinct urge to venture out and wade through the mounds of raked leaves, small mountain ranges, that wait by the shed to be collected.
Fallen leaves litter the hardened ground, a collage of brown and gold, crisp and undisturbed in the stillness. She looks at the trees that line the periphery of the garden. The air is motionless where a tapestry of leaves shimmer in a blaze of copper. In time, the light will fade and eventually soften and dull them. Birdsong reverberating in the garden is clouded by an ache in her forehead.
And then, as suddenly as it began, her reprieve is ended by a heaviness that is relentless.
Her eyes, set deep into hollow and blackened sockets, camouflaged by powder, are blind to the intense colour of this day.
She will arrive soon, she thinks.
She stretches her arm, retrieving tea cups from a cupboard; it is an effort that affects every cell and bone. The crashing

of china, disintegrating, like a nail bomb, drags her screaming from the dark cell she has crawled into. Panic creeps into the room. Cursing the small fragments, she frantically sweeps them into a cluster before they are disposed into a bin.

Placing a plucked cup on the table, she hears the inexorable crunch of footsteps on gravel.

'It's only me mum.' The voice moves through the house, like an intruder.

She is not ready for this. She clings to the cocoon she has inhabited. An anxious wave crashes into her, a foaming and riotous sea, as the invasive sounds from the hallway predict an imminent meeting. She slumps into a chair.

With a laborious effort, she hoists herself from the chair. A dignified posture erects itself, like a rejuvenated yet delicate flower. Standing, hands clasped, an anguished strain pulls at the lines that splay from her eyes. She tries to imagine an air of normalisation around her. She feels a dull sensation radiate from the nape of her neck. There is a panic to her breathing; the air is sucked from the room.

She is exhausted. She picks some fluff from her skirt and wonders why she feels self-conscious.

Her daughter's voice summons an urgency to compose herself. She runs her fingers through her hair and down her skirt; these adjustments are performed and driven by a need to gain an element of control and of self-preservation.

Georgia sweeps into the kitchen, cold air still wreathed around her, clinging to her clothes in defiance.

She kisses her mother. 'It's freezing out there. The traffic was awful. They've got it down to one lane again. They seem to dig up the road for fun. It makes you wonder who plans these things.'

'Would you like tea dear?'

'I'd love a cup,' Georgia says and smiles.

She gulps for air, steadies her hand and pours the steaming tea into a cup and then tentatively into another. It is a ritual she has repeated a thousand times but performed today as if it was her first. She has displayed an assortment of biscuits onto a floral plate.

'Would you like a biscuit?' she asks, as an intoxicating clamour disturbs her thoughts. She must be in control, she tells herself. I will not allow this to beat me.

She sits down. A relief enters her, she assumes Georgia has not detected her unsteady demeanour, encouraging a short-lived smile that fades, rubbed out before maturity.

With a manicured finger, Georgia wipes a crumb from the corner of her polished lips and sips her tea.

'You're looking well, how are things at home?'

'Fine mum, Stephen gets home Saturday morning. He's been in London for a week this time.'

'How is the house coming on?' She plays with the handle of her tea cup.

'Most of the work is finished, thank god. It's been like living on a building site. The decorators start on Monday. It'll be finished for Christmas. You must come and see the house once it's finished.'

She shifts in her chair. 'Yes, I'd like that.'

'In fact mum, why don't you come for Christmas dinner?' Georgia says enthusiastically.

'That would be lovely.' She fiddles with her dress. She has not given Christmas a thought and is reluctant to pore over such a time.

'Are you sure mum? Don't tell me you've got other plans.' Georgia watches her interrogatively.

'No... not at all, I'd like that, really.' She forces a smile, appeasing the moment.

She notices a natural shine from her daughter's cheeks. Georgia has her father's eyes. It is more an observation than an attempt to study her. She takes a deep breath, she has rehearsed her words yet, in their moment of delivery, she feels vulnerable and scared. She must choose the appropriate time with caution.

She stares at her cup, the undrunk tea. Her throat is dry, uncomfortably tight.

'Mum, I've something to tell you.'

Georgia's voice pulls her back. 'Yes dear, what is it?'

'I've spoken to Stephen, and he doesn't mind if I tell you.' She is starting to smile. 'The thing is, well, as you already

know, we've been trying for a baby... God, what I'm trying to say is I'm pregnant.'
There is an unexpected silence.
'Aren't you happy for me?' Georgia sounds like a wounded child. She gazes into her mother's eyes.
'Of course I am. What wonderful news.'
She rises from her chair, scraping it over the floor and embraces her daughter.
'You are pleased for us... Aren't you?'
'Oh darling of course I am.'
The realisation that she will not see this child creeps upon her. She will not experience the transition from mother to grandmother. Tears well up in her eyes and cement the ache in the pit of her stomach. She is reluctant to release their embrace.

She remembers the courteous greetings, her nervous smile.
'How long?'
He moves in his chair, shifting his weight. His words enter her, like a hail of bullets. 'Between three... six months.'
'But I don't feel any pain...'

She cannot remember how she arrived home that day, yet, the numbness that inflicts her has remained ever since, taking root like a mature tree. There has been no release from its anaesthetizing presence, not even the revelation of a new life growing inside her daughter.
'Stephens convinced we're having a boy. He's already talking about taking him to watch Scotland play rugby and I'm only twelve weeks!'
'Your father was the same. It's a man thing.' She hesitates before running her fingers through her daughter's hair. It is unthinkable to neglect her joy.
'You will make a wonderful mother,' she says, retreating to her chair.
'I've had the best teacher,' Georgia says spontaneously.
The words float over to her like feathers.
'Are you ok?' Georgia asks anxiously.
'Of course dear, just a little tired. I haven't been sleeping

too well that's all. I'm happy for you both. It's not every day one becomes a grandmother.' She pauses before summoning a broad smile. In this instant, she knows the opportunity has escaped her, as she hastily pours another cup of dark tea, now watched by a contented Georgia.
She is shining with happiness, she tells herself.
'You must come to ours for Christmas mum,' Georgia insists.
'I will dear. Nothing could stop me.' She breathes deeply and gazes at the steam rising from her cup.
'Good, that's settled then,' Georgia says in an accomplished tone.
She composes herself. Most mothers would savour the news of a daughter's pregnancy with irrepressible excitement and expectation, yet there is a gulf between them. How can she tell Georgia now, today of all days? It has been a lifetime of waiting, her daughter's lifetime. Georgia has the right to know. She regrets the opportunities spurned, like today, another one slides from her, as does time, for now, her body is not her own. She has no influence over this foreign invader; it has entered her uninvited, spreading its destruction, like an oil slick.

She stands at the kitchen sink, looking at the trees, and it is as if she is seeing them for the first time. She scratches the palm of her hand, taming an irritable itch.
She notes that two wood pigeons sit side by side on a branch. She observes the way the light from the fading sun, throws changing and evolving shadows over skeletal branches and bark. She studies the way that thinner branches fan out from singular sturdy ones, like veins and capillaries. Long shadows shade grey slabs, grass, stones, and fallen plant pots, in projected patterns. As the light fades, she wills it to splay its luminance across her garden, so that she can witness, once more, the things she has spent a lifetime ignorant towards.
In this moment, she decides to open a box in her mind's eye, place her secret inside and tenderly close the lid and there it will remain, never to be released.

About the author

In a past life, Dougie has been a dockyard worker, student, musician, and songwriter, playing in several bands, performing live and recording music. He has a degree in Learning Disability nursing and a post graduate diploma in autism. He is a children and young person's learning disability nurse with a specialist interest in autism. Dougie lives in Dunfermline, Fife, with his wife, teenage daughter, older son and hyperactive golden retriever.
The Homecoming is his first novel, inspired by a love of all things Greek, her islands, people, landscapes, sea, light, and ambience all of which are important themes and symbols in his writing.

Printed in Great Britain
by Amazon